T0367611

"Satan cannot DESTROY the church so he decided to JOIN"

One World
Two Views

Karen Fertig

WESTBOW
PRESS®
A DIVISION OF THOMAS NELSON
& ZONDERVAN

WestBow Press books may be ordered through booksellers or by contacting:

WestBow Press
A Division of Thomas Nelson & Zondervan
1663 Liberty Drive
Bloomington, IN 47403
www.westbowpress.com
1 (866) 928-1240

ISBN: 978-1-9736-3495-9 (sc)
ISBN: 978-1-9736-3496-6 (e)

Print information available on the last page.

WestBow Press rev. date: 12/05/2018

Chapter 1

"Where's Dad?" Chad asked as he smacked his baseball into his new leather mitt. He was anxious to practice and felt he would play better than ever with his new baseball glove.

"He's in his study, Chad, but please don't disturb him right now." Christine knew her husband was deeply troubled by all the recent events in their church and he needed to spend some time talking to the Lord about them. She also knew Chad didn't understand, or more to the point, he didn't want to understand!

"But if we don't get outside soon, it will be dark! C'mon Mom, we'll be in before dinner, I promise." His words were shouted over his shoulder as he entered his father's study. It seemed his dad spent more and more time alone in there and he didn't like it. He wanted to have fun and there was nothing he enjoyed more than sports. Watching them or playing them!

"Hey Dad, let's go out and throw the ball around a while before dinner." Chad scanned the dimly lit room and saw no signs of life.

"Dad? You in here?" He turned with a start as his father suddenly appeared. Chad frowned knowing that his father was probably on his knees beside the well-worn desk chair.

"What's going on?" Chad asked with a puckered brow. Martin cocked his head and studied his seventeen year old son. No, it was not time to talk about problems, especially to a hot headed teenager.

"Everything is fine… or will be. I could use some fresh air. Let's go." He grabbed his glove and led the way out to the backyard. It would probably do him good to use up some energy.

1

"I need help with my grounders, Dad. I'm great with fly balls and have a pretty good arm even when I have to throw it to home plate, but those pesky grounders sometimes go right through my legs!" he laughed good naturedly. Martin followed his son outside and breathed in deeply. The Coopers were having a cook out and the aroma of grilling steak made his mouth water. He hoped Christine was preparing something equally as appealing, though she was such an outstanding cook, she could probably heat up tree bark and make it delicious. He smiled realizing it was probably the first one of the day. The church issues gave him little to smile about.

By the time they were done practicing, both felt better. Martin showed his son how to improve his stance to make sure grounders didn't slip by him and Chad, who believed his father knew everything about everything, listened to every tip and did his best to follow the instructions.

Soon Christine was calling her boys in for supper. Everything was on the table as they washed up and Lisa, Chad's older sister was pouring juice in their glasses.

"Slow down, Lisa, you're going to spill it all over the table." Christine chided.

"She's probably got a hot date!" Chad laughed.

"No, I'm sure that's not it! It's a school night." Martin said.

"It's only 6:30." Lisa remarked indicating she did indeed have a date.

"By the time you finish dinner and help with the dishes, it will be way too late to think about a date" said Christine.

"I can dry the dishes when I get home and ..."

"The subject is closed! Maybe another night, but not tonight." Lisa started to argue, but knew it would accomplish nothing. She knew the matter was closed. She also knew she would find a way to make it happen.

"How was baseball practice?" Christine asked hoping to change the subject.

"Chad has a good arm, that's for sure. I think if he can get control of the ground balls coming his way, he will be outstanding!" Martin said with pride, while Chad grinned from ear to ear basking in his father's compliments.

"I have a game Saturday. You're going to be there, aren't you Dad?" Martin had missed several games this season due to meetings and Chad was hurt and angry.

"I'm going to do my best to be there. You know I hate to miss your games, Chad."

"Then don't!"

"It's not as easy that." Chad scowled. He didn't want to know what or who was keeping his father away. In the beginning, Martin told the family about various situations in the church. He did his best to guard the privacy of any member, but he also wanted to pray as a family for each situation.

Perhaps he divulged too much or his children were too young to understand. He wasn't quite sure what he would have done differently. His children seemed more compassionate when they were younger but as they grew into their teens, things had changed. They were a close family and the children took any criticism of their father very personally. As they approached their teen years, they grew more sullen and distanced themselves from many church members.

"Can you believe I heard Mrs. Hunt criticizing my hair style and wardrobe? Just because she dresses out of the 1900's she expects the rest of us to follow in her tracks. Well, there is nothing wrong with my hair or dress and she has a lot of nerve to talk about me." Lisa was in tears.

"I know how you feel Lisa! It's like were a couple of bugs on a stick for everyone to inspect and analyze." Chad added.

"People mean well." Christine consoled without much enthusiasm. She didn't like it any better than they did. There were times she was willing to say goodbye to a member causing problems with their tongue. Martin had to remind her that it was the down side of ministry.

"We can't go anywhere without feeling like there are people in the bushes waiting and watching our every move." Lisa spat. She had just been to the salon to get highlights in her hair and you would think she just shaved her head and grew horns!

"You're over exaggerating, Lisa! You also got lots of compliments on your hair." Martin reminded her.

"I don't know how you stand it Daddy. Why are people so mean? These people are supposed to know the love of God, but they are hateful, backbiting, two faced..."

"You can stop there." Martin would not abide this kind of nasty reaction.

"We need to pray for them." Chad and Lisa exchanged eye rolls. That was always their father's answer. They had earnestly prayed for them, but at some point, they stopped; or at best they changed the structure of their prayers.

It was so much easier when the kids were little. People thought they were adorable and sweet. Martin and Christine were very proud of their children. They were eager to please and very easy to point in the right direction. It wasn't until they began their teens that things began to change. Chad had constant arguments about sports. He began to lie to his father about practice times when he wanted to join a team. He knew his father would not let him miss church to play ball.

Lisa was a different story. She seemed to notice boys the minute she came into puberty, and they noticed her! She was extremely naïve and though she seemed to always see the best in people, she couldn't tell a nice boy from one that would take advantage of her. Though she was less favorable with the adults and could easily point out their short comings.

Lisa finished dinner in a few gulps and headed to the kitchen to wash the dishes. Christine smiled to herself as she had never seen her daughter in such a hurry to clean up. Then it dawned on her *why* her daughter was in such a hurry to be helpful. Somewhere in her muddled little head, she thought she still had a chance to go out on her date. Christine rubbed her temple knowing a headache was about to emerge.

Chad smiled at his sister's audacity. He had overheard her conversation with Jeremy and knew she had full intentions of meeting him with or without her parent's approval. He chewed slowly and grinned at her as she tapped her foot waiting for his dish.

"I think I'll have a second helping!" he laughed.

"Don't you have homework or something?" she scowled.

"Nope."

"Well, I know you have an English test tomorrow that you should be studying for." She harrumphed.

"Okay, Sis, here's my plate." She whisked it out of his hand and sprinted toward the kitchen. He gave his mother a quick kiss and thanked her for a delicious meal as was his custom and then headed for his room to study.

"You know, she still thinks there is time for a date." Christine whispered to Martin as she glanced at her watch.

"Why is it when they were little, they knew 'no' meant 'no.' But now they try to work around every answer!"

"I think it's been too long since you were a teenager, Martin." Christine answered softly to her husband's harsh words.

"I was not a Christian when I was their age."

"Then you really don't know how you would react." Christine had been reared in a Christian home and remembered her defiant times against her godly parents.

"I'm not going to change my mind. If I do, she'll only push more!" He had a point, but she also knew they both had a difficult time watching their children grow up. They were becoming more independent and though that sounded good in theory, it was not easy to let them make decisions.

"Martin, there are so many reasons to say no to our children. We try to protect them and we try to keep them out of the world's grasp, but we need to say yes as often as possible or they begin to believe the world's view that they are missing out." He slumped in his chair and gave her words some thought. He remembered well the arguments with both of his children, and at times they believed life would be fun if it wasn't for all the rules. Without having much maturity at this point in their lives, it was virtually impossible for them to understand.

"What do you suggest?" Martin rubbed his eyes and sighed.

"I suggest we hear her out before we say no. Perhaps there can be a compromise."

"I think we are going to make matters worse, Christine. She is going to feel like she won the argument and maybe she can win the next one too. We are still the parents and she should obey because we are!" he snapped. Christine was silent. Her husband had a fiery temper and she learned over the years to remain calm and quiet when it flared.

"I'm sorry, honey. I think I'm just tired. I didn't mean to snap at you." She patted his hand and smiled making him feel worse. She was a wonderful wife and had a lot of wisdom that he relied on when working through emotional problems that zapped his strength.

"The dishes are done and it's only 7:45." She smiled knowing it was obvious where she was going with this conversation.

"Okay, Lisa. What did you have in mind tonight?" Martin asked.

"Daddy, some of my friends are meeting at the bowling alley. It's just a couple miles away. I'll be there by 8:00 if I leave right now." She folded her hands together and prayed her father would comply.

"You need to be home by 10:00 and that's stretching it." Martin didn't like it. It felt as though he was backing down and he didn't want her to get the impression she could have her way. However, she wasn't whining or sulking and he knew if he told her she couldn't go she would obey him.

"I'll be home by 10:00... I promise! Thanks so much, Daddy!"

"Don't be late!" Christine added.

"If she's late, I'm grounding her!" said Martin flatly.

"She's a good girl, Martin."

"And I want her to stay that way."

View Two

"Why are you troubled?" Portentous asked.

"I have been watching the Parkers" said Ominous.

"Why are they a concern?"

"Martin Parker is a preacher." Portentous cringed involuntarily. How he hated those words.

"There are millions of preachers out there. Most do enough damage to the lost that there is little need to assist them." He smiled evilly.

"This one is different."

"What makes him so special?" Portentous sneered. Ominous took a deep breath. He knew this was *not* going to go well.

"He...ah...prays!" Portentous snarled and viciously attacked Ominous who cowered away defeated once again.

"Do you mean he actually speaks to our Enemy, or does he speak in the ritualistic, religious gobbledygook?" He growled. They were just one acrid breath away from each other and Ominous was still licking his wounds from his last words. A lie would be so much better.

"He appears genuine, though I have not studied him long enough to be certain. I am not the master you are in such things." Ominous knew he could appeal to his vast pride, and Portentous seemed to soften a bit.

"Parkers, you say? Yes, I vaguely remember them. Martin Parker is the pastor of growing congregation as I recall."

"Yes, that's true."

"And what have you done to thwart his efforts?" he challenged.

"I have influenced his congregation to believe unfavorable reports about him and his family. Some believe he is a hot headed man who is trying to make a name for himself." Ominous puffed his chest at his brilliant estimation.

"Excellent!"

"I am also influencing his children. They are teenagers now and are much more attentive when I speak." They both laughed wickedly.

"Good work! You are learning well. We must break down the home!! It is key!! When that is accomplished, the rest will follow like paper in the wind."

"There have been several untimely deaths; some of them are small children. I did exactly as you taught. I told them how cruel the Enemy is. And while they are in the midst of the anguish and pain, they can find no answers. That's when I apply the pressure." He drooled with delight. They nodded their shaggy heads in unison.

"What is his wife like? Have you studied her?"

"Yes, she is a submissive sort. Will not go against her husband no matter how I point out his flaws. She is also like him in... other ways." He dare not say she was also a prayer warrior. He was still licking his wounds from the last outburst.

"How is her husband *bent*?" It was an expression often used between them. He wanted to know how the man was influenced. Was he easily enticed? Was he a man of pride in his appearance or worth? How did he accept rejection? Was he given to rage when his needs were not met? Did he struggle with honesty? Did he run his home selfishly with his needs above the others?

"He is not as lustful as most, though if given the right set of circumstances, he may succumb. He shows more weakness when it comes to his temper. He is used to being the man in charge and forgets from time to time that the heart is deceptive. I do my best to keep him from any introspection that would lead to remorse or confession. He is a man who wants things done and sometimes I make sure he thinks *he* must be the one to accomplish these trivial tasks that keep him away from his calling."

"Good observations! It may take some time, but in due season, we will pull him down." Portentous said with determination.

"Why must we spend so much time on such a small family and congregation?" Portentous shook his shaggy head. He hated dealing with a novice.

"Martin Parker speaks to people about our Enemy, correct?" Ominous nodded quietly, without understanding the point.

"His church also supports missions around the world, correct?" again a small nod was given.

"Must I spell it out for you?" he bellowed.

"Do not be angry! But it seems that we should be spending our time with the mega churches.

"You speak like an idiot! Many of the mega churches have thousands thronging them because for the most part, they are getting a motivational message to keep them happy. They are not taught to be concerned with those who are outside the Enemy's protection. They go home and order pizza, watch their beloved sports, and pride themselves on fulfilling their religious obligation!" he laughed gleefully.

"Martin Parker and his kind are the dangerous ones. They are making a difference one person at a time." He spat. "We do not want his kind to become a mega church with many following our Enemy!"

"Now get back to that family and corrupt them! Work on his anger... break their hearts...cause dissention among the body of believers...mistrust, unrest. Do some damage!"

"Yes, yes, I have a plan!" Ominous always became stronger when he joined forces with Portentous.

Chapter 2

View One

"I hate to tell you, but we've lost another good member." Christine was in tears as she thought of the ugly story someone callously and maliciously wrote on one of the popular websites.

"Why do people believe such junk?" asked Martin, though in his heart he knew the answer.

"It's hateful, that's what it is!" cried Christine as she slammed her fist against the table. They had been through so much already and instead of getting better it was getting worse.

"Don't suggest we go make a visit either because my heart is not in it!" she added

"You know we need to do it anyway." He said softly forcing a kindness that wasn't heartfelt.

"Debra has always loved the church and served in so many capacities. How could she buy into this stuff?"

"Debra's husband isn't a believer and like it or not, we are influenced by those we live with."

"I don't know what *his* problem is. He attends most Sundays and seems to be blessed by what he hears. He certainly smiles from ear to ear when you're talking to him. You would never know he had a problem with anyone."

"He doesn't like sharing his wife with the church. You know ever since she became a leader in the woman's ministry, it has been difficult. He doesn't like her making visits, or having outings for the ladies to get to know each other better."

"The last time I spoke to Debra, she confided that her husband has been using foul language around the church ladies just to get a rise out of them. Of course, Debra is embarrassed but what can she do?"

"I have given her options that will keep the ladies, especially the new ones, safe from that kind of behavior. He's really a very nice man. He claims to be a Believer, but I am doubtful."

"I'm tired of hearing these stories, Martin. I feel like I am constantly defending my family. There is nothing wrong with the way Lisa dresses and I find no problem with her hair for that matter. Yet I hear little complaints about the Pastor's kids."

"Then, let it go! You don't have to defend our children." She didn't want to tell him that she was also defending him these days. It seemed every decision was nitpicked and there was bickering among the members, when they experienced such harmony only a few months before.

"I don't understand what's going on, Martin." He shook his head. He needed to take a walk and get alone with God.

"I'll be back in a little while." He grabbed his jacket from the hook and headed for the door.

"Martin, I think we need to discuss this!" Her voice was thick with emotion and Martin knew it was not the time to talk. Unfortunately, she didn't.

"We'll discuss it when I get back." He closed the door softly as she plunked herself on the couch and began to cry. She wasn't generally given to outbursts of emotion, but this time she couldn't hold back the tears. She felt angry, alone, hurt, and bewildered. She wanted her husband to 'fix' it but he was also confused by recent events.

She knew that you couldn't keep all your members, and people left for various reasons, but this was getting ridiculous. These were people who had been around for a while. They were strong Christians that generally weathered most storms of life. They didn't bail out!

"Mom, are you all right?" Lisa asked throwing her books on the floor beside the couch and rushing to her mother's side.

"I'm fine, Lisa." Her bloodshot eyes told a different story.

"You might as well tell me what's going on. You know I'll hear it from someone." It saddened Christine to see the scowl on her daughter's face as she thought about the church.

"It's nothing that we won't get through." Those familiar words had been spoken by both of her parents in the last few months and she was tired of hearing them.

"I'm going to start dinner, would you give me a hand?" she had no idea it was so late. She opened the freezer door and stared.

"I thought we were going to the Booths for dinner tonight?" Christine closed her eyes and tried to remember what day it was. They had been invited for dinner on Thursday. Was it Thursday?

"Oh yes, of course. I guess I better get dressed." She hoped her husband remembered. Lisa smiled at her and headed for her room. She wanted to look her best. Anthony Booth was a few grades ahead of her and she wanted to appear more mature. She wondered if her mother was going to be upset if she wore a little more makeup than usual.

Martin began walking toward the familiar path he frequented when he felt tied up in knots. Soon he was jogging and praying with each step. What in the world was happening? His children seemed to be more self absorbed than ever. His stalwart wife appeared to be falling apart before his very eyes. Even his deacons and trustees seemed weak and disgruntled.

"Hi Martin." His head jerked up to see one of his distant neighbors running along beside him.

"Oh, Hi Cheryl." He slowed his steps to speak to her. She wasn't a member of his church and though she had been invited for special days, she only came when asked and as far as he knew was not a member anywhere.

"How's Christine and the kids?"

"Fine, how is your family?"

"Me and the kids are fine. At least we will be in another month. I kicked Jason out." She announced as she tossed her pony tail away from her face.

"I'm sorry to hear that." He hated to hear about any family falling apart. Somehow he felt guilty that he never got around to visiting Jason. He was a truck driver and on the road most of the week. He was home on the weekends but that was always a busy time in the life of a pastor. Still, he wished now that he had made more of an effort.

"Don't look so glum. It's all for the best. He was never here anyway so it won't be like the kids will miss him. As long as I get my support check, I'll do just fine." Martin looked the young woman over. It was obvious that she spent time working out. She looked amazing in the tight leotard she was wearing and his mind started to wander.

"I'm still working at the Sports Bar and tips are really good, but with three little ones, the money still goes fast. Maybe you could give me some financial pointers." She smiled widely.

"You must know a lot about money to run a church." She gushed.

"You're right. Sometimes you need to be a magician to make ends meet." He laughed easily.

"Jason wasn't good with money either. I spent mine and he spent his. You really don't understand how a person thinks when you only see them for a few hours a week!"

"I need a man around longer than a weekend, if you know what I mean." She smiled coyly and he knew exactly what she meant.

"He never took care of himself anyway. I mean, look at you. You make sure to get exercise and you look fabulous!" He smiled and hoped he didn't look too pleased at her appraisal.

"It's hard to believe you have teenage kids! You must lift weights besides running." He felt warm and knew his pulse was racing. His eyes began to trace her legs and suddenly it hit him. What was he doing?

"Maybe you would benefit from a visit from my wife. If anyone knows how to stretch a dollar, she does." The smile immediately, left Cheryl's face.

"Speaking of Christine I better get home. I'm sure dinner is on the table. I'll have her give you a call sometime this week. Take care!" He couldn't get back home fast enough. He kicked a stick along the path. He must be losing it.

13

"Lord what is happening? Please help me focus on you. My church is hurting, my family is hurting and I seem incapable of putting a stop to any of it. Show me what I should do?" he prayed earnestly. He had no answer, but he noticed the knot in his stomach was no longer there. There was also a confidence somewhere deep inside that all was under control. He smiled knowing his Father held it all in his powerful hand. He was also grateful for the nudge the Lord gave him in his encounter with Cheryl. When you make the right choice, there is always a reward felt deep in the heart. He smiled and looked heavenward. Thank you Lord… I truly want to please you.

He hung his jacket back on the hook and peeked into the kitchen. There was no one there; nothing cooking on the stove either. He sprinted up the stairs hoping Christine was in their room.

"Hi Honey, I'm home!" he announced in a comedic tone.

"The walk seemed to do you good." Christine was in his arms immediately and as she nuzzled his chest he breathed in deeply. She always smelled good. He grinned as he thought of her cleaning pots and pans or washing the dog and still smelling like a fresh bath.

"What am I missing?" he asked as he held her away from him. She looked far too dressed up for their dinner table.

"You forgot too. We are having dinner with the Booths tonight." He had forgotten.

"Is that tonight? I guess when you aren't looking forward to something; you try to put it out of your mind." He was honest with his wife. The Booths had only been involved in their church for a few months and there were already problems. They were not new to the area, but they seemed to bounce around from church to church over the years. After several conversations, Martin realized Mr. Booth considered himself an authority on just about everything from the Bible to church finance. He was loud and authoritive and pushed his way into every church group handing out unasked for advice. Mrs. Booth was quiet and mousy. She jumped at the sound of his rude voice and was often humiliated by one of his endless stories.

"It's not going to be an easy evening. I've heard Mrs. Booth is not much of a cook." Christine commented.

"Listening to gossip?" He smiled but she knew there was truth in his question.

"Unfortunately, I have had some firsthand experience. She asked if she could make cupcakes as a bus treat. Oh Martin, they were just awful." She giggled in spite of herself.

"They were bone dry and she must have tried to ice them when they were hot because the icing ran off and stuck to the pan."

"Thanks for not bringing them home." He laughed.

"I was afraid she would find out the children's reaction. I don't want to hurt her feelings, Martin. She has a husband that takes care of that." Martin frowned. He had heard Mr. Booth make derogatory remarks about his wife. He held Christine close. He could not imagine speaking unkindly about her. He was blessed to have such a wonderful wife at his side, especially these days.

"Let's try to make the best of it. I'm praying the evening will be beneficial for both families. Maybe if we understand them better, we can be more helpful." He squeezed her and gave her a quick kiss before changing out of his jeans and sweatshirt.

The ride to the Booth residence was quiet, although it was obvious; Lisa had gone the extra mile to get Anthony's attention. Her hair was swept up in a more mature style and her makeup seemed heavier. Her dress was on the questionable side. Martin scowled when she handed Mrs. Booth her coat. Her dress was clingy and on the short side, but there was nothing that could be done about it.

"Everything is ready. Please follow me into the dining room." Mrs. Booth announced. Christine's heart went out to the poor woman as they followed her into the dining room. She walked with slumped shoulders staring at the carpet before her.

"Something smells good!" Christine said hoping to encourage her.

"Don't get too excited. Been married for 30 years and my wife can barely boil an egg." Mr. Booth guffawed. Christine did her best not to shoot him a nasty look.

"Lisa and Chad you can sit on either side of Anthony. Pastor, if you will sit at the head of the table." She sat down heavily and Christine sat in the chair beside her. Poor soul looked miserable. Martin was generally asked to pray whenever he was an invited dinner guest, but Glen decided to pray instead. *"Our gracious, heavenly Father, we are thankful for all the investments you have made in our lives. We thank you for giving us tremendous talents and gifts to be used for Your kingdom. Thank you that we can teach those who know so little about the Bible and show them through our fine example. Amen!"* Martin and Christine exchanged glances at the pious prayer and deliberately made no attempt to look at either of their children. Norma immediately left the table and returned with a plate of dark, dry looking biscuits.

"Norma, these biscuits aren't fit to be served. Get them off the table."

"I'm sorry, Glen, I left them in the oven to keep them warm."

"Nonsense, I would like to have one." Christine decided she would eat one of those biscuits if she choked on them.

"Yes, I would like one too" offered Lisa hoping to appear the perfect guest.

"You don't have to eat them. We usually throw away about half of what she cooks." Anthony and his father both laughed at his joke. The Parker's were silent. Never had they witnessed such behavior. Christine had to hold herself in her chair she wanted so desperately to give Norma Booth a needed hug.

Chad and Lisa exchanged glances as both reached for a biscuit. They were mortified to hear Mrs. Booth treated so poorly. It was appalling! Lisa wondered if Anthony would treat a girlfriend like he did his mother. No thanks!

They filled their plates with meat so tough they had to cut it into very small bite size pieces and chewed until their jaws ached. The potatoes were not cooked enough but there was plenty of butter on the table which made it more palatable. There was definitely not going to be second helpings!

"Well, it looks like everyone has had as much as they can get down, Norma. Bring in the dessert." Glen ordered. Norma obediently set her fork down with a clatter and sprinted into the kitchen, while Martin and Christine fumed. Never had they seen a husband treat his wife with such open disrespect. Christine pushed back her chair and headed for the kitchen to help.

"You don't need to bother yourself, Mrs. Parker. She might be slow and clumsy, but she'll get it out here in a minute." He laughed as he poked his son, while the others sat uncomfortably at the table. Christine ignored him. She didn't trust herself to be polite.

"The cupcakes were such a hit with the bus kids, I decided to make some more." Norma said with a smile. Christine nearly burst into laughter at the sight of the lopsided, near burned little cupcakes with icing stuck to the sides. They were worse than the first batch. Each cupcake was a different size. It looked like she ran out of batter as a couple cups were only about a third full and dark brown. Christine wondered how she would keep a straight face when she served them. Purposefully, she gave herself the small burned one and each of her family members received the worst looking ones. She gave Anthony and Glen the best ones and hoped they would eat them quietly.

"Thank you, Mrs. Booth. Cupcakes are my favorite." Martin gave his son a warm smile at his attempt to honor their hostess. It took several glasses of iced tea, but Martin actually ate more than one of the dry, flavorless desserts.

"How are things going at church, Pastor?" Martin sighed. There was no way he would discuss church business with this brutal man.

"God has been good to us and we are a thankful people." Of course, that answer would not suffice, so Mr. Booth stepped it up.

"How are we doing financially?" he said briskly.

"We are meeting our obligations."

"You got a lot of people that we could get more money out of. I'm not sure you know it… but the Masters have money! And did you know that Charles Hexter is an anesthesiologist? Now that's money!" He tapped a plump finger on the table.

"I was also talking to the Dells and the Price family. Mary Dell's father owns a very prosperous car dealership in Philadelphia. She is an only child and will probably come into a fortune when her father passes." Martin was truly appalled. How did he know so much about his congregation?

"Ha ha, I can see you're surprised! I assure you I am not making this stuff up." He leaned closer and in a conspiratorial voice began again.

"I got this software, Preacher! It would really be helpful for you to get it. It screens people. It's called a Wealth Engine and you can tell what people are worth."

"Oh my!" He was dumbfounded. It felt so unethical speaking of his church members with this man.

"It's perfectly legal, I assure you. It's a real handy tool, Preacher. It's not like looking at credit scores. This software tells you what they own or if they are a CEO of a company."

"Now you take the Flynn family. They dress like a million bucks and have a real nice house, but they are mortgaged to the hilt. Their kids want to go to a fancy college too, so there is no money there." Martin was almost too overwhelmed to speak.

"You need to stop right there!" he managed to say.

"Oh, sorry! Not in front of the kids, huh?"

"Norma, I'm still waiting on coffee." He spat in the direction of his wife. Again, she dropped her fork on the table and ran into the kitchen. She didn't remember him asking for coffee, but she should have known to make it. She decided to wait in the kitchen until it was ready.

"Did you hear that Debra Walston is going to another church? Her husband wasn't worth much, but I know she contributed to the work."

"The Walstons left? When did that happen?" asked Chad. He was friends with their son Kenny and had no idea.

"Ooops... guess I spoke out of turn. Don't you tell your family anything preacher?" he laughed. Martin was fuming.

"We are planning to pay a visit to the Walstons. Please don't repeat that at church. As a matter of fact, don't repeat any of the things you have told me in this room with anyone."

"Sure, Pastor. I was just trying to give you a heads-up, that's all.

If you want the church to grow, you got to know where the money is. Now, you know who to talk to about giving!"

"I would never do that! I preach to everyone and then allow God to touch the hearts." Glen crossed his arms and gave him a disgusted look. He had just given him vital information and instead of being grateful, the pastor seemed upset.

"Maybe we should meet in your office to discuss the rest of my findings." Martin's mouth dropped open as Glen pulled out a thick stack of notes. Apparently, he did his homework. He probably knew more about the church members' finance than they did.

"Call my office and make an appointment. I think it would be good for us to have a private conversation." Glen smiled with satisfaction not realizing Martin wanted to get him behind closed doors so they could have a real discussion!

"Sounds good! I've uncovered some other things you might want to hear about. Not everyone is as loyal as you might think. You need to nip that right away. Shape up or ship out I always say." The Parker's were speechless.

"What you got to do is combat that stuff that's propagated on the internet. Two can play at that game!" Martin didn't want to ask what he had in mind.

"Look at the time!" Christine interjected.

"It's not that late." Glen dismissed her much as he would his own wife.

"I've still got some studying to do." Chad added.

"Suit yourself! Norma! Get their coats!" Glen shouted into the kitchen feeling a bit insulted. The family waited until she returned with their coats before speaking. All conversations was addressed to Mrs. Booth.

"Thank you so much, Norma. You are a wonderful hostess." Christine wanted to tell her how good the food was, but didn't know how to frame it without lying.

"Yes, Mrs. Booth. I think we enjoyed those cupcakes as much as the bus kids did." Martin smiled at his wife. He always knew what to say.

"It was so nice of you to invite us. Thank you so much." Lisa offered and Chad nodded in agreement.

"I'll be making that appointment soon! We'll get our finances in good shape!" Glen smiled. They ran to the car is if chased by thieves.

"I can't remember when I have spent a worse evening!" Christine was the first to speak.

"And to think, I wanted Anthony Booth to notice me! He's a horrible guy! Can you believe the way he treated his mother?" she cried.

"And what's all this about people and what they're worth and whose leaving the church..." added Chad.

"Okay, that's enough! Everyone take a breath." Martin could have added plenty, but he knew it would only escalate things. He felt bone weary and shrouded with discouragement. What a way to spend an evening.

The drive home was quiet with everyone deep in their own thoughts. Lisa fought the urge to speak, but knew her father meant business. No matter how terrible the evening went, he would not allow them to rehash the events.

"Where are you going?" Martin turned the car down a side road which jolted each passenger.

"We are stopping by the Dairy Freeze. I think we have earned a few milkshakes!" Suddenly, they were all laughing. It felt good!

When they arrived home no one seemed in a hurry to part company. They filed into the kitchen and one by one sat in their familiar chairs. Chad gave his mother a rare and unexpected kiss on the cheek. Without a word, Lisa did the same.

"I don't think we say it often enough, Mom. You're the best!" Lisa nodded in agreement.

"I'm sorry, Dad, but I just don't get that family! They were so rude and obnoxious." Chad shook his head and turned to face his father.

"They made me so angry!" Lisa chimed in.

"I could have cried for Norma." Christine added.

"That's where we should begin praying." Chad closed his eyes and gritted his teeth. That was not the answer in his book.

"Listen, I know how difficult this evening was but can you see another side to it?"

"What do you mean?" asked Chad.

"I think I understand." said Lisa.

"Okay, let's hear it." All eyes were on Lisa as she began thinking of all the details.

"Well, look at us. I have never been so glad to belong to our family. Dad treats Mom like a queen compared to the Booths. And I'm sorry, but I have never had food that bad in anyone's home. I mean, there was nothing edible! Not only that, but I found myself wanting to be Mrs. Booth's friend. I have never paid much attention to her at church, but if her husband would speak that way in front of Daddy, then you know he certainly wouldn't be kind to her anywhere else."

"Good, Lisa! Tonight has made you more compassionate and more appreciative!" Chad reluctantly agreed.

"Anything else?"

"Maybe I could help Anthony." Until tonight both kids liked him. He was smart and popular and a pretty good baseball player.

"I think that would be wonderful. You know he's just following his father's example. Maybe you should invite him over for your mother's cooking and show him how a boy treats his mother."

"Only one problem... he'll probably never go home once he's tasted Mom's cooking!" They laughed and jabbed each other in fun for a while then Martin held Christine's hand and she knew instinctively he was going to pray. She held Chad's hand and he took Lisa's.

"Thank you Father for my family that is the dearest on earth to me. Thank you for a wife who is also my best friend. For two wonderful children that mean the world to me. I praise you that they 'get it' they not only see what's right... but have a heart to do what's right. We pray earnestly for the Booths. Help us be a comfort to Norma and a true friend. Help us to show her she has worth. Show

my son how to befriend Anthony. One day he will choose a wife and he needs to treat her with honor. We also pray for Glen. Help me to remain calm when we have our 'discussion' so that You can be seen. We love you, Lord. You alone can touch these hearts. We just ask to be useful vessels! Amen!

When the prayer ended, there was a difference in the faces of his family. They weren't just listening to him pray... they were praying with him!

View Two

Everything had gone wrong! He was so sure he was making a difference but he knew he had failed! What was he going to tell Portentous? He had failed and would pay the price! He searched desperately for a believable lie. Something that Portentous would accept that did not *sound* like a lie. Hmmm. What could he say?

"I don't like the look on your hateful mug! I only want to hear of your success." Portentous always seemed to appear out of nowhere and when he was least expected or wanted. He waited for a few seconds while Ominous shuffled his feet.

"Out with it! Tell me of your success!" he snarled.

"Yes, yes, of course. I was merely thinking of where to begin."

"Why not start at the beginning, you oaf! Wouldn't that be logical?"

"I was thinking of giving you the highlights, but I will start at the beginning. You are right as usual... that would be the most logical place to start." Portentous didn't like the silly lilt in his voice. He was stalling! He was sure of that.

"You certainly understand mankind, Portentous. If given the right set of circumstances, they are all the same." He smiled with pleasure.

"Ah, start there. Tell me what you did worthy of my praise."

"I studied that preacher and though he appears to be totally in love with his wife... I saw some weakness." He laughed gleefully.

"Did he succumb?"

"Not this time, but it is only a matter of time, I assure you." Portentous glared at him. He had not been successful.

"Tell me the story and I will tell you *why* you failed!" Portentous huffed.

"I did exactly as you said. The preacher went out for a walk and I made sure that 'hot' neighbor lady was on the same trail. You would be proud of me. She was going to wear a pair of those grungy, loose fitting sweat pants, but when she opened her drawer I whispered in her ear to wear that leotard that fits her like a second skin. The preacher's mouth was just about watering when he saw her." He laid it on strong knowing that Martin was innocent.

"Continue."

"Yah, the preacher thought she looked really good in that!" he guffawed

"Then she starts telling him that she's getting rid of her husband and she thinks he would be the perfect fit. She even told him she was lonely at night."

"Good work. Then what happened?"

"Uh, nothing much happened after that. I mean he went home and she continued her jogging." Portentous kicked him with a heavy foot.

"Can you do nothing if I am not there to assist you?" he shouted.

"Where did I go wrong?"

"First of all, if I can believe anything you tell me... it sounds like the preacher showed some interest. That's when you push hard! If he seems to back up, you push *her*! She should be easy to push. She loves male attention, which is one of the reasons she is ending her marriage." Ominous realized he missed some great opportunities.

"You should have told her to get closer to him. Perhaps even a slight rub up against him ever so gently so that he reacts to the touch without realizing it has been done on purpose. If he knew that, he would recoil." He grinned. "Did you catch him looking her over?" Ominous was amazed. It happened so quickly, he almost missed it himself

"How did you know?"

"Because he is a man, you idiot! That's when you should have planted some new seeds. He has been discouraged. Discouragement is our friend! You must capitalize on those times!

Ominous didn't want to tell him that the preacher quickly recovered from his first glance and was not listening to him. Perhaps he didn't know how to speak to him... yet.

"Tsk, tsk... you missed several opportunities. I can't be everywhere at once! I rely on you and the others to help get the job done." He chided.

"Anything else? Are you still moving the children further away from our Enemy?"

"They are both pretty disgusted with the church."

"That is not *new* news!" he growled.

"They had dinner with a man I personally planted in their church. Glen Booth will certainly assist the cause!"

"Do tell! I know of Glen and Norma Booth" This could prove interesting.

"He is not a believer and has done damage wherever he is planted." Both laughed hideously slapping each other roughly on the back.

"He has already caused dissention among the people and between hurt feelings and half-truths, he is quite the ambassador!"

"His wife is a believer, you must keep her silent." He warned.

"There is no need to worry. She has been so beaten down she has just enough strength to get her through her day."

"Don't let her fool you! She is connected to our Enemy. She would have resorted to death long ago, but that was before their son was born. He is much like the father at this point, but she still has influence."

"Yes, I've seen her beside her bed in prayer. I thought it was for herself she prayed, but it is for her husband and son." Portentous snarled at the thought.

"Continue to beat her down. Keep whispering in her ear that all is hopeless. She will eventually believe you if you do a thorough job!"

"Anything else to report?" He dare not tell him anything else. He would never hear the end of it if he reported the preacher and family were all praying earnestly for the Booths. No he had nothing else that needed reporting.

"You are also assigned to Debra Walston. What is your report on her?" he snarled.

"You will be happy to hear she left her fundamental church."

"Excellent"

"I am also happy to report that it was largely due to the plant." He puffed his chest feeling important.

"Glen Booth?"

"Yep! He posted some slurry things on the internet and she fell for it. Of course, I did what I could to help her along." He smiled.

"Interesting. I thought she was a little stronger than that."

"She was strong at one point but your advice was priceless! I caused her much distraction and she foolishly discontinued reading that Blasted Book. It took some time to keep her off course but I was subtle. She started getting phone calls every time she opened the Enemy's Book to read. I began the same procedure when she tried to pray."

"Ha! Didn't I tell you? They have no idea what a difference it makes."

"I'm also pressing her to divorce her husband!" Ominous stated proudly.

"He is an unbeliever, though he doesn't seem to know it. Like so many, he is satisfied with learning something new." Portentous knew the type well. They had some religious ideas but never met the Master and seemed quite satisfied with their partial knowledge.

"Yes, indeed! Continue to walk her through the tunnel of time and tell her repeatedly he will never change; therefore her life will never get any better. If you are insistent, you will wear her down."

"Now get back to work! Time is running out!"

"Keep a close watch on the preacher. We need to pull him out of that ministry!"

"Yes, yes... but... how?" He hated to admit his inadequacy but he was not as skilled against such strong forces.

"Haven't you been listening to me?" Another blow to the head of Ominous made him struggle to think.

"Keep him away from that blasted Bible! Do not allow him to actually seek the Enemy in prayer."

"But he has a scheduled prayer time and won't allow anyone to distract him during that time." He stammered.

"Then allow him to pray, but not to pray effectively."

"Guide me. I am not sure what you mean." Ominous closed his eyes and listened carefully.

"When the preacher gets on his knees, bring to his mind the weakest members of his congregation. Help him compare himself to them."

"How will that help?"

"That will help build his pride! He will not think to pray for his own weakness and short comings. He will hardly think of his life as sinful in comparison."

"Yes, that makes sense."

"Next, each time he begins to pray for a particular need, help him to see the situation harshly!" Ominous nodded but Portentous knew he wasn't getting it.

"Listen, you Dolt! When he prays for Glen Booth, remind him of what a brute the man is. He plans to have a meeting with him, make sure you are there! Use Martin's temper against him. No doubt, Booth will make stupid, insensitive comments. Fire Martin up! Make sure the meeting ends with harsh words between them." Ominous nodded rapidly. He got it!

"I myself could make them come to blows! But you are a novice!" Portentous huffed.

"After the meeting, you must work on those kids of his. Tell Lisa she has a great body and she could have a lot more attention if she was willing to show it a bit more! Tell both of the teenagers that their parents inflict their own standards on them because they have control issues. You can make it believable, I'm sure. I want to hear doors slamming, crying and harsh words exchanged!"

"They are all strong believers in the Enemy! They are not easy to manipulate." Ominous thought he should prepare the stage in case of failure.

"Yes, I am aware they all know the Enemy and are His... however, they can be useful to bring down others who have not made a decision to join their ranks. Again, Ominous could only nod half- heartedly unsure where he was going with this.

"Ah yes... I remember a time I actually made Chad swear!" Portentous boasted.

"He swore???" Ominous asked in disbelief. He had been assigned since Chad was a toddler, so he could begin studying him.

"He did not let the words escape his mouth, as many have learned to swear in their minds and it is their heartfelt words, but I knew he did. He almost mouthed the words!"

"You are so gifted! How did you manage that?" Ominous would love to bring them all to this level.

"It is not that difficult. It happens when someone laughs at them or confronts them when they have made an error. You can even see it happening when they are actually trying to speak for the Enemy and are treated unkindly. They are told to speak to as many souls as possible about the Enemy, and though they have good intentions, they are afraid! The Blasted Book tells them not to fear their faces... but I assure you they do. It is not a matter of safety, mind you. They are not going to be thrown into prison for their speaking... at least not yet..." both slapped each other playfully as they laughed at what they knew the world was facing.

"Lisa has kept her mouth shut in order to stay popular with some of the girls in her class. While Chad is fearful the 'jocks' will make fun of him. It's easy to keep them quiet. Just continue to plant ideas!" he laughed gleefully.

"My next report will please you!" Ominous could hardly wait to get back to work!

This was going to be fun!

Chapter 3

View One

"Anthony, wait up!" Chad ran to catch up. The boys didn't have much in common with the exception of baseball. Anthony was hounded by every girl in their class, while Chad was more interested in excelling in sports to spend the time and money most girls wanted.

"Hey, Chad, you looked good out there today!" He said in earnest. Anthony was a good pitcher, but he was not nearly as focused as his coach desired. He was often distracted by the cheerleaders or people shouting from the sidelines.

"Thanks, so were you." They walked in silence for a few minutes, as Chad wracked his brain for conversation. It seemed so easy for his sister, but unless the topic was sports, he had little to contribute.

"We enjoyed coming to your house the other night. Your parents seem nice." Chad fumbled with each word and Anthony noticed.

"You don't have to be polite. I know my parents aren't easy to be around, though my dad can be pretty comical." Chad frowned at the memory. He didn't think his father was the least bit funny.

"Thanks for choking down my mother's cooking! It's pretty bad." It was true but Chad would not dare agree.

"We order out a lot. Maybe we should do that when we have company." He laughed again and noticed Chad was not laughing with him. He grew sober and shook his head.

"My Mom is really a nice person once you get to know her. She's pretty quiet and not outgoing like my father."

"I hope our mothers will get to know each other better. My

mother is terrific." He wasn't sure how to continue. Should he tell him that his mother could cook anything and make your mouth water? That sounded like bragging.

"You will really like my father too once you get to know him. His picture still hangs in the school show case for the most strike outs in a game."

"You're dad was a pitcher?"

"Yep, one of the best! I don't think I'd be nearly as good if he didn't coach me and help me with my game."

"Tell me about your sister."

"She's a pain." They laughed together but Anthony knew he spoke in jest.

"I don't have any siblings so not sure what kind of brother I would be."

"We actually get along pretty well. I mean, I kid her every chance I get but she has grown to expect it."

"Does she have a boyfriend?"

"Not anyone special. She hangs out with a lot of different kids; mostly from church."

"Yah … about church."

"What about it?

"Not so sure I want to do the 'religious thing' at this point in my life." Chad wasn't sure what to say. He never thought of his life as doing some kind of 'religious thing.'

"My dad never talks about religion at home. Don't get me wrong, he gets involved in church once we start going someplace, but it always turns out the same way."

"What do you mean?"

"My dad tends to stick his nose in where it doesn't belong. I think he means well, but he makes people mad wherever we go." Chad could believe that one. Did Anthony understand why?

"Do you think people just misunderstand your dad?"

"Maybe some of it is a misunderstanding, but…" He took a deep breath and Chad waited patiently for him to continue.

"You saw how my dad and mom interact. Most people don't like it."

"Would you?" Anthony's head snapped back. Angry eyes met Chads.

"They always act that way to each other. It doesn't mean anything!"

"Anthony, your mother barely said two words the whole time we were there. I have to tell you, if your dad talked to me like that, especially in front of other people, I would be outraged!" There he said it. Let Anthony get mad. It needed said. To his surprise, Anthony agreed.

"I don't think my dad really means to hurt my mother. He's just done it for so long that it comes natural to him. He can be pretty funny!" He noticed Chad wasn't smiling in agreement.

"Has your mother ever told him how she feels about it?"

"No. I think she said something years ago and it didn't go well. My father is very much in control. Some men are like that. It's their nature."

"It doesn't make it right." Chad said softly. He didn't want to argue but he couldn't let it slide.

"I hope I am the same kind of husband my dad is with my mom. They are really great role models. Not perfect by any stretch of the imagination, but great just the same." Anthony had never heard anyone speak of their parents in such a positive manner. He generally connected with the kids at church who paid little attention to the messages and were there mainly for the social times.

"The Single group is getting together this weekend for some mystery dining. Are you coming?"

"I heard your dad talking about it Sunday. Not sure if it's for me."

"Why the hesitation?"

"No offense, but it sounds kind of lame." Chad bit his lip. He was the one to actually come up with the idea and his dad thought it was great.

"I think it's going to be a lot of fun. I'll tell you what. Why don't you come out this weekend and try it."

"Is Lisa going?" he brightened.

"She wouldn't miss it!"

"Okay, I'll go." He would have to change his ways drastically before Lisa would ever consider going out with him.

"What else do you like to do?" Chad asked.

"The usual, I guess. I like just about any sport. I play video games, mostly on line. I like pretty girls." He laughed.

"Do you like to fish?"

"I used to a long time ago. I haven't been fishing since I was a little kid."

"What about camping?"

"Again, I haven't done that either since I was about ten. As I recall, that was when my parents had the fight over his 'teasing' her." The painful memories resurfaced from the recesses of his mind. He hadn't thought of the fateful camping trip in years. He had never shared the events with anyone and he certainly wasn't going to begin with Chad. He remained silent as the unwanted memories bombarded him.

He had looked forward to the camping trip for months and told his mother he was going to catch enough fish for them to eat dinner every night. Of course, she encouraged him as she packed her biggest skillet. It was the first time he was made aware of his father's brutal treatment of his sweet mom.

It happened after they set up camp. Anthony was anxious to get to the lake and catch as many fish as possible before dark, but his father seemed to be in one of his antagonistic moods. Generally, he waited for it to pass and learned to stay clear of him but he had never actually witnessed his behavior.

"Hold this side of the tent up as I drive the stakes in." he snarled.

"It's too heavy for me." Norma squeaked.

"Then get out of the way!" He pushed her hard and she landed with a thud.

"I'll just go unpack our things." She said quietly.

"Did you remember to bring soap, toothbrushes, toothpaste?"

"Yes, I brought it all."

31

"What about my razor?" Her shoulders slumped. He would surely berate her, though he had told her he would pack his own things.

"No, I thought…" it was all she was able to say before he broke in.

"No?!? Can't you ever do anything right? Why must I always check the list as if you were a child?" She said nothing. There was plenty she could say, but she learned to bite her tongue against this bully.

"C'mon Dad! I want to fish!" Anthony pulled at his father's pant leg. He truly wanted to go fishing, but he also wanted to end this quarrel between his parents.

"Okay, let's go, though I don't know who will cook them if we do catch anything."

"Mom said she'll cook us up a big fish fry if we bring a bunch back!" he smiled as he led the way. He was excited at the thought of fish on his hook. It would be like it was back in the pioneer days. Men brought home fresh food for their families.

By the time they returned with a few fish, Norma had a campfire blazing and coffee brewing for her thankless husband. He threw the fish at her and told her to clean them. She had no idea what to do with them, and though he would never admit it, neither did he.

"I've never cleaned fish before." She said.

"Well then, I guess it's time you learned." He growled.

"Could you show me how?" she asked softly.

"Figure it out woman! I'm not going to lead you by the hand!" She wondered if he had a clue how to scale a fish. She sighed as she took the fish to a stump she used as a chopping block. She cut the heads off and tried to pull off the scales. She pinched and pulled but had no idea how they came off. By the time she was finished, there was not much left to cook. Luckily she brought bread and a jar of peanut butter. She had cut the edge of her fingers and also got barbed by one of the catfish. All in all, it was a terrible experience with little to show for it.

Naturally, dinner was a disaster. Anthony tried not to cry when he saw his massacred fish. After he tasted the greasy remains, he was glad she salvaged so little. If this is what fish tasted like… ugh!! Count me out!

That evening, his mother had enough. She had been mocked and ridiculed from the time they arrived and she couldn't take another nasty comment. She had never been brave enough to give him what for… but tonight she no longer cared!

Anthony was almost as surprised as his father when she began throwing everything out of the tent. When she was done, there was not one single item belonging to Glen that remained in the tent.

Everyone was astounded! No one ever saw this side of Norma. When Glen finally found his voice, it was too late. He swept up a handful of his belongings and made his way into the tent to be greeted by his wife and her fish scaler. She might not have known how to scale a fish, but she waved the sharp edge in her husband's face daring him to take another step.

"Norma, what's gotten into you? You are scaring your poor boy to death!" He knew exactly what to say. She put down her weapon and began to weep uncontrollably.

"If you ever have an outburst like that again, I will put you into a mental hospital and you will never see the light of day again! You mark my words! Anthony will grow up without a mother!" She continued to wail uncontrollably as he threw his handful of clothes her way.

"Get things back in order! We'll be by the fire. When you're done, we're going to need more firewood." He gave her a scornful look and kicked dirt her way as he left.

In her heart, she knew he was smart enough to have her locked up forever. She prayed for a long time and finally left it all in God's hands. She would do anything for her son and would never allow this brutish man to be the only influence in his life.

Anthony knew there was a change in his mother after the camping trip. She became more of a recluse and seldom spoke to his father. She always brightened when he was around and sadly, the older he grew, the less she saw of him.

"Anthony? Hey, Man… are you tuning me out?" Chad laughed.

"Oh, sorry! You asked me about camping and fishing. I thought I answered you." He had no idea where the conversation went after that. He was in a different world. One he was happy to depart.

"We are going camping and fishing in a few weeks. Why don't you come with us?"

"Let me check with my folks first. I'll let you know in a couple days." Anthony gave Chad a quizzical look.

"Why this sudden interest in Anthony Booth? I mean, we've been attending your church for a few months and we barely speak." Chad felt ashamed. Anthony wasn't the kind of guy he spent much time with. No doubt he would have questions.

"No special reason; just thought we probably have more in common than we know and after we were at your house for dinner, I thought I would get to know you better."

"Okay, but you might be disappointed. I don't like Bible studies and I steer away from people who spend a lot of time doing religious stuff."

"Maybe you should give me a list. What's considered religious stuff?"

"You know! I'm not going with you if you decide you want to get people into church. If you want to hang out with the youth leaders and give out tracts on the street, count me out."

"Let's just start with the camping and fishing, deal?"

"Deal!" They parted company and Chad felt lighter than air. He couldn't wait to get home and tell his father what had transpired. For once, he hoped he was actually in his study so they could have a private conversation.

His father appeared pensive as he entered the beautiful study resembling a miniature library. Handsome oak shelving held hundreds of books, articles, and magazines and the room always had the smell of polished wood.

"Hey Dad, I'm glad you're here." Martin brightened at the sound of his son's voice. They had many discussions in this room and most of them were fond memories.

"You're not going to believe the discussion I had with Anthony

Booth today. Well, first I have to tell you that I was praying to make a difference." Chad was animated and his excited hand gestures were sometimes difficult to follow. Martin swallowed the emotion that crept up his throat. He couldn't remember the last time Chad spoke about praying for anyone!

"Okay, let me start at the beginning." Chad took a breath and began again.

"First of all, after spending time at Anthony's house the other night, I got thinking about the kind of family he has you know, compared to the kind of family I have." Martin smiled at his son. Who knew he would make the comparison.

"I couldn't get Mrs. Booth out of my mind. I mean, can you imagine anyone treating Mom like that? At first I was angry with Anthony for laughing at his father's jokes about his mother. Then I figured he was just treating her like his father did and he probably never had a good example to show him the difference."

"That is a very mature observation, Chad. I'm proud of you." Chad beamed at his father's compliment.

"You know how you always tell us God doesn't always answer our prayers the way we think He's going to?" Before Martin could answer, he continued.

"Well, I prayed that somehow I would find a way to be Anthony's friend. I'm not good with small talk so I didn't see how I was going to connect with him. But that's not all! I also prayed that God would help me to say the right things so Anthony would want to hang out with me." Martin furrowed his brow. He couldn't imagine that someone wouldn't want to be his son's friend, though he realized how prejudiced he was on the subject.

"Dad, we have baseball in common. So that's where I started. Then I actually think I made him see that he doesn't treat his mother right. And that's not all. I asked him to go camping with us so we could do some fishing and I'm pretty sure he's going to come!" Martin slapped him on the back. He was almost as thrilled as his son.

"Chad, you will never know what a difference you've made. I had no idea how to reach out to this boy, and you found a way!"

"What's amazing is that I knew when to keep my mouth shut and God seemed to give me the ideas. I mean, I had no intention of asking him to camp with us. To be honest with you, I wasn't sure if I wanted him to go. When the words fell out of my mouth they surprised me almost as much as they did Anthony. And then I knew! I knew that God had put it all together! Martin's eyes filled with tears. His prayer had also been answered. He begged God to give his son an experience with the Lord and He did just that. Many people never experience it! He was incredibly grateful to see God moving!

"I know what you're going to say, Dad. You have prayers answered all the time and have such a close relationship with the Lord. Until today, I had never really understood. He gave his father an uncharacteristic hug. The burdens of the day seemed small in comparison to this great victory!

View Two

Ominous stood outside the classroom. Portentous' voice boomed from within. Just once he would like to please him but today was not the day. There must be something he could say that would help salvage his defeat. Ominous scoured his brain hoping for some report of victory. There were minor successes. He could certainly share them in a way that made them seem much bigger!

He would start by telling him about Debra Walston. She was now going to a very liberal church that challenged her core beliefs. She thought she knew the definition of sin, but this new church allowed just about everything to enter. The music was much like you would hear in any bar or worldly concert. The words could not be understood as it was drowned out by the deafening drums. Ominous laughed as he thought of the musicians standing before the people with smug faces loving the adoring fans. As long as they threw in a few 'religious' sounding phrases, no one seemed to be wiser. There was no worship involved except for a core group that had such basic fundamental values, they could sift through just about anything and still be able to put their heart into the hands of God.

Her husband was now attending church with her, for he could relate to the preacher who seemed much like himself. No more messages to make you uncomfortable or soul searching. The Pastor spoke about doing good for others and staying positive. There was little mention of sin as no one had really defined it. There was little mention of repentance either. If he could keep her there a few more years, she would be of no affect in ministry and her husband would be doomed. Portentous would love to hear that report.

Initially he had a plan to pair up Lisa with Anthony. That could be a real heartbreaker for the preacher. Lisa was innocent and Anthony was worldly and knew his way around girls. If he coached Anthony, he could get her into the backseat of his car and let the hormones take over! He laughed at his own little joke. How did he know Chad would actually have a 'real' time of prayer? Portentous had cautioned him but he didn't listen. Once again, he had given himself too much credit and not enough to the Enemy. Chad was truly one of His.

Quietly, he slipped into the classroom to hear the lecture. As usual, Portentous was eloquent. Words were his specialty. Hurtful words, lying words, confusing words, hateful words, questioning words... they all had their place of usefulness.

"They all suffer with the same malaise — if you peel back the layers far enough you'll find it!"

"PRIDE!!!!!" shouted the class.

"That's right! It gets them every time." He laughed wickedly.

"Questions?" he asked. A timid hand went up and Portentous glared at him. He thought he was thorough in his lesson. What did this dimwit need to have explained?

"Why aren't we just assigned to the lost ones? The ones that are in the Enemy's hands can never be doomed?" Portentous shook his head scowling.

"They are VERY useful! You arouse them in subtle ways. For instance, take John Sharp and his wife Lois. He was a Pastor for a number of years of a growing church. I took it upon myself as a teaching tool to show how easily man is corrupted. The preacher would never consider going to a bar or picking up a girl, ah, but there are much more conducive methods. I planted a troubled church secretary and made sure she needed *counseling.* Of course, she flattered him daily and convinced herself she would be the perfect, saintly woman if she only had a man like him. Then I worked on him. I used his compassion against him. Soon she was in his arms needing to be comforted. I chiseled away at both of them. She longed for this godly man never knowing she would be the tool needed to bring him down. Neither saw it coming. And the spouses!!!!! They fell completely apart. I know if I had given it a little more effort, I could have added suicide to the list!!! It was a victorious day on our side, to be sure!" He gloated. The minions nodded their head in rapturous approval.

Ominous wondered if he should give his report while Portentous was basking in his victories. There was never a good time for a bad report. It was not tolerated for long!

Chapter 4

View One

Chad had several camping ideas he wanted to run by Anthony, but as soon as they sat down together in the hamburger café, Anthony was not wearing his usual smile and Chad instinctively knew something was amiss.

"Hey, don't worry if you don't have all the equipment you need. We have plenty. My dad has extra fishing poles and we have plenty of sleeping bags and blankets.

"Thanks, Chad, but I'm afraid things have changed and you may not want me along."

"What do you mean? Of course I want you along. We've been planning this for quite a while. Don't you want to go?" Chad couldn't believe he would have a change of heart.

'It's … ah… we'll there's no easy way to say this." Anthony stumbled.

"Just spit it out! What's the story?"

"My parents want to come too!" There he said it. It sounded as bad as he thought. The look on Chad's face let him know he was correct in his assumption. No one wanted his parents around.

"They want to go camping with us? But...but… we've got it all planned out. I mean we have a good size tent, but it would be pretty crowded with both of your parents and their belongings."

"Oh, they aren't planning on staying in your tent. No, my dad has an old tent that we probably haven't had out of the garage since

I was ten." He scowled doing his best to keep those memories from creeping in.

"Has he talked to my dad?" he hoped maybe his father would put a stop to it.

"Why would he need to talk to your father? He is planning to go camping and will camp next to your family. You don't have to ask permission for that." Chad sighed and shook his head. It made him sick, and angry! He had been preparing for this camping trip for weeks and wracked his brain for ways he should approach Anthony about so many topics. Now it was all for nothing.

"Hey, man... I really am sorry. I feel the same way you do." He doubted it. After all, they were *his* parents. They gobbled their burgers quickly with little conversation. Neither knew what to do about their predicament. Chad hoped his father would have the answer, but after all was said, he came to the conclusion he would forgo camping.

He searched out his father for answers as soon as he returned home, and believed his father would wholeheartedly agree to cancel their plans. Chad was astonished when his father merely shrugged his shoulders as if he had given an unfavorable weather report.

"Don't you see, Dad? That changes everything!" Chad barked. He couldn't believe how things turned around since his first conversation with Anthony.

"Sit down, Chad, and let's talk about this together." Martin said calmly. He didn't like the recent turn of events, but he had to believe it was part of God's plan. Reluctantly, Chad plopped heavily on the couch with no intention of changing his mind.

"Dad, there is no way I want to go camping with the entire Booth family. Do you know what a disaster that will be? And to think I saw it as an opportunity to help Anthony see things differently." He glowered.

"What makes you think you know more than God?" Martin said firmly.

"I never said that! But you have to admit, bringing his parents along is going to be horrible! We've all seen firsthand how that family interacts!" There was no argument there.

"I'll make you a deal, Chad. I'll keep Mr. Booth as far away from you and Anthony as possible so you have ample time to talk with him."

"How about if we just punch holes in his boat?" Chad laughed.

"How about if we leave the results up to the Lord? Only He can change hearts in the first place!" Martin smiled good-naturedly.

"It's not going to be the trip I was looking forward to, that's for sure!" Chad didn't know where things began to unravel. He and Anthony began to discuss the camping trip every day after baseball and both were getting more excited as the time grew near. He knew something had changed when they met up after practice to get a burger together and discuss camping equipment.

"Dad, you are going to hate this camping trip if you have to spend all your time with Mr. Booth."

"Let me worry about that. You see, just like you have been praying about what to say to Chad and how to be his friend, I have also been praying for Mr. Booth. That's why I think this is all part of the plan. Not your plan and certainly not mine... but Gods!" Chad thought it over and knew his father was right. He didn't want God's interference as he thought through his plan with Anthony. He wanted to have fun and be his friend and hopefully be a good testimony, but he wanted everything comfortably on his terms.

Chad no longer crossed off the days until the camping trip and no matter how desperately he tried; he continued to struggle with the 'new' plan. When the Booth's pulled into the driveway, he involuntarily cringed. Nothing had changed in the least. Mrs. Booth started to get out of the car and nearly got her foot caught before her husband slammed the passenger car door with a thud.

"Who told you to get out? We're going to leave in a couple of minutes so just sit tight." Christine watched from her living room window and shook with rage. He was so cruel she could barely stand it. Martin placed a gentle hand on her shoulder. It wasn't easy for him to watch either.

"I'm going out to greet her!" Before Martin could speak, Christine was out the door. He wondered if Glen Booth would be nasty with his wife if he thought she was out of line.

"Norma! It's so good to see you!" she sang as she opened her car door and pulled her out. She could feel the hesitancy, but she didn't care. The woman desperately needed an advocate against this harsh treatment.

"Thank you for allowing us to tag along." She whispered.

"Not at all! I am looking forward to spending time together. I know so little about you and your family. We are going to have a great time!" She hugged her warmly and noticed the woman practically turned to stone. Obviously, she wasn't used to such tenderness.

"Would you like to come in for a quick cup of coffee?" Norma searched for her husband. Would he be furious to see her standing on the front lawn after he ordered her to stay put?

"Hello, Mrs. Parker!" Glen shouted from the doorway. He and Martin were just coming outside with their hands full of equipment.

"We're just going inside for a cup of coffee. Would you like some?" Christine offered.

"There is no time for that." There was an edge to his voice.

"Like I told my wife, we are leaving in just a few minutes." He glared at her for her disobedience.

"Nonsense, my children are still packing up the car and Martin has to attach the carrier. There is plenty of time." She took Norma by the hand and pulled her past her frowning husband.

"Glen, could you give me a hand?" Martin wanted to get him as far away from the ladies as possible. His face was red with rage and his fists were balled up ready for battle. He would give her an earful later for her disobedience.

"Sure Preacher, I'll lend you a hand." Anthony and Glen helped Martin finish packing the car and soon Lisa was running down the stairs with her maxed out suitcase.

"What do you have in there the kitchen sink?" Chad teased.

"I need all this stuff." Lisa retorted.

"We're going camping, Lisa! It's not a resort. You'll be in a tent."

She ignored him as she continued to drag her suitcase toward the door.

"Whoa! Hold on there girlie! That's way too much stuff to be taking on a camping trip!" Glen admonished. Martin gritted his teeth. It wasn't his business to correct his daughter.

"Daddy, I need everything in here!" She ignored the unasked for rebuke.

"Talk to your mother." Martin said gently.

"No offence, preacher, but why do you need to involve your wife? Don't you make the decisions?" he said accusingly.

"I involve my wife because it is a Biblical approach." He did his best to remain calm, but his accusation was infuriating. Christine and Norma could hear every word from the kitchen as they sipped their coffee. Norma stared at the floor embarrassed for her husband.

"She's supposed to obey you. That's Biblical!" he scoffed.

"And I am to love her as Christ loved the church and gave himself for it. You must read the entire passage. Therefore, I include my wife in these decisions." He said more sternly than necessary.

"Just be sure it's not the way you run the church. I want a man who is confident God is leading him and won't pansy out because his wife doesn't like it." He chided. Martin was abashed!

"Do you have your curling iron in there?" Christine practically ran into the room hoping to avert her husband's attention. She couldn't believe things were going downhill so fast. They hadn't pulled out of the driveway yet!

"No, mother!" she rolled her eyes.

"Give me the general inventory." said Christine.

"Sun tan lotion, week's worth of clothing, bathing suit, flip flops, sneakers," she ticked off each piece on her fingers.

"We aren't going to be gone that long."

"I know but if I decide to fish with the guys, I will want to change out of my fishing clothes." Glen started to sputter as he shifted from one leg to another and Christine knew she needed to act quickly before he felt the need to give more orders.

"Okay, Lisa, give your suitcase to Chad and he'll load it up." She turned on her heel and was out of the room before Glen could speak. Lisa quickly left the room as well as she knew she was about to hear another reprimand.

"She needs to open that suitcase and get rid of about half of it!" Glen bellowed. Martin fought the urge to tell him it was none of his business.

"It's fine, Glen. Let's finish up and get going." He managed to say. How he kept his voice even toned was truly through God's grace.

"I have an idea. Why don't the guys ride together and the ladies ride together?" Christine thought it would give Norma and her more chance to talk.

"Why would we do that?" Glen growled.

"I think that's a good idea." It would be good for Norma, not so good for him.

"I don't see the point." Glen didn't like the idea of someone else driving his vehicle.

"My wife knows exactly where we are going and if we should get separated, she'll be able to find us. Besides, we will want to talk about fishing and camping and the women will want to talk about recipes." Martin laughed.

"Well, don't count on my wife giving you any recipes. You already had a sampling of her cooking and that was a good day." He laughed and poked Anthony but noticed he was laughing alone. He furrowed his brow and looked at his son. Generally, they laughed together. What was wrong with his sense of humor today?

"You drive your vehicle, Glen, and my wife will drive ours. Lisa, you can ride with us or your mom." There was no way she was riding with Mr. Rude. She smiled as she climbed into the backseat with the ladies.

For the next few miles Martin asked Glen questions about hunting trips or fishing trips anything to keep the conversation light. Unfortunately, Glen's stories were accented with gripes and complaints about any and all of his companions. It seemed no one had the abilities he did and he rarely gave anyone a compliment. The boys had their own private conversations that Martin would much rather be part, but he made a deal with his son to keep Mr. Booth occupied. It was going to be a long trip.

The ladies, on the other hand were having a good time. Christine and Lisa never ran out of conversation and after a little prodding, Norma began to relax and join in. She was quick witted and humorous, which came as a great surprise! Soon all three were laughing until their sides ached.

As they neared the camp grounds, everything changed. Norma once again seemed to crawl deep inside herself. Her face was pinched with anticipation of spending time with her husband. Christine was determined to make this the best time Norma ever had.

"It's about time you got here. What did you do stop off for more coffee?" Glen snapped. Christine bit her lip and began hoisting out the supplies. Her husband gave her a 'be-patient-with-him' look.

"You need to gather some firewood so we can get a campfire going." He instructed his wife.

"We can do that." Chad offered and Anthony nodded his agreement.

"Nothing doing! You boys need to help get the tents up." He snapped.

"I think we can handle that, Glen. As a matter of fact, I'll probably get in the way. After all the stories you told, I think I would impede progress." He teased. Glen scowled. Somehow he felt he was the butt of a joke and he didn't like it a bit.

"Putting up a tent is a two man job, preacher. I know you're probably not used to anything heavier than a Bible and a pencil, but if you'll just follow my instructions, we should have the tent up in no time." Martin knew he was deliberately trying to jibe him, but he wouldn't fall for it.

"I would be happy to help you, Glen." He smiled pleasantly. After several mishaps, the Booth tent was finally anchored into the ground. It was obvious; Glen was not the outdoorsman he claimed to be. Martin had to stifle a laugh more than once as Glen held the tent upside down and began pounding stakes into the canvas. Martin finally took over. Glen gave him no credit but merely harrumphed at his efforts, doing his best to criticize every move.

Christine was busy at the campfire assembling their meal. She gave Norma a potato peeler and both women worked in harmony. Lisa and Anthony had caught a few fish and were giving Chad a hard time for coming back empty handed. It was all in good fun. Suddenly, Norma dropped he peeler and said she needed to find a restroom. Christine was alarmed, certain her new friend was ill. She quickly followed after her.

"Norma, are you okay?" she called into the restroom.

"I'll be fine." She was obviously crying. Christine waited patiently praying she would have the right words.

"You didn't have to wait on me. I'm fine." She croaked. Her eyes were bloodshot and her face red from rubbing the tears away.

"Norma, I want to be your friend."

"I appreciate that more than you know." Her lip trembled as she fought desperately for control. She didn't want her pastor's wife to think she was some kind of nut case.

"I know you're upset. I just don't know why." It had been so long since she had a real friend, she didn't know where to begin.

"I don't know how to do things good... you know like cook and such. My husband is embarrassed..." her shoulders quaked and she couldn't continue. Christine hugged her and smoothed her hair.

"Norma, you are a wonderful woman. Don't let anyone tell you different. We are going to spend some time together this week and by the time we're through, you'll be teaching other ladies!" Norma smiled through her tears. She closed her eyes and thanked God again for his timely intervention. She had been so distraught over the last few months that when her husband told her they were going camping it was the final straw. She couldn't face another day of his humiliation. She could bare it in front of her son, as she'd grown accustomed to his abuse; but not with strangers. She had just filled a prescription for her increasing blood pressure and decided to take the entire bottle. Somehow, she kept getting interrupted, but knew that when her husband left for work and Anthony went off to school, she would have her chance.

"I don't know how to clean fish." Norma blurted out as if admitting to a felony.

"I'll show you. Believe me, the first time I ever tried to clean fish, there wasn't anything left to eat." She laughed and Norma giggled like a school girl. How she loved her Pastor's wife! She began to relax a little as they returned to camp.

"Where did you run off to? We're all hungry and the fish aren't going to clean themselves." Norma stared at the fish making no attempt to pick them up.

"You better show my wife how to clean 'em, Christine. She doesn't have a clue!" he guffawed loudly.

"They can be tricky to get the scales off…" Christine began but Glen cut her off in an instant.

"Tricky? Don't be ridiculous! There's nothing to it!" he snapped. Christine could stand no more of the pompous little man. She grabbed a fish and plopped it into his hand. She did her best to remain calm and keep her voice even.

"Martin, we have never had such a woodsman among us before! And to think I was silly enough to bring matches and lighter fluid. I'll bet Glen could start a fire with wet wood!" Martin cocked his head to one side and gave his wife a cautious look. He understood her frustration, but they needed to remember why they were there in the first place. The comment was taken as a compliment and Glen smiled with satisfaction.

"I admit, there isn't much I don't know about the great outdoors." He seemed to be an expert at just about everything and Christine was about to meet his bluff.

"Please show us how to filet these fish properly." she said.

"Let me see what you're using to clean them with. Oh, if only I had brought my own filet knife. I could show you." Norma, jumped into action. She would find that filet knife if she had to tear every piece of luggage apart in the process. Excitedly, she held up the knife.

"Here it is, Glen! I found it for you." She smiled at Christine who understood exactly what was going on. He had no more excuses!

"We'll go get the skillet and oil. I'm sure you'll have them ready before the fire gets hot!" Christine yelled over her shoulder. Norma and Lisa immediately joined her and began pulling the side dishes out of the tent.

"Can you believe he's still trying to get the fish on the block so he can cut the heads off?" Lisa laughed. It was obvious; Glen fumbled around as though he had no idea which was the head and which was the tail. Martin and the boys left him to his misery. No one wanted to lend a hand or be part of the solution.

Glen continued to turn the fish over and over without so much as a slice when all at once he yelped as if someone had shot him. He intentionally cut his finger so he would be off the hook. But Christine was not feeling that generous. As soon as his finger was bandaged she began again.

"I'm sure you've had many injuries out in the woods. Now that you're bandaged, should we continue?" she smiled.

"I can't risk getting an infection. I'm not going to be able to filet them this time."

"Oh, of course, you don't have to do the work. Just walk me step by step and I'll do exactly as you say." Glen's smile faded from his face. He had no idea what to do or say.

"You know, I'll give you instructions when I can actually do the work myself. I mean, you can ask my wife. I'm a perfectionist and I certainly don't want to make you upset with my obsessive ways." He smiled. Martin gave his wife a look that said for her to let it go.

"Oh, sure, I understand." She gave him a look that let him know she understood *perfectly*!

Norma watched Christine deftly filet the fish as though she had been the captain of a ship. She made it look much easier than it was. With encouragement, Norma tried to fillet a couple herself. Lisa and Christine complimented every move she made and in no time they had a wonderful fish fry. Lisa tossed a quick salad and they began dishing everything out. It was wonderful.

Glen had never heard so many compliments given to his wife. He sat stoned-faced and ate in silence for a while, though he noticed his wife was contributing more to each conversation. Neither of them was used to her having such a position among her peers.

As the sun faded from view, Martin pulled out his guitar and began to sing around the campfire. Martin's strong voice filled the air and soon everyone joined in. Christine sang softly hoping Lisa's lovely voice would drown her out. To their amazement, Anthony's voice blended perfectly with Martin's. The others dropped out to listen.

When the song was completed, Martin asked the ladies to sing. Christine shot him a tortuous look. There was no way to blend with Lisa and she dreaded being put on display. Martin did not seem to notice and began to play a familiar tune.

"Oh, I know that one!" said Norma as she began to sing. Martin nearly stopped playing. The beautiful voice stunned all of them.

"Norma Booth! I can't believe what a gift you have!" Christine blurted out.

"I don't think I've ever heard you sing, Mom." Anthony was astounded. Why hadn't she ever sung around the house? He frowned as the answer pounded his mind. What did she have to sing about? He felt deeply ashamed.

Martin played another familiar song and as they came to the chorus, everyone dropped out except Anthony and Norma. The melodious harmony was breathtaking. Anthony had to choke back the tears to continue.

"Okay you two!! No more sand-bagging! I want you both in the choir and you will both be singing duets and solos!" Martin was as surprised as the rest. No one was as surprised as Glen. He had no idea either of them could sing.

"That was absolutely beautiful!" Glen said when he found his tongue. To his surprise, Norma burst into tears.

"Now don't get all teary eyed woman!" Glen huffed.

"I'm sorry! I just can't remember you ever giving me such a nice compliment." Glen couldn't refute her words as much as he would like to argue, she was right.

Something began to change during that camping trip. Glen seemed to have a new pair of eyes. Little by little his tone became more tender. Anthony also went out of his way to be sweet with his mother. Lisa noticed immediately the change in Anthony.

"You can be a real nice guy when you want to be." She giggled.

"Yah, I guess I didn't give you a very good first impression. The fact is... I guess I didn't realize how awful I must have sounded. When you see yourself through someone else's eyes, you see things differently." He stumbled. Chad saw the opportunity and capitalized on it.

"It's not all your fault, Anthony. You were just mimicking what you saw. My dad always tells us how important it is to emulate Jesus in our lives. I don't always think about it either, but when I do it makes a world of difference." Chad and Anthony became close over the next few days and had many discussions about the "real" Christian life as opposed to the hypocrisy often found around them. By the time the tents were packed up and everyone was ready to head home, Anthony and Lisa were making plans to go out. She epitomized everything he was looking for in a girl.

Instead of the girls riding in one car and the guys in the other, Christine rode beside Martin with Chad and Lisa in the back. Anthony rode with his parents. Glen led the way. He still needed to be the 'up-front' guy. But things were remarkably different.

The Parkers noticed with smiles on their faces, Glen and Norma were actually sitting close to each other in the car. So much good had happened from a camping trip that no one wanted to attend! God was so good!

But not everyone was smiling!!

View Two

Ominous traced his steps. He desperately needed to figure out what he was doing wrong. Sure, Portentous would be more than happy to point it out, but that came with a severe back lashing among other dreadful things. He kicked the black sooty air around him and felt totally defeated. Carefully, he checked his list. He was certain he had been given the right people. Glen Booth was a prideful, arrogant, self-made man he could always count on! With only the tiniest bit of guidance, he was a useful tool. Anthony was coming along nicely as well. Norma was a bit of a problem. She truly belonged to the Enemy but was of little use in her present condition.

Portentous warned him of becoming too confident. And now he was paying the price. Was it only a few days ago that he nearly coaxed Norma into suicide? He whispered until he was almost hoarse... 'End it. Nothing is ever going to change! You can't continue this way! Everyone knows you are a nothing! You can't do anything right and you will always face ridicule!" He laughed with glee as she began to search for her pills. She planned to down them all. He all but forgot the prayers of her pastor and his wife as he hated getting anywhere near prayerful people. Portentous warned him about *fervent* prayer. There was no defense against it! Fortunately, few knew it and even fewer participated in it. Once again he had not done his homework. He assumed he knew their weaknesses and could easily capitalize on them.

It had all begun so well. Glen was cooperating wonderfully to his every nudge. He ridiculed Norma from the first morning cup of coffee to the way she packed their suitcases. He supervised but never actually helped in any tangible way. By the time she loaded everything into the vehicle, she was totally depressed and despondent. If only he could get her by herself for a few minutes, he was certain she would follow his instructions and end her life.

He ignored Anthony's helpful disposition figuring he was in a good mood due to the camping trip. He was very chipper and overly sweet with his mother. It was always the small things he seemed to overlook! If he was half the evil enmity of

Portentous, he would have gone to work immediately on the boy. Whenever they had the smallest glimmer of hope, if you were wise... you dashed it out!! He let it slip by him and would pay for his stupid mistakes.

The camping trip totally changed things. Norma had actually sang around the cozy campfire, and now everyone would know the gift in her possession. Anthony had gotten closer to the Parker teens and was influenced to use his singing voice as well. Wait until Portentous found out that Lisa agreed to date Anthony due to his changed demeanor. No longer was he a threat to her moral reputation or a detriment to Chad's weak faith.

If that weren't enough, Glen had actually put his arm around his wife as they drove back home, and the Parker's were having a time of praise for answered prayer!! He could not imagine telling Portentous the news. The only thing missing was Glen's conversion! He must stop that from happening. He must intervene in new unsuspecting ways. He could do it!! He would skip his meeting with Portentous until he had better news to share. He would stalk the entire family until he was certain where to strike. They all had chinks in the armor. It was his job to find it, use it against them and bring them down!

Chapter 5

View One

It had only been a few weeks since the camping trip and already Glen seemed to be reverting back to his old ways. Once again he seemed to be critical of everything from his family to the church. Norma was baffled at his change in behavior. Slowly, he became more agitated and easily provoked.

"There is no way I want my son to be dating that spoiled preacher's daughter. He doesn't need a girl like her!" He spouted off one day out of the blue as he sat scowling before the television. For some reason, he continued to concentrate on every unfavorable detail of the camping trip. He smirked at the thought of Lisa and her overloaded suitcase. Instead of the parents backing his suggestion to re-pack, in his opinion, they gave in to the bratty behavior of their teenager.

Chad was no better. He and Anthony spent quite a bit of time together and he wondered what they talked about. He noticed his son was no longer laughing when he poked fun at his mother. He didn't like it. He wanted Anthony to be tough and a real man! He found Chad's sweet words to his mother discussing. He's a Sissy! Then there was the preacher and his wife. Probably phonies! Oh, they put on a good act in front of others, but he was sure Martin gave Christine 'what for' if she got out of line. He had a strong personality that probably remained hidden from view to the average church person. He probably ruled with an iron fist at home... and well he should!

Glen knew the pastor had no problem making a decision and sticking with it if he was sure the Lord was behind it. It didn't matter if you had a fat wallet or were unemployed; the preacher treated every member with dignity and importance. He would not run the congregation through the Wealth Engine software he'd purchased and had no real idea who could cough up more money if someone put the squeeze on them.

He decided to allow Norma and Anthony to sing in the choir and he looked forward to them singing specials. It made the family look much more important to be on the platform. He warmed to the idea, just as long as his wife didn't start getting a big head about it. He would help her to remember her place!

The Parkers were having troubles of their own. Chad had accidently broken one of Lisa's favorite sculptures that she had made in art class. It had won an award as it was considered the best in her class. It was an accident, but Lisa knew that Chad and Anthony were playing catch in the house when it happened. True to the unwritten sibling code, she would not tell her parents.

"You can glue it together. It's not that big a deal!" said Chad in a 'what's-the-big-deal' tone.

"Sure, it won't even be noticeable if you glue it." Anthony chimed in.

"Glue it?? You two don't have a clue!" Lisa fumed. She wasn't sure what upset her the most. Did either of them realize how important that sculpture was to her? Maybe they didn't like it in the first place. Dumb boys!

Christine was having her own problems with dinner. She rarely needed to look at a recipe but today she just couldn't keep her thoughts together. Her mind raced around in every direction and she didn't seem to be able to concentrate. The worst part was *where* her mind raced! She was not given to jealousy as a rule, but when Cheryl came knocking on their door with a tight, low cut revealing blouse it raised her concern.

"I came to borrow your man!" she said in an airy Marilyn Monroe voice, while she shifted her hips up and down as she spoke.

"He's not home yet. Is there something I can help you with?" her voice had an edge to it and Cheryl responded in turn.

"No, I need a man!" she giggled.

"I have a car problem that I think Marty can easily fix." No one called Martin Marty except his mother. Christine could feel the warmth in her cheeks and tried to remain calm.

"Actually, you would probably be better off asking Dave next door. He's quite the mechanic. My husband generally takes everything to him, as car problems aren't his specialty." Cheryl stood with her arms folded enjoying her discomfort. She knew she looked pretty enticing in her blouse and short shorts and she considered Christine a frumpy house wife in comparison.

"Really? I got the impression he was good at just about everything last week when we were running together." She almost burst into laughter when she saw the look on Christine's face. Obviously, he had never mentioned running into her.

"Don't look so upset, Christine! I was just going to borrow him. I promise I'll bring him back when I'm done with him." She said coyly.

"I'll give my husband the message." Christine could barely get the words to roll off her tongue. When she closed the door, she heard the crash upstairs and decided if no screaming ensued; she would go back to the kitchen and figure out dinner.

"Martin came home late and seemed upset. He had received several calls from church members needing to meet with him. Generally, he had compassion for the hurting, but today he felt angry. Why didn't they ever read God's Word to find the answers? They relied on him to spoon feed them. Another couple called having marital problems and Martin almost told his secretary not to give them an appointment. They hadn't done any of the things he told them to do at their last meeting. What did they want him to do? He didn't have a magic wand to make everyone all better! Maybe some of them needed to go through some trials to strengthen them.

"I hope dinner is ready, I'm famished." He said as he yanked off his tie and plopped into his usual chair.

"It's going to be a while! Maybe you could go for a quick run. I think Cheryl is already out there!" The words startled her as she hadn't expected to say them. Her harsh tone shocked him. Before he could answer, he could hear the commotion coming from upstairs.

"Do we have glue?" snapped Lisa holding her broken statue.

"What happened?" asked Christine.

"It's broken! I didn't think I needed to explain it."

"Don't you use that tone with me, young lady! I can see it's broken. I asked how?!"

"No, you asked *what* happened."

"So, what are you doing? Down here telling on me, Lisa?" Chad broke in.

"I didn't say anything, but I'll bet they can figure it out. I'm holding a broken sculpture and you're holding a mitt and baseball... hmmm... let's see if we can figure it out."

Martin stood for a few quiet minutes watching his family disintegrate before his eyes when all at once he held his hands up.

"Everyone stop! Stop this very minute!" he ordered in his best in-charge voice.

"What is happening to us?" All eyes were on Martin. As they exchanged glances, it was as though they were all in a 'freeze frame' and could view it from the outside. Lisa with her broken sculpture glaring at her brother and Chad glaring back in anticipation of the trouble she was about to cause him. Christine was the first to understand and rushed into his arms.

"You're right, Martin! Look at us! We were having a prayer and praise meeting a couple of weeks ago. It's not like us to be at each other's throat."

"I had the worst day today with lots of mean spirited thoughts." Lisa admitted seeming to catch on.

"I'm with you on that! I didn't even want to talk to anyone today and I'm the preacher!" Martin confessed.

"Don't you see what's happening?" Martin asked.

"I was just thinking about how all that happened at the camping trip seemed to fade. Anthony and I have been arguing about stupid stuff and... well... I'm sorry Anthony." Chad stuck out his hand and Anthony shook it. It was all coming into focus.

"I was just going to say the same thing. If that's not enough, things have changed drastically at home." Said Anthony.

"When we first came home, my parents actually seemed to like each other. My mother still can't cook, but my dad quit hassling her about it. Then he started to make nasty comments about the trip, and everyone who went!" His face reddened as he felt ashamed.

"What *is* going on?" He seemed to be the only one left out of the loop.

"We are experiencing spiritual warfare?" Martin declared.

"What?" Anthony asked.

"You see, Anthony, our Enemy is not very happy with the changes that have been taking place." Anthony's eyes were wide with fear.

"Enemy? What Enemy?" he couldn't imagine what he was talking about! The words had a Sci-Fi feeling he wasn't familiar with.

"Anthony, there is a very dark side to this world. I suppose in a way, it's good we can't actually see what's going on. It would terrify us and yet it would compel us to speak to all we can about our great Lord."

"Are you talking about the Devil?" this was very abstract to him. His mind conjured up a red faced demon with a pitchfork and tail.

"Yes, but he does not work alone. Just as God has angels, the Bible clearly teaches that when Satan was kicked out of heaven, a third of the angels went with him. He doesn't come to us in a scary form or we would all be wise to his ways. Instead, he comes in forms that are pleasant to the eyes." It made sense, though the thought was still a frightening one.

"Don't you believe for a minute that all these things are coincidental." Christine nodded her agreement.

"It all makes such perfect sense to me now. I usually don't have much trouble putting a meal together, but I couldn't remember if I had all the ingredients or worse yet, whether I already put them in! I have been feeling exceptionally scatter brained and tired. I thought about calling your mother to encourage her several times this week and each time something unexpected happened." Christine was holding the phone in her hand to call Anthony's mother, when Cheryl came knocking on the door. What a double whammy that was!

"Dad's right, Anthony. I can see it now! Look how it all adds up. Every one of us can attest to it. Lisa and I seldom have a 'real' argument and I was ready to knock a few more of her sculptures on the floor. You and I have always gotten along and then all of a sudden we're at each other's throats! And that neighbor of ours is acting pretty weird too. I mean all the guys around here know she's hot... but" Christine's eyebrows went up! He wasn't telling something.

"But what?" she demanded to know.

"Well, the other day I was out washing my car and she appears out of nowhere. I hardly know her and she starts asking me a bunch of stuff."

"What kind of stuff?" Marty was as concerned as his wife. He remembered too well how she talked to him as he was taking his run.

"She asked me if I thought she should cut her hair." He sighed not wanting to tell more.

"That does sound kinda weird from a married adult" said Lisa, though she could easily see herself asking the same question.

"Yah, but she also asked me if I was drinking age and when I told her I wasn't, she said I could always have a nip at her house." Christine was boiling. What nerve this woman had!

"She also asked me if I had a girlfriend." He hesitated and realized he should just tell all.

"She asked me how old was the oldest girl I had ever dated. I told her I dated a few girls older than me but not many. Then she told me that older women had a lot to offer a young guy like me. That experience beats age or something like that." Christine was ready to storm out after her but Martin shook his head. They were all a bit too emotional to deal with anything else tonight.

"I almost went to see her one day after I saw her out on a run. I mean, she really looks good in that outfit she wears to run in and ... well... I guess I was flattered that she wanted me to come over to her house." Martin understood and said a silent prayer of thankfulness that his son never went to Cheryl's house.

"Anything else?" Christine was livid. Chad shook his head. He could see things clearly now.

"I'm just so glad I never went to see her. I feel ashamed that at one time I was praying for her and then after talking to her I was the one that needed prayer!" he smiled weakly.

"It's very easy to get caught in a snare, Chad. I council adults much older than you with the same kind of stories. Most never see it coming, but when they do they ignore it or give in to it!"

"This is all new to me! What should we do?" Anthony asked earnestly.

"I know exactly what we need to do." With that, Martin knelt beside their couch and Christine followed. Lisa took Anthony's hand as she knelt beside her parents. He felt a bit awkward at first, but once Martin began praying, he knew it was the answer. He was not accustomed to praying in this manner. The only prayers he heard were at church or the stilted ones his father offered at meal time, when he remembered. This was heartfelt, from the soul, prayer!

Chad, and Lisa both offered prayers as Anthony listened and when they finished, he added a very short prayer from his own heart. It was a wonderful experience. By the time they stood, it seemed things had drastically changed. Lisa and Chad were hugging as were Martin and Christine. He felt a little odd standing there watching, and at the same time enjoyed seeing how this family related to each other.

"Anthony, why don't you stay for dinner? We would love to have you" said Christine.

"Let me call my mom and let her know. Thanks!" Anthony immediately dialed the familiar number and knew his mother was having a rough day. He could hear his father in the background making his snide comments and there was a sniffle in Norma's voice that made him sad.

"I really appreciate the invitation, but I think I'll go home and spend some time with my mom." Christine hugged him and he blushed at the warm display of affection.

Anthony began to sing as he traveled home. His heart was light for the first time in weeks. Pastor was right; there really was something to be said about this whole spiritual warfare thing. He wondered if his mother was familiar with it.

Before he came through the door, he could hear his father's booming voice. He cringed as he remembered the number of times he had laughed with his father and made his own jokes! What was he thinking? He would never let someone treat *him* that way. He figured his mother knew that they were kidding because she was "Mom" and that made it okay! How incredibly stupid!!

"Hey Mom, what's for dinner?" he asked cheerfully.

"What were you expecting... filet mignon?" His dad sneered.

"I'm ordering out. What do you want?" Glen asked.

"What did you fix Mom?" he tried again.

"It's okay, honey. You can order out. My meatloaf didn't come out too good." She sighed. Anthony hated meatloaf. His mind drifted to the Parkers house. They were having beef stew and it smelled delicious, and he was stuck with dried out, bone hard, meatloaf. For an instant, he almost gave in to the heckling of his father. But was immediately reminded somewhere deep in his heart that he had a purpose for eating his mother's awful cooking.

"Meatloaf sounds good, Mom." He pulled a plate out of the cabinet and prayed silently that he would be able to get it down without choking.

"Don't be ridiculous! I'm ordering pizza! Now, what kind do you want?" Glen bellowed.

"Get what you want, Dad. I'm having meatloaf." He cut himself a hefty slice to prove his point and checked the table for side dishes. There was a wilted salad, and some canned green beans. He loaded everything on his plate and sat down next to his mother. He almost started laughing to watch the expressions on both his parents' faces. Both wore an expression of disbelief and rightly so!

Norma dished out a small piece of meatloaf for her own plate and added a few green beans. The salad looked too disgusting and she almost threw it away. She gave her son a smile as he took her hand.

"What's going on?" Glen demanded to know.

"I was just going to thank the Lord for the food is all." Anthony said.

"You better ask him to help you get it down and keep it down." Glen laughed. Anthony ignored him and bowed his head. He took his mother's hand and thanked the Lord for his mother and the food. It was brief and he felt slightly uncomfortable knowing his father's eyes were boring a hole in him. To his surprise, his father became openly hostile.

"I can tell you've been spending too much time around the Preacher and his family. Don't go trying to act all 'spiritual' on me, boy. I know you too well for you to fool me!"

"I'm not trying to fool anyone, Dad." Anthony had more to say, but shut his mouth before he said another word. He knew it would only make things worse.

"For the next few weeks, you just park your behind at home, you got that?" His tone was startling. His face was beet red and his clenched fists looked ready for a fight. Anthony's first reaction was to argue, of course, but again, his heart felt pricked to remain silent. It was all so new to him. He was accustomed to reacting in the flesh and had little dealings with the spirit's leading.

"Okay, Dad." He managed to say. Glen didn't like it. He was expecting an argument and at this point, he would have thrown Anthony against the wall if he dared open his mouth with an objection. He felt cheated! Who was this new mamby-pamby-momma's-boy?" He pushed one more time.

"And I'll tell you something else! I don't want you taking out that Preacher's daughter... Lilly... either. She's a spoiled brat and it's obvious her parents give her whatever she wants. Chad is pretty wimpy too." Anthony gritted his teeth. He wanted desperately to tell his father where to get off, but again, from deep within, he knew to hold his tongue.

"Are you listening to me?" Glen kicked Anthony's chair.

"I heard you Dad and her name is Lisa. We're just friends." Glen stalked out of the room. He didn't actually feel like he'd won. What was there to win? His son didn't give him much response. Still he was in control and that would have to be enough for now.

"I'm sorry, Anthony. I don't know why he's turned against the pastor and his family. Your father has forbidden me to call Mrs. Parker. She is such a lovely person and I was hoping to spend more time with her. I don't know what's the matter with him!" Anthony choked down a few mouthfuls of food and after a big swallow of water, took his mother by the hand and turned her chair to face his.

"Mom, we need to pray for Dad." He began

"Oh, I know he needs prayer…" her voice sounded deflated.

"No, I mean *really* pray! I want to have a set prayer time with you every day after school before he comes home from work."

"Really, Anthony?" she brightened.

"Something happened tonight over at the pastor's house that made me realize what we are up against." Her eyes were wide with amazement as he continued.

"Pastor talked about spiritual warfare and for the first time in my life, I actually understood what it meant. I know what it feels like!" He filled her in on the events that took place before his eyes including each testimony the Parkers gave regarding how they were attacked by the Enemy.

"Oh Anthony, for the first time in so long, I feel like there is hope!" she cried.

"I can help you with your relationship with Mrs. Parker too. I'll just tell Chad and he'll make sure his mother comes over. She was going to call you anyway, but I don't think that's enough. You can talk to her on the phone while Dad is at work, but she shouldn't call when he's home. Instead, she should just stop by!" They talked while they finished dinner, and though the food wasn't good, somehow it didn't matter. It didn't matter at all!

That night while Glen was in the shower, Norma slipped out of bed and knelt in prayer. She felt stronger than she had in a long time. She knew she could lean not only on her Lord, but he had provided her with another arm to lean on. Anthony astonished her with his insight and wisdom. No longer did she feel unaided in this battle. As she prayed fervently for her family, the darkness seemed to fade. She felt hopeful and blessed.

View Two

Ominous' victory was short lived. He started off so well he almost returned early to give his report. He had really gone to work since the camping trip and was feeling pretty smug with the results.

He took his time to research each of his assignments and found some great discoveries. It never occurred to him that speaking to them while they watched mindless television proved invaluable. Their minds drifted in and out as sexual or violent scenes stamped into their unsuspecting brain. It was the perfect opportunity!

He noticed that Lisa was embarrassed by some of the commercials used to capture an audience, but Chad's head snapped to attention whenever commercials with scantily clad girls covered the screen. The internet also lured him from time to time. He was proud that he didn't actually visit the sites, but his heart beat faster and breath came in spurts when he innocently viewed a website that had graphics of almost nude models. He felt he hadn't broken any rules as it was unintentional... but tell that to the image stamped in his brain.

Cheryl was putty in his hand. She loved attention. Any male giving her a second glance was sure to go from first base to home plate in one easy date. The Cheryl's of the world were no problem. There were millions like her. Most came from homes that had already been destroyed. The scenarios were very similar. Cheryl was a second generation broken home victim. Her mother, Rita, had several children by various males. None of them offered to marry her, though several lived with her long enough to scarf up a free meal and perhaps dip into her welfare funds. She trapped one into a brief marriage that ended when Cheryl was in preschool.

Rita came from a home where the father rarely made an appearance. He came home long enough to eat, fight with her mother and on occasion, make another baby. She loved him and she hated him. She married a man much like her father.

He was the father of two of her children but took no notice of Cheryl after he had his first son. With no male attention, she sought for it on the streets, and often in the backseat of her boyfriend's car. She had no understanding of love and therefore could not distinguish love from sex.

By the time Cheryl had reached her teenage years, she left home with James, who was the first man to make promises in exchange for certain favors. Unfortunately, James owned an exotic dancer's club. It was in a seedy part of town where vulgarity reigned supreme. He told her how beautiful she was and how easy it would be to make big money if she would be one of his dancers. Cheryl believed he loved her so was willing to do whatever it took to please him.

He started her off slowly with colorful, scanty costumes. She was to wiggle and jiggle her way around the stage blowing kisses to all the male customers. She loved it! She heard wolf whistles and lewd comments, but to her attention was attention and all was welcome.

The following months everything changed. James told her he didn't have enough dancers in his third tier. He explained that he had set up his club in levels of performance. She was on the first level. It was for beginners who were only on stage for three to four minutes depending on the background song. The next tier spent more time on stage and were expected to throw parts of their costumes to lucky patrons. At the end of the performance, those who caught the costume pieces were allowed to spend time with the performer. His top level dancers were for a specific audience. These girls stripped completely and were expected to go with the highest bidder for 'favors' of their choice.

What James didn't tell her is the reason he couldn't keep this level staffed. He didn't tell her that he gave the girls a tiny percentage of the money. He didn't tell her how many girls had been brutally beaten or savagely harmed. And he didn't tell them how horrible they would feel about themselves in the years to come. Several of the girls who had been used up and spit out... eventually committed suicide. Men considered these dancers the bottom feeders of the world and were replaceable. Apparently, James felt the same way.

Cheryl soon discovered that James only loved James. As she got older, she was replaced by younger dancers and to add insult to injury, he kicked her out of the club as he felt no one wanted to look at a woman her age. Ahh! Those were the easy ones, thought Ominous!

He had managed to revert Glen's thinking. He was not a genuine believer, so was little challenge. He spent many hours speaking to Glen about his so called church family and pastoral family. Glen was coming along nicely. He decided to push Glen into violence. He was sure he could get him to strike his wife or son. He was a coward at heart and could be defeated by any man with a loud voice. But he felt powerful within the walls of his own home. Ominous shook with enthusiasm as he played the scene in his mind.

The problem was the preacher and his family! He had made such headway and then it was dashed as his plan was discovered. To add insult to injury, Chad had actually confessed and repented of his plan to get together with Cheryl.

Before it was over, they were all back on their knees and all his hard work had been foiled! As much as he hated and feared the idea, he was going to have to elicit the help of Portentous. He could not do this alone. He could never remain in the room as they sought help from his Enemy! He tried many times to plant himself firmly and wait until they were done, but none of them could do it. The room literally filled with the presence of the Lord Jesus Christ and no one could stand against Him. It was an awesome, seldom used weapon!

Chapter 6

View One

"I'm so glad you stopped by today!" Norma had no idea that Chad and Anthony orchestrated the meeting. The boys friendship grew stronger every day and Anthony's interest in Lisa also continued to grow. He knew she felt the same way and was probably wondering why he hadn't asked her out. What was he supposed to tell her? He couldn't let her know that his father was opposed to the relationship.

"You look great, Norma! Did you get your hair cut?" Norma blushed under such an unexpected compliment.

"I just snipped it here and there. It gets in my way sometimes." She wanted to tell her that her husband wouldn't give her the money for something he considered frivolous. Of course, he had no problem buying new golf clubs or anything else *he* desired. There was always money for that.

He loved feeling like the 'big man on campus' so when church members decided to go out after church to a local hamburger chain, he insisted on buying for everyone. He pulled out his well-worn credit card and bought for all. No one knew that it was money Norma needed for groceries or bills.

"How are you doing these days?" Christine ventured to ask.

"Actually, I'm doing better than I have in a long time. Do you know that Anthony and I have a time of prayer just about every day? Sometimes he doesn't get home until after Glen so we postpone it until the next day." Christine could read between the lines. She knew Glen would not approve, as crazy that sounds for a person who 'claims' to be a Christian.

"I want you to know how much I have enjoyed listening to you sing. I'm not sure which I love more… your solos or your duets with Anthony."

"I would much rather sing with my son. I hate to be alone on the platform!" she laughed. Christine smiled at her quiet, humble friend. She pressed further.

"How are things with Glen?" Norma wasn't expecting that question. She wasn't sure how to respond. She could list a hundred complaints but she wouldn't do it. Not even to her Pastor's wife.

"Fine." She muttered vaguely.

"Norma, I know things have been difficult. I have never said this to a church member before, but the Lord seems to nudge me that you need to hear it." Norma's eyes were wide with a fearful look. What did she know?

"I think it will give you more patience." Christine took a deep breath and took Norma's small hand.

"I don't believe Glen is a Christian." She was surprised when Norma nodded.

"It is good to have confirmation. I came to that conclusion after our camping trip. I don't know why it never occurred to me before. I guess when someone knows all the phrases and can quote a fair amount of Scripture, you assume they know the Lord."

"I think it is imperative to pray for him. There is a lot at stake."

"I want him to go to heaven too, Christine, and will pray to that end, but I don't understand … what's at stake?" It was frightening to think that maybe her husband didn't have much time left on earth. But how could Christine know that?

"Norma, there has been a lot of turmoil in the church. There seems to be more unhappiness and more faithlessness than ever. People who have always been the backbone of the church seem to be floundering."

"Do you think Glen is responsible?" she clutched her chest. It was unbearable to think that wherever the Booth's attended, the face of the church changed. Things had gotten so bad at one of the church's they attended that they were asked to leave. Anthony didn't know the pastor had asked them to find another place to worship. She was so humiliated she thought about staying home. Oddly, they began attending another church at Glen's request.

"I have been doing some research, Norma. My husband does a fair amount of counseling and it seems that the common denominator with people who are disgruntled is their connection with Glen. Oh, most of them won't actually give his name, but they use the same phrases and tell the same stories. I feel certain your husband is behind it."

"Do you want us to leave the church?" There were fresh tears in her eyes as she thought of once again leaving a fundamental church.

"No, no! I don't want you to leave! I want you to join me in fervent prayer for your husband's salvation and also the church." Norma breathed a sigh of relief.

"Glen is not solely responsible for the atmosphere at church, Norma. Please don't think I am blaming him entirely. But I am convinced, he is a major contributor."

"I was so hopeful when Glen seemed to soften at the camp. When we came home, his attitude was still sweet for a short time. I honestly don't know when it changed but it seemed to happen all at once. One day he was kind and the next day he went back to the way he was before the trip." Christine told her their experience and the discovery they made after their entire household was at each other's throats. It made perfect sense to Norma.

"That explains why Anthony has been meeting with me for prayer. I don't think he has come to the realization that his father is causing the trouble in church."

"Don't be so sure. Anthony is a smart boy and I think he might know more than you think. I don't think he wants to verbalize it, even to himself."

"It is a pretty bitter pill to swallow." She admitted.

"Can I ask you what you've done in the past when Glen has

been nasty?" Christine knew about bullying and wondered what her approach might be.

"I've tried everything. I've apologized, I've cried, I've tried to be sweeter than ever and took blame and responsibility for all that has gone wrong. I don't know what else to do."

"Have you ever threatened him?"

"Why no, of course not. That would be against Biblical teaching, wouldn't it?" Christine was thoughtful. She certainly wasn't trying to break up their marriage, but this wasn't any kind of marriage!

"I hate to ask this… but has Glen ever used any kind of force with you?"

"You mean hit me or something? Why no, though he has threatened to."

"He has threatened to hit you?" She was appalled.

"I don't think he means it. He just has a bad temper when he's mad. He's told me to leave the room because he doesn't want to have to look at me." Christine cringed. She couldn't imagine such treatment.

"But he's never actually put his hands on you in a hurtful way?" she pressed.

"He's never struck me, if that's what you mean. He has shoved me and he has gripped me so tightly when making a point that it left bruises on my arms. But he has never hit me." She knew she must sound pathetic. After all, she was speaking to Christine Parker! She probably had the marriage everyone dreamed of!

"I thought the other day he was actually going to hit me, though. He is more antagonized than ever for some reason. I don't know what's gotten into him. No one can say anything to him anymore without him flying off the handle."

"He sees you as weak and helpless. Maybe he's convinced himself that you would be nothing without him. But you are going to do things differently for a while." Christine needed to speak to her husband before she said too much, but she felt he would agree with her. You didn't stop a bully by giving in to him; not even in a marriage.

"The next time he 'flies of the handle' as you say, I don't want you to take the responsibility of it unless it's definitely your fault. If you have willingly gone against him, that is wrong and you should apologize. If he pushes you, threatens you, or just starts speaking to you in that harsh demeaning tone, I want you to stop him."

"Stop him? Are you kidding me? I would have no idea what to do."

"You're going to put your hand up and say you've heard enough. Tell him to stop speaking to you that way. If he continues, tell him you are going to leave."

"I can't make an idle threat like that. Where would I go? What would I do?" she stammered.

"I don't think it will come to that. He will be so dumbfounded he won't know what to say or do." Norma gasped at the thought. She had never stood up to him. They had arguments early in marriage, but Glen proved she was no match for him. He always won and always had his way.

"You don't know Glen. He will be furious! I don't know what he would do if I talked to him like that."

"I've known many Glen's in my time, Norma. I hate to tell you, but you have helped to create this behavior you now have to live with."

"He won't back down."

"Yes, he will. I am certain of it, because all bullies back down when challenged." She sounded so sure of herself that Norma felt hopeful. She couldn't imagine actually pulling it off, but it was nice to have someone in her corner.

"With that said, I've brought over some of my tried and true recipes that I know you can master. We'll fix this one together and I know your family will love it." She pulled out an envelope with several recipes and laid them on the table. After leafing through several, she pulled out one with a smile. It was fast and easy and she knew even the most inexperienced cook could master it.

"Let's get started. I want to be out the door before Glen comes home from work. And I want you to take all the credit for this meal!" she wagged her finger and spoke with authority.

"I'll take the credit if it comes out good... how's that?" she laughed.

"Deal!" Christine had no intention of seeing her fail. Norma began searching for ingredients and Christine talked while they were cooking. She told her the importance of using spices to give her dishes more flavor. Norma's cooking was very bland as she had no idea the difference between pumpkin spice and all spice.

Soon the kitchen was filled with the wonderful aroma of a great meal. Anthony had come home as they were finishing up and set the table for his mother.

"Okay, the rest is up to you. Remember, I supervised you, but you actually did the cooking, Norma. I want you to take full credit."

"It really smells good, Mom." Anthony chimed in.

"And I want you to remember our talk! Please do as I asked and I guarantee you will get a different result." Anthony looked at his mother quizzically. She nodded thoughtfully as she walked Christine to the door. After a quick hug, Christine headed for home smiling. She prayed Norma would be strong enough to stand up for herself.

"What was Mrs. Parker talking about Mom? Different results with who?" He could guess, but he wanted his mother to fill in the gaps. She told him briefly about their conversation without too many details. She certainly wasn't going to call her husband a bully in front of her son. She still had a hard time believing it would work or if it was the right thing to do.

"Hey Dad, I didn't hear you come in." Glen felt something was amiss. What were they talking about in such hushed tones?

"Dinner is ready, Glen. I just need to put it on the table." He narrowed his eyes as he looked at her. What was she so happy about? As he walked to his place at the kitchen table he plopped himself down and waited to be served.

"I tried a new recipe. I hope you'll like it." She said sweetly.

"If it's anything like last night's disaster, I'm going to ask Pizza to Go to put us on speed dial!" he laughed and poked at Anthony in an attempt to get him involved.

"Smells good, Mom." Anthony said.

"You haven't tasted it yet, boy. Not everything that smells good tastes good!" Anthony waited to see if his dad was in the mood for grace. Not tonight. He plunged his fork into his plate and stuffed in a mouthful. Anthony did the same. It was delicious.

"Okay, Norma. Where did you get this food? Did you order out? Don't try to pass off food you paid for as your own." She stared at him for a moment and realized he didn't want the food to be hers. He wanted to make her miserable for some reason.

"I watched her cook it, Dad. Mom made this herself." He glared at his son and scooted his chair away from the table.

"Why are you hanging out in the kitchen? The kitchen is no place for a man! If I didn't know better, I would think you cooked it. You have a better chance of making an edible meal than your mother!"

"I was only talking to Mom. I didn't cook anything!" Norma and Anthony ate in silence for a few minutes as Glen brooded.

"Can I have a second helping?" Anthony asked. Norma almost laughed as no one ever asked for more of her cooking.

"You can have some later. I need to talk to your mother." Anthony didn't like the look in his father's eye but he nodded respectfully and left the room.

"Okay, Norma. What's going on?"

"What do you mean? It's dinner time and I made dinner." He noticed her voice was strong and took an immediate disliking for her tone.

"Don't you like dinner?" she asked

"It's edible." He snarled. She continued to eat and watched him carefully. He seemed explosive.

"Where did you get this recipe?"

"I got it from Christine Parker."

"Was that woman over here?"

"Why, yes. She stopped in to see me."

"I told you I don't want you hanging around her trying to put on an act just because you're singing now." He was furious.

"She came here. I did not go to her house and I did not call her."

"You getting smart with me?" he slammed his fist on the table making her jump.

"No. I'm just telling you..."

"You're not telling me nothing! *I* tell *you*! I decide when and where and if things happen. You got that, Missy!" he pinned her against the wall with his hand balled up. This was usually the time she cowered but not this time.

"Get your hands off me right now, Glen." She could see the surprise in his eyes. She had never spoken to him so firmly.

"If you don't release me at once, I am going to call the police!" He let her go as if she had slapped him. He had never heard her voice so strong or her stare so intense.

"You wouldn't dare!" he growled but she noticed his voice had lost its confidence.

"I don't think you want to press it. I've had enough." Her voice was calm and clear but there was an air of authority he had never heard before.

"Where is this coming from?" He snapped.

"It is coming from a lifetime of your cruel treatment. I will not stand for it another day."

"Are you threatening me? What's gotten into you? I am your husband! You do as I say!"

"That's right! You are my husband... not my father... not my employer... not my tyrannical ruler!" He released his grip and she sat down, shook out her napkin and began eating as if everything was right with the world. He was speechless!

He plopped onto chair beside her and stared at her as if he had no idea who she was. It would have been comical if there wasn't so much at stake. He took a long gulp of his tea and began munching on the sumptuous dinner she had prepared as he muttered under his breath. He was truly dumbfounded.

Anthony had been listening and praying at the kitchen door but remained hidden from view. He almost shouted in triumph for his mother. He was nearly as astounded as his father. Neither of them had ever known this side of Norma existed.

73

Quietly, he took his place beside his mother, refilled his plate and began eating. Everyone ate in silence, each too deep in thought for conversation.

It remained a very quiet evening with Norma reading a book and Glen staring at the television. Softly, Norma turned off the kitchen light and headed upstairs to get ready for bed. Glen was soon at her heels.

"This isn't over, woman! Not by a long shot! I will not have you threaten me! You got that?" Once again he clamped a vice like grip around her wrist.

"Let go of me, Glen!" she said quietly. She didn't like the look in his eyes.

"Or what? You still threatening to call the police?"

"Only if I have to." She tried to pull away, but he was too strong.

"I think what you need is a little reminder of who is boss around here." He had never actually hit her before, but it certainly looked like the time had come.

"Let me go. I will not tell you again." Her voice sounded more like the Norma he was used to. He could detect a bit of fear and it gave him the courage to continue.

"I'll let go when *I* say, not when *you* say! If you ever threaten me again, you'll be calling the police from a hospital bed! Am I making myself understood?" Glen was shaking with hostility and Norma had never seen him so agitated. He seemed to be holding himself back from his true intent, which was to harm her.

"Don't say anything that you don't want in the police report, Glen." Her voice was a bit more forceful and he couldn't tell for sure if she was entirely serious.

"Hit her... hit her... hit her..." the voice in his mind was so strong he wondered if she could hear it too.

"Mom, are you okay?" Anthony couldn't stand another minute of it. Their voices echoed through his room and although they weren't loud enough to distinguish what was said, he knew in his heart his mother needed him.

"This doesn't concern you, Anthony." All at once, Glen could see the picture through his son's eyes. He had his mother against the wall with one hand bruising her wrist and the other ready to punch her. What was happening to him? He had never hit his wife. He never needed to do anything but scold, ridicule and threaten and she was putty in his hands. He immediately let her go and ran out of the room. In minutes, they heard the squeal of tires as Glen pulled out of the driveway.

"He didn't hurt you, did he?" Norma flew into her son's arms and sobbed her heart out. This was not working! She couldn't do it. She would apologize as soon as he came back.

"I can't stand up to him, Anthony. I'm not strong enough. Christine was wrong. He is not going to change." She cried into his shoulder.

"I think you're wrong. You didn't see his face when I came in. I can't explain it Mom, but it was like he woke up and saw himself standing over you. I could tell he was appalled! That's why he ran out of the room like he did." Anthony and Norma began to pray together and afterwards, he encouraged his mother to call the pastor and tell him what had taken place…but the pastor was not home.

~~~~~~

"Cheryl, what were you thinking?" Martin and Christine were at her hospital bedside. Martin insisted his wife accompany him on this visit.

"I'm no good, preacher! You should know that by now!" she croaked.

"None of us are good, Cheryl. That's why the grace of God is so important." She cried silently as the tears wet her pillow. She was ashamed and embarrassed to find the preacher and his wife at her side. They were good people and she had tried to seduce both Martin and their teenage son for some crazy reason.

"No, you're wrong. Your family is what family should be like. Even your kids are too good for this world. Do you know Chad came to my house yesterday to talk to me?" Christine involuntarily gasped. She remembered only too well their previous conversation.

"Don't worry, Christine. He didn't come to my house to drink or anything like that. No, he came to talk to me about… religion." She rolled her eyes.

"I guess it's pretty pathetic when a teenage boy comes to your door because he thinks you're going to hell! Not that I blame him. I guess after the suggestions and offers I made to him, he couldn't help it." She sobbed.

"Cheryl, Chad came because he wanted to tell you why he is not the typical teenage boy that would have jumped at the chance to take you up on your offers." Martin said as politely as possible. She didn't seem to be listening, but had a faraway look in her eyes, and spoke as if describing a scene.

"I used to be something! When I danced, the room filled with men. Most of them begging for my number. I could have my choice of anyone in the room." She smiled widely as she reminisced.

"The shoes were killers, but it was worth it. There wasn't a man who didn't want me then. But that was then!" the smile left her face as the images faded.

"Look at me now! My husband left me and told me no man in his right mind would want me. I guess he was right!" Christine patted her arm and prayed silently for her. Hopefully, she would be all right in a few days. She had been rushed to the hospital after next door neighbor, Emily, noticed Cheryl's dog whimpering and scratching on the door. Cheryl cared for her little dog as if she was her child so it was odd no one was letting her in. But once it started raining and the dog was still scratching to get in, the neighbor knew something was amiss.

"Emily should have just let me die!" She whimpered.

"And then what would have happened?" Martin asked.

"Then I would be out of this cruel world." She sighed.

"Where would you be?" he asked.

"According to Chad, I would be in hell."

"It's not Chad's decision, it's yours."

76

"Oh, preacher, you've got to be joking! Can you imagine me coming to your church with all those people?" she laughed.

"Yes, I can. There isn't much difference between you and them. They are sinners too. They have found that the Lord Jesus Christ is seeking and saving those who will come to Him." Cheryl crooked her lip.

"Well, I can agree on one thing. There isn't much difference between them and me for some of them. Do you know I actually had some guy come to my door to talk to me and he ended up staying for dinner? I know if I had played it right, he wouldn't have left until morning. What do you think of that?" she waited for shock to register.

"It comes as no surprise. We are all struggling with something. When we don't turn it over to the Lord, it is easy to give in to our flesh."

"I didn't expect that to be your answer." She said honestly.

"If you would let me show you from the Bible..." Martin pulled the Bible from his pocket as he spoke.

"You know, I'm pretty tired. Maybe we can talk another time." It was obvious, he was dismissed. She pulled the sheet under her chin and closed her eyes.

"Would you mind if I pray with you?" he asked.

"Suit yourself. I suppose it's in the preacher's handbook" she smiled. He prayed briefly for her survival and also an opportunity to speak to her about the gift of life through Jesus.

Her eyes were shut tightly, but he saw a tear escape and knew she was listening to his words. He planned to come again tomorrow and asked the Lord to prepare her heart. Martin took his wife's hand and began walking down the long corridor that led to the elevator. Weariness made their walk sluggish and the walk seem longer than usual.

"Martin, your phone is buzzing." He had put his phone on vibrate and paid no attention to the quiet buzzing in his pocket. He sighed as he glanced at the caller's number.

"It's Norma Booth." He frowned. Both of them knew Norma

would never call unless it was urgent… or past urgent!! Immediately, he dialed her number. He wondered if he would need to make a trip to their home to arbitrate, unaware that Glen was not there. His drive took him to a familiar location.

"Hey, Glen! It's been a while. What'll it be?" asked the bartender of the Escape Bar and Grill.

"Give me the usual." Glen smiled at the bartender he knew so well. Everyone called him Jack, though they knew it was a fictitious name. Jack had been in prison years ago and never wanted anyone to know his real identity. Of course, in a bar, people would rather tell their story than listen to yours. That was fine with him. The more liquor, the greater the tips.

"It's been a rough day." He added.

"Trouble at home?"

"Yep! I tell you, back in the day… my mother did exactly what my dad said. We all did. No one dared question him and it didn't matter if he was right or wrong, we did what we were told."

"From what you've told me about your wife, you shouldn't have any problem keeping the upper hand. It's those crazy feminists that can be pretty hard to deal with." The bartender remembered opening the door for one and she bit his head off. Sheesh… you couldn't even be polite!

"She back talked me! She seems to have forgotten her place." Glen smacked his fist beside his cold beer and shook his head angrily.

"Did you put her in her place?

"I would have, but my son came in and looked at me like I was some kind of monster!" There was a hint of sorrow in his voice but he recovered quickly."I don't know what's gotten into her, but I won't tolerate it." Glen guzzled the beer down quickly and the bartender was quick to grab him a refill.

"You just sit here and unwind and I'm sure you can straighten everything out when you get back home." He was the kind of patron every bartender was looking for. One miserable enough to drink away the problem… or at least deaden the misery for a while. Jack hadn't seen Glen in a few months and vaguely wondered why he stopped coming in. He didn't like the guy much, but he was a good tipper and had some funny stories so he tolerated him. He especially enjoyed Glen's abusive tales about his home. He could relate. Jack's time in prison was largely due to an ex-wife who he had threatened and put in the hospital repeatedly. She was whiney and annoying and as far as Jack was concerned, he did nothing wrong.

"Maybe it's time to dump her." Jack laughed. Glen looked at him quizzically. He would never do that... but why? Did he love her? He took a swig of his beer and did his best to put the question out of his mind. He was going to need a few more drinks before the image of his frightened son would leave his brain. He had never hit his mother, so why did he stare at him as if he was some kind of villain? Maybe Norma had put some ideas in the boy's head when he wasn't home. And as far as the preacher and his wife were concerned, they had some answering to do. He was sure the confident change in Norma was a direct result of that snooping preacher's wife. Why couldn't she just leave well enough alone?

"We got burgers on sale today." Jack offered.

"I aint hungry." He snarled.

"Why not? Did your wife learn to cook?" He expected Glen to have some nasty remarks about her cooking, but he just stared at his beer mug and scowled.

"I think she learned a couple new recipes from the preacher's wife."

"Preacher's wife??? You telling me you go to church somewhere?" That was hard to believe from all his experiences with the man. Glen was nasty and arrogant and full of himself. Not the kind of man Jack would have thought cared anything about church.

"Yes, I go to church! I don't know why that surprises you. I know a lot about the Bible too. Just ask me a question and you'll see." He puffed. Jack narrowed his eyes at the man. If he was what you found on the inside of a church, he had no intention of ever attending.

"Don't go getting insulted! I guess I was thinking of the churches I was dragged to as a child." Rick scoffed. Glen glared at him.

"I can't imagine you darkening the doorway of a church." He spat.

Jack narrowed his eyes. Who did this pompous man think he was? As far as he could tell, neither of them were church material.

"Yah, my mother was pretty religious. She wanted me to find Jesus! You know the type. I'm sure you go to one of the liberal churches out there that won't condemn you for stopping in for a drink now and then." To his surprise, Glen's face clouded and he pushed his beer away.

"I need to get going." He slapped some money on the bar and pushed his arms through his jacket.

"No need to hurry! We were just getting started." Jack realized he should have left things alone. Glen had more money in his pocket and it looked like it wasn't going to be spent there!

"Maybe another time." Glen's voice trailed after him as he headed for the door. Glen hurried out the door and started his vehicle not knowing where to go. He didn't want to go home, but Jack had crossed the line. How dare he speak to him that way! He was a dedicated church member! Jack made him feel like a heathen.

Slowly, he pulled his car from the lot as his eyes searched the road ahead. There was another drinking establishment down the road. It seemed to have a lot of younger people hanging around and he didn't think he would fit in with such a crowd, but he wanted at least one more drink before heading home, so he pulled in the lot and found an inconspicuous space.

There were quite a few girls perched around the bar probably looking for someone to buy them a drink. He wasn't interested. He just wanted to spend some time alone with a friendly, bartender who agreed with him, and encouraged complaining customers!

"Hey, handsome! I've never seen you in here before!" Glen barely turned his head and saw a young lady around Anthony's age smiling at him. No way!

"Just came in for a drink and some quiet time." She frowned and made her way to the other side of the bar. He noticed an attractive red head staring his way and he averted his eyes as he ordered a beer. She watched him from her stool and never made a move to speak to him.

"I'll have another!" The bartender snapped open the bottle and placed it before Glen.

"I'm Jason. I don't believe I've seen you in here before, though you might come in on a different shift." He smiled as he pushed a bowl of pretzels his way.

"Just passing through." He smiled feeling a little light headed. He should have known better than to pound them down so fast! He decided to sit in a quiet booth as the bar was getting noisier by the minute. He slid in close to the wall and to his surprise, the red head slipped in beside him.

"Oh, I'm sorry! I guess we both had the same idea!" she laughed.

"It's okay. I'll move."

"I don't mind sharing." She said pleasantly. She was blocking him from escaping and in a few minutes, it really didn't matter. What was the harm?

"I don't live around here, so I didn't know how crowded this place was going to get!" she laughed again and the soft, lilting sound was pleasant to his ears.

"I know what you mean. I wonder if these people are even old enough for a drink!" Glen remarked.

"They look like high school kids." They laughed together and Glen began to feel comfortable with her.

"Jail bait!" he added. She giggled and again he began to feel as if he had known her for a long time. It had been a while since his last drinking binge, and figured the alcohol was to blame for his lack of concern. Immediately, he dismissed his earlier concern. After all, *who would know* seemed to whisper in his ear.

"I really shouldn't be here." She confided.

"I just had to get away from my old man for a while." He nodded in agreement wondering if she was going to tell her story.

"My shift ended early, and I just didn't want to go home yet. It's tough when you are the sole support of the family."

"What's wrong with your husband? Did he lose his job?"

"He's lost every job he ever had. At this point, he doesn't have enough skills or friends to help him secure another position." She sighed.

"So, that leaves everything up to me. Not only do I work a full time job, but he doesn't lift a finger to help around the house either. When I get home, there is laundry, cleaning and cooking to do." Her face reddened as she realized she was divulging intimate information to a total stranger.

"Oh, I'm so sorry! You didn't come her to listen to the woes of a total stranger!"

"Maybe it's easier talking to someone who isn't related to the problem and doesn't even know your name."

"I'm Rebecca." Instead of shaking his hand, she laid a delicate hand on his sleeve. Glen wondered if he should give a bogus name, but worried that he would forget his deception and make a fool of himself.

"Glen" he replied quietly.

They were both quiet for a few moments as they listened to some skirmish at the bar. These were definitely very young drinkers who seemed to have to prove something to someone.

"I don't think this is the place for us." Rebecca laughed as a crowd gathered around a couple young men arguing and pointing to a basketball game on the screen in front of them. Glen nodded and to his amazement uttered the words.

"Where would you suggest?" It was somewhere in his brain, but he never intended to speak the words. What was happening to him? First his fight with Norma that almost escalated into blows, and now sitting at a bar with a strange woman inferring his availability.

"My car is in the lot. Let's just go for a drive." She offered casually.

"I should probably get going." He felt flushed and light headed and was sure if they talked much longer she would take him for an idiot.

"Nonsense, we will only go for a short drive to clear our heads and then you can go back home to your wife and I'll head back home to my husband." She stated as though the matter was closed. Generally, he did not like a woman to make decisions, but for some reason, he enjoyed her taking the lead. Without another word, she gathered her purse in one hand and lifted him to his feet with the other.

"I promise, I don't bite! Well, I don't leave marks anyway!" she laughed and he laughed with her. He walked close behind her, but left enough space between them to examine her figure. He liked what he saw. It made him feel young and virile.

In minutes, they were in her car driving down the highway as if neither had a care in the world. She had a beautiful sports car. He hadn't asked her where she worked and had her pegged for a waitress. He glanced at her profile and creased his brow. There was nothing about her clothing, jewelry, and especially her vehicle that said 'waitress.' "I'm going to take you to my favorite spot, Glen. I think you will like it as much as I do." Within minutes she turned off onto a long, winding dirt road that seemed to go nowhere. Before he could protest, they rounded the corner and he could see a beautiful lake with trees and lush green foliage. It was breathtaking.

"What did I tell you?! Isn't it worth the drive!" she sighed.

"What a beautiful spot! Is this your land?" he asked incredulously.

"It belongs to my father. I come here as often as possible as I love it. I don't know why, but I thought you would love it too." She reached for his hand and he made no attempt to move it. It felt right.

"I should have known the day I brought my husband here and he began looking for something to shoot, that he was not the man for me. I guess when you're young and foolish, you don't consider such things." She turned the radio to a classical station and both sat content as they listened.

"Would you like to walk around the lake?" She opened her door and took a few steps. He was beside her in seconds. It was such a quiet, peaceful place; he barely noticed when she slipped her arm through his. They stopped to watch a heron sweep across the water in search of a fish dinner. She took the opportunity to lay her head on his shoulder as they gazed at the water before them.

"We probably should start heading back." He didn't want to, but the urge to kiss her was overwhelming.

"You to your problems and me to mine?" she said huskily.

"I suppose." He replied; his voice dry and raspy. She turned his face toward hers and kissed him squarely on the lips. To his surprise, he did not pull away but held her tight and kissed her fervently.

"We need to go." He croaked with his last ounce of will power.

"Where do you want to go?" He held her away from him but she pressed herself against him and he felt weak. She took his hand and led him further down the path to a small gate house. He followed her inside like a sleep walker.

"It's okay, Glen. We are quite alone I assure you." She kicked off her shoes and began undressing. He felt shocked, mortified, and pleased at the same time. He felt the urgent need to say no... to stop things from moving forward... but that time had passed.

Chapter 7 View One

Martin knocked on Emily's door. He promised Cheryl he would make sure someone was looking after her little dog.

"How is she?" Emily asked. She had come to understand Cheryl, and had compassion for her. Emily had come from a similar background, and could have easily chosen the same life style.

"She should be home in a few days if everything goes according to plan. She'll be weak, but I think she will be fine" said Martin. He promised Cheryl that he would stop by and check on her little dog. She was fortunate to have such a caring neighbor. Her beloved pet would be in good hands until she was out of the hospital.

"I hope you have been able to talk some sense into that girl, Preacher. She's been quite a mess for as long as I've known her." Emily frowned.

"I didn't realize she was feeling so hopeless. My wife is planning to spend some time with her once she gets home. We certainly are praying for her."

"She needs it!" she said in a haughty voice.

"We could all use prayer." Martin assured her.

"Oh yes, of course. It's just that… well… some need it more than others." Emily said apologetically.

"But you know the kind of life she lives. We have similar backgrounds but I chose the high road and she chose the low, if you know what I mean." She smiled. Martin stood quietly for a few seconds praying for his next words to be helpful. It was obvious, Emily felt superior to her friend.

"I pray I can help her find her way from the broad way that leads to destruction to the narrow way that is available for those who choose Christ."

"Yes, yes. That's exactly what she needs. No doubt she is on the road to destruction. I have stopped counting the number of men that go in and out of her life." She sniffed importantly.

"Can I ask you, Emily, what road are you on?" Martin asked quietly. He wasn't trying to make her uncomfortable, though the question generally did so.

"What do you mean? I don't know what kind of stories Cheryl might have told you, but I assure you we are nothing alike!" Her blushed face told him a different story. He knew nothing of Emily's life and Cheryl had never filled him in, though it was obvious she was hiding something. Martin remained silent which made Emily more suspicious.

"Maybe a long time ago there were some minor indiscretions, but that was a long time ago!" She was furious. Is that the thanks you get for trying to help someone?

"I have always tried to be of help. I don't suppose she told you that we came from the same kind of background! But I rose above it! Okay, so there was a time when I came to one of her parties and things got a little out of hand, but you know how it is, Preacher." She smiled uneasily. He continued to stay silent, while she continued to fill in the blanks.

"Besides, I was probably the best behaved there! Everyone else was drunk and disorderly." She added.

"You haven't answered my question."

"Which road am I on? I'm a Christian, so I am on the right road!" she retorted.

"How long have you been a Christian?" he tried.

"As long as I can remember! I mean, my parents were pretty awful people, but I had a Grandmother who insisted I go to church with her and I went every Sunday like clockwork." She countered.

"It's good to have a Grandmother like that." He smiled thinking of his own.

"I can't say I learned that much, but it's still important to attend, don't you think? I think God puts it on our 'good work' side of the scale." She said.

"Yes, the Bible teaches that we should attend church, but that doesn't make you a Christian."

"Oh, I know there are other things too. You have to keep the 10 commandments and be … uh, good." She shrugged.

"And do you keep the 10 commandments?" he asked.

"I keep the most important ones." She replied.

"Are some more important than others?"

"You have to admit 'thou shalt not kill' is way more important than the one about taking God's name in vain." She said smartly.

"Many people would feel the same way, but God doesn't. It is because we decide what sins are big and what are not. Most people would never be able to recite the commandments and no one has ever kept them except One." He smiled.

"Are you the one?" she asked amazed. She had never met anyone that made that claim.

"No, not me! I've broken most of them at one point or another. I was talking about Jesus."

"Oh, of course!" she replied as if that was understood.

"That's why Jesus came and died for our sins…"

"You're not talking to some drunk in the alley, Preacher!" she interrupted.

"I know Jesus died on the cross. It might interest you to know that I have read most of the Bible and I know the main stories." Martin sighed. He had no intention of making her defensive, but it was generally the reaction.

"I'm sorry Emily. I think you misunderstand my intent." He smiled warmly.

"Just don't want you to put me in the same boat as Cheryl! Now there is a person who needs to hear what you're saying. I don't think she knows anything at all about the Bible."

"Emily, I think you have been a wonderful neighbor and friend to Cheryl and I am grateful she has someone to look after her once she gets home. As a matter of fact, you probably saved her life." Emily blushed and immediately dropped her defense.

"I never thought about it that way, but I guess you're right. She was lucky I was here." Her demeanor changed back to the original haughty, prideful style.

"I should get going, but it was nice talking to you, Preacher." Emily all but shut the door in his face and he stood for a few minutes feeling like a failure. He wanted to speak to Emily about her soul, but she became so defensive, he never had a chance to continue.

His shoulders sagged as he walked the few steps to his vehicle. His mind raced as he dissected their conversation. Was he too pushy? What could he have done differently to keep her from becoming so resistant? He bowed his head and prayed before starting the engine. The answer came quickly. In his heart he heard the answer. *"You planted the seed. Let the seed have time to germinate. Your words will take root if she is open and I will send another to water... in the end... I will harvest the soul."* He smiled as he pulled away.

"Open your heart, Emily! Please just open your heart to the truth!" he said as he pulled out of the driveway.

View Two

"Why so smug, Ominous? Have you some news that will keep me from thrashing you?" Portentous snarled. Though he wanted to hear good news, he would enjoy giving Ominous a good pounding.

"I think you will enjoy my report!" He stood with his chest puffed until Portentous gnashed him hatefully.

"I will decide if you have anything to brag about." He scowled. He did not like the boastful look in his nemesis' eyes.

"I am happy to report due to my constant ridicule and berating, Cheryl is in the hospital. I demanded her to end her life." He remarked importantly.

"When will she be here to torment?" Portentous asked. Ominous cleared his throat and muttered something incoherent.

"Speak up! I did not hear the answer to my question!" he was practically salivating with excitement!

"It appears she will recover." Portentous savagely pounced on Ominous and pummeled him repeatedly.

"This is your good news?! She is recovering? Maybe I should explain to you what a good report consists of, as you have no idea!" he screamed through the darkness.

"She is in a weakened state! I will finish her off once she comes home and no one is guarding her!" He gasped. Portentous loosened his grip.

"She will need to be alone with her thoughts! You must stop the Preacher or his wife and family from visiting! That will only make her stronger and less determined to do our bidding!" Portentous counseled.

"I will be there the moment she arrives. You can trust me to complete the job." Portentous glared at him. There was no confidence in his voice.

"What else have you bungled?" he snapped.

"The preacher made no headway with the other lost soul..." he began.

"Can you be more specific? There are millions of lost souls out there!" he said gleefully.

"I was speaking of Cheryl's neighbor, Emily. The preacher tried to talk to her about our Enemy, but she was too full of pride to listen." He avoided repeating the prayer Martin spoke aloud. Nor did he speak of the praise Martin gave the Enemy once his prayer seemed answered.

"Did the preacher give her Scripture from that blasted Book?" Ominous did not want to admit he plugged his ears. The words were too painful; the hate too deep to listen.

"Yes, but she was not listening."

"Hmmm, do not be so sure! I have been duped before into thinking no one was listening, but that Word seems to boomerang! When I least expected it, it was heeded. You must watch her closely. Do not let her ponder the Word that was spoken." Ominous nodded. Portentous was much wiser than he.

"I have saved the best till last." He grinned evilly and drew a deep breath. He knew he would be commended on this one.

"Well, out with it! I'm in no mood to guess."

"I designed the perfect atmosphere for Glen to *fall*." He giggled in spite of himself. He basked in his victory.

"Glen has a taste for liquor and after his fight with his wife; I whispered the name of his favorite, secluded tavern. He wasted no time getting there I tell you." He and Portentous had a rare laugh together.

"I can see there is more to tell!" Portentous leaned back and closed his eyes. He loved hearing the fall of mankind.

"Yes, there is. You see, I was a bit concerned when Glen left the bar after only a couple belts of liquor so I reminded him that the night was still young and he could use a couple more stiff drinks to calm his nerves after his wife was so horribly disrespectful."

"Do tell." Portentous grinned. Perhaps there was hope for Ominous after all.

"This is where the story gets really good! Glen went to a college sports bar where the girls are loose and willing and drugs flow freely."

"Hmm, I wouldn't have thought Glen would be comfortable there. He is older than the clientele and those youngsters wouldn't attract him. I hope you know what kind of woman interests him!" he chided.

"Yes, I do. As a matter of fact, there was a woman who was prodded there by another of our kind and between the two of us, they were putty in our mitts! Of course, he was a novice in comparison, but I showed him the ropes." He boasted.

"The woman appeared lonely and needy. A wonderful combination for destruction. It took little prompting to get the two of them alone, and the rest is history."

"I want to hear every detail. I want to know step by step how it fell into place." Portentous closed his rheumy eyes and smiled widely. These were the moments they looked forward to. Ominous saw his chance to get on the good side of Portentous and carefully filled in each detail. He spoke slowly and savored each word. He described each miniscule facet with particular attention to Glen's racing heart as he watched Rebecca undress.

"Is Glen feeling sufficiently guilty for his immorality?" Ominous had no idea. He had moved on after the consummation. Was it important? He gave a slight shrug not wanting to taste the wrath of Portentous again.

"You Bumblehead! There is more work to be done!"

"Yes, of course." Ominous said quietly. What was left to do? He had no idea. Portentous filled in the blanks.

"Though Glen is not a true believer, he has been around them for most of his life. He has a moderate moral compass and you will turn up the pressure! Let him know that his wife would never do such a horrible act. Tell him his son will turn on him once he finds out. If that doesn't seem to work, allow him to believe his affair is Norma's fault. Assure him that he is a good man who perhaps has found the woman of his dreams.

"I understand. I will make him miserable." Ominous nodded with pleasure. Portentous continued to outline the plan.

"You must also use Rebecca to bring him down. Tell her that Glen is the man she has been longing for. Get her to call him at home. When the time is right, allow her to come to Glen's house." Ominous clapped his hands. No wonder Portentous was the Master and he the Student.

"What have you been doing to bring down the Preacher and his family?" There was no good news to share. The Parkers were doing well in spite of the constant challenges at church.

"They are difficult people who are strongly connected to the Enemy and speak with Him on a daily basis." Portentous shuddered. His hate was overwhelming.

"Continue to disrupt his preaching. Plant doubt in the minds of those listening."

"It doesn't seem to be enough!" Ominous sighed.

"That's because you don't stay with it! You must chisel away! Whisper to them as they read that blasted Word that it is fairy tales. Puff them up with their good deeds. Anything can be used against them. Haven't you learned anything? We have the power to turn anything useful into a weapon against them." Ominous stared out into the distance. He wished he was as cunning as Portentous.

"Let me break it down for you." Portentous growled angrily.

"When the Preacher or his son are on the internet, you must flood it with as many images as possible of lewd women in sensual poses. Continue to flash those pornographic sites and watch their response. You will be able to detect which ones hold their attention longest. Catch the Preacher off guard on a frustrating day and throw a counseling session his way from one of the prettier church members. Use his weaknesses against him!" he bellowed!

"His weaknesses?"

"Yes, you Idiot! He has a temper, doesn't he?"

"Yes, he gets angry with sin."

"Correct! But you want him to be angry with the sinner! When the lady tells of her abuse, you want him to become angry with her abuser. He wants to protect her. You must use this against him. You must tell her over and over that if she had a man like him her troubles would be over. Help her to seduce him!"

"I'm not sure he would ever do that no matter how I encouraged it." He knew Martin was strong in the Lord and loved his wife and children.

"Perhaps, but he will feel guilty for the thoughts of his heart. Use that! Tell him he should not be preaching for he is more wicked than his congregation. Make sure ugly rumors get back to him about his need to be in charge. If he uses himself as an example, let the hearers see it as boastfulness."

"When he preaches about abstaining from the appearance of evil, make sure the hearers feel he is questioning their spirituality! Let them believe he is an egotistical tyrant who is building a kingdom for himself. Many do, so it is not that much of a stretch!" he laughed at his joke.

"Anthony and Lisa are getting closer. They should be easy for you."

"Yah, easy!" Ominous had no idea what he was talking about and Portentous knew it.

"Again, I will spell it out for you! If you recall, Anthony's father has forbidden him to date Lisa. Therefore, it will be the 'Romeo and Juliet' syndrome when they disobey and meet. Forbidden love seems to make it sweeter! Lisa is often treated as a child as it is difficult for Martin to see her as a capable, young woman. Use that to your advantage. Help her to resent her father for his control. If you can get her to move out, she will be an easier target. Even their good intentions can be used against them. When a child has too many "no's" in their life without other outlets, they feel cheated and suffocated, especially if the parenting is harsh and demanding. Soon, the child feels they will never meet the expectations and stops trying." Ominous nodded with approval. There were so many small things that he overlooked. It was good that Portentous had studied mankind for generations and seemed to know exactly when to put a plan into action.

"Do your best to split up Chad and Anthony. Chad cares a great deal about his sister and will persuade Anthony to treat her properly. We can't have that!"

"What have you done to disrupt the church?" He demanded.

"You will be pleased to know that Glen has done some major damage. You were right. He is the perfect plant to discourage those believers from moving forward. A few weeks ago Glen told many members of the congregation he is tired of being 'scolded' from the pulpit and it was surprising how many nodded in agreement. Funny when they first heard the words spoken, they didn't feel 'scolded' ...but Glen can be pretty persuasive. Don't you wonder why the Enemy wants anything to do with any of them?"

"While Glen is battling his own downfall, you will need to motivate others to take the lead."

"I have that covered. I found a group of women who are supposed to be phoning each other and praying for the needs of the church. What a hoot! Oh, they start with some churchy stuff at the beginning. Nothing worth mentioning, I assure you. But after that, the gossip begins. I can see a few departing in a short time. Some of them even have important positions!"

"Don't forget about the men. The woman usually get the 'rap' for being the gossipers, but I have a news flash... men are just as bad if not worse!

"I didn't consider that!" he admitted.

"That's why you are in the position you are in!" Portentous puffed out his chest.

"And why I am in the position of authority!" he added.

"I will make sure the husbands and wives also share the gossip before they make their prayerful phone calls!" he laughed.

"Good! That will upset the Parkers. Now get back to work!" He snarled and shoved Ominous back into the darkness.

Chapter 8 View One

Norma quietly slid into her slippers and pulled her hair into a tight bun on top of her head. Today was wash day and she took great pains to make sure each piece came out perfectly. Pre-wash stains, paying close attention to blood or grass stains often found on Anthony's clothing. She threw on an old sweat shirt that had seen better days and faded, worn out jeans. Slipping into her ragged sneakers, she shuffled to the kitchen. Something was definitely wrong, but she just couldn't put her finger on it. Her Bible sat on the stand already opened to the Psalms and she began reading. It always comforted her to read the Psalms. After pouring herself a cup of coffee, she walked outside and sat on the porch swing. It was old fashioned and out of date, but she figured she was too, so it just felt right.

"Can I join you?" asked Glen. She nodded and looked at him thoughtfully. Again the thought occurred to her that something was amiss. When was the last time Glen asked her permission for... anything? He expected his needs to be met without asking. Normally, she poured *his* morning coffee, but today his coffee cup was filled, and he poured fresh into hers.

"Are you all right, Glen?" She had considered everything from learning he was dying to finding out he had finally surrendered himself to the Lord and became one of His.

"Fine, why do you ask?" He seemed nervous and uneasy. It didn't make sense.

"Is anything wrong?" she tried.

"No, of course not! Can't I pour coffee for my wife and sit beside her on the swing without getting the third degree?!" That sounded more like Glen and she smiled in spite of herself.

"I'm sorry, Norma. I didn't mean to snap at you." The rare apology only made her more suspicious. Something was definitely wrong; but what? He had been acting strangely ever since their squabble a few days ago. Maybe he was feeling sorry that his anger was out of control. Perhaps it was Anthony's reaction after seeing his father pin her to a wall with a balled up fist. He had not hit her, but it had come close.

"Is there anything you would like to talk about?" she said quietly. It was a general question and she hoped he did not see a motive.

"I was thinking that we should take advantage of such a beautiful day. Is there someplace you would like to go?"

"We could go for a boat ride. We both like the water and it would be very peaceful this time of day." There was no way he wanted to take her near water. It brought fresh memories of the time he spent with beautiful, Rebecca. He could still see her pale skin next to the lush red hair. She was strikingly beautiful.

"I can see you like the idea." He didn't realize he was smiling like a school boy.

"Maybe another time, Norma. I was thinking more of going to an art museum."

"It's too gorgeous to be inside." she answered quickly.

"There is an outside exhibit we could check out. How does that sound?" His attempt to please her was both wonderful and alarming. It had been a very long time since he showed so much attention, and though she wanted to bask in the moment, she wondered what triggered it.

"Of course, we can check it out, Glen. That sounds wonderful." She smiled.

"But, I was going to get the wash started."

"That can wait. Let's eat a quick breakfast and head out." She dismissed the thoughts that plagued her and decided to enjoy the moment. Perhaps this was his way of making up to her.

"Better yet, let's stop by the Egg House and grab a quick bite." He offered.

"Sounds great, but I need to change clothes and do something with my hair."

"You look fine! Grab your purse and let's get going." She loved the spontaneity and decided not to cause any friction. It would take her a while to get changed and apply makeup not to mention getting her hair in order. He would never have the patience for that.

In minutes they were headed down the road with Norma checking the brochure announcing the exhibits. The advertisement was stuck in their mail box and she was glad she left it on the dining room table. There were several local artists displaying their art work and the day was perfect. Who could ask for anything else? Impulsively, she took Glen's hand and he smiled at the gesture.

They were surprised that the parking was congested and already more than half full. Neither suspected there were that many art lovers in the area. Perhaps it was the right timing.

"Would you like something to drink?" Glen asked. There were several food vendors every few feet and you could buy anything from lemonade or ice cream to sausage sandwiches or cony dogs. It was much like being at a fair. Norma bought some roasting almonds from a vendor nearby. The smell was heavenly and neither could resist. Glen bought a large lemonade with two straws and she felt as if they were out of a date.

There were several tents marking the type of artwork found inside. They both appreciated a strong brush stroke and vibrant colors and neither found any meaning in abstracts. They also preferred modern pieces as opposed to some of the work in dated eras, unless of course, it was from the famous.

"Let's check out the local artists." Norma said and Glen readily agreed. They held hands and maneuvered their way through the thick crowds. The tables were full of beautiful painted pieces as well as some exquisite sculptures. Norma began to relax. This was obviously Glen's way of making up for his hateful behavior.

"See anything you like?" The familiar voice was so close to Glen's ear he jerked his head to see the face.

"Wha...What are you doing here?" He could barely breathe as Rebecca stood in front of him looking absolutely breathtaking.

"I'm one of the local artists, silly. I guess we never got that far in our *discussion*." She said amused.

"You paint?"

"That seems to surprise you. I have many talents. You only experienced a few of them." She winked just as Norma came into view. He stood ashen faced as the women looked curiously at each other over.

"Aren't you going to introduce me?" Rebecca asked with a bright smile showing perfect teeth beneath full, luscious lips.

"Yes, of course. This is my wife, Norma." Rebecca raised her eyebrows as her eyes searched up and down the meek woman before her. It was obvious, she had not passed inspection. Rebecca wondered how Glen could have married such a plain, tattered little mouse.

"Nice to meet you." Norma shook hands with the gorgeous, red headed woman who was impeccably dressed. She knew how horrible she must look to this woman. Her fine hair had come loose and blew around her face like a homeless orphan. Her shoes were spotty from bleach spills and her faded jeans looked even worse in the bright sunlight. Though she generally wore very little makeup, today she certainly wished she had taken the time!

"I'm sorry, how did you say you knew my husband?" she asked without glancing at Glen who stood still as a statue.

"I didn't say." She smiled at Glen and realized he was speechless.

"I'm sure Glen barely remembers me, but I came into his workplace to see if I could display some of my artwork there. Some of the local establishments have bought pieces from me as they not only like to buy 'American' as they say, but also like to promote local talent."

"Of course, that's where I met you." Glen seemed relieved, but Norma wasn't convinced. There was more to the story. Of that, she was certain.

"Let me show you around. I think you'll like what you see." Neither Glen nor Norma missed the coy attitude and double meaning. Rebecca slipped her arm through Glen's and began ushering him away from his wife. Norma stared after them for a moment, and then followed a few paces behind.

"You're going to get me into trouble!" Glen whispered.

"Get you into trouble? I am the one who came up with an explanation! I had no idea she was with you. I would have never dreamed for a moment that woman could be your wife!"

"Nora, you're falling behind, dear. I want to show you both my painting." Norma's face reddened and she wanted desperately to go home.

"It's Norma!" she said quietly.

"What do you think?" She held the picture in front of Glen and he sucked in his breath. The colors were magnificent. It was a picture of a nude couple in an embrace. Their body parts melded perfectly, and for all practical purposes they formed one body. The woman's long, curly red hair encircled her waist and hid most of her torso. Some of her hair also encircled the man so his lower extremity was out of view. They were locked in a kiss and you could not look at the picture without thinking of lovers. The couple stood in a beautiful field with lush, vibrant foliage. It reminded you of the kind of picture that could have been taken in the Garden of Eden.

"It's beautiful." Norma sighed.

"Thank you. What do you think, Glen?" it was obvious Norma's opinion mattered little to her.

"Yes, my wife is right. It is magnificent."

"Do you really like it?" she said breathlessly.

"Oh yes. You should get a fine price for it!"

"I want you to have it." She handed it to him as if it were a baby in a cradle.

"Oh, no! I couldn't do that" said Glen in a hollow voice.

"I *want* you to have it. I can see how much your wife likes the painting and I think it a beautiful picture of true love. Don't you think so Nora?"

"It is quite beautiful, but Glen is right. We couldn't possibly allow you to give it to us." She was astounded. According to Rebecca's story, she barely knew Glen. There was obviously more to the story. She tried to give her husband the benefit of the doubt. After all, Rebecca was certainly memorable. Perhaps she flirted with Glen in order to make a sale and he was feeling uncomfortable with it.

"Okay, if it will make you feel any better, you can have this remarkable painting for the mere price of twenty dollars." She waved her arms and spoke dramatically as if auctioning off the painting.

"It's worth more than that!" Glen remarked.

"Yes, it is, but I insist you take the painting home with you and perhaps place it in a special place in your bedroom." Norma turned crimson at her remark and Glen could feel heavy sweat beads pouring down his back. Rebecca shoved the painting into Glen's hands and pointed ahead of her.

"The cashier is over there." She pointed to the well-built man behind the cash register. It was obvious he spent time lifting weights and had a rugged, though not too studious look.

"Sold another one Chuck." She hollered and smiled at the cashier.

"But… but…" Glen stammered.

"Not another word! Take it and enjoy." She turned to assist another customer leaving Glen and Norma to stand alone with the painting.

"Come on Glen. Let's go pay for the painting and get out of here." Norma urged. She couldn't stand there another minute. He followed mutely after her and felt foolish handing the cashier twenty dollars."

"I think there has been a mistake. This painting goes for a hundred dollars easily. She has already sold a few others similar to this one." He frowned.

"What are you trying to pull?" Glen wanted to throw the painting on the floor and run, but that would make him look guilty!

"Rebecca, get over here!" the man shouted across the room making all eyes turn in his direction.

"I assure you, that is the price she asked us to pay. I am not trying to *pull* anything. I think we should just forget the whole thing and be on our way." He added.

"Nonsense! You will do no such thing!" Rebecca stood tall and sniffed the air importantly.

"I wanted this couple to have the painting and *I* decide the price of *my* artwork! You are here to collect!" Chuck glared at her but she held her ground.

"We'll talk about this at home!" he snarled.

"There is nothing to talk about. I painted the picture. I set the price for twenty dollars. He gave you the twenty dollars. End of story!" she snapped.

"This painting is worth more than twenty dollars."

"Yes it is. I'm glad you can see some things have value!" The sharp words seemed to permeate the air and all was silent for the moment. Rebecca snatched the twenty dollar bill from Glen's hand and slapped it on the table.

"Thank you for admiring my painting. Hope you will enjoy it as much as I enjoyed painting it." She smiled at Glen as he tucked the painting under his arm and headed outside.

Norma walked silently beside him trying to sort out all that had transpired. The pieces didn't make sense. She glanced several times at Glen who seemed to be lost in his own thoughts. She wished she knew what he was thinking.

"Is there anything else you want to see?" She wanted to head home and he was equally ready.

"I think I've seen enough." Her voice had an edge to it and Glen pretended he didn't notice. He had no answers and had no idea how he would ever be able to put this behind them.

The drive home was uncomfortably quiet. He tried desperately to think of topics they could discuss just to concentrate on something else, but the elephant remained in the room and no one wanted to speak of it. He hoped Anthony would be home. It would give both of them someone else to talk to and new conversation.

"What are we going to do with the painting?" Norma blurted. She hadn't intended to say it out loud, but it spilled out anyway. He bit his lip and struggled with an answer.

"We can put it anywhere you would like." He said brightly, hoping to sound nonchalant. She wanted to tell him to put it in the trash.

"Can I ask you something, Glen?" Norma decided to have it out with her husband. Something didn't smell right about this whole situation and she decided to get it out in the open.

"Oh look, Anthony's home!" he sang. Before she could get another word out of her mouth, he parked the car and practically tackled his son. He was desperate to get away from his wife's questions.

"How was practice today, son?" He asked brightly.

"We didn't have practice today. It's on Tuesdays and Thursdays." said Anthony.

"Is that right? Has it always been Tuesday's and Thursdays because I thought it was more often than that." Anthony looked at him quizzically. He was speaking far too rapidly and seemed out of breath.

"I can show you my schedule if you want to see it." He said jokingly.

"Yes, why don't you show me your schedule? I want to make sure you read it right. After all, I would hate to think all your team is off somewhere waiting for you and here you are at home!" Again, his racing voice had an unfamiliar pitch. Anthony stared at him, waiting for him to hyperventilate!

Glen took his son by the arm and led him into the kitchen. Anthony had no idea what was going on, but it was apparent his father was trying to get away from his mother for some reason.

As they were talking, Norma appeared in the kitchen with the painting tucked under her arm. Glen pretended not to notice.

"Hi Mom, whatcha got there?" he asked good naturedly. Her eyes never left her husband's as she answered the question.

"Your father and I went to an art exhibit today. We got a really good deal on this one as your father knew the artist." Glen's face reddened and he rubbed his eyes with the palms of his hands.

"Why don't *you* tell Anthony the story? It always seems to confuse me!"

"There is no story to tell. I think the woman explained things very well. She came into the place where I work to display her artwork and we had a brief conversation." Anthony furrowed his brow. There was deception in his father's voice and quite obvious his mother wasn't buying the story.

"Yes, Anthony. This woman, who only met your father briefly at his work, seemed to be so taken with him that she gave us this painting for twenty dollars."

"I only met her one time, Norma. I swear!" That much was true, but a very small part of the story.

"Can I see the painting?" It was still tucked under his mother's arm and he figured it couldn't be very good if she was only asking twenty dollars for it.

Norma hesitated. The picture was very sensual but not vulgar. She actually wanted to see her son's reaction to such a piece. Carefully, she laid it on the kitchen table and unwrapped it. Anthony's eyes said it all. He blinked a few times and his mouth dropped open slightly. It wasn't the kind of picture the family gathered around.

"Wow!!" He finally exhaled.

"Not exactly the kind of picture a stranger gives a man for twenty bucks, huh?"

"She gave the painting to both of us." That was stretching it and he knew it. Rebecca treated Norma like a non-person and practically swept him away from her as soon as she could.

He watched the tall, leggy red head size up his short, non-descript wife and knew what was going on. There was no comparison. Unfortunately, Norma looked worse than usual with her thin hair flying around and her 'scrub woman' apparel. He felt embarrassed for her and equally for himself. He could see his wife through her eyes and felt a bit humiliated by her appearance. He should have allowed her to fancy herself up a bit. But he had to face facts. He could have sent Norma for the best 'make-over' and on a scale from one to ten she would still be a three. Ah yes, Rebecca was definitely a ten! She was more beautiful in the bright sunlight than she was in the shadows of the bar. Today he could see the brilliant green eyes against the mesmerizing cascade of red hair.

He had vowed to never see her again. He had taken Norma to the exhibit as a grand gesture. How could he have known she would be there? He knew very little about her. Today he found that she not only had beauty, but also talent. He was more drawn to her than ever.

Without a glance toward his family, he took the painting from the table and headed upstairs. He decided to place it on the wall over their bed. His palms were sweaty while he drove the nails in the wallboard but he was determined. He smiled as he thought of the dreams he would surely have after gazing at the painting before he nodded off.

Sure, Norma was going to pitch a fit... let her. As long as he was the man of the house, he could put anything on the walls he saw fit.

He noticed each time he hit the hammer against the nail; there was an increase in intensity. He felt angry. He threw the hammer against the wall with a thud. He picked up the painting and sprawled across the bed to gaze at it again. It made him feel a bit light headed and giddy. He ran a finger across the female's form and his heart beat faster.

He closed his eyes and retraced each step he took with Rebecca starting with an innocent drink and ending in her arms. He was amazed that she seemed so drawn to him.

One thing they had in common was their spouses. The man she called Chuck was equally as plain as Norma! He laughed to himself as he thought of the two of them. Maybe they could get together once he and Rebecca left them. He shook his head. What was he thinking? Rebecca had given no indication she would leave her husband. Sure, she spoke of his inadequacies, but he figured she was just doing a little complaining as many spouses do. It meant nothing.

He hugged the painting close to his chest and let his mind drift. Rebecca wanted him to have that painting. She could have chosen several other pieces, but this is the one she wanted him to have. The reasons were obvious. Her husband said she made more than one of these paintings. He wondered if they had the same painting above their bed.

"Hey Dad, can I interrupt you?" Reluctantly, he laid the painting on the bed and motioned for his son to come in.

"You need something?" He wanted to get back to his daydream of Rebecca.

"I was wondering if I could invite some kids over tonight to watch a movie?"

"I suppose so. What time would they be coming over?"

"I thought 7:30 or 8:00 would be a good time. That way everyone would have had their dinner and Mom wouldn't have to make anything extra." Glen nodded. There was a time they would have enjoyed a laugh about Norma's cooking, but those days had past.

"Is your mother cooking dinner now?" He asked.

"I think so. She's got pots and pans on the stove so I guess she's cooking up something for us." He smiled. Anthony wondered what had happened today. His mother was sniffling in the kitchen as she cooked and his father was here in their bedroom with this sensual painting.

"Boy, Dad, that's some painting!" Anthony remarked.

"Do you like it?"

"It's very well done. I guess that's why I don't understand why the artist gave it to you for such a cheap price. I can tell it disturbs Mom." He added.

"Now look! I don't have to defend myself to you or her either for that matter. The woman wanted us to have the painting and I think it was a very nice gesture. End of story!" he snapped.

"You don't need to get defensive with me, Dad. I was just talking out loud. Surely you can understand why Mom might have a problem with it." He came to talk to his father about another matter and it certainly seemed unlikely that he would get the response he was looking for. Maybe he would bring it up another time.

"Was there anything else?" he asked impatiently. Anthony shook his head. He wanted to talk about Lisa. He knew she would not sneak around to see him and he didn't want it that way either but he knew his father was wrong about her and her family and he wanted to see her with his blessing.

"Out with it, Anthony. I can always tell when you've got something more to say."

"I don't think this is a good time to talk."

"Nonsense! It is the perfect time to talk. Your mother is busy in the kitchen and I've got no place to go." He patted the bed welcoming his son to sit beside him.

"I wanted to talk to you about Lisa Parker." Martin scowled. He had enough of *that* family and their interference.

"I don't know what you have against her, Dad. She's a really nice girl and I think I have the right to date any girl I want." He hated to sound so brash but he knew for whatever reasons, his father respected that tone. Oddly, Glen smiled at his son. He liked the feisty attitude.

"I admit, you are growing up!" Glen slapped him on the back and grinned. Lisa was a pretty girl and growing more womanly every day. She wore just enough make up to enhance her best qualities. Her clothing was never tight or revealing, but any red blooded male with good eyes would be drawn to the tall, curvy teenager. Immediately, his mind drifted to Rebecca. He wondered if his son had the same ideas when it came to Lisa. Glen smiled at the thought. Wouldn't the preacher have a meltdown if his daughter succumbed to temptation with his son? Somewhere in the recesses of his heart, he found joy in the thought.

"Maybe your right, Anthony. Just because Lisa is the preacher's daughter shouldn't make her taboo! She's just another girl as far as I can see. She doesn't have a halo if you know what I mean." He poked his son for emphasis.

"She's a great girl, Dad." Anthony wasn't sure where his father was going with the conversation, but he wasn't going to let him talk badly about her.

"Tell you what… if you want to start going out with her, feel free. Just remember her father is against you teenagers having any fun whatsoever!! I feel sorry for his family. They probably sit in the room with the kids when they are on a date! I wouldn't be surprised if he didn't sit between you!" He laughed at his snide remark.

"You can bring her here if you want some privacy. I promise your mother and I will stay out of your way! It's ridiculous to overprotect!

You have to trust your kids sometime or they will just rebel. Am I right?" he poked him again.

"The pastor is pretty protective but he is not unreasonable. No, he doesn't sit with us when I go over to their house." He didn't let him know how often either the pastor or his wife came through the room when he was visiting Lisa. It made them aware that their conduct could be seen at any given time and they were never left entirely alone. He vowed he would do the same for his own children. Glen's face hardened. He did not like to hear his son compliment the Parkers.

"Hey, I'm glad you trust me, Dad. It means a lot to me." He added hoping to change his father's grim expression.

"You're a good kid. Why shouldn't I trust you? Besides, I've lived long enough to realize that if a person wants to get into mischief, there is very little anyone can do to stop them." He hoped his son didn't realize he was speaking of his own personal experience.

"I'm sure you're right, but it's still best to put up all the safeguards possible to keep from going down that path." Glen stared at his son for a few moments and felt tears behind his eyes. His son was a better man and he knew it. Anthony felt uncomfortable under his father's gaze. He seemed troubled and he was certain part of it had to do with the painting lying on his parent's bed.

"We better get downstairs. I'm sure dinner is about ready." He glanced at his watch and hopped off the bed. His father trailed behind him. It was going to be an uncomfortable dinner and Glen stiffened his jaw as he headed toward the table.

Dinner was on the table and though it was a decent meal, everyone seemed to have difficulty getting the food down. Anthony noticed there was almost no communication between his parents and both seemed to stare at their plates. There was an occasional sniffle from his mother followed by a harrumph from his father. All and all... a most unpleasant dinner.

Anthony helped his mother clear the table and put food away hoping everything would be in good order as his guests arrived. Lisa was to bring the movie and Chad was bringing sodas for everyone. They had plenty of popcorn to go with it so they seemed to be in good shape. Chad was bringing over a new guy from church that he wanted to introduce to the group. He was very excited for everyone to get to meet Colten McDaniel, as he was quite an athlete. Not only did he 'letter' in just about every sport he entered, but he was also a very good student. He wasn't expecting the tall, well built, good looking young man who could have been on a magazine cover.

Everyone seemed to flock around him and questions were fired off from every direction. You would think a celebrity had joined them. Anthony asked nothing and fumed that Lisa seemed to be mesmerized by him.

"What was it like living in California, Colten?" Lisa asked.

"My friends call me Mac. Colten is also my Dad's name." He said.

"Okay, Mac, tell me about California." Lisa felt like a child speaking to someone famous.

"It was a lot nicer than when I lived in Jersey, that's for sure. I love to surf and there is no place to do that around here!" he laughed good-naturedly.

"I've watched the guys on surf boards! It's amazing to watch them ride a wave!" Chad commented.

"It's a blast! Don't get me wrong, it takes a lot of skill to stay on a board like the real surfers do, but it's fun no matter how long you last!" Anthony asked no questions and couldn't wait to get the movie started to shut the guy up. It was getting very annoying!

The movie was enjoyed by all and they continued to chat about every aspect of the film while munching on their snacks. Colten was the first to look at his watch and realize the time.

"Man, I need to get going! I've got to get up early tomorrow for practice. Anyone need a ride?" Chad was the first to respond.

"That would be great, Colten, I mean Mac. My mom dropped us off as she needed the car tonight. It would save her a trip." Anthony was furious! There was no way he wanted Lisa riding with Mr. Wonderful!

"I don't mind taking you home!" Anthony interjected.

"Hey, I don't mind, besides, you have other guests." Colten interjected. Anthony could barely conceal his anger. What nerve!

"You don't mind hanging around for a while, do you Lisa?" asked Anthony brightly. Before she could answer, Chad shook his head.

"Thanks, Buddy, but that really isn't necessary. I know Lisa has a test tomorrow, and I have a little bit of homework to finish so we'll just hop in Mac's car and see you tomorrow. Lisa looked a little pained, which pleased Anthony, but Chad ushered her out the door before she could speak for herself.

When everyone had finally cleared out, Anthony immediately, called Lisa. He was fuming and would barely let her get a word in. He accused her of *wanting* to leave with Colten and before it was over, she hung up on him. Fine with him! He stomped his way to his bedroom and could overhear his parents arguing. Maybe his father was right. Women are pains! They need to be kept in their place!

As he drifted off to sleep, his mind seemed to wander off into a dark arena. He dreamed of following Lisa to a sleep over she was having with some of the girls from church. After they slipped into their pajamas, and began painting their nails, he and some of the guys from his baseball team arrived at their door. Anthony had a beer bottle in his hand and when no one answered the door immediately, he threw the bottle against the door splattering the contents. A couple of guys were pretty drunk and began howling next to the window.

"Let me in, or I'll huff and I'll puff and I'll... how does the rest of that go?" he laughed hysterically and the other guys laughed with him as if it were the funniest line ever! Suddenly, the door opened and the guys were pulled in.

"Stop yelling or someone will call the police!" Lisa laughed. She looked fantastic in baby doll PJ's and he began pulling her to the couch. His heart raced as his dream took a sensual turn.

By the time he woke up, his mind was in the wrong place! Still angry, instead of shaking off the dream, he closed his eyes and thought of each detail. He could see himself grabbing Lisa inappropriately, and speaking roughly to her. Part of him knew he needed to stop and pray, but instead he continued to feed his hungry, fleshly side and found it to be insatiable.

The Booth household wasn't the only one in turmoil. As soon as Lisa hung up on Anthony, she lit into her brother with a vengeance.

"Now look what you've done! Anthony is furious with me!" she snapped.

"That's his problem. I think he's just jealous because everyone paid so much attention to Colten." He countered.

"I wouldn't like it if Anthony had taken another girl home, so I guess I shouldn't be upset with him. But he started yelling at me like it was my fault and my decision."

"C'mon, Lisa, no one took you against your will."

"What was I supposed to say? You did all the talking for both of us. Was I supposed to offend Colten or make my boyfriend mad instead?"

"Well, in the first place, I have never been able to make you do anything. Besides, you could have said you wanted to stick around and help clean up or something. You didn't have to go. I think you *wanted* to go!" He said.

"I didn't think of that. And maybe I did enjoy Mac, but I didn't know it would make Anthony so upset!"

"You know, Lisa. I think Mac likes you, but I have to check him out."

"Check him out? What does that mean? I don't need your approval!" she spat.

"I don't know if he is a Christian. I invited him to come watch the movie so everyone could get to know him better and also to find out where he stands."

"So, where does he stand?"

"I don't know. He never commented on the movie and everyone was asking him so many questions that it became impossible to get back to the topic."

"What makes you think he's interested in me?" She felt very flattered. After all, he had the attention of everyone in the room.

"Trust me, he is interested. But you aren't available anyway... remember... Anthony?" he chided.

"Yah, we'll see!" Lisa had never given Colten a second thought, though she thought he was very interesting. She wasn't the kind of girl who had more than one interest at a time. Besides, she was a small town girl and he had lived in several fast paced cities. He would surely tire of her if they ever were to spend time together.

She had also heard through the rumor mill that Colten was known as quite the player! He had an eye for pretty girls and was known to be dating more than one at a time. If that weren't enough, she had also heard that he dated girls that were known to have loose morals. Surely, that would be reason enough! But it wasn't!

From the dark world, Portentous and Ominous were smiling widely! Portentous shadowed Ominous, as the opportunity was at hand to move forward with their destruction plan.

Portentous schooled those who waited in dark places to learn how to bring devastation to those in their watch care.

Quickly, he brought images to Anthony's mind that on other, prayerful days, he was able to dismiss without much effort. But today, he was filled with the fleshly side of his nature. Ominous watched with fascination as Anthony seemed to listen with interest. Portentous warned him to push gently. A nudge here, a vile thought along with a depraved picture worked wonders. Lust was difficult for the most virtuous to resist. He learned to maneuver his victim in tiny steps that were almost imperceptible. He found if he prodded slowly, while a person was more vulnerable, they were putty in his hands. Many victims found themselves in situations they would have sworn would NEVER happen to them. Ominous guffawed in spite of himself. Even the most proclaimed 'saint' of the Enemy, spent about half the time necessary to overcome their flesh! Ominous and Portentous often listened in as Pastor's gave advice and counseling from their own empty well. Those that the Enemy loved were a miserable lot agreed Ominous and Portentous. What riches were at the Enemy's fingertips for those who claimed to love Him.

View Two

It was definitely time for a "field trip" for the minions in Portentous' charge. Reluctantly, Ominous tagged along hoping to find some flaw in his mentor's teaching. He would be flogged for pointing it out, but he was well acquainted with pain and it was worth it to humiliate the pompous Portentous.

"It actually takes very little to get them off course! Sometimes you will have to team up to get the job done. Tell Susie to call Patty while she is trying to read or pray. Make sure Susie mixes a little gossip or slander in with her prayer requests. As difficult as it may be to listen to them pray or watch them read that blasted Book, you must continue to divert their attention. Interrupt their thoughts as they try to study or memorize. Cause as much disruption as possible... phone... texts, doorbell, anything will cause their minds to drift or wander. They are not nearly as bright as you might think."

"What if they continue to read or pray anyway?" a hideous dark image asked.

"Everything can be used against them! As they are reading a passage, tell them they will never measure up to that Book!"

"But some know they don't measure up and have been bought back by the Enemy." Ominous and Portentous cringed at the thought. Those would always be in His care and they could never be doomed! However, they could still be useful!

"Then you tell them over and over how undeserving they are. Tell them that they are hypocrites! Tell them their shameful behavior will never lead anyone to the Enemy! Bring to their remembrance every sinful act they have done. Discourage them! Play those unwanted memories over and over in their heads until they become depressed and useless!" the advice was received with loud applause and obnoxious laughter.

"Portentous is absolutely right! Mankind is no match for our skills!" he interjected hoping for his own applause.

"Unfortunately, you have little to contribute! You have repeatedly bumbled your assignments and are an embarrassment to the cause!

"Oh really? Have you forgotten what I did to Glen Booth? You were pretty excited about that report as I recall!" He stated smugly taking his chances that Portentous wouldn't throttle him for his exuberance.

"I was referring to Cheryl. I keep looking through the darkness for her. As I recall, she was on her death bed, but she is not here! You let her slip out of your hands and now that preacher is trying to encourage her. I call that a DISMAL FAILURE!! His voice echoed through the air, making everyone take a step back including Ominous.

"Have no fear! The preacher is going to have his hands full in the coming days." He smiled.

"Do continue, Ominous... and this better be worth hearing!" he gnashed on him making him squeal in pain. Ominous recovered quickly and decided with so vast an audience to weave the story into creative exaggerations and perhaps a lie or two.

"First of all, let me comment on Cheryl. We shall be welcoming her any day now. Her doctor is also in my watch care and I have drawn him into the misuse of prescription drugs. He barely makes it from day to day and it is affecting his work and his home life. Cheryl has worn him out with her constant calls, so he upped her meds and she is taking more than necessary. At this point, neither of them seems to be able to function." He guffawed.

"Take note of this!" Portentous instructed.

"If you are smart, you can cause the same kind of domino affect!"

"Yes, if you are smart!" Ominous puffed his chest and continued.

"Glen has accepted Rebecca's sensual painting that will hang like a black cloud over his bed causing major problems in his already fragile marriage. I arranged for Rebecca to be at the same art exhibit as the Booths. And speaking of the Booths, Anthony has succumbed to my temptation to dismiss his antiquated thoughts of purity. He seems to be memorizing a very erotic dream that will help me to bring him down. And last but not least, there is a new arrival in the midst. Our own dear Colten McDaniel."

"Mac? He is now part of the equation? How did I miss that one?" Portentous bent over in hideous laughter. Mac was indeed one of their most destructive ones.

"I got Colten Sr. fired again!" said Ominous importantly.

"Again? What for this time?" asked Portentous.

"Same thing... it's always the same thing!" he howled. Colten J. McDaniel, Sr. was an older version of his son and still turning heads wherever he went. He was handsome, smart and very gregarious. No one seemed to question his credentials, for if they had they would find most of them to be bogus. He had actually never attended college, though he had transcripts that appeared legitimate. He also had an eye for ladies of all ages. If they appealed to him, he cared very little how old they were. He was a master at getting hurtful information that could be used against them in case they ever wanted to cause him problems.

"A woman, no doubt!" laughed Portentous.

"Yep, but this one really bit him good!' they all laughed waiting for the rest of the story.

"Colten Sr. has been in this predicament before. You know, where the young lady decides to blow the whistle on him. Many times she is someone who works at the same company. Of course, Colten has much more influence, so he tells her if she decides to blow the whistle, she will never work again. He will make it his personal goal to keep her from working anywhere in the field." He admired Colten's ability to maintain control of the situation.

"So, did he find one who wouldn't keep her mouth shut?" asked Portentous.

"That's right! This one sang like a canary! But, oh the song she had to sing!" Ominous had to take a few deep breaths to continue.

"He told the young lady that she would do as he said or she would find herself out of a job, but she would not comply. Instead, she told him they would see who was leaving! Colten laughed in her face and called the CEO of the organization, who he had just played 18 holes of golf with that morning. While she stood aghast before him, he told the CEO that reluctantly, he had to dismiss his secretary as she was substandard to what was necessary for the position." He waited a few seconds to build the suspense.

"To his surprise, he was called to the CEO's office to discuss the unexpected dismissal. Colten grinned evilly at his secretary and told her to find herself some boxes and be gone by the time he got back. Angrily, she charged out of his office and he was a little disappointed that she did not leave in a puddle of tears. Generally, he had broken anyone who did not do as he wished." Ominous paced around the area for a few seconds with every evil eye fastened to him, waiting to hear how the story ended.

"Imagine his surprise when he entered the CEO's office and found his secretary sitting in a chair opposite the CEO. Colten began sputtering... outraged that his secretary could think for a moment she could go toe to toe with him. 'I don't know what this gal has been telling you, sir, but I have documented her poor performance and am within my right to have her dismissed. She has been here long enough to know the chain of command sir and has absolutely no business coming to a busy man like you! That should tell you what kind of person we are dealing with! She obviously has some mental issue...' but before he could continue, the infuriated CEO stood to his feet with a look of fierce anger. He raised his hand to shut him up. To his great surprise the woman began to speak. 'This is the man I was telling you about. He told me if I didn't do what he wanted he would fire me. I told him I was married and I would not do as he asked.' The CEO glared at Colten. 'Sir, you can't believe this woman! You just give me a couple days and I can have sworn evidence that she has been doing favors for many of the men here so they would overlook her poor performance. We need to fire her for the good of the company.' Colten thought it was over and he had won when suddenly the CEO reached for the hand of the young lady. 'You have a great deal of nerve Mac! How dare you speak of mental issues and doing other men favors!' said the CEO. "I am so sorry for what this vermin has put you through! 'Thank you, Daddy!' she replied as Colten stood there horrified. 'There will be someone fired today, Colten, but it will not be my daughter Christie. You obviously didn't know that or you would never have slandered her. Unlike you, she graduated at the head of her class. I checked you out, and the colleges you claim to have attended have never heard of you. My daughter is professional enough to want to make it on her own and has never given you her maiden name. She has also told me about your behavior and she took the liberty of checking out some of your previous employers. I would suggest you take the boxes you asked my daughter to fill and remove every trace of Colten McDaniel from this place and if I ever hear your name mentioned anywhere; I will let them know I would not hire you to sort mail! Now get out!' the laughter was deafening.

"He and his family have relocated within miles of the Parkers and they were immediately asked to attend the church by one of the crazy door knocking people. The preacher showed the man his need of the Enemy and asked if he had ever asked to be forgiven of his sin. But old Colten is a man full of pride and excuses. He told the preacher he had done something like that when he was a little kid attending church, but in truth it was only lip service. The only reason he is attending this fundamental church is because he is interviewing with a prominent man in the congregation and will use it to win him over. Mac junior has already been embraced by the teens as he is as winsome as his father. The girls are already vying for position and I have decided to get him together with Lisa Parker. If I can bring her down, it will break the preacher's heart. There is nothing like a scandal in the church, especially if it is at the top!!" HA HA HA!!

"Just make sure none of them actually listen to the preaching! That could be dangerous!" Portentous warned.

"Not only will I make sure they don't listen, I will make sure all those around them are mesmerized by this new family. Mac is very involved with numerology, astrology, crystals, tarot cards, the occult, everything and anything but church!" Ominous decided to push things a little more for his captive audience.

"I guarantee by the end of the summer, the Booth's will be divorced, Glen and Rebecca will be seeing more of each other on the sly, and Rebecca's husband is big enough to put Glen in the hospital! I also guarantee there will be a child born out of wedlock to one of the teenage girls. If I play it just right, I intend the victim to be Lisa Parker!" He would do his very best to make sure it happened!

Chapter 9

Cheryl downed a few more pills and slipped into her bath. Although it relaxed her, she stressed over the plans she had made with Christine Parker. She shook her head. Why had she allowed the preacher to talk her into going to lunch?! She tried to call and cancel but no one was picking up and besides, it was getting too late to cancel unless she had a really good reason. If she cancelled pretending to be sick, Christine would come rushing over with some soup or something. Maybe she wouldn't answer the door. She would apologize later. She laid her head back and shut her eyes. In a few minutes she was fast asleep.

Christine always seemed to have so many interruptions no matter what she planned to do for the day. There were constant phone calls and often she had to turn her phone off when she was with guests. Her husband's schedule was worse than hers. It was a wonder they had time for each other or their children at times. Fortunately, her husband had clear boundaries and learned how to balance his home life and the demands of the church to give his best to both. Christine did her best to maintain the speed limit. She was going to be late, but knew Cheryl would not be ready when she got there. Lisa had seen Cheryl in the grocery store and was very worried about her. She seemed to be in a trance and her appearance was startling. She appeared to be lost, and Lisa saw her wandering from one isle to another stopping nervously at the drug section.

"Can I help you find something?" Lisa offered the disheveled woman.

"I wasn't taking anything. I was just looking!" She looked at Lisa as though she were about to be arrested.

"No, of course not. I just thought maybe I could help you find something."

"It's not on the shelf! It figures they keep it locked up. You don't know how to get the stuff behind the counter do you?" she cried.

"I really need it. I mean, my doctor is out of town and I dropped some of my pills on the floor and can't find them." Cheryl pleaded.

"Do you want me to ask the pharmacist if he can get you a few more pills until your doctor gets back?" Lisa had never heard such a crazy story, and wanted to get an adult involved.

"No, he won't help me! I've asked him, but he insists that I go to an urgent care or something. But I won't do it! They cost you an arm and a leg. Not that he cares! They are supposed to be here to help when you need them, but he won't do it!" she wailed.

To Lisa's horror, Cheryl collapsed to the ground weeping and pounding the floor like a small child in the middle of a temper tantrum. The pharmacist came rushing out to help the distraught woman and Lisa left without another word. The scene was etched in her mind as she recalled the details to her family that evening.

After hearing the story, Christine would not take no for an answer when she called Cheryl. The woman was in a desperate situation and needed help. It is very difficult to reach out to people in that state of mind. She pushed everyone away with the exception of a boyfriend or two that might be willing to share their drugs. None of her neighbors had seen her in days and when Martin called her neighbor, Emily he got an earful.

"I'm done with that kook!" she hissed.

"Try to help a person and what do you get? I'll tell you what… an ungrateful, nasty, lying, thankless…"

"She's sick, Emily. We need to help her." He interjected, hoping to stop her tirade.

"I'll say! You know the authorities came and took her kids. Don't know why they didn't get the dog too. I was afraid to tell them. They would probably just put him in the dog pound."

"I'm so sorry to hear that."

"Well, you can't blame them! She is unfit as a mother and I assure you they should have been taken from her long ago. She is too unstable to raise kids!" she huffed.

"I've done all I can for her, preacher. You know she never even offered to pay me back for the dog food? I don't know if she's even feeding that poor dog at this point. She used to dote on him like it was her own kid, but now he can scratch the paint off her door and he'll be lucky to get back in the house."

"When did you see her last?" Martin asked.

"When I returned her dog to her. You know I went out and bought some pretty expensive dog food and gave her the rest of the bag and she practically slammed the door in my face. Didn't offer to pay me back and never said a word of thanks. That's gratitude for ya!"

"She owes her life to me!" she spat.

"I am certainly glad you called the paramedics." Martin said quietly, though Emily was barely listening.

"I could have called the police on her many times, but being a good neighbor, I tried to look the other way when she made hair brained decisions that I knew would cost her! She's in for trouble if she ever pulls a stunt like that again. I'm not going to help her again!"

"You would allow her to die?" Emily softened at the thought.

"No, I wouldn't go that far. But I won't take care of that pooch again. She better find one of her boyfriends or something. I'm out good money for taking such good care of that dog and not even a thank you!" she began again. Martin puckered his lip. Why couldn't people do a good deed without expectations? It is great to receive thanks, but he hated to see how many became bitter when they didn't obtain one.

After Martin's conversation with Emily, Christine was determined to take Cheryl under her wing and nurture her as much as possible.

Christine knocked again using her fist. She was determined to have a talk with Cheryl. She could hear her dog whimpering inside and it worried her.

"Cheryl, it's Christine Parker." She shouted. She put her ear to the door feeling ridiculous. She hoped there were no nosy neighbors watching. As she pressed closer, she could hear the sound of running water. She said a quick prayer and then broke the screen door. Fortunately, the inside door wasn't locked and she was able to get in easily.

Water flooded the hallway and was rushing into the kitchen. Christine followed the stream of water leading her to the bathroom. There she found Cheryl lying motionless at the bottom of the tub. Quickly, she pulled her over the rim and began CPR. She fumbled for her phone and dialed 911. By the time she heard a voice, she was practically hysterical. She begged them to hurry and continued CPR until they arrived.

She prayed silently as the paramedics worked on her lifeless body. She noticed the disgusted looks they exchanged. Two athletic looking females and one tall, solid black man had been dispatched. They had been to this address a few weeks ago and it was obvious they didn't think she was worth their time. It angered Christine.

"If there is anyone you would like to call, I would suggest you do that." The one in charge told her.

"I'll call my husband and have him meet us at the hospital." She received a cursory nod and again Christine flared.

"I hope you will do everything in your power to help revive this woman."

"We're doing what we can. You know people like her keep us pretty busy!"

"People like her? What does that mean? You don't know her or what she's been through in life. Are you her judge and jury? Is she not worth the effort?" It was not like her to speak out so strongly. Suddenly, she remembered the last time she felt this angry and oppressed. She knelt beside the couch and began to pray. At first, she could barely concentrate, but she forced her mind to go before the Throne of Grace. She could feel the warmth of His love as she poured her heart out to Him. As she prayed, a smile came to her lips. It was as if she were standing in the warmth of a sunbeam on a cold winter day. She begged the Lord for Cheryl's life.

"Please Lord, give me one more chance to bring her into your Kingdom" she prayed earnestly. She was too engrossed in prayer to hear Cheryl begin to cough and sputter until the black paramedic smiled at her and gave her a gentle nudge. He was a Christian and understood her prayer perfectly.

"I think you've been heard." He grinned. Instantly, she was on her feet.

"She's still pretty weak. Would you like to ride in the ambulance?" he offered.

"Yes! Thank you so much!"

"You're welcome." He shook her hand and told her he would also be praying for her.

"My name is John Dunbar." She nodded her appreciation as she called Martin and left a message with his secretary. She knew he had quite a few counseling sessions booked for the day so she wasn't quite sure when he would be able to respond. As she spoke to the church secretary, Cheryl began to cough. She looked completely bewildered. Where was she? What was happening?

"It's okay, Cheryl. You're going to be alright" Christine whispered as she patted her hand.

"What's happening? What have I done?" she moaned.

"It's okay. I think you slipped in the bathtub." The story didn't ring true to any of the hearers, including Cheryl.

"Please stay with me!" she clung tightly to Christine's hand and she decided she would stay by her side until her husband arrived.

"You're going to be just fine. I'm going to stay with you and Pastor will also be arriving a little later." She said softly.

"He's probably going to be angry with me this time. It seems like the hospital is the only place we see each other."

"He'll be happy to see you. We have all been concerned for you." She closed her eyes tightly allowing the tears to roll down the sides of her face.

She seemed to drift off to sleep and Christine used that time to speak directly to the paramedic.

"Did you think she slipped and bumped her head?"

"No, I think her system is full of drugs! We did a tox- screening and I assure you, she was feeling no pain when she got into the bathtub." Christine ignored the haughty attitude.

"What happens now?"

"Guess that's up to her doctor. She will have to be in the hospital at least overnight." Christine was determined to help this young woman. She began to pray and though it was a struggle to stay focused, she forced herself to concentrate. Once again, she felt the eerie sensation of a dark presence. To the amazement of the paramedics, she began to pray aloud.

"Lord, please make your presence known! I pray you will protect Cheryl from the evil I feel surrounding her." The paramedics exchanged glances and she knew they dubbed her as some kind of religious fanatic. But Christine's prayer was immediately answered. There was a release as if someone had her head in a vice grip and let go.

"There seems to be something oppressive around whenever I try to get close to Cheryl. I know it sounds fanatical, but I had to pray aloud just to keep my thoughts together!" She spoke directly to John, hoping he would understand.

"Normally, that would sound a bit on the fanatical side to me, but I have to tell you, I was praying with you and felt the same kind of pressure. I was one of the first ones to arrive on the scene the last time we came to this address and it was almost eerie. She kept saying that she was afraid to die but it was almost is if she was carrying on a conversation with someone else. First she would say she wanted to die and then she would start crying and ask me to help her. She was frantic." He shook his head in remembrance.

"I am usually a pretty compassionate guy and so are my team members, but for some reason, we all seemed to snap at each other. We usually work well together and each person knows what they are responsible for. As I watched my team perform their duties, it was obvious; the sense of urgency was missing."

"I imagine it happens when you find a drunk in an alley." Christine said thoughtfully.

"Yes, sometimes. I know each life has value, but when you see someone waste their life it angers you! The worst ones for me are drug dealers, wife beaters, child predators and the like. Sometimes you have to force yourself to help them."

"I can understand that." said Christine.

"This is different. Sometimes when you deal with people that are part of the occult world there is an oppression that comes with it. But this lady… I don't know her story. She just seems to have lost her way."

"Cheryl, can you hear me?" John tapped her hand gently as he called her name.

"Wha..what's happening?" Her blood pressure was dropping and John needed her awake so she wouldn't slip into a coma.

"You're going to be fine, Cheryl. You'll be back on your feet in no time!" he said.

"What difference does it matter. Just leave me alone." She whimpered.

"Now you listen to me, Cheryl. This life is not all there is. You won't slip out of this life and be done with it. There is another life that awaits you and you are not prepared for it." John's voice was stern making Cheryl cry in earnest.

"I'm afraid of what's waiting." She admitted.

"Then fight! Fight to stay on this side, girl!" She nodded without opening her eyes and held tightly to Christine's hand. Suddenly, she stopped crying and began speaking, but the conversation was not with John or Christine.

"You're right! I'm no good and never have been. I will just end up hurting my kids more if I stick around! Yes, they are better off without me." She tried to pull her hand away, but Christine held on tightly.

"Your kids would be heartbroken if anything happened to you, Cheryl! They would spend the rest of their lives wishing they had been around to stop you. They would blame themselves! Is that what you want?" Christine said harshly.

"No, no, I don't want to hurt them! But they are going to realize that I was a bad mother… so bad they were taken away from me!" she wailed.

"Cheryl, they love you. You love them. It's not too late to make changes."

"I never make the right choices, can't you see that?" she sobbed.

"Those days are over! You can have a fresh start! A clean slate! My husband and I will help you." Cheryl wiped her eyes and listened to Christine's cheerful voice.

"Think of the best day you've had with your kids. Holding them as infants and smothering them with kisses." Cheryl smiled. She truly loved her children and could faintly remember snuggling them close and showering them with hugs and kisses.

"You can have those days again, I promise. You've been off track, but we'll help you get on track again. Why even your little dog has missed you." Cheryl's eyes widened. She hadn't given her precious dog a thought for quite some time.

"We'll have those kids back in your arms in no time."

"Do you really think so?" she asked hopefully. Her eyes started to glaze over and a frown began to form. John noticed it immediately as well as her blood pressure.

"Cheryl, don't you listen to no lies! There are too many people who love you and want the best for you. You are a mighty lucky lady! God has surrounded you with His care givers. You listen up, girl!" he added.

"But, I've tried so many times before and …"

"Hush now! Don't you listen to that nonsense! God loves you and wants to see you do something with your life. Why I was worse off than you are at one time. They found 'ole John Dunbar in a drunken stupor. I didn't even want to get sober. I just wanted to die."

"Then you understand, don't you?!"

"I understand that I almost let myself believe that lie. I thought I would always be 'ole drunken John Dunbar with no reason to live. But I was wrong, and so are you."

"But you're a doctor and I'm just a…."

"I'm a paramedic and learning to become a doctor but that's a long ways off. Can you imagine that? I was an old drunk before God got a hold of my heart and changed my life."

"See Cheryl, God has a way of finding the broken things, like us and if we will let Him, He will show us the way to find the best things in life and not only that, but He will also show us how to make sure we are ready for the next life." Cheryl's eyes sparkled with excitement. Could the same thing happen to her?

"You know when I was a little girl I wanted to be a veterinarian." She smiled.

"Sounds kind of silly now." She looked away from both of them.

"What's silly about a dream for a better life? And doing something that would help a little animal too? No, that's not silly at all. What's silly is not following your dream and believing a lie."

"That dream seems like a million years ago. I'm not as young as I used to be."

"There is always time to pursue your dreams. I know that for sure!" he laughed. Cheryl seemed peaceful as she listened to John's deep voice of assurance. Christine remained quiet as John quoted Scripture and then sang a beautiful hymn in his rich, baritone voice. It was a comfort to all of them.

Suddenly, Christine's phone began to buzz in her purse and she grabbed it quickly hoping it was her husband.

Martin was having a very difficult day and prayed his wife would not be the bearer of more bad news. He glanced at his schedule and there were at least two more counseling sessions ahead. His secretary had taken the liberty of ordering lunch as she knew he would not have time to leave his office.

"Is there any way you can meet us at the hospital?" Christine asked quickly.

"What's going on?" he asked hoping the emergency was not life threatening.

"I'm sorry, Martin. Let me fill you in." Briefly she gave her husband the details.

"I'm afraid it's going to be a while before I can get there. It's been quite a disturbing day."

"Is there anything I can do?" He smiled at her concern. Christine was such a wonderful wife who always tried to be the best helpmeet possible.

"I'll fill you in when I get home. Pray that I will be useful to the cause of Christ today." He wondered how much information to share.

"How much do you know about the McDaniel family?" He asked tentatively. They were relatively new to the church and were making friends quickly.

"Not much, really. The Longs knocked on their door and apparently Mr. McDaniel made a profession of faith when he was a child. I don't know about the rest of the family. Mrs. McDaniel has already asked me about getting involved, and their son is making a hit with all the teens. That's about the extent of what I know."

"Make sure Mrs. McDaniel is not put in charge of anything for now."

"Is there a problem?" Kate McDaniel asked to be put in charge of the Teen Spectacular coming up in the next few months. She seemed to have some great ideas and let Christine know she enjoyed taking full control of a project.

"I'll know more after my meeting. I don't want you put in an uncomfortable position. It's always best to go slow with new people." Christine agreed. She didn't have a strong personality, so when those who were stronger seemed to push their way into a project, it was easier for Christine to give them the lead, though it didn't always have a happy ending.

"I will meet you at the hospital as soon as I can. Cheryl sounds relatively stable at the moment and we'll pray that we can really help her this time." He added. Martin prayed silently as he thought of Cheryl and the many others he knew that led similar lives.

"Pastor, Mr. Ryan is here to see you." His secretary buzzed.

"I'll be right there." Martin took a deep breath and exhaled slowly. This was going to be a trying meeting. Mike Ryan called for an appointment days before and it was obvious he was quite upset. He was known throughout the church as a negative person who seemed to concentrate on the dark side of any day. He began talking before he was seated and Martin closed the door before the entire office was disrupted by his outburst.

"You need to help me, Pastor. I'm a patient man, but I'm not about to put up with this!" he huffed.

"Calm down, Mike. Let's start from the beginning and we'll figure this out together." Mike shook his head and took a breath. He wanted the pastor to understand and he knew if he didn't calm down, he would miss the point.

"How much do you know about the McDaniel family?" he asked.

"Not very much. They haven't been coming long enough to get to know people and ..."

"But they've been coming long enough to weasel their way into everything!" he interrupted.

"People seem to like them. Maybe that's why it appears they are moving quickly into the church family." Martin said, but there was something that didn't quite sit well with him either. He was generally a pretty good judge of character and there was something about Colten McDaniel that disturbed him. Until Mike called to discuss his concerns, he was too busy to give it much thought.

"Now, what's this all about?" It was generally easier to deal with the men who made appointments as they weren't as emotional and got to the point much quicker.

"Okay, it's like this. Steve Winters has finally posted the position I've been waiting for and I thought for sure I would be the only likely candidate. After all, I've put in my time and worked hard. I thought Steve had his eye on me for the position too."

"Yes, you've certainly shown yourself to be an exemplary employee and I know Steve thinks a lot of you." Mike's face reddened as he thought of his chances blowing out the window.

"Then this guy from nowhere shows up in our church and who does he make himself known to? Steve Winters, that's who!" He snarled.

"McDaniel has him over to his place for dinner, buys golf tickets for him and if that's not enough, Kate McDaniel takes his wife to some swanky restaurant and they are exchanging recipes and then Kate finds out Steve's daughter is getting married and she is practically the wedding planner! She is making the flowers and altering dresses! How am I supposed to compete with that?" He finished breathlessly.

"Do you really think Steve Winters can be bought?"

"It's more than that? The families are becoming friends!" He said sorrowfully.

"You're friends too." Martin pointed out.

"I can't afford to buy him golf tickets and my wife and Kate McDaniel have nothing in common." He sighed.

"Why are you here, Mike? You certainly don't expect me to put a stop to a new friendship."

"Pastor, you might think I've lost my mind, but I have to tell you, there is something about the McDaniel clan that bothers me." Martin would not comment and the room was silent for a few minutes. Finally, Mike broke the silence.

"You may not like what I'm going to tell you, but please hear me out." He pulled some notes from his pocket and continued.

"I've done some checking on the McDaniel family and I've got news for you. They aren't what you might think. There is a reason they move around so much. Colten McDaniel has had his share of problems. Most of them he has created himself! He's been fired for many things including lying to his boss. He has been caught cheating. I mean cheating on everything including his wife."

"Those are pretty serious accusations, and even if they are true, his past is really none of my business or yours for that matter. I won't allow you to come into my office and make such allegations!" Martin said.

"Listen, preacher, I'm not just trying to run the man down because I think he's trying to take a job away from me. It's much more than that. I think you know me better than to think I just run my mouth on people!" It was true that Mike was not knows as a tale bearer. He had a negative point of view, but he was not a gossip.

"Pastor, my son spent some time with Colten, Jr. or Mac as they call him and he came home pretty shaken. Mac is into heavy metal and the occult. The parents are too according to their son. Did you know that before these people came to our town they lived in Massachusetts?

"And that's a problem?" Martin was getting weary of the conversation and wanted to get to the hospital to see Cheryl. He needed Mike to get to the point if there was one!

"Let me tell you what Kate McDaniel did in Massachusetts. She was a Medium!

That's right! She had her own help line that people called to have their fortunes read! In the meantime, Colten worked in a brewery, and also helped to set up web sites. I'm talking about pornographic sites!"

"Maybe that's why they left Massachusetts. Maybe they are no longer practicing and decided to move away from that atmosphere and start fresh." Martin felt warm all over and a bit nauseated.

"My son says they still have all Kate's paraphernalia. They keep it hidden so church people won't see it. Kate still does readings and still has loyal callers who want their latest fortune read. When my son said the occult was wrong Mac told him that occult means obscured or hidden not evil!"

"You've got to do something about this. This is not what we need in the church. Don't we have enough trouble day to day without inviting this kind of stuff in?" Martin rubbed his eyes and thought about the accusations. This was not something he could let slide.

"I know you think I'm just burned up because of the job situation, but truthfully, it's more than that. Colten has a reputation with any female that will look his way and I can show you he's been fired for it. Kate doesn't seem to care anything about his extra marital affairs and has earned her own money through her Medium practices. Mac on the other hand has also followed his father's footsteps when it comes to the opposite sex. He told my son he has never had a relationship with any girl that didn't end up in bed." Martin gritted his teeth as he thought of his own daughter. Like the rest of the teen girls, Lisa thought Mac was good looking and athletic with an outgoing personality... quite the charmer.

"The worst part is that Mac put doubts in my son's mind. After all, when you meet such a fine looking family who seem to have reasonable explanations for what they do, it makes you feel a little different. Kate seems religious and certainly does not remind you of a witch! Colten and Mac are both the kind of guys that seem to know how to get close to people." There was concern and anger etched on Mike's face. As much as he wanted the job with Mr. Winters, the situation was much deeper.

"Maybe you should do a series on the occult for the youth. We certainly don't want to see anyone headed in that direction." He added.

"Let me give it some thought and some prayer. I appreciate you letting me know." Martin felt bone tired and in no mood to make a hospital visit. Of course, that would not prevent him from going.

The two men prayed together and Martin began gathering his briefcase and hospital ID as he headed to the parking lot. He would not be back today and wanted to make sure he had his sermon notes with him.

As he headed to his car, he realized he would need to stop for gas...another nuisance keeping him from his destination. He decided he would grab a cup of coffee to drink on the way. He was definitely in need of some caffeine!

"Hey Pastor, I was thinking of stopping by before I went home, but I didn't have any appointment and wasn't sure how busy you might be today." Martin smiled weakly at Steve Winters as he approached.

"How's it going, Steve?"

"Ya got a minute?" he asked.

"I'm on my way to the hospital." Martin hoped he wouldn't try to detain him, but Steve was a corporate executive who was used to having his own way.

"I won't take but a minute of your time. I just have a question." Martin sighed and hoped he would not be delayed. He glanced at his watch.

"I've only got a couple of minutes. Walk with me while I get some coffee and we'll talk." He forced a smile.

"I'll get straight to the point. You know I've been grooming Mike

Ryan for a significant position in the company and I think he deserves it. He's been with the company quite a while and is a good employee who has earned the right to move up the ladder." Martin sighed. He didn't want to open this conversation here in the gas station.

"But then Colten McDaniel shows up at our church and I have to tell you, he is pretty impressive. He's polished and seems to know how to handle himself." He folded his arms and waited as if waiting for an answer.

"Well, what do you think? Have you spent any time with Colten or Kate? My wife and I have and we have been pretty impressed with the whole family."

"If you're asking me which man should get the job, I would ask for a resume as you would for anyone looking for a job and then you need to call his references and check him out thoroughly, especially if you are comparing the two men."

"Oh, Colten has had some very impressive positions. He has given me some great references."

"Have you called any of them?"

"No, I haven't gotten that far. I just wanted your take on the man. I trust your judgment, Pastor and I may be a little clouded. Don't get me wrong. You know how I feel about Mike Ryan, but it will take a little grooming to get him qualified to fit the position and Colten seems to be a few steps ahead." Steve was sorry the Pastor could not spend some time discussing the matter, for he was deeply troubled. Pastor could surely help him sort it out.

He wanted to tell him that though Colten was very likeable and captivating, there was something that didn't sit well. From the time Colten shook his hand and gave him his resume he began to feel uncomfortable. He was generally a very clear headed man who could make snap decisions if needed, but today he felt muddled and unfocused. Colten's answers seemed relevant at the time, but as he tried to remember his responses, he might as well have recited nursery rhymes. It made no sense.

During the interview, Steve had to continually check off the questions he asked as he couldn't be sure he had already asked them.

And the final disturbing piece was the odd drop in temperature. He found himself turning up the thermostat, though the day was relatively warm and Steve liked cool weather. It seemed foolish to ask, but he decided to ask Pastor about the strange events surrounding his interview.

"Let me get back with you Steve. You're not going to make a decision today and I need to check some things out before I give you an answer." Steve gave him a quizzical look, but Martin was not sharing.

"Call me when we can talk without interruptions." Steve called over his shoulder as Martin sprinted to his car.

View Two

"If Cheryl comes out of the hospital this time, you will no longer be of any use, and you KNOW what that means!" Ominous whimpered in spite of himself. He didn't want to be sent to the lowest abyss.

"She is as good as dead! She has been listening to my voice! She would have drowned in the bathtub if that annoying preacher's wife hadn't intervened! I continue to tell her she is no good to anyone and needs to end it all." He said proudly.

"Then why isn't she here!" Portentous thundered.

"In due time, I promise!" Ominous said more decisively than he felt.

"What else do you have to report?" Portentous sneered. He hated Ominous, as hate was his most prominent emotion!

"The McDaniel's have joined the Parker's church and let me tell you, the tide is already turning." He said gleefully.

"Continue" Portentous said warily. He was tired of half-baked promises that held little value.

"Mac has already made a name for himself in the youth group and has put serious doubts in the minds of the teens. Some of them struggle with their beliefs and wonder if they just believe what their parents have told them. Mac has made the other side of life sound so appealing and promising and will lead many astray. Of that I am certain!" Ominous boasted.

"Excellent!" Portentous said in rare praise.

"Kate McDaniel had a tea party at her home as a getting-to-know-you gathering, and most of the women were impressed when she began reading the tiny tea leaves floating in their cups. Of course, she is a master and few seemed uncomfortable." There was a thunderous clap of approval by all those listening in.

"Kate began by speaking to Allison Hammond who is having both marital and child related problems. People are such saps for compassion." Ominous giggled.

"She told Allison that she could foresee grave problems ahead. It was such fun to observe! Kate told this woman that she needed to let go of her past heart ache. It was as if Kate grew up with her. Imagine Allison's surprise when Kate told her she knew she had attempted suicide last year!"

"Yes, another one you let get away as I recall!" Portentous hissed as Ominous continued pretending he had not interrupted.

"She stared at Kate as if she was a god before crumpling into tears. It was great!" Ominous pounded his chest in delight. Of course, after hearing Kate's profound statements, the other women gathered around to hear more. They were like a bunch of cackling hens vying for the rooster's attention!"

"Listen up! When the occult is brought into an atmosphere such as a church, it must be handled delicately. Kate promotes herself as a spiritual person who has been given a rare gift. If you didn't know better, you would think she worked for the Enemy! After she wets their curiosity, she begins to craft her skill to the unsuspecting. She starts off slow and watches the reaction. If there is someone in the crowd who vehemently opposes her, she discontinues and waits for another opportunity. Believe me, most people fall victim to her discourse." Portentous spoke with authority.

"Remember, even the most stalwart can fall victim. For example, if a child was lost and the parents feared for their safety, would anyone care whose mouth the answer came from as long as the child was rescued! Of course not! Then there is room to tantalize with more observations and knowledge of the past." He added.

"Humans are incredibly curious which makes them dabble into things they should leave alone. Just ask Adam! Ha! When they are baited, they easily succumb. And don't forget, they seem to think of themselves as much smarter and wiser than we know them to be. Once they get a taste for the unknown, they often become mesmerized!" Portentous continued which irritated Ominous immensely.

"As I was saying... Kate made her rounds spending a little time with each woman and giving her a little taste of her knowledge. She was wise enough to leave Christine Parker off the invitation list as she would have put a stop to it and the women would not feel comfortable asking Kate for more juicy details with their pastor's wife listening in. Laura Johnson could have been a problem, but when Kate gave her a hug and told her she knew there was a scar on her back made by her step father in one of his tirades, Laura just stood dumbfounded. Kate assured her that these 'gifts' were from heaven and they need not fear." Ominous voice boomed in competition with his nemesis.

"When the ladies left Kate's house, they practically worshipped her! They told her how blessed she was to be given such power." Ominous cleared his throat and continued.

"Kate asked the ladies to keep the information to themselves as there are many who don't understand the rare gift she has been given. She also let them know she would be happy to visit each lady personally to give them more insight to their particular situations. Of course, if they talked about her gift in the church, she would surely be asked by many to discontinue using her talent and the women would suffer from her silence."

"I also am happy to report Rebecca and Glen will be meeting again soon. When Glen bought her painting, his address and phone number went into the computer. I will make sure Rebecca discovers it and either shows up at his door or at the very least, sets up a new rendezvous with him. Rebecca's husband will also have access to Glen's address and phone number." He emphasized with an evil grin.

"I'm not sure which one will be visiting Glen first!" he guffawed. Ominous paced the perimeter importantly waiting for all eyes to be fixed on him before speaking. He cleared his throat loudly and spoke with authority.

"Let me outline your next assignments. First and foremost you will make sure Cheryl arrives for torment immediately! You will also make good on your promises to bring down that fundamental church you have been assigned to! We have given you the tools necessary to complete your assignment including the addition of the McDaniel family who clearly works for us! Your failures will no longer be tolerated and you know what that means!"

"But... but you have already seen the progress I have made ..."

"A novice could have made the same progress! I have practically walked you through each step and still you have failed!" Ominous could hear the whispers and venomous speech all around him. He did his best not to shake.

"I will make good on all the promised I have made. You will see! I will exceed your expectations!" he puffed his chest and strutted on shaky legs hoping to change their minds.

"I have plans I have not shared. You will see! I am no novice!! You will be pleasantly surprised!" Ominous would bring Cheryl to them if he had to cut her throat himself. He was going to have to step up to get things accomplished. What would score him the most points? Ah, yes... bringing the church down would be paramount! Everything else would fall like dominoes. He needed to get his strategy together to fully manipulate the McDaniels. They were moving too slow.

Lisa and Mac were also big on his list. Lisa had never kissed a boy but Mac was persuasive, and loved a challenge. Ominous would have to press him harder to take away her purity. He also decided to push Rebecca's husband harder. Though he shivered with delight to think of destroying the Booth's household, it was even more appealing to have Glen hospitalized. With any luck, he too would be on death's door. He trembled with excitement when he thought of the possibilities.

Chapter 10 View One

Martin opened his car door slowly and willed his feet to obey. He prayed for Cheryl and for God's intervention in her life, but Cheryl was not the most pressing issue. His conversation with Mike Ryan confirmed his naggings suspicions.

When Colten McDaniel first came through the doors of the church with his handsome family, it seems the entire church welcomed them heartily. Colten drove an expensive car and the family could have been on the cover of any magazine. They were well dressed, warm and friendly. Who could ask for more?

After the first service attended, the family lingered a while to speak directly to the Pastor and his family. Martin glanced at his wife and saw the same apprehension. Kate had her cornered and although Christine appeared friendly, there was something about her stance that suggested wariness. Kate was friendly, but forceful. Colten's conversation mirrored his wife. Both seemed capable of any task including preaching. Martin thought perhaps they were just enthusiastic people, but in his heart of hearts... he knew better. His conversation with Mike dispelled any lingering doubts. He would need to address this immediately! He chided himself for dismissing his niggling concerns.

He pushed the thoughts from his mind and concentrated on Cheryl. She was in good hands with Christine at her side. He prayed silently as he pushed the elevator buttons. Cheryl was in ICU until she could be evaluated. The staff knew Martin on a first name basis so frequent were his visits. As soon as Christine saw her husband, she flew into his arms.

"Oh, Martin, I'm so glad you're here." She said softly. This reaction was totally uncommon in a public place. Christine had been reared in a home that did not show outward displays of affection, and Martin was often troubled by it in his early days of marriage. She never held his hand or put her arms around him in public and seemed embarrassed if he so much as kissed her cheek in front of others.

"Is everything all right?" he asked. He led his wife to a deserted section of the waiting room and sat close to her stroking her hand.

"I'm sorry, Martin. I don't know what's wrong with me." She wiped her eyes with the back of her hand. She related the entire story including the conversations Cheryl had with her, John Dunbar and someone who appeared to be unseen.

"I've never seen anything like it, Martin. She actually spoke into the room as if someone else was with us and the worst part is that I felt the presence too!"

"I have to agree with your wife. This lady was not only speaking to someone but she was getting answers!" John Dunbar entered the room unexpectedly and reached his hand out to Martin.

"John Dunbar" He said. The men shook hands and John wasn't sure if he should continue on his way. He didn't want to interrupt.

"What do you think, Martin?" Christine's eyes were wide with confusion. Martin leaned forward holding his head in his hands and closed his eyes. He didn't want to think about the answer. He KNEW the answer. John sensed Martin's reluctance to continue the conversation.

"Cheryl could use some company about now. Why don't you table your talk for later and spend a little time with her before the doctor shows up and chases you off?" He smiled good naturedly and led the way to her room.

"Hello Cheryl." Martin spoke quietly into the room as he entered.

"Oh, Preacher! I'm so embarrassed to see you again... here!" she muttered.

"Did they fill you in? Did they tell you that I'm a nut case that tried to take her life? Well, maybe your wife should have just stayed out of it and I would be out of this horrible life by now."

"And then what?" He had asked her that question before, but she had no answer.

"Maybe all that happens is that you go back to ashes again."

"And if you're wrong?" She whimpered and shrugged her shoulders. She was a pitiful sight and John, Christine and Martin were each touched by her frailty.

"I'm Dr. Sawyer. I'll need you to give us a few minutes please." He was a no nonsense doctor who gave the attending nurse a furrowed brow. There was only one person allowed in ICU at a time and he would scold her later for allowing three people at the bedside.

"You can decide which one of you will see her once I've completed my examination." He pointed to the rules listed on the door in bright letters.

They returned to the familiar waiting room and engaged in light conversation. John told them how he became a paramedic and the transformation that happened in his life once he became a Christian. He had a fascinating way of telling his story and Martin made note to have him give his testimony to his congregation.

Suddenly, a crash cart flew by them and an alarm sounded "code blue." John jumped to his feet and sprinted down the hall. Each of them prayed the race was not to Cheryl's room.

"We're losing her!" Dr. Sawyer's voice was heard above the racket. John entered the room and stood close by in case his assistance was needed. Somehow, Cheryl had pulled out her IV and had landed with a thud on the cold hospital floor.

"Just let me die!" she gasped. Without another word, John raced back to the waiting room to find Martin.

"She needs you, Preacher. She needs you now. I don't know how I'll hold off the rest of the medical team, but she needs you more than she needs them." He said breathlessly as Martin sprinted alongside him to her room.

Martin had faced this situation more than once and it was never easy. The medical team worked frantically to get Cheryl back into position in her bed and inserting her IV. Martin did his best to stay out of their way and while the crisis was at hand, they barely noticed him. But after everything was adjusted, they became aware of his presence.

"You need to leave, sir. Only the medical team is allowed in these conditions."

"He needs to have a word with her." Martin appreciated John's intervention. After all, he was considered part of the team and was obviously well respected.

"There is nothing he can do for her. She needs to rest." snapped the attending physician.

"Just let him have a word with her. I promise I will stay right here beside him and we will be out of here in just a couple of minutes." John gave her his best smile, and she gave him a cursory nod.

"Cheryl, can you hear me?" Martin whispered.

"Oh, no... am I still here?!" she cried softly.

"Cheryl, you need to listen to me carefully. There is hope for you. Jesus died to pay for your sin."

"Yes, Jesus" she repeated weakly after him.

"He knows none of us can make it to heaven without Him. Cheryl, when He died, He died for you! You can't imagine how much He loves you."

"I am not worth His love" she cried.

"Neither am I." said Martin.

"You? You're a good man. He's got to be real proud of you! At least He has a winner!" she said sadly.

"You're wrong, Cheryl. I can't make it without Him either. But He has changed my life and He can change yours too. We are all sinners in the need of a Saviour."

"I'm not like you. I'm a bad person. They took my kids! That's how bad I am!" she whimpered.

"None of us deserve His gift. None of us!"

"Think of it this way. If we were throwing darts and you landed within two inches of the bulls eye and I landed within one inch, which one of us hit the bulls eye for a perfect score?"

"Huh? Well, neither of us, but you came closer."

"Did you ever hear the expression 'a miss is as good as a mile?"

"Yah, so?"

"So God's heaven is a perfect place because He is perfect. The only people who can be with God are those who are perfect. And the only way to be perfect is to have the righteousness of Christ."

"How do you get that?"

"By knowing you're a sinner."

"Tell me something I don't know!" she said sorrowfully.

"Then you must understand that Jesus Christ is the one and only way to heaven because He said so. The Bible says in John 14:6 "I am the Way the Truth and the Life; no man cometh unto the Father, but by me.""

"I don't think anyone ever told me that before. I thought it was about doing good, living right and stuff like that." She said.

"Do you really think Jesus can forgive me?"

"He forgave me! I sure wasn't worthy of it." John piped in excitedly. He could see the conviction and understanding on her face and prayed she would come to the Saviour just like he had done so many years before.

"I feel so miserable and worthless" she admitted.

"You're exactly the person Jesus is looking for. He came to seek and to save those who are lost."

"What should I do?" it was obvious she wanted to pour her heart out to the Lord.

"There are no 'magic' words, Cheryl. God is looking for a heart of repentance and brokenness. He will gladly receive you if you will ask for his forgiveness and receive His gift of everlasting life."

"It sounds much too simple." She admitted.

"Man thinks he can win God's heart, but only through Christ the payment for sin has been made." Cheryl's countenance changed as the words penetrated her mind and heart. Immediately, she began praying and telling the Lord how sorry she was for her life and asking Him for forgiveness. While John and Martin listened quietly, Cheryl trusted the finished work of Christ and in turn received a regenerated heart and spirit.

After Cheryl had cried, prayed and trusted the Lord for her soul, Martin prayed as well. John was a vocal man who interjected from time to time just to praise the Lord with Martin.

"Let's go tell Christine. She'll be so excited!"

"You go get her. I'll wait here." John smiled down at Cheryl's bed as tears formed in his eyes.

"I was worried about you, girl. Truly worried! But you listened to the right voice this time." He chuckled.

"Aint no one gonna pluck you out of His hand! It's going to be okay no matter what!" John was so excited he had to remind himself that he was in ICU. But ICU reminded him where he was as Cheryl's vitals beeped across the screen. He gasped as he watched the monitor. Someone called for a crash cart and John hurried to Martin's side to keep them from entering the room.

"What's happening? I don't understand!" Martin and Christine exchanged worried glances as John peeked his head in to see if the team was able to stabilize their patient. She was not responding.

"I'll let you know something as soon as can." He assured them as he pointed toward a small office used to speak to immediate family following surgery. Christine reluctantly followed her husband. Her excitement was stifled by the new turn of events.

After thumbing mindlessly through a few magazines, Martin began to pace. This was taking far too long and he was very concerned. He prayed for peace for all concerned and decided to get them both some coffee. Christine walked with him to the vending machine to stretch her legs. To their surprise, John was standing outside Cheryl's room staring at the floor. It didn't look good!

"How is she doing, John?" Martin's voice startled him and he looked up with tears in his eyes.

"She didn't make it" he said sorrowfully. Christine gasped and Martin pulled her close. They were anticipating a celebration.

"I was thinking of how we could speak to her case worker and get her kids back. What a testimony she would have had to inspire others." Christine choked.

"We can still celebrate" said John.

"Do you realize how close she was to entering eternity without Christ? We can celebrate her decision and her home going! I'll bet she's thanking the Lord Jesus right now! Mmm mmm, what it must be like for her! I envy what she is seeing!"

"Me too!" Martin admitted. Christine brightened, though it was difficult to see passed the young woman's death.

"There's nothing more to do here, Preacher. Why don't you and the Missus go on home? We'll get in touch with next of kin and I'll let you know about the arrangements. I'm sure her relatives will want you to hold the funeral" said John.

"I suppose you're right." Martin glanced at his watch. It was much later than he thought.

"Let me call Lisa and see if she got my earlier message. She was to start dinner for me so we should be able to eat soon after we get home." She rubbed Martin's weary shoulders affectionately as she spoke and Martin scratched down his number for John. He wanted to stay in the loop as arrangements were made and relatives contacted.

As they walked to the parking lot, Christine decided to call home again. When she left so many hours ago to have lunch with Cheryl, she didn't know how long she would be gone. She hoped to have a long talk with the misguided woman. She made one of their favorite casserole dinners and Lisa was to put it in the oven by 4:00. Everything would be ready by the time they arrived.

"Hello, Chad, let me talk to your sister" said Christine.

"Lisa's not here Mom." Chad replied.

"She's not? She was supposed to be home right after school."

"Well, that was before Mac asked her to go to get a soda with him." He laughed. Christine glanced at her watch. School was dismissed by 2:30 and it was going on 6:00. Lisa knew better than this!

"Go in the kitchen and see if dinner is in the oven." She ordered. She hoped Lisa might have stopped home to carry out her assignment.

"Nope. There is something sitting on top of the stove covered with foil."

"Okay, turn the oven to 350 degrees and put the dish in the oven."

"How long is it going to take to cook? I have plans tonight." Christine was in no mood to discuss his evening plans. When were her children going to get it through their heads that 'plans' had to be checked out with parents *before* they happened. They were not to be made and then inform the parents!

"We'll talk when I get home. If your sister arrives before your dad and I, make sure she knows she is to remain home until we get there. No one is to go anywhere!" Chad knew by the sound of her voice that she was in no mood to argue. He hoped Lisa hadn't ruined the evening for both of them.

Christine drove a little faster hoping to beat her husband home. She was definitely having a talk with Lisa. This was totally irresponsible of her!

To her surprise, she could see Mac's car on the highway ahead of her. He was speeding and weaving in and out of traffic. She was horrified! The proximity of her daughter to the driver indicated she could not possibly be wearing her seatbelt. Christine was fuming! She prayed for their safety as she did her best keep up with them. She did not want to risk a ticket, but she also did not want them out of her sight.

Traffic was heavy at this time of day and she had no intention of weaving in and out of the four lane highway. Her fingers hurt from gripping the steering wheel. In a few more minutes, she completely lost them. Or perhaps they lost her! She continued to search each lane for Mac's vehicle in vain. There was nothing to do but continue to head home. She slowed her pace knowing she had lost them, however, when she pulled into the driveway, Mac's car was sitting empty in front of the house.

"Lisa, where are you?" Christine shouted into the living room. She was furious, shaken and bewildered. Mac was sitting on the couch flipping through a magazine, looking completely relaxed, as though he had been there for hours.

"Hello, Mrs. Parker. I came to see Lisa. I hope that's all right." He jumped up to greet her and gave her his best smile and she stared at him in disbelief. Did he think she would be fooled into thinking he just happened by?

"Have a seat, Colten." Christine narrowed her eyes at him. She did not tolerate deceit. He sat down as if nothing at all was wrong. However, Lisa knew better than to pull an act on her parents. Christine met her in the kitchen.

"The casserole isn't quite done yet, Mom. Do you want me to make a salad to go along with it?" Christine wondered how far she would play this charade and decided to find out. If her daughter decided to begin lying to her, she would nip it at once.

"How long has it been in the oven?" she asked. Lisa looked at the timer on the stove. There was still another thirty minutes left.

"Looks like it will be done in about thirty minutes." She smiled.

"Is it okay if Mac stays for dinner? We want to ... um... study together" Christine was fuming but before she could answer, Martin walked through the kitchen door.

"Something smells good! I'm starved!" he smiled as he laid down his brief case and pulled off his tie.

"Hello, Pastor." Mac walked into the kitchen as if he was part of the family. Martin greeted him warmly.

"Dinner will be ready soon. Do you care if Mac stays for dinner?" Lisa asked. There was an awkward silence as Martin detected his wife's demeanor. Something didn't seem quite right but he was too worn out to think about it.

"It's fine with me if it's okay with your mother." He offered. Christine's silence was noticed by all and Lisa had no idea why her mother seemed put off. As far as she knew, no one knew she had been out for hours with Mac. When she sailed into the kitchen to put the food in the oven, she found Chad had beat her to it and also set the timer. She hollered up the stairs to thank him but did not realize her mother had already called home. Lisa assumed Chad was hungry and getting a jump on dinner.

"Sure, you can stay." Lisa and Mac exchanged curious glances at her hesitant answer.

"Hey Dad, you got a minute?" Chad called from the top of the stairs. Martin sighed. He was too tired to think at the moment and hoped Chad had nothing urgent to discuss.

"I'll call you when dinner is on the table. Go relax" Christine urged. As soon as he was out of the kitchen she began again.

"How was school today?"

"Fine"

"Did Chad have practice after school?" Lisa had no idea.

"Yes, there was a special practice called today. It lasted for quite a while. You know the coach wants us to be ready for Saturday's game!" Mac chimed in.

"If Chad had practice, how did you get home?" she quizzed, never once taking her eyes of Lisa.

"I brought her home. I hope that's okay" said Mac.

"Why weren't *you* at practice?"

"Oh, it was more for the outfielders. I generally pitch so I didn't have to be there." He lied.

"I would think your position would be more vital than the outfield. Odd that the coach didn't insist you stay."

"Well, I hate to brag, but I'm a pretty good pitcher and the coach is pretty lenient with me." He smiled. Lisa stared at the floor looking very uncomfortable. Christine decided to capitalize on her discomfort.

"Why were you so late getting dinner in the oven? I was hoping to have dinner on the table by now?" She folded her arms and looked intently into her daughter's eyes praying she would not lie to her. Lisa could not hold eye contact under the piercing stare.

"Oh, that's my fault too, I'm afraid." Mac jumped in.

"We have a huge history test tomorrow and we started studying the minute we got here. I'm afraid Lisa didn't see the note until she entered the kitchen to get us a drink." Christine was floored. Not only did Mac have a ready lie each time she asked a question, but there was not a hint of a blush on his cheek, nor any hesitancy. She noticed he looked directly into her eyes without flinching or showing uneasiness.

Christine was about to expose the whole ruse, when she noticed her daughter's embarrassment. She scurried around the kitchen placing glasses and napkins on the table. She did not add to the conversation, neither did she correct anything that was said.

"I think it's ready, Mom. Do you want me to let Dad know?" She wanted desperately to be away from the kitchen and the conversation. With her mother's nod, she raced to the stairs to call her father and brother to the table. She hoped to change the subject as soon as they arrived, if she could swallow the lump in her throat long enough to ask them questions.

When everyone was seated, Martin blessed the food and began passing the rolls and iced tea.

"How was your day Dad?" Lisa asked eagerly as soon as he stepped into the kitchen.

"It's been a long day." He sighed. He didn't really want to discuss Cheryl's death with Mac in the room and certainly wouldn't discuss his visit from Mike Ryan. However, he thought it might be a good time to get additional information from Mac.

"So, Mac, tell us about your life prior to your move to our area."

"I suppose we have moved more than the average family, but then again, my family is not average." He laughed at his little joke and Chad laughed with him. Lisa bit her lip and stared at the food on her plate. She had never seen this side of Mac and it was totally unappealing to her.

"Head hunters are constantly calling my father and offering some ludicrous amount of money if he will go to work for them. He turns down jobs all the time as he knows my mom is tired of moving." He bragged.

"What firm brought your father here?" Mac's face reddened as he was caught in his own web of deceit.

"I... uh... am not sure which job he's going to take. He's been offered more than one and hasn't made a decision yet." It was obvious to everyone except Chad that he was lying. Martin knew he came to their area in hopes of *finding* a job.

"I haven't had a chance to really get to know your mother yet. I am looking forward to spending time with her" said Christine.

"You'll love my mom. Everyone does. She's good at just about everything and people seem to be naturally drawn to her."

"Yes, she seems quite talented. I know she has expressed a desire to get involved with church activities."

"That sounds like Mom. She can do anything from designing brochures to writing programs for you. And you should see her type! Her fingers fly across the keys."

"Did your mother work outside the home before coming here?" asked Christine.

"She's had a few jobs, but my dad doesn't really like her to work. Besides, he makes enough money that she doesn't have to do that." He was becoming more uncomfortable with the questions regarding his family. He enjoyed bragging about them, but he had gotten himself into trouble in the past for sharing information that was detrimental, especially concerning his mother.

"It's good to know there is someone so talented in our midst." Christine hoped she didn't sound too condescending.

"We will have to have your family over for dinner sometime."

"Dinner is delicious as usual." Martin did his best to remember to compliment his wife. If he had learned anything in counseling couples, appreciation was one of the number one faults of husbands and wives.

"Thank you Martin. And thank you Lisa for remembering to put it in the oven for me." Chad gave his mother a confused look. She knew that didn't happen.

"Lucky for you I was thirsty or we would all be hungry right now." Mac laughed.

"What does that mean?" Chad asked without a smile.

"We were studying and I asked Lisa for a drink. Good thing too or we would be ordering a pizza." He grinned at Chad conspiratorially.

"You were studying here with no one home?" Martin frowned

at his daughter who knew it was absolutely forbidden to have boy in the house without supervision.

"Oh, we weren't alone. Chad was here and you know Chad... once we got started talking about sports we forgot all about studying." Lies rolled off his tongue as easy as water.

"I think we should study another time. I'm not feeling well" said Lisa. She couldn't stand another minute of this. Surely, her mother was going to expose the lies and her stomach churned in protest.

"Oh, sure. I understand." Mac said... though he didn't understand at all.

"Do you want to walk me to my car?" he asked.

"Yah, okay." She said hesitantly. She just wanted this night to be over, but in her heart she knew it was far from over. Her parents would be waiting inside for an explanation.

As soon as they walked out the front door, Mac spun her around and tried to kiss her. She pulled away as if he were a stranger. Truthfully, he felt like one.

"Don't be uptight, baby. I think we're in the clear. Your parents seemed to buy my story." He said proudly as he pulled her close again.

"How could you lie to them like that?" She said angrily.

"What do you mean? We were in a tough spot, but I pulled us through. Don't be upset that you can't think as fast on your feet."

"What's that supposed to mean? Do you lie to me too?" she said as she pulled away from his grasp.

"I have no reason to lie to you. I respect you and I care about you more and more each day. I just didn't want your parents to come down on you. That's all." She softened as she looked into his soulful eyes. She couldn't believe the most popular boy she had ever known was so attracted to her. It made her heart beat a little faster.

"Can't I have a kiss good night?" His breath was on her face and she felt her resolve slipping away.

"If you want me to go back inside and tell your parents that I was not telling them the truth, I'll do it for you. I would do anything for you, Lisa." He pulled her close and this time she didn't resist.

"I want my parents to like you and they won't if they think you are dishonest with them."

"Shh… it's okay. I will make things right between us. Besides, I can be pretty irresistible, don't you think?" he laughed and she laughed with him.

"Now, about that kiss." She stood like a statue as he bent down to kiss her. Just then the door opened.

"Lisa, Mom wants to talk to you." Chad's voice interrupted them and Lisa pulled away from him.

"I'll see you tomorrow." Mac blew her a kiss and got into his car. Things had not gone as expected. He called his friend Thomas to report.

"Hey, I'm just getting started. Don't count me out yet!" he laughed. Lisa would have been appalled at the discussion.

Mac had only been in school for a short time before he became one of the most popular guys there. He seemed to fit with any crowd. He was such a chameleon that he could hang out with the guys who used drugs one night and go to church the next morning.

After an evening with a wild, unruly group of guys, he was challenged to date Lisa Parker. According to this group, she would not date anyone who was not in church and even more specifically, in a fundamental church! Lisa turned their heads, but not enough to want to attend church.

Sometime during the evening, when they bet on everything from who could shoot the basketball from the farthest distance to who could drink the most beer, Lisa's name came up. He was first challenged to take her out, but that didn't seem to be enough. He was charming enough to get a date from just about any girl. Then they raised the stakes.

"I'll give you $100 bucks if you can get her to smoke or drink and I'm not talking about soda and cigarettes."

"I'll do even better. For $500 bucks, I'll get her to leave the church and all her puritanical ways!" Mac was feeling pretty sure of himself after a night of drugs and alcohol.

"How long do you think it will take?" the guys were all checking their wallets. They came from substantial homes with lots of money.

"With a girl like Lisa, you have to move slowly, or you'll scare her away. I have to win her trust and then I'll make my move." He grinned slyly.

"I'll give you three months!" said Thomas who was generally in charge.

"I won't need that long!" he said confidently.

"How will we know you're not lying?!"

"Oh c'mon, when a girl's reputation is ruined how fast does that go through the school?" Mac snickered.

"Yah, and with a girl like Lisa, it will really spread like wild fire. The promiscuous girls will have a field day! There is nothing they love more than slandering other girls!"

Thomas gave Mac a hard time, but it only made him more determined to win Lisa over, break her, and then dump her. It was his usual method and quite honestly, he was growing bored with it. He never met a girl that meant anything at all to him. Sometimes it concerned him that he had never loved any of them. He spoke to his mother about it. Of course, she told him that he had not yet a girl worthy of his time and talents. Both parents encouraged him to do "whatever makes you happy." In truth… nothing really made him happy. His family moved so often, his friendships were always surface ones. There was no one he stayed in contact with after moving as one person meant as little as the next.

Lisa watched his car pull away from the driveway and reluctantly headed back to the house as if going to an execution. She walked slowly as thoughts tumbled through her mind. She was upset to hear Mac lie so easily, but when he said he was trying to protect her because he cared so much about her, she melted.

She took a deep breath as she entered the kitchen. Her mother's eyes were blazing and she knew it was going to be a long evening.

View Two

"Did you really think you could hide?" Portentous growled. He kicked Ominous viciously until he rolled into view. By now, a repulsive crowd had gathered all hoping to add to any painful situation. Most of them had no idea what had happened, it mattered little to any of them. They only wanted to be part of the torture.

"I was not hiding. I was preparing my report." Ominous lied.

"Let me save you some time... I will ask the questions! Your answers will determine your fate!" he hissed. Portentous strutted like a district attorney closing in on his victim.

"You said you would coerce Cheryl into committing suicide!"

"Yes, and she did!" Ominous interrupted.

"Is that so?"

"Yes! You should have seen me! I whispered over and over that she was a loser! I reminded her that she was an unfit mother and her kids would be far better off without her! I told her she could never change as she has tried before and never succeeded." He puffed out his chest as he reminisced.

"I told her to take her entire prescription and even had her mix medications just to be sure. Then I watched her slip into the bathtub and danced when I saw her head slide under the water! I was spectacular!" He almost took a bow in his excitement.

"THEN WHERE IS SHE???" Portentous bellowed, shaking the entire assembly.

"What do you mean? She hasn't arrived yet?" Ominous croaked?

"Do you see her anywhere?" Portentous and the other minions were beginning to circle making Ominous very nervous.

"I don't understand. I was there watching as she slipped under the water. I am quite certain she is dead!" He said in bewilderment.

"You have that fact correct. She is indeed dead! However, she is NOT here. How do you explain that?" Portentous snarled. Ominous had no explanation and stood in fear of his hateful companions.

"Did you stay with her until her spirit left her body?" Ominous shook his head.

"I was quite certain she was dead, and I proceeded to my next task. You know I am working quite successfully with Mac to break Lisa Parker. Oh you would be very happy to see how she is succumbing to his masterful lies." He grinned.

"Has she lost her purity?" Portentous asked.

"It is just a matter of time." Ominous said with confidence.

"Unfortunately, you have run out of time!" Portentous announced.

"You were to bring back a good report or deal with the consequences! As I see it, you have failed in every task! You see, Cheryl is not among us because you were too stupid to complete the job! That preacher's wife intervened and now we have lost her!"

"My task was to make sure she ended her life!" Ominous voice shook with fear.

"Yes, you idiot, she did finally succumb to the first death! You unfortunately left her in the hands of the Enemy's people. And for the record, let me also remind you that we lost John Dunbar because of your debacle. He was lying in an alley in a drunken stupor! He should have been 'easy pickens' as they say, but again, you did not stay on task until the job was complete and what happened? I'll tell you what happened! Not only did we not get John Dunbar, but he now works tirelessly for the Enemy and was instrumental in keeping Cheryl from coming to us!" The circle was getting smaller around Ominous and he could feel the power of their hate as they closed in.

Ominous wished he was more like Portentous, but he had never mastered his fear of the Enemy. When the Enemy's people sincerely prayed, he had to flee. He could not bear it! He wondered if Portentous honestly did not fear the Enemy. But there was no honesty here, so he could not be sure.

"I see no reason for you to remain in your post when there are so many others willing to bring mankind to their knees! You have nothing to report that would cause me to change my mind!"

"Wait! I have more to report!" Portentous hated Ominous but if he had something newsworthy he was interested in hearing it before making his final decision.

"Kate McDaniel has already made her mark in the Parker's church. At this very moment, she is lining up women to tell their fortunes. Of course, she is not touting herself as a fortune teller! But she is giving these women information that will make her the most popular woman in the church. No longer will they go to Martin Parker for advice or council. Instead, they will council with Kate. I predict a great percentage of the church will fall away from their fundamental beliefs of the blasted Word and succumb to her talents." His comments were applauded and Portentous nodded in agreement.

"Anything else you wish to share before I decide your fate?" Portentous hissed. Ominous knew he better come up with something remarkable or suffer the consequences.

"If things go as I have planned, we will be receiving Glen Booth into our midst." Portentous huffed and Ominous pushed further.

"Let me clarify. *Today*, Glen Booth WILL arrive! I will allow nothing and no one to interfere." He promised.

"Hmmm, I'll tell you what I'm going to do. I will give you the opportunity to bring Glen Booth to us but it must happen today! If it does not happen, I will consider it your final failure! Do I need to spell it out for you?"

"No, no! I understand perfectly. It will happen just as I have said!" Ominous was not certain how he would make it happen, but knew it was his only hope.

"Is there anything else you wish to share?"

"I...I don't think so." He said quietly. His confidence was beginning to wane and he could not allow that to happen. Too much was resting on his success.

"There is one more assignment you could take to add positive points to your atrocious negative reports." Ominous nodded eagerly. He was in desperate need of something to change his course.

"John Dunbar has been asked to give his testimony at the Parker's church."

"And you want me to stop him? You have nothing to worry about! I will make sure he never speaks there!" Ominous sighed with relief. That was a relatively easy assignment. There were so many ways to put up road blocks. He could distract a driver and cause an accident, or he could distract him in any number of ways.

"No, I don't want you to stop him. As a matter of fact, I want his testimony to be heard by all those who think they have no hope. I want him to be elevated before the people. I want them to want to be just like John Dunbar!" said Portentous firmly.

"I don't understand." Portentous glared at him. Everything had to be spelled out!

"Let me instruct you step by step... you fool! First, you will allow this man to share his testimony. However, if there is any kind of invitation for others to become part of the Enemy's camp, you will thwart it. You will cause distractions everywhere. You will tell the losers listening that they have tried religion or programs or medication and nothing has ever worked. Tell them they are doomed and will look like fools when they fail again, but this time they will have an entire church laughing at them."

"Yah, I can do that. Is that the assignment?" It seemed to simple and without purpose.

"Shut up, you imbecilic Moron! I will send several others to help you as you are incapable of working alone. Now my final point. After John gives his long winded speech blah, blah, blah, you will begin to work on him. I want you to bring some of the people from his past back into his life." Ominous wanted desperately to ask why, but he did not want another beating so remained quiet.

"Bring Vontrice back into his life. She used to be his girl and she is still a mess. I have deliberately allowed her to continue her dismal life knowing she would be useful at some point." Ominous was beginning to understand.

"Vontrice has always been influential. If the truth be known, John still has deep feelings for her he had buried deep within his heart. He had not thought of her in years, but Portentous knew the mind of man. It would take very little to get him back in her grasp.

"If you are successful, you should have Mr. Dunbar lying in an alley in a drunken stupor just like they found him years ago."

"Yes, yes... I can make it happen!" Ominous swore.

"What are you waiting for? Get going!" Portentous shoved him and all those within close proximity gnashed on him as well.

Portentous hoped he would be successful but in truth, he had no intention of sparing him. On the contrary, he laughed fiendishly. It would be a feather in his cap to send not only Ominous, but Glen Booth to the deepest abyss! His actions would surely make him more powerful!

Chapter 11 View One

John was excited to give his testimony to Pastor Martin's congregation. It had been quite a while since he spoke publicly and he felt a bit nervous. He made it a point to witness to any who would listen to him about his Saviour. No matter the response, John remained friendly and loving to everyone. He was called "Preacher John" by some and worse by others, but his testimony was inspiring and he lived his faith before all who made his acquaintance.

He decided to write out some of the details of his conversion as he was afraid his memory would fail him as he stood before a group of strangers. He knew his testimony was powerful and sincere and he prayed it would give hope to those listening.

He remembered the day and hour he trusted the Lord, but other details were fuzzy. He chided himself knowing his earlier drinking affected his memory. He wanted to tell people there was no enjoyment associated with his drinking days, but that would be a lie and everyone would know it. Yes, there was 'pleasure in sin for a season.' There was no denying that. But the problem was nobody knew how long that season would last and nobody realized what it would cost them in the end.

His sobriety also cost him a few things. There were members of his own family that no longer spent time with him. His brother had died in a car accident and though he was not given many of the details, he knew that his blood alcohol content was over the legal limit. He also knew his parents received a law suit from the driver of the other vehicle who managed to survive when his brother crossed the yellow line, but would be wheel chair bound for the rest of his life.

And then there was Vontrice. He shook his head sadly as her image unfolded in his mind. They were in love with so many things in common. Sadly, one of them was their love of alcohol. Vontrice promised him many times she would stop drinking, but she could not seem to stop. He understood completely, as he could never have stopped if it hadn't been for the Lord's intervention. He tried desperately to help her find the Saviour, but she was not interested.

"So, you think you're better than me now?" she shrieked when he refused to drink with her.

"I aint better than nobody! Never said that!" he began.

"Then have a drink with me and then we'll have some fun." She plopped on his lap and kissed him passionately. It was difficult to refuse her, but he loved her enough to want her to find what he himself had found. A new life in Christ!

"Tricey, you know how I feel about you, girl!"

"Show me!" she challenged as she kissed him again and began unbuttoning his shirt.

"I want you to listen to me." He said pulling her away to look into her beautiful brown eyes.

"Don't want to listen. No more talking! Let's see some action!" she giggled and began again to remove his shirt.

"Don't you understand it's because I care so much about you that I want you to listen?" Vontrice folded her arms and narrowed her eyes. What happened to the fun loving John she enjoyed spending time with?

"If you're going to start preaching to me again, you can just leave! Leave and never come back! If I want to talk to a preacher, priest, or rabbi, I know where the churches are! I don't need you to tell me how to live my life or look down on me because I want to have fun!"

"But you're fooling yourself and you know it! How many times have I held you because you've been too sick to leave alone?"

"I didn't say I haven't overdone it from time to time, but I'm doing okay!" she retorted haughtily.

"I thought you loved me!" she added.

"I do!"

"Then why are you trying to change me?"

"Vontrice, I love you, without alcohol."

"You should love me no matter what... like I love you. How many times have I stayed with you when you've overdone it?" she reminded him.

"And I thank you! But I don't want to be that person and neither do you. I could have died in that alley if someone hadn't come to help me. I am lucky the ones that stole my money didn't decide to end my life that day." That was a painful memory for both of them. John was passed out in an alley, and Vontrice was too hung over to go looking for him. It took a few days before she knew what happened to him.

She was happy that he wasn't hurt and wanted to celebrate with him as soon as he came to her house. She told him she had been too sick to search for him and was happy to know someone had come to his rescue. However, everything changed when he began to witness to her.

"You sound like one of my Papa's old buddies. He used to get drunk as a skunk and then start crying and singing religious songs. He was pathetic!" she scoffed.

"I'm sure when he was inebriated he realized how pathetic he looked and remembered his commitment to the Lord is my guess."

"Well, guess again! Papa's buddy was nothing but a drunk! Couldn't keep a job or provide for his family. Everyone felt sorry for his poor wife and kids."

"He was nothing but an old fool! And if you think I'm going to listen to any religious talk, you're a fool too!" she spat.

She walked out of his life and he never heard from her again. It broke his heart but he knew it was probably for the best. He wasn't a good man when he was with her. She could break his resolve every time.

He shook his head as he reminisced. 'nuff of that' he said opening his Bible. He prayed earnestly that God would give him the words to say that would speak to hearts. It wasn't enough to hear about an old drunk and the life he led. These people had stories of their own. What they needed was hope! What they needed was change! He could provide that and his heart beat faster at the thought.

The old grandfather clock in the living room chimed and he realized he would have to make his notes later. An unexpected call from his mother late the night before rearranged his day. It had been so long since her last call; he almost didn't recognize the number. At the last minute, he snatched the phone from the cradle and was surprised to hear his mother's weak voice.

"John, can ya hear me boy?" the voice was old and fading away.

"Mamma?" The sound of her voice brought instant worry.

"Yes, it's your Mamma. I need you to do me a favor."

"Of course, I will if I can" said John.

"I need you to take me to the doctor tomorrow morning."

"Are you okay, Mamma?"

"I guess the doctor will decide on that." She never admitted to being sick even if she couldn't get out of bed. She told her children she was just napping whenever they came to check on her. Fortunately, John had an older sister that could do the cooking and cleaning when his mother was ailing.

"If you can't take me, I'll cancel it. I'm sure I'll be fine in a few days. I just need to get rested up is all. Can't a body take a rest in the middle of the day without everyone fussing and making doctor appointments!" she complained. He would have to call his sister to get the rest of the story.

"No, no, don't you cancel. I'll be there in plenty of time to get you to the doctor." He wanted to get an early start. Mamma lived only a few miles away, but he had some questions of his own to ask. He certainly wasn't going to depend on her version.

Doctor Samuel Chase had been their family physician for years, and though he was getting older and wanted his sons to take over, Mamma would see no one except Doc Sammy. She said she would quit going to the doctor if he ever gave up his practice. She wasn't going to trust her health to anyone's youngins no matter if they had credentials or not.

Mamma was in worse shape than he imagined. She leaned heavily on a cane and had to stop to catch her breath every couple steps. He noticed a wheelchair in the corner of the living room but his mother would have nothing to do with it. She was going to be mobile and no one was going to make her an invalid. The topic was not up for discussion.

John wished he had come earlier. This was going to take much longer than anticipated and he wondered if he would have a chance to speak to Dr. Chase alone. Painstaking steps were made in tiny paces and he was beginning to run out of patience. His mother was a hard headed woman and John admired her in many ways. Maybe it was this kind of determination that kept an old woman moving so many years past her prime.

She was immediately ushered into a private room to wait for the doctor and John began thumbing through a magazine to occupy his time. Her earlier comments raced through his head. He was surprised when she asked for a ride to her appointment, but didn't realize she had never intended to call him. She thought she was dialing her son, Quinten. Their phone numbers were nothing alike including the area code. Quinten had moved to Jersey several years before. She almost hung up as she didn't want to be a burden to him when she hadn't had contact with him for so long.

"Is there a reason you don't stay in touch with me, Mamma?" John asked quietly.

"Not anymore, I suppose. You have proven yourself, John. You're a good boy! All that drinking is behind you and you have finally done something with your life."

"Thank you, Mamma." John smiled at the rare compliment.

"I guess I just didn't want to be disappointed is all. I have seen too many people go on the wagon for a while only to fall off and hurt everyone around them." She sighed.

"Like I try to tell anyone who will listen, I didn't get on the wagon. I don't know where I would be if it hadn't been for Jesus." She patted his hand and smiled at him like he was still a little boy. She had gone to church in the earlier days of her life, but she married an alcoholic who infected all their children. He was a functional drunk. He went to work every day, and seemed to be able to get the job done, but when it was quitting time, he was the first one in line at the local tavern. Every night he closed the place down and came staggering home. If his children wanted to spend time with him, they knew where to find him.

When his children were old enough to drink, their father bought them their first beer. With their predisposition to alcohol, it didn't take long for most of them to become alcoholics as well.

John remembered the night he came home to find his father sitting on the couch with beer bottles lined up around the coffee table. He thought he had indigestion and John followed him into the bathroom to help him look for antacids. He doubled over in pain and told John to call his mother who was asleep in the next room. By the time they rushed back into the bathroom, he was dead on the floor. His mother shook her head and called an ambulance. No one seemed surprised at his funeral and there were very few tears shed.

"Thanks so much. I appreciate you getting me in on such short notice. John's head jerked at the melodious sound of the familiar voice.

And there she was standing before him. She still had the perfect figure but when she turned around John nearly gasped. Her beautiful face had several stitches and it was obvious by her swollen eyes, someone had done this to her.

"Vontrice?" he said softly as if tasting the name on his tongue.

"John? Oh John!" she ran into his arms and he held her as she cried her heart out. The nurse stood impatiently waiting for her to pay her bill. The disgust on her face enraged him.

"Excuse me, could you pay your bill so I can assist other patients." Vontrice had no money and intended to ask for more time to pay the debt, but John snatched the bill from the woman's hand and gave her his credit card. Vontrice was going to object, but she had no idea how she would pay, so remained silent and allowed John to once again come to her rescue.

"Aren't you just my Knight in shining armor!" she smiled and his heart melted just as it had years ago.

"Who did this to you?" he asked keeping his voice low.

"It doesn't matter." She couldn't look into his eyes as the feeling of shame overwhelmed her.

"It will always matter. *You* will always matter." She hugged him and they sat quietly together without speaking. It was one of the things he loved about her. He knew lots of women who couldn't stand silence. They could talk about nothing for hours. Vontrice was different. He didn't realize how much he missed her until now.

"Excuse me, you wanted to speak to the doctor?" her words were icy and John decided immediately this nurse would also be part of his conversation with Dr. Chase.

"He can see you for a few minutes while your mother is dressing." Vontrice got up to leave, but John grabbed her hand.

"Don't go anywhere. This won't take long I promise." She seemed reluctant.

"I'll take you home and we can talk." He added hopefully.

"Sure why not." She plopped back down and smiled up at him. She had nowhere to go and no ride to take her, so why not? John stepped in front of the nurse and walked into Dr. Chase's office.

"I have a few questions if you don't mind." John got right to the point. He knew his mother would be furious to find him asking questions about her and he didn't want Vontrice to get away from him either.

"Can you fill me in? Is my mother okay?" his words tumble out in a rush.

"Your mother is remarkably well for her age. She needs to take better care of herself and eat properly but that is a common complaint for people her age. She can't digest greasy foods and I know she loves them. Her bones are getting more brittle, but she won't use a cane. Her heart is getting weaker and she is forgetful, but that is also due to her age. All in all, she is doing very well."

"That is a surprise. Generally, someone has to hog tie her to get her to the doctor's office and that's only after she is too weak to protest."

"It surprised me when she called for an appointment. It wasn't her daughters that called. She made the appointment herself."

"Maybe you have missed something. Mamma wouldn't call unless something was ailing her big time. It doesn't make sense."

"I agree, but the tests I ran on her all came back with fairly good results. I would just keep an eye on her. Sometimes, when they get to be this age, they start thinking more about their own mortality and begin wondering if something might be wrong with them. It's really not uncommon." John nodded, but it sure didn't sound at all like his mother.

When he returned to the waiting room his mother and Vontrice were deep in conversation. His mother laughed and soon both women were laughing together hysterically. It was a pleasant sound.

"Look who I found in the waiting room, John!" announced his mother.

"It's so good to see you again, Vontrice" said John.

"I've invited her to lunch, is that okay John?" his mother asked sweetly.

"Sure it is. It will give us all a chance to catch up a bit." He smiled.

"Could you take us to the Fried Green Tomato?" It was one of his mother's favorites and strictly against her diet. There was not an item on the menu that didn't pass through the deep fryer including the desserts.

"Oh, I love that place, but I'm afraid I'm a little short today. I wasn't expecting to go out to lunch." In truth she didn't have the money to get her to the grocery store either, but she could never share that with anyone.

"Let me treat both of you ladies." Vontrice held up her hand, but his mother slapped it down playfully.

"If John wants the pleasure of treating his favorite ladies, we will not deprive him of the privilege" said his mother.

In a few minutes they were all settled into John's car headed for his mother's favorite restaurant. Vontrice sat in the backseat just behind the driver and John stole as many glances as possible as he drove down the road.

No sooner had they found seats when a waitress came rushing to the table to greet them. Everyone knew John's mother as she came as often as possible to enjoy the same food she prepared for her family when she was well.

"Mamma Dunbar!" the young woman exclaimed.

"I know it's been a while! I want to order for my family today. I will have greens and okra and also some smoked ham to go with it." John and Vontrice smiled at her. Mamma always took charge and loved it.

Lunch was enjoyed by everyone including the staff that made their way from time to time to check on Mamma Dunbar. It was obvious they all loved her. Before long Mamma's eyes were closing and it was time to get her home for a nap.

Vontrice and John helped her to bed promising they would get together with her in the next few days. She kissed them both and told them how much she enjoyed lunch.

"It was almost worth that doctor visit just to get to go to lunch!" she giggled through sleepy eyes. They tiptoed out to the living room and sat on Mamma's worn out couch. Everything in the room was faded, outdated and falling apart... just like Mamma.

"Thank you for such a lovely day" said Vontrice, though the same words were on John's lips.

"Are you doing okay, Tricey?" No one had called her that since she stopped seeing John.

"I'm doing, don't need to worry" she said a little too quickly.

"I never want to see marks on this pretty face again!" He held her chin in his hand and she kissed him. Everything else seemed to fade except the beautiful girl in his arms.

"Oh, John, how I've missed you." Her voice was soft and husky and he closed his eyes and stroked her hair.

"I've missed you too." He admitted.

"Why don't we celebrate finding each other again?" She brightened.

"Oh, I couldn't eat another bite." He said.

"I was talking about going to my place." As soon as the words were out of her mouth she was sorry. She didn't want him to see how she lived. There were men's clothing scattered across her bedroom floor and she wasn't sure who might be there.

"I have a better idea. Why don't we go to my place and talk" said John. He was in no mood for any more surprises. If the person who harmed her was there, he might end up in jail.

"Excellent idea!" she agreed. John was beginning to worry. Obviously, he still had deep feelings for her and bringing her to his home was not the smartest idea.

The ride to his house was quiet. Vontrice hoped she had not made a mistake getting together with John. Sure, he was the best guy she had ever been with, but things had changed drastically when he came to know the Lord. She loved and admired him but could not see herself living that kind of life.

"I don't suppose you have anything to drink, do you?" she ventured.

"I have soda, juice, sparkling water, milk… what'll ya have?" he smiled knowing she was waiting for another choice.

"Maybe you have some cider that's gone hard!" she laughed softly and he smiled at her as he poured two glasses of his best purified water.

"This is actually good." She smiled.

"The stuff that comes out of the spigot smells like rotten eggs and is sometimes a weird color." She wrinkled her nose.

"Yah, the water that comes out of my tap is much the same as yours. Sometimes they put in some chlorine to fool you, but it doesn't fool my stomach." They drank in silence for a few minutes each gathering their thoughts.

"Tell me how you are *really* doing, Tricey!"

"Just doing day to day. That's all a person can do." She sighed.

"I don't like seeing you hurt. No one should lay a hand on you!" He was getting more upset as each word became louder. She took his hand softly into hers and kissed it as tears spilled over onto his hand. He pulled her to him and she could hear his heart beating like a drum. Somehow the sound settled her nerves.

"Such fine, strong hands!" she whispered with her eyes closed.

"Vontrice, it hurts me to see you this way."

"I've been doing alright taking care of myself." They both knew it was a blatant lie.

"Yah, I can see that" he said sarcastically.

"There's never been anyone else, John Dunbar. Lord knows I've tried to replace you but I know I'm fooling myself." Her breath was on his face and he was starting to feel intoxicated with the nearness of her.

"There's never been anyone else for me either." She kissed him and pushed him gently back on the couch. As she continued to kiss him she began to undress. He reluctantly pushed away from her embrace.

"Can't do it Tricey!" he sighed.

"What? I don't appeal to you anymore?" there was more hurt than anger in her voice and immediately he pulled her close.

"It is taking every bit of will power I can conjure up to stop us."

"Then, why stop?" she said playfully.

"Because as much as I love you ... always have... always will... I love the Lord Jesus Christ and I know I will break His heart if I do this. I owe Him everything, Vontrice. I owe Him everything!" he closed his eyes and thought of the day he had been forgiven. No, he would never walk away from the Lord.

"So, we're back to religion again." She quickly buttoned her blouse and reached for her purse. It was time to get out before he started preaching.

"Please listen to me." She turned to give him a sharp rebuke, but as she looked into his soulful eyes, something within her melted.

"John, my sweet John, why can't you just accept things the way they are?"

"You have stitches in your face and a black eye, and you don't see any reason for change?" he was truly astonished.

"I can't be something I'm not, not even for you!" she cried.

"No you can't. Do you think I could have changed by myself?"

"Probably not, but there are lots of agencies out there now. You could have joined AA and went through their program."

"But that wouldn't have changed my heart. That was changed when I met the Lord. He changed my wants."

"Does that mean you don't want me?"

"Vontrice, I want you more than words can say. You're a wonderful woman and I want you to be *my* woman…"

"But?"

"God wants me to be equally joined together with a woman of faith."

"Then I guess I'm not the woman." She could feel her mouth quiver as she spoke the dreaded words.

"You could be." He kissed her cheek and stroked her hair. He could feel his resolve fading away.

"I don't think so. But thanks for lunch and the ride. I'll pay you back for the doctor bill when I get paid." She had no idea when she would ever have any money but she had to get away from him before it was too late. She had no intention of becoming a religious fanatic!

John begged her to stay or at least let him drive her home, but she was out the door before he had his keys. She slammed the door behind her and he stood staring after her in a daze.

"Lord I know I made the right decision, but it was a very hard one for me! It would have been so easy to just give in. She feels so right in my arms and yet I know I represent You with every move I make and I don't want to bring any dishonor to You. Please guard my Vontrice. Keep her safe until she is reached for you!" he prayed. He stood to his feet feeling hopeful. He was grateful he made the right decision.

Chapter 12 *View Two*

Ominous was running out of places to hide. Not only was Portentous searching for him but he had many others searching as well. It would only be a matter of time before he was found and then what would he do? He shuddered as he thought of his fate.

"How could I fail so miserably?" He chided himself. He had such great plans for those placed in his charge. True, he allowed Cheryl to slip through his bony fingers at the last moment, but he fully intended to bring John Dunbar to his knees. He blamed Vontrice; not that it would make any difference to Portentous. He orchestrated their meeting precisely, even allowing her former boyfriend to use her as a punching bag a week before. Normally, she would not go to the doctor as she had no money for one, but he knew if her face required stitches, her vanity would require her to go to the hospital for sure.

It took quite a bit of persuasion to get Mrs. Dunbar to make a doctor appointment. Ominous repeatedly told her she was deathly sick and would die if she didn't see a doctor. If that weren't enough, he told her that her children would not find her for days and her rotting body would attract rats that would consume her. She was deathly afraid of rats, as they ran rampant in her grandmother's house when she was a child.

Everything was coming together nicely. Vontrice and Mrs. Dunbar had back to back appointments with Dr. Chase and there was no doubt everyone was excited at the reunion. He salivated as he watched John and Vontrice interact. Surely, he would succumb to the pleasures of his former life once the opportunity was presented.

After lunch the next trap was set. Mrs. Dunbar was exhausted and ready for a nap. Vontrice made her move and soon they were back in familiar territory. She had spent many nights in John's apartment, though it was now clean and tidy with new furnishings. Ominous could see the desire in both of their eyes as they drew nearer to each other and was excited as Vontrice began to lure him into intimacy with her. He had no idea the man could have such restraint. There was a moment when he filled John's head with the pleasure that could be his if he would allow himself the indulgence. But it had ended in failure!!

Maybe if Vontrice ended up in the hospital he could get her to end it all. But he had little hope after his failure with Cheryl. Perhaps he could persuade John to hunt down Vontrice's attacker. Nah, he would probably just start preaching to him.

He had some good news to share but doubted it would save him from the awful fate awaiting him. He had been successful with the Rebecca, Glen, triangle. He encouraged Rebecca to pay Glen a visit but when she seemed reluctant, Ominous decided to work on her husband, Chuck. He wasn't the brightest man, which helped immensely in Ominous' manipulation. He whispered over and over how Glen was about to ruin his marriage and after he became thoroughly enraged, he finally found the information he wanted on line and headed to the kitchen to grab a beer. It was a hot day and he decided to stock the fridge with his favorite brew. Standing next to the sink, he downed two in a row and snapped open another one as his thinking became more fuzzy.

After the fifth beer, he knew he could conquer the world and would start by taking the smirk off Glen Booth's face. He tried to push the whole incident with his wife's painting out of his mind, but today it was strangling him. He smiled as he thought of snapping Glen Booth like a twig! It was a good thing Rebecca was out of the house today. He would deal with her later. She was making a fool out of him and he wouldn't stand for it another day.

By the time he gulped down the rest of his beer stash, his vision was so impaired, he could barely read the directions to Glen's house, but somehow he made it. Squealing into the driveway sending trash cans flying, he stomped on the brake and opened his car door. Unfortunately, he forgot to put the vehicle in park and had it not been for smashing into the side of the garage, there was no telling where the car would have lodged.

"I've come to pay you a visit Mr. Booth!" he slurred.

"We got ourselves some unfinished business and I aim to settle it right now!" With Anthony at his side, Glen rushed to the kitchen window to investigate the commotion.

"Can I help you?" Norma had just returned from getting the mail and barely recognized the brutish man pounding on the garage door. The inebriated man seemed vaguely familiar but she couldn't place him.

"I came to settle the score with your husband!" He could see Norma did not remember him so he continued.

"You got a painting from my wife that might as well be a self-portrait of your husband and my wife together and I for one have had enough!" he growled. Norma gasped as recognition formed in her brain. Of course, this was that dreadful woman's other half.

"I hope you aren't too fond of the joker you married, 'cuz I'm about to put him in the hospital and if he's the wimp I think he is I might be able to put him in the grave!" He laughed at his joke.

"You need to leave before I call the police!" Norma's voice quivered as she stood between the man and her home, and would not budge.

"I got no beef with you, lady, though I got to tell ya, after looking at you, I can see why your husband would go for a hot woman like my Rebecca." Norma blushed with anger and humiliation. What nerve! He certainly was nothing to look at either!

"If you don't leave at once, I am going to call 911!" she announced firmly. Chuck snatched the phone from her hand and threw it into the bushes.

"Get lost, you little mouse!" he snapped. He was tired of looking at the tiny waif of a woman and beat once more on the garage door.

"Last chance Booth! You coming out or am I coming in to get you?" Glen stood paralyzed as the door few open and in seconds Chuck grabbed him by the collar and threw him into the garage.

Instantly, he began pummeling him. Glen was no match for the brutish man who threw blow after blow until he fell to the floor unconscious. Anthony called 911 as his mother ran into the garage to help her husband.

She was like an annoying gnat to the hulk of a man beating her husband to a pulp. When Anthony tried to come to his father's rescue, Norma ordered him back inside to watch for the police. Anthony's fear was greater than his allegiance to his father and he remained inside watching for the police to arrive.

Convinced he had killed the man who lay motionless on the garage floor; Chuck staggered back to his car and jerked it into gear. The fender was dented and the headlight was broken on the driver's side, but the car was not disabled. Chuck peeled out of the driveway, running over the rose bushes and laying a strip of rubber across the sidewalk.

"Dad are you okay?" Anthony asked as he knelt beside his father.

"Huh...yah boy, I'm okay. Get me on my feet and back into the house before our nosey neighbors call the police." He said through bleeding lips.

"I've already called them" said Anthony.

"No, no, call them back. I don't want the police involved." But it was too late. A nearby cruiser pulled into the driveway before Glen could get to his feet and were beside him with their little spiral notebooks waiting for statements.

"It's okay, officer. It was just an accident. My family just panicked a little. We don't need the police here!" Glen said unconvincingly. It was quite obvious the man had been in a fight and was not the victor.

"Just sit down, sir. Everything is going to be all right. We have another unit in pursuit of the person who did this to you." Glen closed his swollen eyes and let out a painful breath.

"Did you recognize your assailant, Sir?" asked the policeman with pencil poised.

"It was just a disagreement. Nothing to get excited about." Glen could barely get the words out. Each painful breath convinced him he had broken ribs.

"We've run the plate. Belongs to a Charles Benson." The policeman reported.

"No need to pursue Chuck. We're friends and we'll get this hashed out without your involvement."

Ominous grinned as he thought of the outcome. It had a rare happy ending for him. Chuck was sure he had killed Glen and therefore resisted arrest. He was too inebriated to realize the folly of outrunning the police and therefore continued to run. He was not familiar with Glen's area and did not notice the warning signs. Not only was there road construction ahead, but the bridge was out as well. As Glen made a hair pin turn around the curve, he nearly ran down one of the construction workers. From that point, he completely lost control and careened over the bridge. In midair he vaguely wondered if it was the end... It was.

Portentous greeted him with many dark, hissing minions who could not wait to begin his tortuous eternity. Perhaps he had been too hard on Ominous. If he could keep bringing tortured souls to them, he would defer judgment.

Chapter 13 View One

"Norma, the last person I want to see is the Preacher! Call him back and tell him I'm not able to have company yet." Glen could not get comfortable in any position. There were few places in his body that did not ache. It hurt to talk, it hurt to move, it hurt to think! He had never been quite so miserable in his life. Yet, he insisted he would mend at home and would not go to the doctor in spite of his wife's pleading.

"Too late, Glen, I'm here and you are in no condition to throw me out." Martin said with a sheepish smile.

"Don't mean to be rude, Pastor, but I really am not up to talking." Glen said through painful breaths.

"I can see that. It's a good thing I brought Earl with me." Glen narrowed his puffy eyes to get a better glimpse of the stranger standing in the middle of his bedroom with Martin at his side. He recognized him as a member of the church, but had never actually met the man.

"I'm Dr. Adams, Glen. Pastor asked me to come with him, as your wife says you are refusing medical help." He said solemnly.

"Just need to rest up a few days. I'll be fine." Glen said in a hoarse whisper. He was already so fatigued he knew he would not be able to continue conversation. He hoped the man had at least brought some pain pills with him. That would be worth the visit.

Glen allowed Dr. Adams to listen to his heart and gently run his hand across his chest, arms and face. He winced at every touch and thought he would blackout when the doctor wanted to listen to his breathing placing the stethoscope on his back.

"How bad is he?" asked Norma wringing her hands.

"I can't be sure without x rays, but I am fairly certain he has a couple of broken ribs, a deviated septum and possibly a fractured eye socket." Norma wept softly and Martin patted her shoulder. The poor woman was on the verge of a breakdown but Glen wouldn't budge. He didn't want to tell them that he was terrified Chuck would return to finish the job. He fully expected him to pull a gun on him before he was through. It was best to heal up and stay away from him. He felt safe in his home, though he didn't know why since that is where Chuck found him.

"I'll heal up and as you said, without x rays you can't be sure of anything."

"I've treated enough broken bones to identify one with my hands." Dr. Adams assured him.

"We'll get a restraining order against that awful man and maybe I will feel safer." Norma cried.

"That won't be necessary." Martin interrupted.

"Yes, I know they aren't worth the paper they are written on so I've heard, but I will feel better just the same. We need police protection!" said Norma.

"It won't be necessary. The man that attacked you died in a car crash trying to outrun the police." Glen would have clapped if he could have stood the pain. Norma bowed her head and asked forgiveness for her feelings toward her husband's assailant.

"Mr. Booth, with the injuries you have incurred, I would advise a thorough assessment. You could have internal bleeding." He wasn't deliberately trying to scare Glen, but he needed to know the severity of his injuries. To everyone's surprise, Glen had a complete change of heart.

"Get me dressed, Norma. I think I will follow Dr. Adam's advice." Norma did not question her husband, but immediately began finding easy to wear clothing. Of course, he was not about to tell anyone how fearful he was to go to the hospital. Perhaps he had watched too many movies where victims were hunted down and killed in the hospital while the unsuspecting slept. Not that Chuck could pretend to be a doctor. That would be too unbelievable!

Martin had a word of prayer with the Booths and followed Dr. Adams outside. Both were pleased that Glen decided to get checked out and both were puzzled at his unexplainable change of heart. Martin was sorry to see the elation in Glen's face as he heard of Chuck's death. It was another indication of Glen's heart. When a person is entering eternity lost, it should bring heartache to the hearer.

Chapter 14 View One

John nervously paged through his notes. He knew what he wanted to say, but he had never excelled in public speaking, and English was not his best subject. When he was in a comfortable atmosphere, he spoke in short choppy sentences without much structure. It was hard to remember to use all the adverbs and adjectives necessary to form a good sentence.

He had to think about words that the congregation would relate to. He often used the expression "Are you jiving me? Or we're just chillin today." He realized many would not understand what he was talking about and the subject was too important for him to cause confusion.

John prayed earnestly that his words would be used mightily for the Lord. As he prayed, he began to feel uncomfortable. It was a relatively cool day, but he was perspiring and feeling a bit nauseated. Was he coming down with something? Should he call the Parkers and tell them he was not going to be able to share his testimony? The urge was so great to call it off that had he not been in tune with Lord, he would have missed it. His head snapped up as he remembered the last time he had such strong feelings.

John's brother, Lincoln, was a missionary in Bulgaria and John briefly visited him a few years ago. He was very inspired how his quiet brother, Linc could preach excitedly to these people who were very confused about the Gospel.

One night during his stay, a lady came to Linc's house to warn him about his missionary endeavors. It seemed that he was winning more and more of her converts to Christ, and Melba was outraged.

"You don't belong here, Mr. Missionary! These people are fine in my care and I don't want you talking to them anymore." She warned.

"Sorry, Melba, but I can't comply. The Lord has sent me here to speak on His behalf and that's exactly what I am going to do." He was kind but firm.

"I've come to warn you! If you decide not to heed my warning, it is on you!" she screeched. He smiled at her as she rattled her maracas and chanted something in her native tongue. John could feel his skin prickle and watched for Lincoln's reaction. After the door was closed John grabbed his brother's arm.

"That woman is scary, Linc!"

"She is at that." He laughed more at his brother's feared expression than her warning.

"Don't be afraid of her. She is to be pitied. I have tried to reach her, but I think she is too far gone."

"What does that mean?"

"I think she is so far into the occult, she can't find her way back." John shivered at the thought.

John and Linc had spent hours putting a plan together to reach many of the bush people who lived off the land and no concern to anyone. But the day after Melba's visit, both John and Linc became ill. Both were burning with fever and both were extremely nauseated and shivering.

"That woman put some kind of hex on us, Linc! Are we going to die?" Lincoln would have laughed if it didn't hurt so much. John was a very new believer and had never experienced such things.

Without a word, Linc slid onto the floor and began praying. It hurt to speak and he would much rather pray in his mind and heart, but his brother was in need of prayer as well and he wanted him to see the power of the Mighty God they served.

"Lord, you know my heart. I love these people, but Melba has them fearful to walk away from her and her lies. I have seen your power since I first came here, but John has yet to experience it. I'm asking you to be high and lifted up so all can see Your glory!

Melba thinks she is powerful, but she is less than a flea compared to Your might. If you see fit... I pray that you will completely heal John and I right before Melba and her followers eyes. I promise to shout the glory to my King and Saviour! Amen!" Lincoln slipped back onto the couch and both he and John fell into a fitful sleep.

The following day Melba came with her band of frightened people who did her bidding. She had heard that John and Lincoln were both very sick and she told the people the sickness would be unto death if the gospel continued to be shared.

John was amazed as he watched Melba circle the people and shake her maracas. He could see many of them tremble with fear. They considered her a goddess who could bring you favor or great harm.

"Let's go outside and meet our guests." Lincoln spoke through parched lips.

"You go, I'm too sick!" said John.

"It's okay, just trust me John."

"You said that to me when we were kids and I almost drowned in the river!" John laughed in spite of himself.

Slowly, both men stood to their feet and walked out onto the front porch in their bare feet. John noticed his brother searched the crowd with pity in his eyes. The love he had for these people was obvious.

"Are you ready to go home and take your meddling brother with you?" Melba snapped. John was unsure if the question was asked of him or Lincoln.

"I am not going anywhere. I have come with a purpose and I will stay as long as the Lord requires me to do so and that's a fact." He smiled at her glaring face.

"Then prepare to die!" she screamed, holding her arms in the air for emphasis, while the onlookers braced themselves believing John and Lincoln would disintegrate before their eyes.

"As in the days of Elijah, I pray for a miracle. John and I have asked that you make us well and strong before these people." Lincoln's voice was strong and powerful and his words were said with such force that even the leaves on the trees were gusting from his strong prayer.

"I am not only well, but strong with the Lord's power today." With that, Linc walked toward a sturdy black pine tree and with one hand, bent the top portion of the tree to touch the ground. The crowd, including John, gasped. This was definitely not a sick man!

John was so mesmerized by his brother that he didn't realize his joints stopped aching and his fever was gone. Often, when you focus completely on something it takes your mind away from the pain you might be experiencing. John stepped off the porch and stood beside his brother for support.

"I can't remember when I've felt better!" he shouted and pounded his chest for emphasis. Linc smiled in approval.

"I don't believe you! You are both going to die and nothing can stop it!" she laughed fiendishly.

"You're wrong, Melba! The Lord is on our side!"

"As you can see, we are both feeling strong and healthy." John interjected.

"There is more than one way to die!" She motioned for one of her converts and he stood before them with an old fashioned pea shooter commonly used as a weapon among the people.

"Do as I say!" Melba ordered the frightened man. He shook his head and slipped back into the crowd.

"Do as I say before something befalls *you*!" she warned.

"Do not threaten these people, Melba!" He began walking toward the man who was doing his best to disappear into the group.

"Jesus loves you! You do not have to live in fear! He sent me here to tell you about Him and His great love that is available to each of you." Lincoln placed his hand on the would be shooter's shoulder and the man began to cry.

John did not understand the language, but it was obvious the broken man was nodding at Lincoln and desperately wanted a new life. He was worn out by the hostile existence under Melba's frightful command.

"I'll set your house on fire! I'll poison your well! You better listen to me if you know what's good for you!" Melba cursed and stomped her feet.

"Lord, show these people your power! Give them a demonstration of the Almighty!" Lincoln shouted into the air. When nothing happened, Melba laughed and began to scoff and curse God shaking her gnarled fist into the air.

"If your house is on fire, there will be nothing this god or anyone else can do!" she screeched.

No sooner had the words escaped her mouth than a gigantic cloud burst came from nowhere pummeling them with torrents of rain and hail. John and Linc began singing praises to the Lord while the crowd huddled their soaked bodies together.

"That's *my* God, Melba! That's *my* God!" shouted Linc over the sound of the storm. John heard the people pleading with Melba, but could not understand what was said.

"Ha ha... they are begging Melba to make the storm stop! They told her to call on *her* god to make it go away!"

"What is her answer to their request?" John asked.

"She is telling them that a little rain won't hurt them." Ha laughed.

"Let us see whose God is greater!" Lincoln shouted as the storm picked up intensity. The hail was accompanied by great claps of thunder and lightning.

"You're a dead man, Mr. Missionary! Do you hear me... A DEAD MAN!" she screamed. She yelled something to the rest of the people and they began to run as if shot from a cannon.

When the crowd dispersed, there was one man still standing in their midst. It was the man who was supposed to kill Lincoln with his poisonous dart.

The man stood with his head bowed for a few seconds and then slowly walk toward Lincoln. He knelt at his feet and laid the poisonous dart and shooter on the ground. Though John did not understand his words, it was obvious he was asking for forgiveness.

Linc raised the man to his feet and embraced him as the man wept uncontrollably into his shoulder. It was difficult to console the man, though Linc continually patted his back and spoke softly.

In the end, Tokono gave his life and allegiance to the Lord Jesus and eventually began his own work sent out by Lincoln to others in the bush.

John shook his head in remembrance. What a miracle he had seen! God had intervened in a powerful way that changed many lives.

In the months to come, Lincoln wrote to tell John it was discovered Tokono was actually Melba's grandson. Though she had not left her false teaching, she was no longer a threat. She loved her grandson and could never find it in her heart to poison his well or burn his home. Linc was hopeful that through her grandson, Melba would embrace the truth.

John drank deeply of his coffee to take the chill from his bones. Yes, he remembered the last time he felt this way. There was no doubt in his mind; there was some kind of spiritual warfare going on. He didn't expect everyone to love his testimony, but he knew in his heart that someone did not want him to speak.

He began writing down more Scripture to go with his outline. He prayed that he could encourage those who were feeling desperate and confused. Images of Vontrice came to his mind and he wiped the tears from his eyes as he thought of her. How he wished he could say the right words to open her heart to the Lord. Even as he prayed the worry lines in his brow increased. What would it take? God knew and was working behind the scenes even as John prayed, Vontrice was leafing through the paper in search of employment.

"Face it girl!" said Vontrice to the image in her mirror.

"You should have stayed in school and developed some skills!" she turned her face from side to side and sighed. What was she going to do when she was no longer young and attractive? Those days were coming soon, especially if she continued to stay with abusive boyfriends.

She was about to throw the paper into the trash when something caught her eye. There was a small ad for a part time person to work in an art gallery. It was more than a cashier job. They were looking for someone with a trained eye for artwork. She had been a very good art student and her teachers complimented her constantly. She also displayed some of her art in a small local gallery and sold a few pieces.

She wiped the tears from her eyes as she thought of her wasted life. What had she done since high school? If she had applied herself, she could have gotten a scholarship, but she was more interested in parties and boys with promises to love her. Stupid, stupid, stupid!!

She applied fresh makeup to hide any signs of cruelty and tucked the newspaper under her arm. It wouldn't hurt to investigate. Hopefully, the employer was a man. She knew how to charm them. Maybe she could sweet talk her way into a job.

She wasn't familiar with the gallery, and knew little of the east side of town. She would have to take the bus as she had no money for cab fare. She rehearsed her qualifications that were mostly bogus but could not be easily checked out and smoothed her skirt. She should have taken the time to press it! Too late now!

She walked the few blocks to the address in the paper. She didn't want questions asked about her mode of transportation. Soon Vontrice stood in front of the small gallery and wished she had time to stop at the liquor store. She shook her head at the thought. Surely, she would be immediately dismissed as a job candidate if she showed up with whiskey on her breath. Besides, she had no money for such an indulgence.

She took another look through the window and saw a beautiful, red haired lady standing next to the cash register. Was she the owner or an employee? Again, she smoothed the stubborn wrinkles from her skirt and tentatively opened the door.

"Good morning, and welcome to Art Works. What can I show you today" Rebecca said brightly.

"H-hello" Vontrice stammered. Her tongue seemed to stick to the roof of her suddenly dry, parched mouth. In desperation, she placed the newspaper on the table. The job was circled in red.

"You would like to apply for the job?" asked Rebecca. Vontrice nodded in relief.

"You do realize you will have to speak to do this job." Rebecca laughed breaking the tension in the air.

"Of course. I'm sorry. I guess I am out of practice."

"You're out of practice talking? Oh my! That doesn't sound much like the person I'm looking for."

"No, no. I'm not out of practice talking. What I meant to say is that it's been a while since I looked for a job." The two smiled at each other and Vontrice began to relax.

"I'm Rebecca. I am looking for a confident woman who can help me buy and sell artwork. What makes you think you are the right candidate?" Vontrice knew she was challenging her, and took a deep breath.

Instead of giving her an answer, Vontrice began to look more closely at the artwork that was either hanging or displayed on tables.

"This is a beautiful sculpture, but if you want to catch the attention of all who come through your doors, you need to arrange it a little differently." Rebecca rubbed her chin and scrutinized the arrangement.

"I arranged that myself." Vontrice sighed. Of course, she would have to pick something that might offend the owner.

"The sculpture itself is exquisite. But it is not getting the attention it deserves. For instance, the sculpture has some beautiful gems embedded that seem hidden in this lighting. But, if you place a light above it, the gems will shine like diamonds." With that, Vontrice moved a floor lamp next to the table, and turned on the top light fixture. She maneuvered the lamp to spotlight the sculpture and immediately, the gems shined brilliantly.

"Excellent! You know, I have been disappointed that it has not attracted more attention. That is exactly what it needed." Feeling inspired, Vontrice took a few more steps and noticed several wall pictures displayed in no particular pattern.

Without asking Rebecca, she began rearranging them. She angled two of the small paintings to accent the two larger ones. Her adjustments were much more appealing to the eye and Rebecca smiled at her.

"Let's talk!" The ladies talked at length. Vontrice revealed very little about herself in comparison. Rebecca told her she was a recent widow and it was apparent she was not grief stricken.

Vontrice left smiling after they negotiated a starting salary. Her hours were flexible though there would be times she would need to meet with an art dealer to help choose pieces that would fit Rebecca's store. She was so excited and wanted to share her news with someone. She called John as soon as she returned home.

"That's fantastic news, girl! You are very talented and this is a golden opportunity for you to show what you can do!" John said earnestly.

"Well, it's a start. But I am planning to show my boss some of the paintings I've done. I hope she will like them." John smiled and thanked the Lord that this could be a new beginning for her.

"Do you have anything framed?"

"That costs money, John. No, I don't have frames for them." Suddenly, John thought of a proposition.

"Tell you what. If you'll come to church with me on Sunday to give me some moral support, I'll go with you to frame a few of your best pieces to show your boss."

"John, you know how I feel about going to church!" she said exasperated. He would not take no for an answer.

"Yes, I know, but I'm making it easy for you. You don't even have to stay for the sermon if you don't want to. I just want you there when I give my testimony. I could use a friend in the audience." He added.

"You just want me to be there for your testimony? I can leave after that?" she sighed.

"Just want you there for moral support. No matter how bad I mess up, I know there will be at least one person who has my back!" he laughed and she laughed with him.

"Okay, John. You win!" she said.

"That's my girl." The words came tumbling out of his mouth before he could stop them and there was silence at the other end of the phone.

"I'll see you Sunday." Vontrice hung up before he could detect her tearful goodbye. She would always be his girl and she would always love him. She just couldn't figure out how he could love her! They had little in common these days. He was excited about the Bible and church and none of that fit her schedule. She envied him. He was happy and productive. Not everyone was a drunk or drug user who needed to be converted. She tried to tell herself that she knew lots of people who were happy with their lives but that was at first glance.

She had been friends with a girl in high school that came from rich parents and had everything money could buy. Her parents were considered the 'jet-setters' of the day and when they got bored with the USA they traveled abroad. Her friend, Char seemed to be having the time of her life. Of course, she was only a teenager at the time.

One day when Vontrice stopped by to visit her friend, she found Char's mother, Dee Dee home alone. She was invited in for a quick snack in case Char returned from the mall early, which was highly unlikely!

Dee Dee quickly put a snack of brownies on the table and the two began to chat. Vontrice was in awe of Dee Dee and hoped one day to live in the same wonderful lifestyle.

"I would be so happy if I could do all the things that you and your family get to do. You've been practically everywhere and you have the best of the best." Said Vontrice.

"Yes, we've seen and done more than most people I know." Dee Dee said with no enthusiasm in her voice.

"You're living the dream!" Vontrice gushed.

"I suppose you're right." Dee Dee said with the same flat tone to her voice.

"You don't seem happy! I don't understand that. I would be elated! What am I missing?" Vontrice furrowed her brow and thought about Dee Dee and her family. Her husband was a stock broker and very devoted to his family. Char made good grades and would probably win a scholarship for her achievements. Her brothers were also good students who were also conscience of their health. All of them exercised and none of them had any use for alcohol, tobacco or drugs. They were a model family in many ways. Almost too perfect!! So what was the hesitancy?

"To tell you the truth, Vontrice, I don't know what is missing. You know when you're young, you think that if you have all the money you need, good health, vacations wherever you want and that sort of thing that you would finally feel like you've arrived. You would be truly happy!"

"And you're not?" Vontrice couldn't imagine.

"I'm disappointed. I have everything. Don't get me wrong, I'm grateful, but... well... it doesn't satisfy." She finally managed to say.

"I would be satisfied!" Vontrice quipped.

"You say that because you haven't experienced it. I *have* so I know what I'm talking about!" Vontrice thought she was wrong. It must be something else. Maybe her husband wasn't attentive enough or something!

A few years later, she ran into Dee Dee at the grocery store and she was not only happy but appeared exuberant! The two talked about old times and caught up with each other. Dee Dee did most of the talking. Vontrice had little to tell of a life that was on a downhill slope. Dee Dee's husband had been made a partner in his firm and they continued to travel. Her children were all married and she loved being a grandparent.

"Ah, so that's what made the difference! You have grand babies now and that has completed your life!" Vontrice was sure she found the answer.

"You're half right!" Dee Dee laughed.

"I absolutely love my grand babies. They sure put a smile on our faces. But that was not what made the difference in my life." She took Vontrice by the hand and looked straight into her eyes.

"I found the answer, Vontrice, and I can't wait to show you." With that she pulled a small Bible from her purse and began to show Vontrice Scripture. Dumbfounded and a little embarrassed, Vontrice leaned over the meat counter and wondered how she could end the conversation. Vontrice was barely listening as she worried people would see them huddled around a Bible in the middle of a grocery store! As Dee Dee turned to the next Scripture, Vontrice decided to make her escape.

"Oh my, look at the time!" said Vontrice.

"It was really nice running into you and maybe we can discuss religion some other time. I have to get going! Please give Char a hug for me." Vontrice quickly hugged her and made a bee line for the check out.

"Can I call you Vontrice? I really would like to finish our conversation." Dee Dee shouted behind her.

"Sure, I'll call you!" Vontrice shouted over her shoulder. Dee Dee sighed. She was so excited about her new relationship with the Lord that she was sometimes too enthusiastic. She should have learned from her lesson with Char. She practically hog tied the poor girl into listening. She wanted desperately for her family to understand what had taken place in her life. She smiled as she remembered those days. She didn't want to depend on God to get the job done. Her children had always been respectful and obedient and she tried to use that to coerce them into salvation. Thankfully, her wise Pastor helped her to see that she could not force them to believe. And mercifully, the changes in her life brought about the interest and then the conversion of her entire family.

Vontrice struggled with the concept that Dee Dee was in need of anything. There was no question she was as excited as John about her new found religion, though why she wasn't complete without it baffled her. She tried to imagine her life without alcohol. She couldn't. John told her God would change her 'wants' but she didn't believe him. Maybe when she was old and had no desire to party anymore. But John told her how dangerous it was to wait.

"Most people who think they'll come to the Lord in the eleventh hour die at 10:30!" She told him she would take her chances and the look on his face broke her heart. She hated to hurt him, but felt she had no choice. Maybe things were about to change in her life. If she did well in her new position, who knew how far she could go! She might open her own art gallery someday. Maybe God wasn't unhappy with her after all.

She began to hum as she walked toward home. She had no money for bus fare and wondered how long it would take her to walk home.

Hopefully, she could convince Rebecca she was a sports enthusiast and enjoyed walking and running. She certainly couldn't let her know she was broke. If the weather held out, she could walk to work for quite a few weeks before it would be too cold. Rain would be another problem. She would be a mess by the time she got to work if she walked in the rain. Even with the best umbrella, her hair would be wild and unruly by the time she arrived.

By the time she arrived back to her apartment, she was exhausted with aching back and burning feet. She was definitely out of shape! She slumped down on the thread bare couch and wondered if she could find an apartment closer to work. Unfortunately, that took money. She would probably get evicted anyway now that she threw her abusive boyfriend out.

The next problem was her wardrobe. Barefoot, she scuffled to the closet and began inspecting. She threw hanger after hanger on the floor in frustration. Shorts, tank tops, faded jeans, sweat shirts and several pairs of sneakers. Great! She found very little that could be worn to work, especially when images of Rebecca came to mind. During her interview, she noticed the impeccable business suit with matching heels. Of course, the necklace and ear rings complimented the suit perfectly. She quickly placed the questionnaire on her lap to hide her wrinkled skirt. She thumped her forehead and concentrated on a solution.

There had to be an answer to her problem. Her eyes scanned her bedroom and suddenly, an idea popped into her head. She pulled the bedroom curtain down and gave it a careful inspection. In all honesty, she had never liked the cream colored curtain with rust colored threading. But today she could see it as a skirt! Carefully, she walked through the apartment looking for other fabric that could be recycled into something more useful.

She laughed as she looked at the lacey kitchen curtain. She pulled it down and draped it around her neck. With little alteration, it would make the perfect shawl. The shear fabric was perfect.

Carefully, she pulled open each bedroom drawer searching for anything she might have missed. Her ex-boyfriend left a white dress shirt and a few shirts that could be altered to fit her.

She didn't know how Rebecca would feel about trendy, unconventional outfits, but she was about to find out. If she could make them stylish without appearing bizarre, she might be able to pass the first week. If she was careful with her paychecks, she could add a few more outfits slowly to her wardrobe. She sighed with relief. She was determined to make it happen! Now she just had to figure out what she was going to wear to church tomorrow.

Chapter 15 *View Two*

Portentous excitedly approached his newest prodigies. He hated them all, of course, though there was a certain amount of pleasure in their obvious admiration. He would enjoy torturing them if they did not understand or adhere to his training. With a prideful swagger he entered the room. He puffed his shaggy chest and exhaled a rancid breath.

"I have decided to give a bonus to whoever gives me the best answers today. If you are chosen, I will aid you to bring strong delusion to someone of significance." The minions applauded and a small fight broke out among the contenders. Portentous watched excitedly, hoping they would tear each other to shreds. They did not need to know he had not made the decision but was told what to do by a higher authority.

"We must condemn them at a faster pace!" he bellowed.

"I check the census hourly and they are coming at a rapid pace." Quipped one of the students. Portentous pummeled him repeatedly for his comment. This one definitely would not be a contender.

"That's the problem with many of you. You are satisfied! You forget that the Enemy loves them and continues to woo them no matter how close they are to finding their way to us!"

"And don't forget those who are willing to give their lives for the Enemy's cause! They carry the Enemy's love in their hearts and continue to pursue the lost ones no matter what it costs them. We have lost many at the last moment because one of you forgot your mission!"

"When we lose one at the last moment, we all pay the price!" Portentous had been brutally beaten for trusting Ominous. He was almost sent to the furthest part of the abyss along with others who had disappointed their hateful Master.

"Now for the test." Portentous strutted around the room importantly and cleared his throat.

"There have been several assigned to break down Martin Parker's family and ministry. More than one is assigned to the entire Parker family and of course, the extended church family. But things are moving too slowly."

"Why is there such urgency for this particular family and their church? What makes them different?" You might ask. Normally, Portentous would attack such a question, but instead he decided to elaborate for the dimwitted.

"There is great urgency for many reasons. You can't see into the future, but if you are smart, you can definitely see the necessary signs. This particular church appeals to every member to speak to as many as possible about the Enemy. They have been instructed to memorize the truth in that Blasted Book that will cause many to bow the knee to their new revelation. They have been taught to love the Enemy more and therefore are a threat to our cause!"

"Tell us how you would stop them!" Portentous noted the one speaking. He would definitely be assigned once properly programmed.

"Divide! Divide and Conquer! Find their weakness and push them toward the things that will render them useless! Don't forget that even those who appear to be faithful and stalwart in their faith are no match for you. Shake their faith to the core!!"

"Could you provide examples?" asked another student.

"You must watch them carefully. What do they derive pleasure from? How do they live when no one is examining them? Those that are undisciplined are the easiest to prey on. They are all easily distracted but that is not enough. You must break down their faith!" Portentous smiled as he thought of those he himself had broken.

"Find out what worries them. If it is health issues, then whisper constantly that their health could very well be in jeopardy. Make every pain count! They have short memories. Use it!! Tell them they most assuredly have a life threatening blood clot. When they have a simple cold, tell them their lungs are going to fill up with fluid and kill them. Worry them over their finances! Worry them over their families! Tell them they have been too soft or too hard on their children and it is their fault when they make the wrong choices."

"You are certainly the Master of this!" said another student. Portentous gave him a rare smile as he continued his discourse.

"Above all, make absolutely sure that whenever something unfavorable happens in their lives to tell them repeatedly that it is our Enemy's fault. He truly doesn't love them as He says He does or they would not have such pain and displeasure. I have taken down missionaries, preachers, evangelists and prayer warriors with those words! Sometimes it takes time to wear them down, but if you are consistent, it will pay off."

"Pay no attention to the words they say to other believers. Some are merely parroting words they have heard. Instead, watch them! Have they stopped reading the Blasted Book like they once did? Do you hear them getting in touch with the Enemy? Watch for every clue! Do they seem depressed? All can be used to crush them!"

"Is it possible to bring them to us?" someone whispered carefully not wanting to be identified.

"NO! It is not possible!! But it is possible to doom all the lives they have touched! Sometimes that is equally as rewarding."

The Minion Report:

Who is moving up in ran ks today? Speak up if you have done something noteworthy! If not... perhaps I will condemn you today!" Although, they were all condemned so it made little difference.

"Let me report" they shouted in unison pushing and shoving their way to the front. Each believing their report was far above the others.

"I am assigned to Jeremy Johnson and though he belongs to the Enemy, he has not walked with Him in a number of years. Somehow, when I was not paying close attention... he found his way back! Of course, I could not let that happen!" He heard the sounds of boos and hisses as he spoke, but knew he was about to turn things around. He was careful to mention Portentous in his speech.

"Portentous taught me the value of watching and waiting for the perfect time! I did exactly as he said." He gritted his jagged teeth, hating to give Portentous credit, yet fearing his wrath if he did not!

"Jeremy humbly made his way back to church and was received with open arms. Soon the pastor asked him to give his testimony to a group of struggling men. The men sat in rapt attention as he gave his testimony and some believed they too could conquer their problems by giving themselves to the Enemy." Portentous gave a rare smile as his name was spoken.

"I waited for just the right time and began to place obstacles in his path and then I watched to see what drew his attention. I tried many subtle devices. It is amazing what some find appealing. For Jeremy, it was not found in a woman's face, figure or style. It was her sense of humor! Can you imagine??? And then I knew I had him. She was not a believer, but in time, he no longer cared." He guffawed.

"I too have learned from Portentous" sputtered another minion hoping to gain some points.

"Distraction is a wonderful tool, but make no mistake... most of them are not nearly as trusting in the Enemy as they appear in church! They can very side tracked on the internet or reading posts by unbelievers. Soon, they begin to re-evaluate their own experience. I SCREAM at them that it is all a big joke! In the end, they will go back into the ground and that will be the end!" He laughed gleefully with other minions cheering him on. "I tell them to get all they can each day as if it is their last! For some, I just keep them out of the Blasted Book and into gaming, movies, television, friends... it doesn't really matter as long as they are preoccupied! I have had tremendous results!!!"

Another smug minion demanded to be heard a he fought his way to the front.

Karen Fertig

"Let me tell you a story that I have repeated over the ages" he drooled. "I watch some of the Enemy's best converts and even allow them to speak in the Enemy's name. Then I begin to infiltrate ... in time, they begin to concentrate on themselves. I let them know that they are desirable and they could have what they want if they will just show some booty...take a little walk on the wild side! I tell them to shake their *money maker* as many are willing to pay to see!! STUPID are these people!!! They are putty in my hands. While they are collecting their few coins, they're children are watching! Not only are they confused, but it totally devastates those that were once witnessed to. Everything falls apart like a cheap tent!" he laughed. Imagine when they stand before our Enemy!! They will have to watch as people trip over their disgusting, confusing life into HELL! BWAAAAHAAAHAAA

Chapter 15 View One

Martin rummaged through the bathroom cabinets in search of migraine medicine his doctor recommended a few months ago. Though he was not one to take medication of any kind whether over the counter or prescribed, he found that if he didn't catch the headache at the very beginning, he paid the consequences. After spending a day flat on his back, he decided to follow the doctor's orders. He had a busy day planned, as usual, and he couldn't afford to be down with a migraine. It seemed the days blended into each other with more than one person could possibly accomplish.

"Oh, Martin, you're not getting another one are you?" Christine watched her husband down a couple pills with a glass of water and immediately her heart went out to him. He worked tirelessly and she had to pray constantly that she didn't begin to resent those who took advantage of his kindness.

"I'll be fine. I think I caught it in time." He smiled hoping he was correct in his assumption.

"What can I do to help?" She massaged his back and neck and he closed his eyes and enjoyed the warmth of her touch.

"Can you meet with the trustees and show them the church budget, then go to Chad's baseball game? Oh, and don't forget to meet with Mrs. Palmer who just lost her husband a couple of months ago." Of course, he was joking, though she might be able to spend some time with Agnes Palmer. He loved the dear lady, but she had a way of holding on to you and keeping you for hours. She would put her arm through his on his arrival and the conversation would go on endlessly as he grunted an answer or two when he could get a word in. She was elderly, lonely, and had hundreds of stories to tell. She was also a strong prayer warrior and there were times Martin called her to ask for additional prayer when he was making a hard decision. She never asked for details and he was grateful there was not a lot of explaining necessary.

"I can meet Agnes if you would like." She sighed. She too knew meeting her would end any other plans for the day.

"That would really help."

"What time will you be home tonight?" she asked tentatively. There were so many issues to talk about and never enough time to discuss them. She handled as many situations as possible but there were some things that she knew Martin needed to take the lead on, but when he arrived home weary and spent, she refrained from adding anything else to his day.

"My plan is to be home in time to eat and attend Chad's baseball game." He searched his wife's face for unspoken problems, but she quickly smiled and kissed his cheek.

"Have a great day, Martin. I'll see you tonight." He waved as he pulled out of the driveway and she slumped down in her chair to finish her cold cup of coffee. Forget about working on the quilt she wanted to give as a Christmas present to her mother. That would have to wait for another day.

Martin did not have the opportunity to meet with Kate and Colten McDaniel as he had planned. It seemed there was crisis after crisis the last few weeks and his schedule was overflowing. It made him uneasy. Every time he spoke of calling Colten, his phone seemed to ring with yet another problem needing his immediate attention. Martin was determined to speak to them before John Dunbar gave his testimony. He wasn't sure why he felt so adamant until he began praying for John. Somewhere in the recess of his heart and mind, he knew the McDaniel's were in direct opposition of both the testimony and preaching that would be heard that day.

Christine was dealing with many of the same feelings as her husband. It only became worse once Lisa began taking an interest in the younger Colten McDaniel everyone referred to as 'Mac.' He was handsome, energetic, gregarious and courteous, yet she prayed constantly he would not be part of her impressionable daughters' life.

Yesterday, when he knocked on the door and asked if Lisa was home, Christine fought the urge to tell him she wasn't there. Of course, she wouldn't lie to him, but she certainly didn't want him spending time with her. Fortunately, Lisa had an appointment with her piano teacher and though she asked Christine to cancel it, she would not.

"I'm thinking of dropping the piano lessons anyway." Lisa said. She really loved playing, but her time with Mac overshadowed anything else these days.

"Oh, you don't want to do that! Those lovely hands were made to play beautiful music." Mac told her as he held a delicate hand to his lips. Lisa blushed with pleasure. Christine blushed with anger! Sensing her mother's displeasure, he immediately let go of her hand and followed Lisa into the living room.

"I would be happy to drive Lisa to her lesson for you, Mrs. Parker." Mac offered.

"How sweet of you to offer, but I am heading that way myself so it really won't be necessary. Besides, it really isn't out of my way and I plan to stop at the grocery store before heading back home." Her voice sounded excited and she knew she was speaking too quickly. It was apparent she didn't want him driving Lisa anywhere.

"We probably should be going soon." She added. Lisa frowned at her mother and wondered why she was so rude to this handsome young man who was the epitome of everything a girl could ever ask for.

"I just wanted to spend a few minutes with the prettiest girl in school." Christine rolled her eyes as she trailed behind them into the living room.

"Could I offer you a soda or something?" Lisa looked annoyed while Mac grinned at her. He was well aware that she didn't want them to be alone.

"Thank you for offering, but as I said, I am not planning to stay." Lisa and Mac plopped on the couch in close proximity.

"Is there something else you wanted, Mrs. Parker?" he thoroughly enjoyed her discomfort, and it was apparent, they were both anxious for her to leave the room. Reluctantly she did so as she shook her head muttered something indistinguishable.

"Sorry my mother is acting so weird! I don't know what's gotten into her!" Mac almost started laughing at her naivety. No doubt she would be putty in his hands… if he could ever get her alone. He loved a challenge and it would be part of the gratification to not only break this girl's heart as well as her purity, but he also felt a sense of power to know the preacher and his wife were no match for him.

"She's only trying to protect you." He smiled.

"From what… you?" Lisa laughed.

"Ah, she sees the wolf in me that you don't see. She knows if I ever got you alone, you would succumb to my irresistible charms." He winked at her and she could feel her heart thumping wildly in her chest.

"Oh, please… I'm not a twelve year old with my first crush! I would never 'succumb' to anything no matter how charming you are." She giggled nervously.

"I'll bet you haven't even had your first *real* kiss yet." She blushed and wanted to change the subject. He would truly think of her as a twelve year old if she answered honestly. He laughed sensing her uneasiness. Narrowing his eyes, he cocked his head to one side and spoke more seriously.

"To tell you the truth, Lisa, I'm kind of glad you haven't. I want to be the one to give you your first *real* kiss along with other pleasures we can enjoy together." His face was so close to hers, she could feel his warm breath as he intended to give her a passionate kiss right then and there!

"Lisa, we need to be going. Thanks for stopping by Colten. Perhaps you can visit another time." Christine walked into the living room and stopped dead in her tracks as she watched the skilled teenager advancing toward her daughter. Evidently, he intended to kiss her had she not entered the room.

"I'll walk you to the door." Lisa squeaked her voice tight and raspy. Mac grinned once again at Christine, as though they had a secret between them.

"It was nice to see you again, Mrs. Parker." He walked closely behind Lisa and when they were out of earshot he whispered.

"Maybe next time."

"Thanks for coming over. I'll see you tomorrow." Lisa smiled at him hoping her wobbly legs wouldn't give her away. She peaked through the binds to watch him strut with confidence down the driveway.

He couldn't wait to share his encounter with his buddies and would definitely spice it up a bit once he had every listening ear. There was no doubt he would win the wager. It was going to be almost too easy!

Before he reached his car, Chad and Anthony walked toward him fresh from their baseball practice. Neither Anthony nor Mac smiled at each other. Chad was the only one who seemed happy to see him.

"Hey Mac! Sorry I wasn't home when you got here. Did you forget I have practice after school?" he slapped him playfully on the arm.

"Uh, actually, I came to see Lisa." He said more to Anthony than Chad.

"Oh, I'm surprised she was home. She has a piano lesson today." It was obvious Chad was disappointed that it was Lisa he came to visit.

"I got to see her long enough to make plans." He lied.

"You're welcome to come in if you want." The tension between Mac and Anthony was obvious. Chad liked both of them and situations like this made him uncomfortable.

"Thanks, Chad. Maybe another time. I better get going." He waved as he jumped into his sports car and headed out of the driveway.

"Hey, Mac, could I have a word with you?" Anthony asked. Mac stopped and waited for Anthony to approach. Neither of them looked happy.

"What's on your mind?" Mac asked.

"Listen, Mac. I know guys like you. You aren't really interested in Lisa. You just like the chase! You like the adrenaline rush you get from trying to break them." Mac narrowed his eyes. He didn't like Anthony and he certainly didn't want him to get in the way.

"I know you like Lisa. Let's just say... let the best man win." Mac grinned.

"And then what? You'll just move on to your next conquest." Anthony snapped.

"That's none of your business. You're not her father and you definitely aren't her boyfriend. Like I said, Lisa is free to choose whoever she wants to spend time with."

"I don't want you seeing her." Anthony snarled.

"You listen to me. I will see who I want, when I want, whenever I want, and believe me you can't stop me! And if you are stupid enough to try, you will be the sorriest guy I know!"

"Are you threatening me?" Anthony was ready to pull him out of the car when all of a sudden he withdrew his hand and stood as still as a statue gazing into Mac's dark, menacing eyes. Somewhere deep in his mind he felt frozen and afraid.

"You mean nothing to me, Anthony; therefore, you are of no interest to me. However, you need to understand you are no match for me, and like my parents who never let anyone get in their way, I do not tolerate threats. I will plow right over you to get what I want, but make no mistake... I will have my way." Anthony could not find his voice and felt confused, weak and slightly nauseated. Mac smiled knowingly at his victim. He was one of many.

"Anything else, or do we understand each other?" Mac scowled. Anthony shook his head and Mac squealed out of the driveway. Chad rushed to his side, and though he was missing some of the details, he knew in his heart that he needed to speak to his parents about the unsettling encounter.

Unfortunately, Martin was not available, so Chad relayed the information to his mother which only increased her anxiety. There was no one she could speak to about it but her husband and the Lord and she was having difficulty getting in touch with either one about the matter.

Martin got home in time to wolf his supper down and race to Chad's baseball game. He hoped to relax together as a family but something was definitely amiss. Lisa sat with arms folded muttering monosyllables when asked a question. She seemed upset with her mother and Martin tried to ignore her sullen attitude for the moment. Chad seemed to be spending quite a bit of time boosting Anthony's obvious anxiety. He glanced at his wife several times but she only smiled and gripped his arm. Something was troubling his family and he needed to get to the bottom of it when they arrived home. He prayed for the necessary energy!

Oddly, Mac was not at the game and neither were his parents. Lisa asked Chad if he knew why Mac was missing which led into another ugly exchange.

"How should I know?" he spat angrily. At the moment they were losing the game due to Mac's absence. His coach yelled at the entire team as if it were there fault Mac was missing. Their coach hated losing more than anyone on the team and losing the game would only make it worse. If that weren't enough, Anthony's lack of concentration was alarming. Generally nothing got past him, but today he was lethargic, moving in slow motion, if he moved at all.

Lisa also watched Anthony's movements with concern. There was no doubt something had happened in her driveway between Mac and Anthony, and though she thought dating Mac would make her the envy of every girl in school, she would never date a bully. Besides she still had feelings for Anthony and this incident forced her to analyze them. He had come a long way since their camping trip and when she thought about their fight, it occurred to her that Mac was at the root. She could see but not hear the exchange between the two young men facing off in her driveway. She got chills when she recalled the look on Anthony's face in response to Mac's statements. She also noticed her brother's wild eyed look at Mac and his race to support Anthony who seemed on the verge to collapse.

Wild cheering brought Lisa from her reverie. Unfortunately, the cheering was from the opposing team who had won the game. Anthony was limping off the field with Chad close behind.

"Something is definitely wrong with Anthony. I'm going to talk to him." Martin jumped from the bleachers leaving Christine and Lisa to pick up their things.

"What's going on, Mom? Do you think Anthony is okay?" she asked quietly.

"I'm not sure what's going on, but I trust your father will be able to help him. Something is definitely wrong. Did you see him just stand there while the ball hit him?" Truthfully, Lisa was so engrossed in her thoughts; she didn't see anything happening on the field.

Martin caught up with Anthony and Chad quickly as Chad was blasting him for losing the game. The coach was pacing behind them waiting for his turn to give the entire team a good tongue lashing. Martin stepped in just in time.

"That's enough, Chad." His voice startled both boys, and Anthony had never been happier to see his pastor. He fought the urge to rush into his arms and sob his heart out.

"Pastor, I don't know what's wrong with me, nor do I have an explanation for what happened out there!" Anthony quaked.

"It's okay, Anthony. Let's sit down and talk about this." The coach folded his arms and glared at Martin. He had a speech prepared that included benching Anthony if he ever repeated today's performance.

"I would like a word with him before you take off" Coach Adams bellowed.

"This is not the time." Pastor did not wait for a response but led Anthony into a deserted hallway where they could talk uninterrupted.

"Is it okay if I listen to his explanation?" Chad asked as he approached. He knew he overreacted and felt badly for spouting off.

"Maybe you can help me explain, Chad. You were there when…" he looked away unable to finish.

"Why don't you begin and if Chad is aware of any missing

pieces, he can let us know." Pastor's voice felt warm and comforting and Anthony began to relax for the first time since his encounter with Mac.

Martin listened intently as Anthony described the ugly exchange that seemed surreal at this point in time. There were times he could not describe the details and fear crept into his voice as he remembered the ominous feeling of impending harm.

"Did Mac threaten you?" Martin asked.

"Yes...no... I think so."

"I'm sorry, I can't really tell you what he said, but I know he means to harm me."

"That doesn't make any sense, Anthony. Sure, he's a pretty big guy but you are too. Why would you fear him?" There was no mistaking the terror in Anthony's eyes as he described each detail he could remember. Anthony stared at the floor and shrugged his shoulders.

"What did he say to you?" In truth, Anthony couldn't remember the words. His fear seemed unreasonable and unjustified ...nevertheless, it was *very* real!

"He said I didn't know who I was dealing with and he said he got what he wanted and I would be sorry if I got in his way." Martin and Chad waited for more, but there was nothing else Anthony could add.

"You had to be there." He said softly almost in a whisper.

"I was there, Dad, and I can tell you I saw something happen that I can't explain either." Anthony brightened. Maybe he wasn't a crazy coward after all.

"I didn't hear what Mac said, but I can tell you I saw something in his face that made you shudder. I have never seen a look like that on anyone's face in my life." Chad shook his head and wrapped his arms around himself.

"You saw it too? I can't even describe it." Anthony added.

"Try!" said Martin. He needed more details to come to the correct conclusion.

"This is going to sound weird, but you know how when you're watching a scary movie and maybe the guy looks like a normal guy but he isn't? Well, I know it sounds inconceivable, but for a few seconds he didn't look like Mac anymore." Anthony nodded in agreement and Chad did his best to describe what he saw.

"It was like one minute he was Mac... the great looking guy that can charm the socks off anyone, and in the next few seconds, everything changed. His face was distorted and his eyes were... uh... different! I can't explain it, Dad! He was different."

"He was terrifying!" Anthony blurted out.

"It was like he wasn't Mac for a few seconds. His face was crimson with anger and his eyes were like daggers. Anthony's not kidding. He was pretty terrifying. It was just for those few seconds that everything seemed different. I ran up to the car as it sped away, but whatever happened was over and Anthony was standing there shaking. If I hadn't grabbed him I know he would have fallen to the ground."

"He said he was like his parents and none of them tolerated threats. No one gets in the way of the McDaniels!" Martin closed his eyes and sighed. He knew in his heart the boys weren't exaggerating.

"Anthony, I want you to spend some time in prayer about this situation. My family will also be praying. Mac or his parents are no real threat to you or any other believer. I have some important decisions to make as well. It's all going to be okay." Anthony breathed a sigh of relief. He trusted his pastor and after they had prayer together, he felt more like his old self again.

Christine and Lisa were waiting on the bleachers as Chad and Martin joined them silently. No one spoke of the incident on the field on the way home though no one seemed to be in a talking mood on the drive back. Martin tried to sneak a peek at his daughter and wondered if he banned her from seeing Mac, if she would rebel. There was no doubt the boy was very desirable to the entire youth group and he prayed for wisdom before he approached the subject. Oddly, Lisa was the one to come to him instead.

"Dad, can I talk to you for a minute?" she asked as soon as they entered the house.

"Of course, Lisa, what's on your mind?" He ushered her into his study where they could talk alone. Christine decided to make some coffee as they rushed out of the house too quickly to have dessert and she had made brownies. She needed to keep herself busy as she contemplated whether to approach Martin with her own concerns.

"Dad, something happened today that is bothering me a lot." She paced a few moments trying to find the right words.

"Mac came to see me and you know I am quite fond of him. He's funny and intelligent and..."

"Very good looking?" Martin added.

"Well, yes, he is *very* good looking but that's not enough for me. I mean I know I would be the envy of every girl in the school, but something happened today and, I don't think I want to see him anymore." Martin almost jumped for joy and did his best to remain silent as there was more she needed to say.

"What happened today that changed your mind?" he asked cautiously.

"He didn't know it, but I was watching him through the window and he and Anthony apparently had a fight. Not a fist fight, but a verbal one."

"I see." She continued to pace and finally flopped down on his lap as she did when she was a little girl.

"Oh Daddy, it was awful and kind of scary!" she cried into his shoulder. He hugged her trembling body close and stroked her hair.

"Tell me what you saw." She struggled with the details just as Chad and Anthony had, but in the end, the description was the same.

"There was something menacing about Mac and I know Anthony felt it too. Should I be afraid?"

"No sweetheart, you don't need to be afraid. But I am in agreement that you need to break ties with Mac. There is more to it than I can share with you right now, but I assure you, it is in your best interest to stay away from him."

"But he's in our youth group and is Chad's friend too. It's not like I won't be seeing him in church and at school."

"I want you to be kind to him but distant. If he asks you to go anywhere, tell him you need to call your parents first. Tell him that we are a very busy family and you have to check in with us before you make any plans." Lisa thought that would sound reasonable and began to relax a bit.

They walked out of the study together and Martin headed for the kitchen with the aroma of fresh coffee and brownies in the air. Lisa sped up the stairs and dashed quickly into her room shutting the door behind her. She didn't want to talk about the situation anymore and knew her brother would want to discuss it with her.

As Martin entered the kitchen the phone rang and Christine gasped with surprise. They had been trying to reach the McDaniels for quite some time and to her amazement, Colten was on the line for her husband. Placing her hand over the receiver, she mouthed 'it's Colten McDaniel' and handed Martin the phone.

Christine noticed her husband was not getting a word in edgewise and only grunted a few 'uh huh and I see' into the conversation. Within minutes he cradled the phone and shook his head.

"What in the world was that all about?" she asked.

"He called to let me know that although he and his family wanted to be there to hear John Dunbar's testimony and of course, my message, they would not be able to attend."

"He's never called before when they missed church. Why now?" Martin rubbed his chin and shook his head. These people were a mystery in many ways and he wished desperately he had answers. Unfortunately, they kept their distance most of the time. They were friendly and kind at church but he could never really get any of them alone.

"He said they had a crisis to attend to and he would explain later. He wondered if we could postpone John's testimony and I told him we couldn't do that. He said if we could wait until next month, he could have twice the people coming to hear him." They exchanged glances and finally Christine blurted her true feelings.

"I think he wants to postpone the testimony in hopes John doesn't get the chance to speak. I know how awful that sounds but I think he's lying about everything." Her harsh words startled Martin. His wife generally saw the best in everyone and was always there to pick someone up and give them a second chance when others wrote them off as a lost cause.

"What difference would it make if John's testimony were postponed?" they exchanged nervous glances and finally Christine said what they both were thinking.

"I think they can somehow prevent him from speaking. I know how crazy that sounds, but that's the way I feel." To her surprise, Martin nodded.

"Did you ask to meet with them? Maybe you can get to the bottom of all this. I hate feeling this way about anyone, but no matter how hard I pray, nothing changes."

"I don't want them to become members of our church." Said Christine.

"I don't believe they ever will."

"What makes you think they won't join? They say they are believers."

"Yes, they say they are, but I have asked Colten the name of the church they attended and he gives me very generic names of churches. Do you know how many churches are called 'Christian Church' and when I ask him his former Pastor's name; he can never come up with it. I have also asked Kate and the name she gave me is not listed on any of the churches I've tried."

"You know, I asked Mac one time about the church they attended and he also gave very vague answers." Christine remarked.

"Ever since I told Colten I wanted to meet with him and Kate to discuss some issues, he has been unreachable. I tried to ask him before we hung up but he beat me to it. He said he knew I wanted to meet with him and he was desperately trying to find something open on his calendar."

"I don't want Lisa going out with Mac. I'm not sure I want Chad hanging around him either, but I know for sure I don't want Lisa spending time with him.

"I think that has solved itself. Lisa has decided not to pursue a relationship with the charming young man." Christine closed her eyes and thanked the Lord for answered prayer.

For the remainder of the evening, Christine told Martin about her meeting with Agnes. She was the one who benefited the most from their meeting. Agnes seemed to have a sixth sense concerning sensitive issues the church faced and commented on things she couldn't possibly know without the Lord's intervention.

She mentioned praying fervently for John Dunbar and told Christine that she was very excited to hear his testimony as she had never felt such an overwhelming urge to pray for someone she had never met. Confident that he was going to say something life changing for his Lord, she knew the battle for souls weighed in the balance.

"It's a bit troubling that John's name keeps coming up. He told me a few days ago that he is prepared to speak and if I would like, he could also preach."

"What did you tell him?"

"You know, I feel that John has the message that needs to be heard and I am anxious to hear him speak. I love that bit of southern accent he has and there is something about John. He speaks so plainly there will be no one leaving confused."

Chapter 15 ᵞiew ᵀwo

"What do you have in place to foil tomorrow's big day at Parker's church?" Portentous snarled. He was in a particularly nasty mood as he had been given orders to stop John Dunbar from giving his testimony. It infuriated him as he had already given instructions to allow John to speak and ruin him afterwards. Although the orders came from the top, he despised following them. In his opinion, he was equally as important as anyone on this side of the world. Perhaps one day he would be the Leader and Omnipotent One!

"Ah, you will be very pleased with my report." Bombastic gloated. He was newly assigned to the Parker's and the others that Ominous had failed to reach. Though many were searching for Ominous, he seemed to be staying one step ahead of the ugly crowd. His luck would run out soon and his fate would be worse for hiding. In the meantime, he had to put up with the smirking Bombastic who seemed to think he would move up the chain of command. Due to his hateful persistence of another high profile ministry, he was able to get approval to climb the ladder of fleeting success and if he was successful in his present mission, Ominous would be reporting to him. The two glared at each other, the hate burning in their rheumy eyes.

"John Dunbar is far too ill to preach tomorrow." He strutted and puffed out his chest.

"Is he hospitalized?" Ominous snapped.

"No, he is sick in bed at home."

"Does he have some kind of plague? Perhaps something that will take his life?"

Bombastic knew better than to lie. Of course, he was not permitted to touch John's life in such a way and Portentous knew it.

"I am sure he will not be well enough to attend, however, I have also made provisions that if he does show up, his opposition will be too strong for him to make a difference."

"Details!! I am not a mind reader!" Portentous growled. He regretted his words as soon as they were spoken. He did not want to admit he did not know all things. His pride would not allow for such an admission. According to Portentous he knew everything and would one day be ruler of all. He spoke the words softly into the ears of the other minions as he could not afford to be overheard.

"Kate and Colten McDaniel along with young Mac, have decided to take their next step of allegiance. Therefore, they will do our bidding as they have been promised a great reward for their efforts." Portentous doubled over with heinous laughter and all within earshot also gave thunderous applause.

"If Mr. Dunbar is so foolish as to come to church, Kate and Colten will discredit him in such a way that no one will have anything to do with him or his testimony. And just to add a little topping to the cake, I have let Kate know that John visited his brother in Bulgaria and both he and his brother, Lincoln, became very sick. Kate will tell the church that he has contracted some deadly and very contagious disease such as Ebola. Believe me there is enough panic right now to start a riot. Once people take a good look at the black man shivering and sweating, they will order him out of the church."

"Maybe they will have him shot!" added a voice close by.

"There are many other things in the works that will proving me to be worth much more than anticipated. For instance, I am newly assigned to the Booth family. My predecessor started the groundwork but was too stupid to know how to put a plan into action. I however will finish the task he started." Portentous could barely contain himself as he watched the pompous idiot. Did he actually think he would take his place in the line up? He was far more powerful and would show it if need be.

"John Dunbar's old girlfriend, Vontrice is now working for Rebecca."

"How does that help our cause?"

"I will have the two of them conspiring to 'get their man' and perhaps make it a challenge. Rebecca should have no problems winning Glen Booth as he is already putty in her hands and after John Dunbar is humiliated and run out of the church, he will find comfort in Vontrice's arms and his old friend... alcohol!"

"And I have not forgotten Ominous' bumbling efforts to ruin Lisa Parker either. Oh, yes, there is nothing but disaster ahead of them all!" he shouted into the wind hoping his victory speech could be heard in every part of the abyss.

"Talk is cheap. Rewards only come from winning over your opponents. True, you have prepared a good plan, but until you come forth with results, it is just more pompous words and I am weary of listening... SO GET TO IT!!!!!!!!!!!!" He punched Bombastic as hard as he could and enjoyed watching him limp away.

"Let me give you all a warning! Be careful about your hopeful boasting. Until the job is done, there is nothing to be excited about. Many have slipped through our fingers because they failed to take into consideration those who work for the Enemy. Did you notice in all of Bombastic's bragging he never mentioned Agnes Palmer? Maybe he sees her as an old lady who could do no harm, but he is dead wrong!

"Agnes Palmer must be pushing eighty! She is frail and now that her husband is no longer there for her, she is quite lonely with no one to check in on her to make sure she is all right." The minions obviously had no understanding.

"She is one of the most dangerous women in the church." His comment was met with snickers which infuriated Portentous.

"SILENCE!! I will explain to you imbeciles before you make complete and total idiots of yourselves, which by the way, I will not tolerate while you are under my tutelage." Immediately, there was complete silence and Portentous pounded the air before him as if he had an invisible opponent.

"Agnes Palmer and Donna Rodgers are potential weapons against us. Ominous was incapable of sustaining damage to these enemies as like you, he did not see the big picture." He harrumphed.

"These two women spend a great deal of time in the Enemy's blasted Book and if that were not enough, they also speak daily to the Enemy and He speaks to them." The frightening looks were visible on each repugnant face. They were starting to get the picture.

"Only the bravest ones can bare to spend time with these two women, as at any given moment, evidence of answered prayer might be revealed. It is with great difficulty I have been able to spend time with this kind. Thankfully, there are not many to contend with, but even the weakest of them can return back to their first Love and can be used greatly by the Enemy thwarting our advances." He shuddered at the words remembering the time he boasted of defeating a prominent Sunday School Administrator who was living immorally. Believing his mission had been accomplished; he moved on only to find the man had confessed his sin and became strong in his love for the Enemy. Soon he was on the mission field winning hundreds to the faith. His error nearly sent him to the deepest abyss!

"Remember your weapons! They are forgetful of the Enemies daily mercy and love. They are selfish Beings and focus on themselves. Use it! Tell them they should have gotten that promotion! They should not have financial problems! Create havoc in the family. Discourage that young mother at home that she is wasting her life! Drugs and alcohol are great tools, but food can work as well. Let her gain another fifty pounds. and she will be looking for anyone to give her a compliment. Help him to compare what he has at home to that sharp office gal. Tell them over and over that the Enemy has allowed them to be sick. Use every problem they face and tell them that their powerful God could have stopped it if He wasn't so hateful!"

The minions were salivating with the thoughts of defeating their assignments. Each one was sure they were capable of utter destruction. Portentous would not admit, even to himself, that there were limitations. He too was afraid of the power these Beings possessed. It was a mystery that anything 'Holy' could take residence within these corrupt mortals, but he knew it was true. The Word, and even the Enemy Himself lived within them. Many did not grasp the concept and relied on their old corrupt nature to see them through the storms of life. Rarely did they find the ones that realized the gift bestowed to them. But the ones that knew... the ones that understood... they made Portentous shudder and flee.

Chapter 16 View One

John struggled into his well-worn suit wondering how he was going to speak in the next couple of hours. His head was throbbing and his stomach lurched with every step. There was no possibility of food this morning. The mere thought made him reach for the trash can. He sprawled across the bed holding an ice pack to his head and began praying.

Glancing at his watch, he knew it was decision time. If he didn't act soon, there would be no time for Martin to prepare a message for his congregation. As he gingerly curled his body into a ball, he reached for the phone. To his amazement, it began to ring.

"H'lo" John whispered into the mouth piece.

"John, its Linc! I called to pray with you before you speak today!" the happy voice of his brother Lincoln put a smile on his face despite the growing urge to empty his stomach of last night's dinner.

"Linc, I wish you were here Bro." Lincoln pressed the phone closer to his ear trying to hear the faint voice of his dear brother.

"I wish I could be there too. I would love to hear what the Lord is going to say through you today." John couldn't muster a response. He lay quietly with the phone in his hand.

Somehow, over the miles, Linc knew his brother was in trouble. No wonder the Lord woke him up in the middle of the night to pray for him. It was more than encouragement he needed. He was in desperate need of prayer.

"Hold the phone close to your ear and listen to me." John mutely obeyed and though Linc had no way of knowing if he was still on the line, he began to pray.

"Lord Jesus, my brother is in desperate need. I know for sure that is why you woke me up to call him. You have given him a specific task today and he is going to fail if you don't intervene. There are lots of folks that need to hear what you want my brother to say on Your behalf. I believe today could be the day that someone is looking at their last chance to make a decision for You! I know I can offer my dear brother nothing, but I also know You are the Master Physician. I beg you to touch John. I ask that you not only touch his body, but that you give him clear thoughts and strong, sound words... Your Words from Your Book for this special day. I thank you that you heard me and that You will have Your perfect Will! Amen.

When Linc began his prayer, John closed his eyes and allowed the prayerful words to sweep over his mind and body.

"Thank you, Lincoln, you're my favorite brother." John croaked.

"I'm your only brother" he laughed.

"That's what makes it easy" John said with a smile.

"Lay still for a spell, John. Just allow your mind to speak in Psalms and prayers to the Lord and wait on Him." John nodded and Linc felt like they were together. He had no way of knowing if anything had changed, but he had done all that God would have asked him to do and was satisfied that whatever the outcome, it was God's will.

"I'll call you later to hear how things went today. Maybe I'll catch me a little nap before I call you."

"I appreciate your prayers, big Bro." John closed his eyes and tried not to move. The nausea had subsided and he thought it was due to his remaining perfectly still.

"Don't know if I am going to be able to speak. Woke up very sick!" He grunted into the phone.

"Are you dressed and ready to go?"

"Yes."

"I'll call you back in an hour to check on you."

"I need to call the preacher and let him know what's going on." John murmured.

"What you going to tell him? You don't know yourself what's going on." Linc laughed. John didn't answer and in a few more minutes, Linc could hear the slight snoring and hung up. He continued to pray for his brother and was reminded of the time they were both violently ill as a result of the hateful Melba.

"Lord, Lord, what you going to do through my little brother today?" Linc laughed. He felt perfectly calm knowing His Sovereign God had it all under control.

John slept for almost an hour and when he awoke, it all seemed like a dream. Had he truly been so sick just a short time ago? He questioned whether he actually spoke to his brother or whether it was part of the dream.

He jumped out of bed and smoothed some of the wrinkles from his pants and shirt. He grabbed his Bible and his notebook containing his testimony and message and headed toward the door. He said a quick prayer that Vontrice would be there today. She had not promised him, but he was hopeful. It was hard for him to prepare his message without thinking of her. She would be surprised to know the tears he had shed over her.

There was no time for breakfast and it surprised him that it was even an option. Was it only a short time ago he thought he surely had contracted some horrible, life threatening plague?

He smoothed his hair back with his fingers and took one final look at himself in the mirror before heading to the church. He was out of time and no matter how he wished he could shower and put a better shine on his shoes, it was too late. Before he made it to the door, the phone rang. To his surprise, Lincoln's voice greeted him.

"You still home, John? You better hustle or you're going to make that pastor pretty nervous! He laughed good naturedly.

"Linc, It's good to hear your voice" said John excitedly.

"We'll catch up later, I just called to check in on you, but you're going to be just fine in that pulpit today!" John felt the Déjà vu experience.

216

By the time John reached the church he was not only feeling well, but he felt empowered! He had prayed and prepared and was confident it was the message God wanted him to speak. What he was not expecting was the overflowing parking lot. There were parking attendants doing their best to assist guests. People were parked in the grass and along the roadside. If people continued to come, they would be knocking the doors of their neighbors for additional parking spaces.

As soon as John walked through the doors Martin greeted him and ushered him into his office. It was apparent neither was expecting such a large crowd.

"I didn't expect the entire town to show up!" John said sheepishly.

"I admit I am pleasantly surprised. Many calls and fliers have been sent out to promote this day, but you never know what to expect. Sometimes people cancel at the last minute and there is really no way to tell what the attendance will be for any promotion."

"I am very excited to hear you speak to us today, John. I know you are the man of the hour!" He smiled warmly at John and both men prayed before entering the crowded auditorium.

The choir was spectacular and John had to hold back the tears when Martin sang "Were it Not for Grace." It was the perfect setting for him to begin his message and you could hear a pin drop as he stood erect behind the pulpit.

"Grace... that's what I found when I reached the end of myself. When I was sure I was no good to nobody...I found His Grace!" John swallowed hard and continued.

"You know why some of you haven't found it yet? You don't know you need it, or you still think there is something else out there." He shook his head as he peered over the crowd.

"You feel like a nothing and a nobody? Good! You're exactly what the Lord can use! Haven't done much right to begin with and can't relate to some of those perfect people in the Bible? Can I tell you that with few exceptions, you'll be able to see the blemishes on every one of those Bible characters! God changed their lives and used them and His Grace will do that for you!

"I love to read about Joseph, 'cuz he's one of my heroes. Joseph started off with this coat that showed he was the *preferred* one in his family. But you know he didn't get to wear it for long. Can you imagine his surprise when one minute he was wearing his favorite coat and the next time we see him he's standing in his underwear crying out to his brother to let him out of the well?" John laughed in spite of himself.

"Joseph's servant's robe was left in Potiphar's wife's hand. But Joseph remained righteous and in the end he wore a kingly robe when Pharaoh made him the second most important man in Egypt. And today, Joseph wears a robe of righteousness given to him through the Saviour. Ah, it is such a beautiful picture. Maybe not one your life resembles." Every eye was fastened on John as he continued revealing Biblical truths.

"Let's talk about Noah. You may not be able to relate to a man like him who did what God asked without any former visual of what he was making. He just obeyed. Most of us can't obey for a month... but Noah obeyed for the one hundred twenty years it took him to build this floating zoo! Maybe you can relate to the people standing on the outside of the ark? Maybe they was just minding their own business and came by to see what the crazy man was doing? You may have just come by the church to hear what crazy 'ole John Dunbar has to say. You may be on the outside of the ark looking in. Like Noah, I want to warn you." John stopped and silently asked the Lord to touch each listening ear.

"I talk to people all the time and do you know what lie they believe more than any other? They believe they still have time. Do you know the man lying in the hospital bed still thinks he has time? The man that took off for work today believes he'll be home in time for supper! Scoffers today say the same words as you read in the Bible. 'They have been predicting that Jesus is going to come back for as long as I can remember' they tell me. I have to tell them that we are one day closer than we were yesterday."

"Imagine the day that they were all assembled outside watching crazy Noah pounding away on that big 'ole ark. Some may be laughing. Some may be just curiously standing by. I don't believe everyone was making fun of him. There may be some that thought of doing what Noah said, but they wouldn't go against the crowd."

"Now imagine if you will that first drop of rain. Can you feel it touch your face like a little mist out of nowhere? Imagine the silence as that first drop turns into a shower. Now I want you to pay close attention!" John walked across the platform making eye contact with as many as possible. Eyes were riveted on the speaker.

"Can you see the young mother climbing a tree with a baby in her arms? She screams out to Noah to help her! She tells him she is willing to die, but PLEASE take in my baby! She climbs higher into the branches as the limbs tear at her clothing. Please open the door to the little ones… to the ones that were not scoffing but merely puzzled. We are not a bunch of criminals! We just didn't listen. We thought we were safe! We thought there would be time! We are listening now! Please, please, please … Noah… I beg you to open the door." John could hear someone weeping, as he continued.

"I believe Noah also wept for he did not shut the door, the Lord shut it." He finished.

"Today may be the day the door shuts on your life. No one will be able to open it after it has shut. No one can pay you out or pray you out. It will be over!"

"You may not be knocking on the door, but Jesus said 'Behold, I stand at the door and knock' This may be the last time He knocks on your heart's door."

"Isn't it about time for you to let go of that life you think is your own? Your best day here on earth pales in comparison to what awaits His children. Oh, but what awaits those who have not allowed Him to come in!" John wanted to gather the entire congregation in his arms and lead them all out of their captivity. If only he could help them to see that they were imprisoned.

As John began to pray, several people came forward and Martin greeted each of them warmly. They were taken to a quiet place to speak to those who could show them the way that leads to eternal life.

Suddenly, Kate McDaniel appeared out of nowhere and began to shouting at the top of her lungs.

"Everyone get out! The church is on fire! Follow me to safety." Several ushers looked to Martin for instructions as panic set in. Immediately, people reversed the direction from the front of the church to the exit doors.

"Listen to me. You are safe. Please stay in the auditorium while we check out the situation. I promise you are not in danger." Martin spoke with conviction and though he had no idea if there was a fire raging out of control, he knew deep in his heart that Kate was trying to stop the service. He was also given assurance that the people were safe.

It was obvious the people were torn. He noticed for the first time how many ladies looked to Kate for instruction. He didn't know about their experience with her. The gift they thought she possessed. They struggled within themselves to know who to follow. Fortunately, many of the husbands were in charge and most would not budge.

Martin quickly left the pulpit and instructed his pianist to continue playing. He nodded to John who once again stepped behind the pulpit and began speaking.

"Can you understand there is a fight going on for your soul? Can you feel the Enemy pulling your mind away from the Lord? This is not a coincidence. Who's going to win this one? Oh the devil doesn't want to lose you! He's causing a distraction and a diversion. That is one of his tactics. It must be that someone who is about to commit his life to God is nearer to death's door than I imagined." Several people who stood indecisive turned back to the sound of John's voice.

"That's right. You're heading the right direction now." John chuckled.

"Think of it this way… if the building were on fire, where are you going to end up? This would only be the beginning of the fire for your soul!"

Christine was in tears as she watched Devon Rodgers come forward weeping. She still struggled with her memory, but one thing was certain. She did not know the Saviour and she knew she needed

Him desperately. Christine led her to a quiet room where they could search the Scriptures together for the truth that she needed.

Devon told Christine how troubled she was over her memory loss and Christine assured her that it was more important to know where she was going than where she had been. It seemed to be the right answer.

As John continued to speak, Martin caught up with Kate McDaniel. He thanked the Lord for the time of prayer he had before John came to speak. Normally, he would have been so upset that he would have wanted to shout at the smug face standing before him, but instead he knew he was looking into the eyes of one who had somewhere along the lines given her allegiance to the dark side. Kate changed her demeanor as he approached and appeared fearful and distraught.

"Oh Pastor, we've got to get the people out of here. Colten has already called the fire department and it is not safe for those who remain inside. If you want to continue the service, please do it outside." She begged.

"Where is the fire? Take me there." He said calmly. She furrowed her brow and took a deep breath. This was not going according to plan.

"It is far too dangerous. We must escape at once!" She took him by the arm hoping to lead him away, but he gently pulled away from her grasp. For some reason, her touch nauseated him.

"We must get this building evacuated before anyone gets seriously hurt." She commanded. Please come with me and help me take the people to safety!" She reached for him again, but he pushed passed her and decided to find it himself. She seemed to be stalling and his patience was growing thin.

"It started in the teen classroom." She yelled over his shoulder as she raced back to the auditorium. Perhaps with Martin out of the sanctuary, she could finish what she started and stop the service. Just as she was about to enter the auditorium, one of the deacons stopped her. She gritted her teeth glaring squarely at the older gentleman. She never liked him and the pretense was wearing thin.

"You need to go outside and wait for the fire department."

"What??? Why me?" she fumed. How dare he block her way! She was not finished causing confusion.

"Because you called them." She glared at him for a moment and decided to push her way back in. But he was stronger and had no intention of letting her pass.

"You're not getting back in there. I don't know what you had in mind, but I can tell you it aint happening! I know the junk you told my wife, and I told her she was to stay away from you."

"You don't know who you're dealing with, mister!" she sniped. She had hoped to make inroads with the deacon's wife Char, and thought because they were both from the hills of Virginia they were dumb, unsophisticated people.

"I got me a pretty good idea and I can tell you this... you don't know who you are dealing with either. I know we don't come from no highfalutin station in life, but the Lord didn't mind that when he saved me. He has assured me that 'greater is he that is in me than he that is in the world' and you can't win against Him!

Kate took a deep breath and narrowed her eyes. She smoothed her beautiful dress and brushed a few strands of hair from her forehead. For once, she stood dumbfounded as she had nothing to say against the power of his words. She needed to find Colten and team up against them.

In the meantime, Martin found the smoldering remains of the fire and though it had not gotten out of control, the damage to the teen department was extensive. The chairs, tables and white boards were charred and smoking. The room was directly under the anterior part of the auditorium and if the ceiling gave way, no doubt the pulpit and a good portion of the pews would be greatly affected. For a fleeting moment, Martin wondered if the people should evacuate.

"I think everything is in control, Pastor." Martin turned to face Mike Ryan who held a fire extinguisher in his hand.

"How bad was it?" Martin dared to ask.

"Could have been worse but fortunately I got to it before it got out of control."

"Do you have any idea how the fire got started?"

"Yep, but no one will believe me." Mike sighed. It seemed like the entire congregation loved the McDaniel family and if he reported anything negative, he was bound to be seen as jealous. Everyone knew he and Colten had both interviewed for the same job and Mike had not hidden his feelings about the entire McDaniel clan.

"Try me."

"I can't really prove anything, but I saw the young McDaniel boy coming out of this room laughing with his parents about some inside joke." That certainly didn't prove they set fire to the room, but maybe there were more incriminating details.

"I smelled smoke the minute they headed up the stairs and though I wanted to follow them to see what they were up to, I decided to take a look at the room first. Glad I did too because the waste can was on fire and it had already spread onto the carpet. By the time I ran back with the fire extinguisher, it had done more damage than I expected."

"Do you think Mac set the fire?"

"I do." Martin nodded.

"I'm thankful you were here!" Martin said earnestly.

"If I were wearing my jacket, I would have tried to put it out with that, but I didn't really have anything to beat it out with. Besides, I wasn't thinking straight when I saw those flames." Mike admitted.

"Did you hear any of the conversation as the McDaniels left the room?"

"Nothing that really made much sense."

"Tell me what you heard."

"Kate and Colten were holding hands and thanking someone for allowing them to be used to further their cause." Martin was speechless.

"It was weird as it didn't seem they were actually talking to each other, but just talking into the air to nobody!" he finished. Martin could feel the hairs standing up on the back of his neck. He knew in his heart who they were talking to.

Sirens could be heard in the distance as the local fire department responded to the 911 call. The frantic dispatcher prayed silently that the fire had not caused much damage as Pastor Martin was his own dear preacher and he couldn't bear to think of the church in a blazing inferno nor the lives of those he knew so well to be in jeopardy.

The woman placing the emergency call seemed frantic and painted a picture of utter destruction. According to the trembling voice, the church was a fire ball and there would surely be many casualties if they delayed. According to the caller, they were going to need all units to respond.

Of course, the plan was to create as much chaos as possible. One fire truck could be easily sent on its way once the situation was understood, but if several showed up there would be no way to draw attention away from the confusion.

Mike and Martin hurried outside to meet with the firemen careening into the church parking lot with siren's blaring. Mike called the fire department to let them know the fire was out and they need not dispatch any other emergency vehicles to the church.

"Thank you for responding so quickly. I'm sorry, for your sake, that this has been a wasted trip."

"No problem! It is always good to see things in control. I have to say the dispatcher was a little shaken when he sent us out. We were expecting quite a blaze." Martin silently thanked the Lord that this was not an emergency and all were safe.

"Do you mind if I take a look around to be sure?"

"I can take you to the room where it started." Mike said as the fireman followed behind him.

"I called the station and there will be no others coming out. Our dispatcher has also cancelled the ambulance that was scheduled to come. Someone certainly panicked." He smiled. Martin smiled through gritted teeth as he realized he must deal with the truth of the situation.

"You go on ahead, Mike. I need to make an announcement to my congregation." Martin prayed things were under control inside and no one left the auditorium.

He hurried into the sanctuary and was greeted by Christine who threw her arms around his neck impulsively, which was totally out of character for his proper wife.

"Martin, I have never seen so many people come to Christ at one time! We are running out of personal workers!" she laughed.

"That's wonderful news!' He said as the excitement gripped his heart.

"John just continued to move the people with his testimony and the Scriptures. He is a remarkable man."

"Where are the McDaniels?" he asked suddenly wondering what other chaos could be brewing.

"I don't know. Someone said they had some kind of emergency and they left."

"Hmmm, they said they had some kind of 'crisis' and would not be able to be here today. Instead, they came and did their best to stop the service."

"What are you going to do about them?" asked Christine.

"I am going to ask them to leave the church. I will not tolerate another minute of this!" Martin exclaimed.

"How will you explain *that* to the people?" Like any church, people left for a variety of reasons. Some were offended by Biblical preaching, while others were looking for socialization and did not want to be bothered by any do's and don'ts that were taught. Martin may mention a family's departure to the staff, but rarely from the pulpit. This situation, however, was going to be very different. Kate and Colten made a point of inviting most members of the congregation to their beautiful home for dinner, lunch or an after church get together and it was obvious, most enjoyed their attention. They would probably not leave without causing problems; perhaps even a church split!

"Maybe it would be best if we could get them to leave of their own accord." Said Christine thoughtfully.

"Not sure I see that happening!" Martin needed to approach Kate about the fire and though he would not be able to prove Mac set it, he could at least address her alarming 911 call.

"I think there is a way." Christine smiled.

"What did you have in mind?" There was no doubt God put this wonderful woman in his life for many reasons. There was no one on earth he trusted more. She was the only one who could set him straight when needed, and her encouragement and support was vital to his ministry.

"Okay, we're not actually saying the words, as it is too eerie to think about. But if we are right and I believe we are... how would you go about discouraging them from being a part of our church?" Martin rubbed his chin and furrowed his brows.

"I think we should have them over and invite Agnes Palmer." She smiled as his face brightened. Understanding began to permeate his mind.

"Of course! A real time of concerted prayer could be invaluable! Prayer is always a tremendous weapon, but the stakes are higher on this one."

"We should invite Steve Winters and the deacons and their wives as well."

"As much as I hate the idea, I'm going to have a meeting before the meeting." Martin decided to tell those that would be invited for prayer why it was imperative to pray fervently for the outcome of their time together. If they were successful, he would not have to ask the McDaniels to leave. They could not stand to stay!

John interrupted their conversation as he excitedly raced to see Martin. Martin reached out his hand, but John had him in a bear hug and practically lifted him off the ground.

"Sorry you were not here to witness what the Lord did today! It was truly miraculous! Although, if you hadn't taken care of the opposition, it probably wouldn't have happened at all!" He handed him several names that would need additional follow up and wiped the remaining tears from his eyes. He had sincerely prayed for the people who would be within earshot, but the Lord exceeded his expectations.

"What exciting new! I will certainly listen to the recorded message!" Some of the names were familiar, but most of them had been invited guests.

The service had been over for nearly an hour, yet people remained in the auditorium smiling through tears for all that had taken place. Some had seen their loved ones come to the Lord after years of waiting and no one was in a hurry to leave.

"Can I be frank with you Pastor and tell you that the last time I witnessed this kind of thing, I was on the mission field with my brother Lincoln. He called me this morning and prayed with me. I think he knew I needed him. And here I was all but willing to give it all up just 'cuz I woke up sick!" He didn't tell him he could barely move and that it felt like an elephant was sitting on his chest.

"I'm so thankful that didn't happen!" Martin said sincerely. He would have loved to see the people move like this after one of his messages, but in end... it wasn't really John's words that moved the people. It was the power of the Great God they served.

"I believe I was sick for the same reason, preacher." John confessed.

"We were dealing with a very unpleasant situation. Not everyone was happy with our message and one of the prominent leaders did her best to stop us. I didn't know how far she would go to make her point, but I worried that she would poison both of us!" He shook his head in remembrance of that fateful day.

"I learned something that day about my brother, too. I was a green horn compared to him as he had already weathered a few storms before I arrived on the scene. His faith had been tried and proven and I'll tell ya, there aint nothing like it! When you see the opposition fall when you're standing alone, there is no other explanation than God arrived! Ha-ha!" Martin thoroughly enjoyed listening to John and it bolstered his own resolve as he thought what faced him in the days ahead.

"What are you planning to do about the opposition you are facing?" he ventured to ask. Martin filled him in quickly and John asked if he could be part of the prayer meeting.

"My brother would be glad to join us if you would like him to." John offered.

"I think that would be a wonderful idea. As a matter of fact, I am going to call some of our missionaries to join with us!" Martin was growing more excited as he thought of some of the missionaries he knew who had seen God do some miraculous things first hand.

"Isn't it just like God to show His power against whatever comes our way?" The three rejoiced together... but not everyone was happy!

View Two

Portentous was in a particularly foul mood as legions of his sinister contemporaries vied for position. If he were to keep his slippery place of importance, he would have to find fault with each of their boastful conquests. He listened carefully for every detail of their victories. He would not allow any to compete with him nor move up in rank. There was too much at stake. After much wailing and flogging, one of them made his way to the front of the group to gloat.

"I have no failings to share, but I do have a generous portion of victories!" Bombastic smirked with delight.

"I'll be the judge of that. Of course, I must always take in consideration that you are lying!! But of course we are ALL liars from our own evil Father!" Portentous laughed before soberly continuing.

"Just give us the highlights! If I need more information, I will stop you." He snarled.

"But of course! I have been entrusted to several humans referred to as 'affluent' but deep within, they are all the same. Sometimes, I grow bored with them as they give me little challenge." He yawned.

"Enough of your boasting! Let's hear the details!" someone screamed from the back ranks. Obviously, somebody who wanted his turn to share.

Bombastic ushered them closer to the dark abyss. The sound was horrifying and gleeful smiles could be seen by all.

"I hope you remember the rich man spoken of in the Blasted Book! I alone defeated him!" Bombastic puffed his shaggy chest and strutted as he spoke.

"Ancient history!" Portentous snarled.

"I am merely setting the stage! He is one of millions I have personally doomed!!! Do you remember his first words as he got a taste of eternity? He wanted Lazarus to come and cool his tongue from the tormenting fire! How strange these humans are! He thought he could order Lazarus around as he did on earth."

"Yes, they are a pretty dull witted lot, aren't they!" Portentous agreed.

"Some of them think they are Atheists! But that is something they made up themselves. There is no such thing!"

"But many do not believe in God. Doesn't that make them Atheists?" asked one of Portentous' new students.

"NO! They have been created in such a way that they MUST worship... however, due to their free will, it is up to them *who* or *what* they will worship. But make no mistake, they are all worshipping something. It often takes a very small nudge to get them off course and most worship themselves in one way or another.

"As I was saying, the rich man was one of my first victories and after these thousands of years, I have perfected my craft! I do not make the mistake of walking away too soon. I admit, it is uncomfortable sometimes, but I have learned persistence pays off!!"

"Is there a point to this insidious charade?" Portentous glowered. He was gaining far too much attention and Portentous decided to tell one of his own victories. Bombastic glared hatefully as Portentous began speaking with all eyes on him.

"The rich man is child's play! I on the other hand doomed a man that was once very close to making a decision for the Enemy!" He cleared his throat and puffed out his shaggy chest. He never tired of telling the story and it always brought the same thunderous applause.

"I am speaking of a notable king who had all the power, prestige and wealth any king could obtain. But, after acquiring everything his world had to offer, he found himself unsatisfied. He could not put his finger on the problem, so Paul did it for him. Our attempts to kill this man were foiled each time! Those who call themselves Christians should have hated him! Ah, alas, he once worked for our side, though he was not aware of it at the time!" He sighed.

"I wanted to set him on fire! I wanted to slit his throat and watch the blood run into the streets! But he was untouchable! We all did our best to discourage him. There were a number of times he was beaten, shipwrecked, stoned, left for dead, and robbed! Every evil I could think of was thrown at him, yet he would not submit! Imagine a mere mortal that would not succumb! Fortunately, these are few and far between and almost unheard of in today's world! Yet, he stood tall and straight before King Agrippa and without hesitation, stuck a bony finger in his face and told him his fate!"

"Listen as I repeat the most delightful words you will ever hear... 'ALMOST THOU HAST PERSUADED ME!' The room once again exploded with applause.

"Yes! I have doomed several members of one of the largest churches in the world! It took time, but it was well worth it." He bellowed.

"Who knew that this small time preacher would grow a thriving ministry that could be heard in several languages and countries? In time, he was not only on the airways, but had his own televised broadcast. It seemed everyone was tuning in to hear him. It made me cringe! It made me angry! It made me SICK! I vowed I would do something about it and I did!" He laughed triumphantly.

"They become powerless when their ego gets in the way! I appealed to his flesh and in time he began to believe me. He thought he actually had the power himself to change people and the world around him. I told him he should be keeping a large percentage of the donations made to his broadcast as there would not be a broadcast without his talents and abilities!" The room exploded with laughter and Portentous allowed him to have his moment of glory.

"And then you exposed him?" someone asked.

"No... it was too soon. You must have patience if you want the BIG victories!" Bombastic sneered.

"He began to have followers that practically worshipped him. At first he seemed a bit embarrassed, but in time, he began to believe his own propaganda!

There were people lined up just to have him touch them!" Bombastic had to wait until the laughter died down before he could continue. It was obvious; everyone was excited to hear the report.

"In time, his wife found him intolerable. She knew him too well to treat him like a god no matter what people believed about him... not that he cared! He could have his pick of any number of mesmerized females. It was a wonderful day when she left him"

"And then you exposed him?"

"Patience! You must have patience!"

"Tell us how you took him down!" cried the crowd.

"Tell us... tell us... TELL US!!..." The crowd screamed in unison.

"I found the perfect way to humiliate him and give the Enemy a major 'black eye' as they say!" he giggled.

"I was teaming up with Ominous at the time and he had surveillance on this poor widow woman. Now Ominous, as you know, was not the keen expert that I am in discouragement, and humiliation. He thought she was barely worth his time and trouble. But this woman inherited a great deal of money and as you can imagine, her popularity increased on a daily basis! All of a sudden, everyone wanted to know her and help her."

"You mean they all wanted to help themselves!" laughed Portentous.

"Exactly! The poor little woman had nothing but her little television set and no one offered to take her to church. It was easy for her to get sucked into the broadcast! Her views became his views and she all but forgot what she had been taught as a child. After all, church people let her down and even the preacher could not find time in his busy schedule to visit with her."

"Gotta love 'business'" Portentous howled!

"Yup! So Ominous nudged her to give her gigantic fortune to the broadcast ministry! I made sure the media covered it and it was sensationalized to the max! Everyone seemed to know about the widow woman and her generosity to the ministry!"

"And then???" Excitement filled the air as they anticipated the final blow. Portentous had to hand it to Bombastic. He certainly knew how to paint a picture!

"Yes, then I took him down!" The cheers were deafening and Bombastic took a bow.

"The preacher's name and face were on every tabloid as I discredited him. Picture after picture displayed the misuse of money. Cruises and other expensive trips were presented on every magazine rack. The media ran rampant with the story. Bombastic could not be more pleased! They depicted the little widow living in a hovel with nothing in the cupboards and an empty fridge. The only furnishings were a thread bare chair and a cot to sleep on. Of course, with technology, the media superimposed a home found in a ghetto to replace her humble but livable little house. The widow was also transformed into a weak, helpless woman confined to a wheel chair. The article waged war on "Men playing God" who robbed the widows of their money. As an added bonus, the preacher's mansion with servants and heated puppy pool was also on the cover. And it would not be complete without showing the preacher with scantily dressed woman. The embarrassing picture showed the preacher splashing several nearly naked and very young ladies while his Bible lay opened, wet and obviously discarded nearby.

"I did not stop there! I continued to provoke the public to speak out against such conduct and though they are also disgusting creatures, they begged for his head... and got it! The man is in jail today and the majestic kingdom he built for himself is in ruins!"

"I hope he enjoyed his day in the sun!" They all howled together in delight!

"And that is how you get the job done!!!!!!!!!!!" Bombastic shouted as he took a prideful bow.

Chapter 17 View One

It took Martin nearly two weeks to invite all those he deemed necessary for the 'fervent prayer' time he knew was necessary to drive the darkness from his church. Christine made several phone calls before she realized that if word spread throughout the church it could cause more problems. Those who were not asked to come may feel that the Parker's thought they were not worthy to come to a prayer meeting! People could be very easily offended and it was a constant battle in ministry to make sure everyone felt equally loved and worthwhile. Martin understood her concern but knew it was essential to go forward.

"Those we are inviting are the kind of people who will not be broadcasting it to the rest of the congregation. They are humble people that want to join in prayer" said Martin.

"I don't believe they would deliberately tell someone, but word gets out fast. They can't exactly lie if asked why they were at the pastor's house on Tuesday night!" He nodded in agreement.

"If Kate and Colten get wind of it, you know they will surely use it to cause more division!" Again he had to agree.

"I suppose the best thing to do is to tell those we are inviting that we will explain everything when they come over and that it would be best to keep the meeting under wraps." He hated the secrecy but also understood the concern.

The problem was solved by Steve Winters who seemed to have the same concerns. Mike Ryan wasted no time announcing his finding to Steve and who he believed staged the fire in the teen room, Steve had given more concerted prayer to the situation. Mike never asked Martin if he confronted Kate but he knew the circumstances better than almost anyone and chided himself for the fear that crept up his back each time he knelt in prayer. There was something sinister about that family in his opinion and though he would like to find out more about it, he was also fearful.

Steve thought it would be best to have the prayer meeting at his house, and after Christine voiced her concerns to her husband, it seemed to be the perfect solution. No one would expect Kate and Colten to be invited there and most of the people involved held positions in the church. All in all, it did not appear suspicious or "excluding" in view of those who were asked to attend.

When the day finally arrived, Christine received several calls early in the day. Each person reported the same symptoms and each one felt they were in no condition to attend the meeting. Martin considered postponing the prayer meeting, until John Dunbar called.

"Pastor, have you heard from anyone scheduled for the meeting tonight that has come down sick?" John always got right to the point.

"Why yes, we have had several calls!"

"You call each one of them back and tell them to show up anyway, even if they have to drag themselves out of bed and come in their pajamas!"

"What's going on, John?" Martin asked.

"I know exactly what's going on. I guess after the third time, I should be an expert on the subject!" John quipped.

"I'm not following you."

"I feel just like I did when I was on the mission field with my brother Lincoln. I almost forgot about it until the symptoms came on me again when I was asked to preach at your church. Then when I woke up this morning, I recognized what was happening to me! I know the others won't understand it, but you must tell them they are not sick…at least not the way they think of sickness!"

"But what if they are?"

"Then I will personally check them out and send them home! Remember I am an EMT Pastor."

"How can you be so sure?"

"Because I have the same symptoms!" John's head was pounding and he felt the urge to vomit every time he spoke, but he remembered only too well the last time he felt that way.

"Just get them all gathered together and I'll call Lincoln. He'll know what to do." John felt too weak to continue, but willed himself into his shoes and jacket and painfully, left his house. He knew he was right and vaguely wondered why Martin and Christine were not afflicted.

By the time he entered Steve Winters' home, he was not only exhausted, but shaking with pain. Maybe this was not such a good idea after all. He glanced around the room and knew most of the people before him were in similar shape.

"I've got Lincoln on the line, John. Just take a seat anywhere and I'll put him on speaker so everyone can hear." John lowered himself to the floor as he could not imagine taking another step without losing consciousness.

"H'lo everyone! This is Lincoln Dunbar here in Bulgaria! Now, I know this is a very important meeting and you are all very necessary pieces for success. I hope it is obvious to you, as it is to me, that your sickness is not from something you caught and it can't be cured by a pill." Lincoln laughed. It seemed that only he and the Parkers remained untouched.

"Pastor, I want you and Christine and anyone else who is still able to move to put your hands on those who are ailing. Don't misunderstand me, I know there is no power in your touch, but these who are afflicted can benefit from your prayers and placing a hand on their shoulder connects you to them and we'll all pray for the Power Source … our Heavenly Father… to minister to them. Give them your comforting touch." Lincoln spoke quickly as was his nature and Martin, Christine and Steve Winters circled each affected person and prayed fervently. By the time Martin closed in prayer, Lincoln began to pray for all of them.

"Lord, I bring nothing to the throne of grace that you don't already know about, but you've told us to come to You, and here we

are… desperate for You. We have gathered for a divine purpose and no doubt we have hit some oppressive opposition! Thankfully, You are greater than anything we face. How marvelous it would be to foil the enemy's plan to stop us from prayer! We will not be defeated because we are not in charge, You are!" When Linc ended his prayer, all was quiet in the room. John was the first to speak.

"Thanks, Bro! I appreciate you so much!" John wiped the tears that seemed to run down his face. He had never been an emotional kind of guy before he became a Christian. Now, he had to fight tears on a daily basis. Whenever he began to sing a tune in his head, the thoughts of his own unworthiness would engulf him. It no longer embarrassed him and he felt sorry for those who seemed to have 'gotten over' how the Lord interceded on their behalf.

"Pastor, I know you customarily close in prayer, but will you lead us off?"

"I think you already did that!" Martin laughed good-naturedly.

Once again the room grew still and Martin prayed fervently for the situation they faced. He was tempted to add other concerns, but decided he would keep the focus on the immediate need. When he finished, Christine began to pray.

By the time she finished, John had pulled himself off the floor and was on his knees beside Steve's well-worn sofa. His prayer began softly and the longer he prayed the more fervent he became. The sound of his voice seemed to fill the room and it was obvious he was no longer afflicted.

When he finished praying, Steve Winters prayed. John smiled as he echoed their prayers. It was almost as if each person was given a number so they would know when it was their turn to pray. It was beautiful to hear the hearts of those who were in touch and in tune with the Lord. Martin took Christine's hand and gave it a gently squeeze as the excitement in the room continued.

After the last person prayed they remained on their knees. No one was anxious to end this sacred time and Martin allowed all participants to linger as they felt the urge to continue in prayer. As people rose from their knees and sat quietly waiting for the others to finish, Mrs. Winters crept softly into the room.

"There are refreshments in the kitchen if anyone is interested." She whispered. Soon the kitchen filled with all who had participated, and though so many had come to the house feeling miserably sick, plates began to fill with food.

"My goodness, I thought I was going to have to waste my little luncheon with so many who came feeling so poorly." She smiled.

"I'm hungry as a horse!" John announced.

"Can you send me some of that?" Lincoln asked through the phone.

"You don't even know what it is!" John laughed.

"Now, little brother, you know if it's food, I'm interested! And if it's American food…count me in!"

"I wish we could send it to you! But I'll tell ya what I'm going to do. I'm going to eat your share!" John and Lincoln laughed together.

"How is everyone feeling?" Lincoln asked.

"I have to tell you, I worried a bit about bringing all these sick people to my house!" Steve said.

"But you would never know any of them were sick."

"I've been through this before and though it is such a relief to have those awful symptoms pass, I still feel like someone punched me in the stomach!" John said and the others nodded in agreement.

"When I was asked to crawl out of bed and come anyway, I thought Pastor had lost his mind! But then the Lord reminded me of all we have been through. I have come to trust the pastor and if he says to come… I come!" Agnes laughed. Martin wished he had a congregation full of people like Agnes. She told him once that she felt akin to Gideon or Joshua and wondered if the walls of Jericho would fall today in obedience or whether a committee would be formed to discuss their options as the enemy slayed them.

"I'm so glad I did. I have never witnessed anything like this in all my life!" she smiled.

"There is something I wanted to share with the group!" Agnes continued. She seemed troubled and hesitant to speak.

"Go ahead, Agnes. We're listening." John encouraged.

"I ran into Kate McDaniel a few days ago and she said some troubling things to me." Christine exchanged pensive glances with her husband as she continued.

"She has never liked me and has made it clear that she does not desire a friendship between us. Personally, I wouldn't have it any other way, though I know how that must sound." She sighed.

"Generally, whenever she sees me, she nods curtly and moves on. That's why this was such a strange conversation." She took a sip of her tea as all eyes focused on her. She hated to be the center of attention and would never want to create drama, but this was the right setting for her to speak frankly.

"She said there was nothing people like *me* could do to people like *her*. I asked her what she meant and she told me not to play games with her."

"I tell you there is something wrong with that family." piped in Steve Winters.

"She told me it was a shame we couldn't be friends, but she knew me better than that. Said that she would hate to see an old woman put in so much time and trouble over things that I should leave alone." Martin could feel the hair on his neck prickle and his heart began to race.

"Do you think she was trying to scare you?" asked John.

"That's exactly what it sounds like to me!" said Steve.

"I surprised her when I told her that the things I put time and effort into have always been a blessing to me. I told her that over the years I have found what a wonderful, powerful and all knowing God I serve. She said she understood completely as she too had full allegiance to the wonderful, powerful god."

"For a few seconds we just stood staring at each other. She broke the silence. She smiled at me and said that it was a shame we had a fire in the church and hoped we would not have any other mishaps. She said though we had a beautiful church, so many things can go wrong. It could have been faulty wiring or plumbing. I told her it was not our building but belonged to God and He knew how to keep it safe."

"I think she's threatening us!" Steve was getting worried.

"I'm not worried, are you?" Agnes took time to study each face. Sadly, many of them appeared frightened.

"I think we need to be careful we don't see spooks and evil around every corner!" said Mrs. Winters.

"I know my husband has his own reasons for wanting to believe the worst about these people, but I have to tell you. Kate McDaniel has been very kind to me and seems to want to be helpful." Steve had never mentioned it to anyone else, but when Colten came for the second interview, things took a definite change for the worse. Steve told Colten he had been a good candidate and he had carefully considered hiring him, but after carefully examining each candidate, he decided to hire Mike Ryan. He was not expecting the angry response which included a threat that his business would be closed in the next year due to his lack of leadership and ignorance. Steve asked him to leave and was deeply troubled.

"I think these people are ... dangerous!" Steve shook his finger at his wife wishing she would see things his way.

"I don't know if I would go that far, but I will say that at one point I asked Kate to come inside and perhaps we could pray about some of the issues. She recoiled as if I had asked her to stick her head in the oven!" said Agnes.

"It intrigued me that she wanted no part of it, so I went a step further. I took her by the hand and began to pray."

"What was her reaction?" asked Martin.

"She pulled her icy hand out of mine and glared at me. She said that before it was over, there would be many in the need of prayer! Then she stomped off!"

"What do you think, Pastor?" John asked.

"I really don't know the McDaniel family very well and I won't make judgments based on here say and conjecture."

"But Preacher, you know as well as I do that one of them set that fire and look at the way Kate spoke to Agnes!"

"I'm saying until I know more, I will treat them as misguided folks in need of prayer. In the meantime, we will pray that the Lord shows them their need. They aren't beyond His reach!"

"We are not gathered here to pray against the McDaniel family. We are here to pray for power in the midst of this situation."

"Then you are admitting... we have a situation!" Steve wanted Pastor to spell it out for everyone.

"I believe our church is in the need of prayer. I want each of you to believe that God is faithful! If any of these accusations are true, we are going to trust our Lord who is stronger and will circumvent *anyone* or *anything* that stands in the way of building this work for the Lord."

"You're right, Pastor. Look how sick we were just a few hours ago. It's a miracle any of us even made it here today." said Agnes.

"A miracle is right! Can't you see that God is in this?" John added excitedly.

"I think we are in for some exciting times ahead, but it's going to be okay! Long as we stay faithful and moving forward... it's all going to be okay!" John clapped his hands together and shook his head.

"So what's next, Pastor?" Christine knew he was holding back but there was no point in creating panic.

Suddenly, Lincoln spoke and it startled them as they had forgotten he was still on the line.

"Pastor, I know many people like the McDaniels. Now don't get me wrong, I'm not praying for harm to come to nobody... for sure. But you are dealing with some very powerful elements, I assure you."

"If that is what we are facing, how have you handled it?" Martin felt he could use the advice of someone who had victory over this kind of situation.

"I would gather these people one last time and pray specifically for this family. You need to pray with compassion for their souls and you need to pray with compassion for the church that the Saviour gave his life for. So... Steve... when these people come to mind I want you to say these words in your heart...'these are people for whom the Lord gave his life' it will help you see them through different eyes."

Steve nodded his head feeling ashamed. When you think of people in that light, it changes your heart.

Dishes were set on the table as one by one people returned to their knees. Fervent prayer was extended once again but this time with specifics. By the time prayer had ended, the room was peaceful and calm. But it was *anything* but calm in the McDaniel household.

Chapter 18

"Can you believe the nerve of that broken down little woman?" Kate spat.

"She actually thinks she is stronger than I am… than *we* are!" she snapped.

"Why are you so upset, Mother? What does it matter what any of them think?" Mac hadn't seen his mother this angry since his father had unexpectedly lost his last job.

"I'm talking about Agnes Palmer! She must be a hundred years old and yet everyone treats her like she just walked off the mountain with God on her shoulder!" she screeched.

"By the way, you aren't exactly winning either, my son! I haven't seen that preacher's daughter in your car, or in your bedroom for that matter."

"In time, Mother, in time. She finds me irresistible and I can see her weakening more each time we are together." He gave her his best eye roll and scowled. He knew how to win the girl over and didn't need his mother on his back.

She decided not to tell him about her conversation with Lisa Parker. He and his father would be furious to know she got involved in the situation. She hadn't planned to speak with Lisa, but after her conversation with Agnes, she decided to go shopping. Buying expensive jewelry always lifted her spirits. Sometimes she purposefully bought something extravagant and completely out of her price range. Part of the thrill was knowing Colten would be furious. Of course, the attention was priceless. She knew all eyes were on her as she strutted around with her sparkling, expensive jewelry and exquisite wardrobe. It made her a bit heady to think about it.

After her encounter with Agnes, she marched herself into the most expensive jewelry store she knew and began harassing the poor, young sales girl. The manager, who had experienced firsthand the offensive woman's anger, quickly stepped in. Though she despised Kate, she was not willing to lose a sale. She displayed the most expensive pieces in their showcase and flattered the self-indulgent woman each time she tried on a piece. She was admiring herself in the mirror as she clasped a large, diamond medallion necklace. She giggled as she read the back side of the medallion. "Mother of the World" was inscribed in beautiful scripted lettering that looked hand engraved. It was designed to make a mother feel that she was the most important person in the world to her family. But Kate read it as though the wearer was the mother of all things in the world. She liked the thought. It made her feel powerful and important.

Ignoring the babbling sales clerk, she turned the mirror to see her reflection at every angle and saw Lisa Parker admiring some of the jewelry in the case behind her. She narrowed her eyes as she watched the naïve, young girl. It astounded her to think of Lisa's innocence. Mac told her he was sure Lisa had no experience with boys and could barely conceal his excitement. He would be her first! Their eyes met in the corner of Kate's mirror and Lisa was the first to respond.

"Hello Mrs. McDaniel." Lisa thought she was one of the prettiest ladies she ever met and today she looked exceptional.

"That's absolutely gorgeous!" the brilliance of the diamond sent sparkles to the ceiling.

"Why thank you, Lisa. I think it is a lovely piece!" Kate smiled through gritted teeth.

"Are you shopping too?"

"Just window shopping. I love to look at the new pieces that come in. I guess jewelry is my weakness." Lisa laughed.

"You should have Mac come in with you so you can select something. He would like that. He is really very fond of you, Lisa. I hope you realize that."

"Oh, I could never allow him to buy me something in this store! Everything is so expensive, and besides, we are just friends." She could feel the blush on her cheeks. She did not want to discuss Mac with his mother.

"That's your choice, Lisa. I know he is my son, so you will think I'm partial, but Mac could have any girl he desires and he has chosen you." She made him sound like Prince Charming scanning his kingdom for a desirable mate.

"I agree! Mac could have his choice. But I really don't know him very well and I am not really looking for a steady boyfriend." Kate looked as if she had been struck. Who was this young girl anyway? Did she think she was too good for her son?

"Why don't you come to our house for dinner tonight and get to know him better? I'm sure your parents hover over you whenever you have male company, but I assure you it won't be that way at my house. You can relax without someone watching your every move!" Now Lisa was angered. Her parents loved her enough to watch out for her. There were times she resented it, but in her heart she knew the truth…most of the time.

"I appreciate the offer, but I have plans tonight, perhaps another time." She almost told her she would have to check with her parents before she accepted the invitation, but felt Kate would use it against them.

"Let's make it another day this week. I won't even tell Mac I've invited you, just to surprise him." She laughed conspiratorially.

"Thanks for inviting me. That is very kind of you." Lisa felt uncomfortable and wanted to leave the store but Kate took her hand and gripped it firmly.

"I know your parents treat you like you were a two year old. They seem to make all the decisions for you and your brother. What worries me is that they don't value your opinion and choices. You are practically a grown woman, Lisa. You are smart with a good head on your shoulders! There is a time to let go and trust your children. I can't see that happening in your household!" Lisa wanted to argue, but she had used many of those same arguments herself. Kate had a strong grip on Lisa's hand and as she stared into Kate's eyes, she could feel those old arguments come to life in her mind. She felt the irritation and hostility as if she was in the heat of the moment again. The longer Kate talked the more they seemed to intensify.

"My parents are a little over protective but it's because they love us." Lisa's words sounded hollow and distant.

"Hmmm, I think it's out of pride! They wouldn't want you to make them look bad. After all, the Pastor thinks his kids should be perfect!" Lisa remembered telling her father the same things a few months ago.

"He knows Chad and I aren't perfect..." she was beginning to lose her resolve and Kate could taste victory!

"I heard through the grapevine that growing up you were never allowed to spend the night with anyone outside of your family. And that your parents have always told you what you can wear and check to see how tight or how short. The list is endless! How do you think that made the other parents feel when they asked you to come to their house?" She watched Lisa's face as she hurled each accusation. She could see a faint nod.

"After all, what happens when you grow a little and your favorite dress doesn't have much of a hem? And God forbid that you gain a few pounds and your favorite sweater becomes a little too tight! I'm sorry, Lisa. I'm not trying to speak unkindly of your parents. It's just that they have such ridiculous rules for you to endure!" Lisa nodded her agreement and Kate smiled warmly at her.

"We must allow our children to think for themselves at some point! Mac has never disappointed me and I have given him as much freedom and liberty as possible."

"Children need to make their own decisions, with our guidance of course, or they will be incapable of making decisions when we are gone. Or they will not learn to trust their decisions as they have never had to rely on their own judgment!" Lisa thought Kate was one of the smartest women she had ever talked to. She spoke to her as if she was an adult... a *smart* adult!

"Why don't you give me a call sometime this week and let me

know when you can join us for dinner. I promise to have all your favorites and then you and Mac can spend some quality time together. He has internet in his room and would enjoy showing you some of the games he likes to play." Lisa nodded and Kate released her grip. She hugged her warmly and Lisa left the store feeling dizzy and more than a bit irritable toward her parents.

Kate walked out of the jewelry store with a new necklace and a certainty Lisa would be over for dinner very soon. She knew she laid it on thick, but when she felt the girl succumbing to her veiled comments, she knew she had won! She fully intended to get her to Mac's bedroom and she giggled as she thought of Mac teaching her games on the internet.

"Mac will teach you some games all right… adult games that you will love until shame overtakes you." She laughed.

Lisa left the store with her head spinning and had full intention of speaking to her parents. She was, after all, almost an adult and should be able to make her own decisions.

As she headed for the parking lot, she was greeted by Anthony.

"Lisa, wait up!" he shouted from the curb.

"Hi Anthony, I was just heading home."

"Are you okay? You seem upset." Her face was pinched and he recognized the angry look as he had seen it firsthand.

"No, no, I'm not upset. Just have some unfinished business at home to take care of." She smiled.

"Are *we* okay, Lisa?" He asked quietly.

"Of course, why wouldn't we be?" He looked so forlorn her heart went out to him.

"It's just that… well… I think of you as my girl and maybe I'm way out of line." Lisa stared at him for a moment and realized how far their relationship had come in the past few months.

"You know I am very fond of you, Anthony. I enjoy your company."

"But you don't think of me as your boyfriend. And please don't say you're a boy and you're my friend so that makes me your boy friend." She laughed as he took the words out of her mouth.

"I really do like you Anthony. I certainly have no one else that fits the description of boyfriend either, so let's just leave things as they are." She stammered.

"Leave things as they are? How are they?" She didn't know how to answer. He looked so sad that she wanted to tell him she would be his girlfriend, but that seemed like a dumb reason.

"Is it Mac?" he ventured to ask.

"No, it is not Mac. We are just friends." Anthony fought the temptation to speak unkindly of him. Lisa would feel the need to defend him and that would only make him angry.

"Can I walk you home?" He asked hoping to spend more time with her.

"Sure. Let's walk." He walked close to her but fought the urge to take her arm or hold her hand.

Soon they were talking and laughing like they did before the McDaniel family arrived on the scene. Both were feeling more light hearted by the time they reached her house.

"I have the deepest respect for you, Lisa. I honestly don't know another girl like you. It's not just because you're so pretty. I admire you. Girls today think they should be making adult decisions and the guys I know will help them along hoping to corrupt them." Lisa looked astonished.

"You would have to be in a guy's locker room to understand. Guys tell what they've done and to who! I used to be one of them. But I have to tell you. You have been blessed to have parents that love you so much. You've been around my parents. Can you imagine what would have happened if I had been a girl instead of a guy? My father wouldn't protect her and my mother wouldn't have much of a say. I've seen your father in tears for the youth group, Lisa. Can you imagine how broken hearted he would be if it were you or Chad?" Slowly, Kate's speech began to diminish in her head. Anthony was right! She had wonderful, caring parents! Impulsively she hugged Anthony. She couldn't believe how stupid she could be!

"Thanks, Anthony!" He enjoyed the hug but had no idea what prompted it. Just then the door opened and Chad stuck his head out.

"Hey Anthony! Want to stay for dinner?" Lisa nodded her

approval and ran past both of them to the kitchen where Christine was dishing out spaghetti and meatballs.

"You're the best, Mom" she hugged her and Christine hugged her back hoping to keep the bowl of spaghetti from dropping on the kitchen floor.

"Well, thank you very much! You're not so bad yourself!" she giggled.

"Can Anthony stay for dinner?" Chad shouted from the living room.

"If it's okay with his parents." Anthony immediately called his mother before she prepared too much food and soon they were all settled in the living room.

It was like old times with Lisa and Anthony... as it was before Colten McDaniel arrived at school. She berated herself for listening to Kate McDaniel and decided to put some distance between herself and the entire family.

Kate continued to wait for Lisa's call and to make matters worse, Colten was in a dark, troubling mood and though Kate tried, she could not get to the bottom of the problem. Every time she hinted around, he became enraged and they began to argue.

"I think it's time to leave this area." Colten snapped. He did not get the job from Steve Winters and though he had several promising interviews, nothing was materializing. Kate was actually telling fortunes in a nearby town under a fictitious name but the money was not the same as when Colten contributed.

"Maybe Dad's right. I'm ready to move on." He was experiencing anxiety as well, but Kate wouldn't hear of it. She would not be defeated!

"Nonsense! We will not be driven away! If and when we leave, it will be our decision to do so." She screamed.

"Can't you tell it's not the right place? These people disgust me and I want to get away from them."

"Of course they disgust you. That's hardly the point. What's going on, Colten?"

"If you must know… I didn't get the job with Steve Winters. He hired that ridiculous Mike Ryan!

"That's ludicrous." Kate threw her head back and laughed loudly. She remembered Mike as a scrawny little man who seemed to be afraid of his own shadow.

"Do you want me to handle Mike Ryan? Believe me when I get done with him he will be happy to work for you if he can work at all!" she laughed again.

"It's more than Mike Ryan." Kate took him by the hand and narrowed her eyes. She hated weakness!

"Spill it, Colten. What's going on with you?" Colten wasn't ready to tip his hand, but he knew things were not going according to plan.

"Listen to me, my Darling! We are winning! Do I have to burn the church down for you to agree?" He smiled at her and shook his head. She was really something! He loved her and he hated her. She was selfish and spoiled but when she set out to do something, she was relentless and no one better get in her way!

"Maybe I'm just tired." He offered. Kate thrived on new challenges, while he was content to bask in past achievements and relax.

"There is still a lot of work to be done, Colten. I can't do it all myself!"

"I pull my weight! I do my fair share and more!" Colten retorted, though his words sounded hollow to his own ears.

"Now you listen to me! Once again, I am going to fix everything, as usual, and then I expect your full cooperation! You and Mac both better shape up! I want Lisa Parker over here this week! That should take care of whatever is left of that preacher and his happy group of believers!" she hissed. She felt unusually riled as she snatched her purse and slammed the door behind her. She felt angry and needed to find a target for her hostility.

To assuage her anger, she needed to do something BIG! Something worthy of her talents. She made a mental list. First she would pay Mike Ryan a visit. That would be fun. If she played her cards right, she could put him out of work permanently. She would have to do a little homework on him first to find his weaknesses. Next she would visit Steve Winters to let him know her husband would be able to begin work with him next week after she got rid of Mike. She hadn't forgotten about Agnes Palmer! Perhaps she would break into her home and totally vandalize it. That should give her a heart attack!

She balled her hands into fists until the nails bit into her skin. It wasn't enough! Maybe the final act would be to set the church on fire. The weather was turning cold and on their shoe string budget, they would have to meet in the parking lot! That would show them!

She slowed her steps and unclenched her fists. Kate smiled at her decisions. We'll see who leaves town!

Her tires screeched as she bounced out of the driveway and headed down the road. It felt good to have a plan! She glanced at her watch and discovered it was almost five o clock. No doubt Mike Ryan would be leaving his office and heading to his car. She couldn't wait to confront him. She sped through town barely stopping for red lights or stop signs, pulled her car into one of the VIP spaces and hastily threw open her car door denting the expensive car in the next space.

"I would like a word with you!" she shouted across the parking lot as Mike headed toward his car.

"I got nothing to say to you, lady." Mike scowled.

"Good, then I'll do the talking." She sneered.

"Get away from me or I'll call security." He warned.

"You really are a little mouse of a man, aren't you?! Don't worry. I'm only planning on talking to you, unless of course, you won't heed my warning."

"Warning? Warning about what?"

"Let me spell it out for you. My husband was the perfect candidate for the job you are now enjoying. He is twice the man you are!" she glowered.

"I guess Steve Winters didn't think so!" he spat.

"The point is… you are going to step down and allow Colten to take the job."

"You're nuts, lady! And I don't like threats!"

250

"I'm sorry, you misunderstand me. I never make threats... at least none that I can't carry out!" she laughed.

"Now listen and listen good! You are going to step down from your current position and you are going to let Mr. Winters know you were not the right candidate from the job."

"And if I don't?" There was fear in his heart and he had no idea why.

"I assure you don't want to find out! I don't make idle statements. Let's just say you are no match for me or my family and so many things could go wrong for you." He frowned and appeared puzzled as she went straight to the point.

"Your wife has had some mental issues. I know the people of the church are not aware of it, but by the time I expose it... I will make sure you are to blame! I might go as far as to accuse you of your own mental illness. I assure you, I am very convincing and you will be hard pressed to find employment anywhere once I'm through!"

"How do you know about my wife?" he asked with a quivering voice. As far as he knew, only the pastor knew about their situation. His wife had a mental breakdown and had to be hospitalized. It was the most agonizing time in their life and he couldn't imagine that Kate McDaniel knew anything about such a private matter. She ignored his question.

"If that's not enough, I am willing to let people know about your drug addiction!"

"You're crazy! I don't have a drug addiction!"

"You recently stopped using a prescription drug to reduce your chronic back pain..."

"What are you talking about? I took pain meds prescribed by my doctor. It's true he has reduced the dosage as I was having a reaction, but... but... how would you know anything about that?"

"Yes, he reduced the dosage when you started hallucinating like a man on LSD!" she laughed.

"That's a blatant LIE!"

"By the time I finish spinning the story, it will be of a mad man who has taken too many drugs and is such a terrible husband his wife had to be hospitalized before she had a complete nervous breakdown!"

"No one would believe such horrific lies!"

"Are you willing to take a chance on that? You forget that I am very popular among the women in the church and many are astounded at my knowledge of their situations. I have been very helpful as well. Don't forget it was Colten and I that found Devon and brought her home.

"Yes, you brought home Devon, but she's not the same girl! Maybe you had something to do with that too?" he scowled.

"That is none of your concern. What *is* your concern is doing as I have asked you...politely... before things get out of hand."

"Now that I have made myself clear, I want you to march yourself into Steve Winters office and let him know of your decision to step down!" She smiled smugly.

"That won't be necessary." Kate clutched her throat as Steve Winters stepped up behind her. He had heard most of the conversation and his bright, angry red face spoke volumes.

"Maybe it would be best if I stepped down, Steve. I won't have my wife's condition exposed and it's not worth taking a chance of another hospitalization. She is much too fragile for any of this."

"It's okay, Mike. It would not be in Kate's best interest to propagate these stories as it will gain her nothing. I have no intention of hiring Colten now or ever! And I have every intention of exposing this conversation to the Pastor."

"Perhaps you should rethink your decision, Mr. Winters. I know things about you and your company that you would not want exposed either!" she challenged.

"If you've done your homework, you will know that my business is above board and has nothing to hide. My books are open to anyone who wants to see them. You can do that when you have been honest!"

"That might be so, but like most things that get reported, it only takes a small twist to go from honest to corrupt. I assure you, I can make that happen with very little embellishment." She laughed. Steve was so angry he could have knocked her to the ground. He immediately began praying and the Lord reminded him of the time spent on his knees with other church members for such a time as this.

Kate was aghast when he took her by the hand and holding it firmly in his, he began to pray, out loud, right there in the parking lot. She struggled to pull her hand away, but Steve held it tightly in his.

"Lord, our dear sister, Kate, seems to be in the need of prayer. I ask that right now in this parking lot she gets a glimpse of who you are! May she know your power and strength! Mike was shocked to watch Kate as Steve prayed! She seemed shaken and on the verge of tears.

"Let go of me!" she screamed! After Mike recovered from his complete shock, he began to relax. No longer was Kate in control of the situation and it was obvious by the fear in her eyes, this experience was tormenting her.

"I'll let you go after I have my say!" His hand was like a vice and she had no choice but to listen.

"You go home to your husband and tell him it's over! I'm not entirely sure of the situation, but I do know this, Kate. We have had enough. Like Elijah, I am willing to call down the power of heaven to stop this... this...scheme of yours and I dare say; you won't like the result."

"Now who's doing the threatening?" she snapped.

"I'm sorry you see it as a threat. That was not my intent. I am merely putting a stop to *your* threats!"

"You are all a bunch of fanatical, crazy people! You should all be locked up... from the Pastor to the nut that gave his speech while the church was on fire!" she exploded.

"I won't spend another minute with any of you!" she screamed as she pulled her hand out of Steve's grip.

"Threaten me, will you! You'll be sorry for those words Steve Winters!" she raced to her car and careened through the parking lot at with her accelerator to the floor. She drove through the gate damaging the fence and tearing off the lift gate arm.

"What do you think she'll do next?" Mike's fear was returning with a vengeance.

"Can't say for sure, but I think she got the message." Mike wished he was as calm as his friend and employer. She scared the wits out of him!

Chapter 18 *View Two*

"Get in here immediately!" screamed Portentous.

"What's the trouble?" Bombastic shook with fear. The list was endless of his misdeeds and he couldn't be sure what Portentous knew, though he had no intention of admitting to anything.

"I hate it when these stupid mortals go off in another direction! I thought you had the McDaniel family at your beck and call! There is much work to be done and they are more experienced than most!"

"What seems to be the problem?" Bombastic dared to ask. Portentous stuck him forcefully knocking him to his knees.

"If you were watching as I have commanded you, we would not have such problems!" Bombastic shook under the sneer of his giant enemy.

"Kate McDaniel has been calling out in desperation! Why have you not given her direction? She can only achieve minimal success without our intervention!" Bombastic cowered away before Portentous could deliver another blow. In truth, Bombastic heard her cries and enjoyed her torment too much to answer.

"I was enjoying her misery!" Portentous smiled at the thought. When the McDaniel's had served their purpose, they would come to this place of torment and he and Bombastic would be eagerly waiting!

"We have given her time and attention. This is the time to push her! She has had some particularly evil thoughts that she might not generally yield to, so let her know it is time!" Portentous knew that other minions were watching and he called out loudly.

"What are the three 'D's that will bring mankind to its knees?" He asked. The reply reverberated throughout the room.

"Discredit! Discourage! Demoralize!" they shrieked in unison.

"Excellent!" Portentous strutted arrogantly around the other minions and exhaled an acrid breath before he began another exhortation. Bombastic listened cautiously to be sure he was following the criteria as well.

"When studying these mortals you must remember they fall into three basic categories." Bombastic hoped he would not be asked to disclose them, as he would be throttled if he spoke incorrectly.

"You must watch closely! They may be able to fool each other, but they cannot fool us!" he growled.

"You will find the Believers, the Unbelievers, and the Make-believers!" He laughed.

"Why are they difficult to tell apart? The Believers go to church and the Unbelievers do not, correct?" asked one of the more impervious minions.

"You would think that would be so, but alas it is not that simple, for you see they can often mimic one another." All eyes were on the prideful Portentous and he seemed to grow larger before their very eyes as he continued.

"Sometimes Believers do not connect with others that could help them on their journey to our Enemy. I give applause to those who have thrown road blocks into their paths and screamed doubts into their minds! Then there are the Unbelievers. If they are the bold type, they are easily spotted. They are the ones that discredit the Enemy with their unproven theories. But keep in mind, there are many Unbelievers that are tossed about in search of truth. If you are wise, you will stick close to them so they do not slip out of our grasp!" Shaggy nods and soft curses were heard from those who shared the experience.

"The Make-believers are the most difficult for both sides. These are the ones that must be studied. There are Make-believers in the pulpits and teaching classes. They know much theology and know all the correct terminology and catch phrases the Enemy's people are so fond of shouting. Don't be fooled by those who give a hearty 'Amen' to the speaker. Sometimes they feel it is required, others enjoy the spotlight, however brief. Many Make-believers have been at this task for so long, they are not aware themselves that they do not belong to the Enemy. The feel good messages have lulled their soul to sleep. But I warn you... the Unbeliever and the Make-believer, are only one step from joining with the Enemy. You must NEVER let down your guard! AM I CLEAR???"

Bombastic hated studying these people. He had been caught off guard more than once when someone began praying earnestly for the Enemy to save their soul, and he shook with fear as he felt the Enemy approaching to snatch the humbled heart away.

How could he tell Portentous how frightened he was of the Enemy? He wondered if Portentous was as fearful. His mind drifted to the time he shouted to a young man to end his life. He could almost taste his death, when suddenly, the man began praying with all his heart and the Enemy came to his rescue.

He was blinded by the heavenly sight of the great King and Redeemer snatching the pitiful young man into the palm of his hand. It was too much to witness. The utter beauty of the man's deliverance made Bombastic weak and he began tumbling back to the dark portals of the doomed.

"Remember, we are not defeated! Many love the broad way that leads to destruction! They do not realize the bridge is out and they will soon fall into our waiting hands!" Cheers echoed throughout the room and Portentous knew they understood!

"Where shall you begin?" Portentous was still in his 'teaching' moment and waited impatiently for Bombastic to report.

"Do not let Kate lose her resolve! She has had moments where she believed she was on the wrong side! She is afraid of Steve Winters and that Preacher. Now is the time to use her anger for our purposes!" Bombastic nodded, though he had no idea how to proceed.

"Tell me your plan for success!" Portentous could smell fear and looked forward to pummeling him for his stupidity.

"I will assure her... she is on the winning side!" Bombastic spat, desperately seeking a plan. There was a frigid air of silence before Portentous began speaking to his students.

"Beware that you are not the dolt Bombastic has clearly shown himself to be. He has not thought ahead and therefore has no hope of winning this battle." Bombastic began to sputter and speak, but he could not think clearly and knew he would only make things worse. Clearing his throat, Portentous continued.

"Kate must carry out her threats." Bombastic had no idea what threats she made as he was not there to hear them.

"With any luck, Mike Ryan's wife will join us soon. She has regained some of her strength, but Kate can easily push her over the edge. Kate needs to meet with her within the hour and begin her undoing! Kate must tell her that Mike is going to lose his job as he is not capable of handling the responsibility; furthermore, it is all her fault! They are in dire need of money due to her medical bills. Mrs. Ryan must be convinced there is no hope for her mental instability and as an added bonus; she must blame her husband for her fragile condition. Tell her If Mike was any kind of husband, he would have helped her when she first began to show signs of her unstable state." Bombastic shook his shaggy head in agreement. This was going to be fun!

"Next, Kate must rally some support. There are many women in the church that think she has some kind of godly gift. She must sow discourse quickly!" Bombastic nodded and looked to Portentous for details.

"She must appear devastated! The preacher, Mike Ryan, Steve Winters and anyone else in authority must appear to be heartless and hateful people who have caused her mental and physical anguish. Mix a little truth with the lies so it is palatable." Bombastic waited for more as Portentous was on an evil roll.

"Listen as I weave my lie...Kate must tell the people of the church she has been accused of setting the fire to the church when, in fact, she was the one who reported it! The preacher is a mean spirited man that his children and wife fear! The church staff also has seen his misconduct and is fearful to report it. Make sure Mrs. Ryan's mental health is exposed! If that is not enough, tell Kate to put her arm in a sling and state that Steve Winters pushed her down in the parking lot and told her to get out of the church and out of the area!'"

"Brilliant! You are Brilliant!" laughed Bombastic anxious to put the plan into motion.

"The church plans to meet for prayer...good... we will be there to make sure their voices go no further than the ceiling. Most of them will never notice!" They laughed hysterically at his joke.

"Then, when all those that the preacher deems as his 'prayer warriors' come together, Kate is to set fire to the church. Colten and Mac will bolt the doors from the outside and no one is to get out! NO ONE is to escape including the McDaniels! I am tired of working with them and I think it is time for them to get their 'just rewards!" BWAHAHAHAH!

Chapter 19 View One

Steve wasted no time calling Martin and quickly relayed the situation. They both knew that Kate would not take this lying down. Once again, it was time for fervent prayer. Martin sought the Lord for guidance and in his heart he knew it was going to be a show down! There was no telling how far Kate would go to wreck and ruin the church, and there was nothing he put past her. In answer to his burdened prayer, he called John Dunbar. He had grown to love the man and knew he and Lincoln would be his best advisors.

In turn, John called his brother and they prayed together fervently for the Lord's intervention. Lincoln was always the calm, peaceful one who brought serenity to any situation.

Martin had asked John to meet with him in his office as soon as possible, and John slipped on his shoes as he was saying goodbye. The sense of urgency was overwhelming.

As he headed down the familiar route to Martin's church, he thought once again of the last time he had been there. What a time that was! His preaching had been powerful and moving and the opposition was almost as strong. He shook his head as he thought of Kate screaming the church was on fire. She was a piece of work to be sure!

John stopped to zip his jacket, as the air seemed to have turned chilly. He was glad he grabbed his heavier jacket, though he always had to fight the zipper on this one. There seemed to be little threads hiding somewhere that lodged in the teeth making him wiggle the zipper until it finally zipped! He was concentrating on his problem when he looked up with a start.

"Vontrice!" he smiled. The sight of her always made his heart beat faster.

"John Dunbar! I thought you was about to run me over!" she laughed.

"Never! Well... never intentionally!" he laughed easily with her.

"I was hoping to run into you." She said nervously.

"You don't have to run into me. I have a phone. You have the number." He teased.

"Funny, I thought of calling you several times but then I decided that if I was supposed to talk to you, I would run into you."

"Then it looks like you are supposed to talk to me. That suits me just fine!" He could tell she had something on her mind and it seemed serious.

"Can we sit down?" He glanced at his watch and knew the preacher was waiting on him, but Vontrice would always take priority with him. He knew if he told her he was meeting with the pastor, she would not detain him and he may never find out what was bothering her.

"You're really something John Dunbar! Do you know that?" Her eyes filled with tears and he had no idea what brought about this kind of emotion. He remained silent and waited for her to continue.

"Let's just say... you owe me some picture frames."

"WHAT?" He took her by the hand and looked deeply into her dark brown-black eyes. Could it be true? Did she come to church as he had asked?

"Yes, John, I came to church. I heard you preach! I was astounded! You were magnificent up there!" Tears rolled down her cheeks and she fought for control. She didn't want to break down completely, but that day was etched forever in her mind.

"Girl, I just spoke the words the Lord gave me to say. Nothing magnificent about me...everything magnificent about my Saviour!" he chuckled softly.

"Yes, you're right. I could see myself for the first time just like the Lord saw me. When you talked about Noah, I thought of myself climbing the highest tree trying to escape. But there is no escape, is there!"

"Sometimes I wish there was Vontrice. I wish everyone I love could magically understand what the Lord did for them that day on Calvary and come willingly to Him." He sighed.

"There were so many responding to your invitation to come to the Lord that you didn't see me."

"I can't believe I didn't know you were there! I looked over the crowd hoping to see you. I though you decided not to come." He was still missing the point.

"I *did* decide not to come. After our conversation, I tried to put you out of my mind and heart for good, but I just couldn't do it. You made it clear you could not build a future with me in my present state and I resented it. I don't know why. I guess it just sounded so final." She handed him a flyer with his picture on it and he looked surprised.

"I found it in my door. I guess the church wanted everyone to hear John Dunbar preach!" she smiled.

"I had no idea." He said honestly.

"It was the strangest thing, John. I could have sworn I threw it away, and when I went to the kitchen to get a drink, it was on the table!" she laughed.

"I threw it away again and this time I was sure it was in the trash! Then the funniest thing happened. I had also thrown away an empty jar and decided it would be a good jar to empty grease into. You remember how much I love bacon!" she giggled and he nodded. She loved bacon and would tell him there was going to be bacon in heaven and it would be healthy to eat!

"I pulled the jar out of the trash and put it on the table while I was cooking my bacon and eggs and once again it happened!" She shook her head at the memory.

"That little flyer was stuck to the bottom of the jar!" John laughed with her.

"Guess you were getting tired of seeing my ugly mug!" said John.

"All I can tell you is it worked! I ate my breakfast and decided to go to church and hear you preach before I found the flyer stuck to my pillow!" she teased. Then her face grew serious as she continued.

"John, I couldn't take my eyes off you as I watched you open the Bible and preach. As I said... you're really something!" she took both of his hands in hers as she continued.

"John, I understood! I got it! I finally got it!" she smiled.

"You mean...?"

"Yes, I spoke to your pastor's wife, Christine. She showed me verse after verse and for the first time I understood and saw my need!" John couldn't hide his tears from her. He held her close and they cried together as onlookers walked by them in confusion.

"I want you to come with me." He grabbed her by the hand and glanced at his watch. He was definitely going to be late, but Martin was going to be excited to hear the news.

Vontrice was surprised to find herself at the Parker's home sitting with Martin and Christine as if she were family. Christine welcomed her warmly and had no idea the relationship that existed between the two seated next to each other. John did not hesitate to thank Christine for personally speaking to Vontrice of her need of Christ. He could not have asked for a more knowledgeable person to speak to her.

Soon Steve Winter arrived and a few minutes later Agnes Palmer rapped on the door. Agnes was happy to see Vontrice as she remembered the pretty young lady who listened intently to John as he preached. There was no doubt in Agnes' mind that Vontrice heart was breaking with conviction. She was the first to hug her before she left the church that morning.

"What are we going to do, Preacher?" Steve had been pacing as he listened to the small talk. Though he was excited for Vontrice, it was hard for him to focus. His heart was racing as he thought of Kate McDaniel standing in his parking lot making threats to Mike Ryan. She meant business. There was no doubt about that.

"Could I interject?" John asked.

"Of course!" said Martin.

"Linc told me that he had been praying even before my phone call. We talked about how Melba, I guess you would consider her the local witchdoctor, manipulated the people with fear and power. You should have seen those poor people gathered around her. She was like a goddess to them. They believed everything she told them without question until Lincoln showed up with the gospel! It came to a showdown and Lincoln is sure it will be the same with Kate." All eyes were glued to John including Vontrice.

"Linc said he believed her first step would be to gather the women around her for support."

"But they would never believe her over the pastor!" Steve argued.

"Don't be so sure! She has gained a lot of support in a short period of time. Don't forget she was the one to find Devon and bring her home. There are many women in the church who think she has a *gift* that most don't understand."

"I understand her *gift* better than she thinks!" Martin quipped.

"But Martin, do you really think she can cause that kind of division?" Christine asked.

"I think it's already happened on a small scale." He replied.

"What do you mean?"

"I have had more than one counseling session with a woman who has remarked about Kate's gift. When I didn't embrace it, they seemed a bit insulted. There are those who discontinued their appointments and have turned solely to Kate for advice." Christine clutched her throat. That seemed incredulous!

"But, they would never do anything destructive! If Kate spoke hatefully about you, she would lose all credibility, don't you think?"

"I'm not so sure how far things would go. No, I don't think they would help her throw rocks through my windows, but she might be able to persuade them to stand by while she did." Christine shook her head. She loved the ladies of the church and didn't want to believe they could get involved with anyone who would go against her husband.

"Melba also became violent. She would have poisoned us but the Lord continued to protect us. My brother says he thinks she will gather support and then march either here or the church."

"And then what?" Steve asked.

"Not sure! She could vandalize or set the property on fire.

Anything from dumping something harmful into the baptistery to poisoning the drinking water, I suppose."

"Oh my! Don't you think you are being a bit unrealistic? Those are pretty strong statements!" Vontrice exploded. She wasn't part of the church but couldn't imagine anyone doing something so horrible to a church or its people. Before anyone could respond, there was a knock on the door. Steve pulled the drape slightly to see who was making the ruckus.

"Hello ladies, how can I help you?" asked Martin cordially.

"Pastor, we have come to stop the bullying! I have just come from the hospital where Kate McDaniel received stitches in her arm and is now wearing a sling for her dislocated shoulder!" Evelyn screeched. Of course, Evelyn would be the spokesman. If there was a problem in the church, Evelyn would be somewhere in the mix. She was known as a 'pot stirrer' and seemed to love controversy. She had made numerous appointments with Martin and every meeting was filled with drama. She complained about people asking too many questions if she missed church or felt slighted when no one asked where she was. There was no pleasing her. The only person she seemed to be close with was Kate.

"I'm sorry to hear Mrs. McDaniel has been injured, perhaps she fell or…"

"No, she didn't fall! She was pushed! And do you know who hurt this fine woman? Steve Winters, that's who!" Just then Steve stepped into view and the Evelyn glared at him.

"What did you do, come to see the Preacher so he could hear your side of the story? Well, facts are facts and Kate has been injured thanks to you!"

"What facts are we talking about?" Steve couldn't believe the accusations!

"Kate told us that she came to your establishment just to have a word with Mike Ryan. She wanted to see if Colten could assist him in any way being that *he* is the man with the experience! Before Mike could answer her, Steve ran her out of the parking lot and told her he had made his decision and didn't need a meddling woman to come and make trouble!"

"Did you ask Mike if that was true?" Steve was both angry and hurt. He had known most of the women for years.

"She told us that Mike wouldn't speak against you as he just got this big promotion, and when she tried to speak to you, you pushed her and she fell down hitting her arm on the curb. Poor thing called me to ask for a ride home as she felt too weak to drive."

"I know Steve is probably a big donor in the church, Pastor, and you wouldn't want to do anything to upset him, but if you recall, this is not the first time Steve has lost his temper and harmed someone!"

"Do you remember last fall when some poor homeless man was hanging around the church looking for a hand out? Steve told him he needed to move along and when the man put up some resistance, Steve pulled him away from the building and shoved him down the sidewalk! Poor man!"

"You have made some pretty nasty allegations, and I have heard enough. Let me set you straight on the poor homeless man. He was a known child predator and was hanging around the church waiting for the kids to get on the buses. Steve had seen the man before and decided to speak to him and let him know he needed to distance himself from our kids or we would call the police. The man had been drinking and got belligerent with Steve. I didn't want to upset the congregation and make them worry about their children, so we never exposed the problem. Thankfully, Steve made it go away!" Martin prayed that his anger would not get the better of him.

"Now, let me explain the situation with Kate. She came to see Mike Ryan but it was to tell him to step down from his position and allow her husband to take the position." Steve interjected. He dare not say more as he didn't want to expose Mike's wife.

"I guess it's your word against the word of an injured woman." Evelyn said haughtily.

"You're wrong about that too. You see, there are cameras in my parking lot. I put them in a few weeks ago. I can easily replay the tape from the time Kate arrived on the scene. She flew into the parking lot damaging the car next to hers. You can't hear the conversation she was having with Mike, but I think body language will speak for itself." His statements were met with silence. Obviously, Kate had not known there were cameras. Perhaps she investigated before he had them installed.

"The tapes will also show that Kate was never pushed nor did she fall down. The only time she was touched is when I asked that we pray together. Her reaction will be worth the price of admission!" Steve said. The women were beginning to squirm and it was obvious some were having a change of heart.

"I believe I can clear this up right now." Steve snapped his fingers remembering the pushy salesman that spoke endlessly of the modern security system newly installed to his business property. Steve was vaguely listening but remembered watching the tutorial that gave specific instructions how to see what was on camera with just a touch.

"If the salesman is correct, and if I can figure out how to access the system, we can view it on your laptop Pastor." Everyone crowded around the laptop as Steve began reading the instructions. Soon they were in business. They could view the parking lot and surrounding area and with a few clicks, Steve could back up the tapes until they saw Kate careening into the parking lot and sideswiping the car next to her.

"She said the damage was done on her way out as she was so distraught and in a great deal of pain." One of the women whispered to Evelyn.

"Notice her stance in front of Mike Ryan." He swung the camera around to get her facial expression. It was obvious she was the one in control of the conversation. Her arms were flailing about as she spoke and more than once she tapped on his chest making her point.

"I want you to see Mike's face as she threatened him." He wasn't sure how much to divulge but he wanted desperately to make the point. He glanced at the pastor and knew it was best to keep the rest to himself.

"Now, here is where I joined them. They did not see me approach and though I could not hear what Kate was saying until I got closer, I knew she was making some kind of threat."

"Like you said, you weren't close enough to know what she was saying so you can't really say she was threatening him. She is a dainty woman and he is quite a good sized man. Do you really think she could threaten him in any way?" Evelyn spouted without much conviction.

"I didn't hear the beginning of the conversation, but I heard most of it. But let's continue watching." During the next few minutes of the film, Kate spun around and in time it was obvious she was enraged. Her face was red and her hands were flailing the air as she spoke.

Steve purposely, moved the camera so all could see his facial expression. He silently thanked the Lord he did not appear angry. Even when he took her by the hand it appeared to be a warm gesture. Her reaction, however, was very telling. There was no doubt she was screaming at him and doing her best to release herself from his grip. When Steve closed his eyes and began praying, it left no doubt. Kate was fuming.

When she pulled her hand free, she once again began to point her finger as she screamed at them. Steve magnified her face as large as possible as she made her final threat. Steve slowed down the film so they could decipher the words ... *"You are all a bunch of fanatical, crazy people! You should all be locked up... from the Pastor to the nut that gave his speech while the church was on fire!"* There was a collective gasp from all.

"I'm so sorry Pastor... Steve... I guess we all jumped to conclusions! I must say, she really was very convincing." said Amy Weir. She was the last to go along with the crowd and now she was deeply ashamed.

"Maybe I should pay our injured lady a visit!" Martin did his best to hide his aggravation.

"I doubt she will still be there. She said she had some errands to run and they couldn't wait no matter how she was feeling." Evelyn piped in.

"I think you should stop by the church, Pastor." said John. He started to argue, but the look on John's face changed his mind.

"Would you like to go with me?" He asked.

"Sure. Would you mind dropping Vontrice off when we're done?" He wasn't sure that was the best idea, but he had brought her along and didn't want her to walk home, especially after all she had seen and heard.

They drove in silence for a short distance each deep in thought. Pastor prayed he would be able to approach Kate McDaniel without losing his temper. His children could attest that nothing angered him more than a lie. The punishment was always more severe and they could not remember a time when they had lied that it was not found out.

John could not shake the feeling that something was very wrong at the church. He tried to dismiss his thoughts, but he could not make the hair on his neck lie down! He prayed he was wrong.

Vontrice was confused and astonished as her mind raced across the details of their meeting. She had no idea who Kate McDaniel was and didn't think church people could do the things she had been accused of. That was just the hypocrites, not true believers, right?

As Martin pulled into the church parking lot they heard an explosion. Screeching to a halt, they jumped out of the vehicle and ran toward the sound. They could see fire pouring out of the basement window and John ran for the hose while Vontrice called 911.

Martin's anger subsided as he raced around the building and found Kate sprawled on the ground bleeding profusely. He yelled for John, as it was obvious, she needed a paramedic.

"Kate, Kate, can you hear me? Stay with me!" Martin pleaded. He could not tell how badly she was burned and had little knowledge of treating burn victims. John, however, sprang into action applying cool water to her blistering burns.

"It wasn't supposed to happen this way! I should have been victorious!" she seemed bewildered and lost consciousness several times. John gently coaxed her back each time with reassuring words and gentle strokes to her hair.

She was rushed to the hospital with second and third degree burns. No longer would her face, arms or legs be beautiful and it was very likely she would lose her hand and forearm due to the gasoline can explosion. Her life hung in the balances as a team of doctors worked frantically.

The fire to the church had no real impact. A small storeroom with old hymnals and VBS materials were destroyed, but little else. John's hunch had been correct. Kate had every intention of burning down the church.

Colten and Mac had been called to the hospital and their conduct was startling. Neither seemed concerned for Kate but Colten immediately began firing questions to Martin about the church fire. Was he going to press charges, if in fact he knew unequivocally, Kate set the fire? Was Martin planning to expose the event to the church?

"The doctor can see you now." A baffled nurse mumbled. When neither Colten or Mac responded, Martin was losing his patience.

"Why don't you check on your wife? Anything else can be discussed at a later time." Martin said. Colten's face remained angry as he shuffled off with Mac in tow.

"Now there's something you don't see every day! His wife is in ICU full of monitors and IV and his concern is whether you are going to tell anyone?" John shook his head.

"What's *with* that family?" said the aggravated nurse as she walked away. She had never experienced so little concern in all her days of nursing.

Martin waited until the doctor finished speaking to Kate's family, and then as they were led into the ICU, he approached the doctor.

"Excuse me, I am their Pastor and wondered if you could give me some information on Kate. Is she going to be all right?" The doctor folded his arms across his chest and shook his head.

"I certainly hope so. She's going to need quite a few skin graphs and in the next few hours we will know if her hand and forearm will need to be removed." Martin winced. It was an awful price to pay.

"I'm so sorry to hear that. We will be praying for her and the family." Martin assured him.

"Yes, they are certainly all in the need, preacher. I mean, there is no doubt this was a beautiful woman, but her husband seems appalled that we would suggest surgery to remove her dying limb, even if it is vital for her survival!"

Colten and Mac spent little time in the ICU and Martin never saw them leave. He glanced at his watch and only minutes had gone by from the time the doctor gave his diagnosis to their departure.

"Is it okay if I slip in there for a couple minutes? I just want to pray for her and perhaps she can hear me." Martin asked.

"Of course. Just put on the mask and gown before you go in." cautioned the doctor.

Martin stood beside Kate's bed and prayed fervently that somehow he could reach this woman. He had little understanding of the McDaniel family and though he had his suspicions, he had never come to terms with them. It seemed so outrageous and medieval in his mind. He preached about the occult and warned his people to stay as far away as possible to anything resembling it. It was dangerous to all... not just the teenagers.

The burns on Kate's face and arms were quite severe and she was barely recognizable. Her face was charred and filled with fluid giving her a ghastly appearance. He leaned close to her ear and began to pray. He was taken aback when she turned rigid and tried to move her head away from the sound of his voice.

"It's okay Kate. No one is going to harm you. Please listen to me."

"No, no, no!" she whimpered.

"Kate, you can't win. Do you hear me? No matter what you have thought to be true, you cannot win! It is impossible! Please allow me to tell you the truth." He whispered.

"No, no, no!" she cried softly. Suddenly, her monitor began beeping and the nurse came running.

"I'm sorry, but you need to go now. She needs to rest." Martin nodded and leaned close once more.

"Kate, I will be back to see you and together we are going to see you through this!" He stated firmly.

The next day Martin and John decided to pay the McDaniel men a visit. Martin was appalled that neither of them had been back to visit Kate. The doctor had been frantically trying to reach Colten as it was clear, Kate must have surgery to repair her hand and forearm. Gangrene was setting in, and it was unclear whether the skilled doctors would be able to save the affected areas.

"If you have any idea how to contact her husband, it is imperative that we find him. She is in no condition to sign for herself and I will operate without signature if it comes to life and death. However, it is best to have a cooperative family with something this drastic."

Prompted by the doctor's concern, John and Martin rode in silence to the McDaniel residence. Colten had not found work, so they felt assured he would be home. Mac had not come to school according to Martin's son, Chad.

"Colten, it's the Pastor, are you home?" Martin shouted when no one came to the door.

"I'm going to check the garage for a car." John said as he peered through the small glass windows.

"Nope, no car." He announced.

"You think they're on their way to the hospital?" Martin asked.

"Don't think so, Preacher." Martin watched John take a small tool from his fingernail clippers, and push it into the garage door lock. He turned the knob as if he had his own key.

"I think this is breaking and entering, John."

"Not if we didn't come to steal." John laughed.

"Not sure the police will buy that." Martin smiled. He was uncomfortable with the scene, but they were desperate to find Colten.

"Well, will you look at this!" John opened the kitchen door that led to the garage and whistled.

"Looks like they've been busy guys!" said Martin as they surveyed the interior of the house. Everything was gone. The cabinets had been emptied and there were only a few remnants of furniture scattered here and there.

"I can't believe they left! How could they do that to their own wife and mother?" said Martin.

"I know how heartless it is, but tragically, I've seen this before.

Sometimes it's because loved ones don't know how to deal with it. But I think it's a different story with the McDaniel's." Martin furrowed his brow. He had not dealt with this before, at least not on this level.

"Did you see the look on Colten's face when he saw his wife?" John asked.

"To tell you the truth, I was talking to the doctor so I didn't see his reaction. I know they left in a hurry."

"Colten looked angry and disgusted. You know, I don't believe these people have deep feelings for each other. I can't imagine he wants anything to do with a woman who is less than beautiful and nothing to do with a woman who has lost most of her arm." Martin couldn't argue but it seemed so calloused that he had a difficult time with the concept.

"I wonder where they're headed?" said Martin as he opened an empty kitchen drawer.

"Look at this, Pastor." John found a scribbled note left on the coffee table. There was a faint phone number and a Massachusetts address.

"You suppose it's a relative?"

"Let's call it and find out." Martin dialed the number and a young man answered.

"Hello, I am trying to locate Colten McDaniel and wondered if he might be headed your way." Martin wished he had given his conversation more thought before dialing.

"Who is this and why are you asking?" came the curt reply.

"I am a friend of his and I need to speak to him."

"Who is this?" Martin was sure the man was about to hang up.

"I am his Pastor and..." John shook his head knowing it was a mistake.

"Don't ever call this number again." the phone banged in his ear.

"That was stupid of me! I should have known better than to identify myself that way!" Martin chided himself.

"You probably weren't going to get any information anyway. Maybe we can look up the address and see who lives there." Martin folded the paper and stuck it in his pocket. It would have to wait. He needed to get back to the hospital and check on Kate.

John offered to ride along as his shift would begin soon and he also wanted to lend support to Martin as he spoke to the doctor about this strange situation. They wasted no time getting to the ICU unit and asked specifically for Kate's attending physician.

"Dr. Chase is in surgery, but should be able to speak with you in a couple of hours." The nurse checked his schedule and made a note of Martin's request.

"Would it be all right if we peaked in on Kate McDaniel?" John asked.

"Oh, she's not in there. As a matter of fact, Dr. Chase is performing her surgery as we speak. He just couldn't wait any longer. Her temperature was rising to a dangerous level and if he waited, she could lose the entire arm." Martin sighed heavily. He decided to call Christine and have her meet him. He just wanted to hold her in his arms and let her know that if she were to go through a car windshield and scar her beautiful face, he would still love her to the debts of his soul. He thanked God again for placing her in his life.

There was nothing to do but wait... and pray. They prayed first of all for Kate's survival. Martin also prayed for wisdom as he would be the one to tell Kate her family had forsaken her. Christine shed angry tears as Martin repeated the sad story of Colten's departure as his wife's life weighed in the balances.

It was obvious; the McDaniel family was an illusion... nothing but smoke and mirrors! They fooled just about everyone in the church. The appeared polished, educated, and talented and it seemed many were vying for position to be close to this gregarious clan.

"It's hard to believe this woman set fire to the church not once but twice! How will she survive the news?" said Christine.

"The news about her family or about her condition?" He didn't know which would be more devastating.

Kate came through the operation without losing her entire arm. Skin grafts from Kate's thighs were challenging. They needed enough skin to apply to her cheek and neck and nose. Her legs and arm were not as damaged and would probably heal with moderate scarring.

Martin peaked in on her and soon John and Christine joined him. They held hands around her bed and prayed fervently for her. The more they prayed, the more agitated Kate seemed to become.

"Do you think she knows we are here?" Christine asked.

"No, she's still under the anesthetic. But I think we are dealing with other outside forces who do not want us here." That was the kind of talk that gave Christine shivers. She knew very well that there was a dark side who hated all those who loved the Lord, but most people never give it much thought.

Christine continued to shake her bandaged head and made small incoherent, muffled sounds as they prayed. It was heartbreaking to see the once beautiful woman wrapped up like a mummy.

"I wonder what's going through her mind?" asked John. But he too would shiver if he were able to read her thoughts, for Kate was terrified. She dreamt of seeing herself before a mirror and watched her face become distorted as her arms and legs became as those of an insect. She cried as the image began to disintegrate before her.

"You are no longer useful. You have no service to perform. You will die alone and in great agony!" laughed the hideous voice.

Chapter 19 *View Two*

"I'm waiting...where are they????" Portentous screamed! Bombastic shuddered as he thought of his fate. He had been confident he could do a better job than Ominous. But that was the problem with all the contenders. PRIDE! He knew the fate of Ominous and was sure he would follow if he did not have the right answers.

"In time, Portentous. Kate is in the hospital with deadly wounds."

"Deadly wounds? Explain yourself!" Portentous breathed deeply and exhaled a rancid breath.

"I can't wait until she sees herself! You won't want to miss it! She is burned beyond recognition! Her entire arm and legs have been burned away. Even her luscious hair has been scorched and mutilated." Portentous gave him a quizzical look. There were lies mixed with truth, as always.

"It will cost you if you are lying to me!!"

"Perhaps I am being overdramatic, but I assure you, Kate will be devastated the first time she takes a look at herself. She is quite hideous! Completely disfigured!" Comparatively speaking, it was the truth.

"But if she thinks her burns are severe and painful, she has nothing on earth to compare to what awaits her." They both doubled over in ghastly laughter.

"I have driven her family away, but they won't get far. I have sent them to the "Watcher" in Massachusetts. He will abuse them and send them to us in due season." Again gruesome laughter filled the air.

"Ah, if only we had more of them. The "Watcher" you sent them to is extremely useful. He appears to be an educated business man with wealth, prestige and just enough fame to keep his doors busy with those on their final journey." The Watchers were the most influential people in the world who had long ago given themselves over to the darkness that loomed before them. Those like Portentous and Bombastic controlled their every move. The bargain they made allowed them to own most of the earth's treasure. When anyone snooped too closely, those that might want to expose their findings could never prove them and were eventually considered 'conspiracy' theorists. Those brave souls were often left in dire straits as the Watchers owned the media and publicly turned their bravery against them. Many were missing, or proven frauds with false documentation. This method sent out a warning to others before they became a problem.

"I want a full report once they get to Massachusetts. I want every detail! They loved hearing each horrific step the Watcher used. They were brutal and clever and very resourceful. They had a knack for making people suffer beyond the original scope Portentous could ever hope for. They were masterful and useful and their eternity would no doubt be at the very bottom of the abyss.

"I told him to take his time as I knew you would be pleased to hear each aspect." Portentous nodded his rare approval.

"I can't wait to hear the report! Perhaps I will schedule some time to attend as the Watcher torments them. He is quite remarkable for someone who is not actually ... one of us!" He grinned evilly recalling some of those tortuous moments.

"Yes, by the time he sends them to us, we will barely recognize them at all!" Bombastic agreed.

"Bring Kate McDaniel to us... it is time for her to pay her dues!" smiled Portentous.

"Can't we watch her suffer for a while?" Bombastic asked.

"Why? Are you so *&#@ Stupid that you don't realize the agony she is in pales compared to her eternal torment?" Portentous snarled.

"No, of course not! I was only thinking of that preacher and his family. They will mourn her passing and torture themselves that they allowed her to pass without reaching her." Portentous rubbed his chin. He hadn't thought of that.

"I will allow it, but beware! If for any reason that preacher or John Dunbar persuades her to join them with the Enemy... Your head will roll!!!! Now get out of my sight and create havoc!"

Chapter 20 View One

Vontrice walked slowly to work. She was thankful to find such a wonderful job and for the first time, realized that the Lord had allowed her to land secure this position. She had a great relationship with Rebecca, who was teaching her how to buy, and price items for her store, while she continued to mentor her in displaying each piece. She prayed that she would be instrumental in leading Rebecca to the Saviour, though she knew it would be challenging. Rebecca showed no interest whatsoever in spiritual things nor did she have any desire to hear.

One night after a late closing, Rebecca surprised her by bringing out two champagne glasses and filling them to the brim. She also cut some fresh bread and gouda cheese and after setting the tray before Vontrice, plopped down on the sofa and kicked off her shoes.

"Help yourself, you deserve it." smiled Rebecca. Vontrice was overwhelmed. She had already received two raises in the short time she was employed and had never been treated so well by any employer... especially a woman.

As they relaxed together they began sharing their lives with each other. The champagne loosened their tongues more than usual and at some point Vontrice asked her how she had become a widow.

"Oh honey, I was glad to be rid of him. I mean, I certainly didn't want him to die in a car accident, and I didn't do a dance at the funeral, but I must admit, I haven't shed a tear either." She laughed softly. Vontrice had no idea what her response should be. She had never seen anyone with such a glib attitude for a deceased partner.

"Was he an artist?" she asked.

"Oh my no! He wouldn't know a piece of artwork from a door knob. He was more of an accountant. He paid the bills and little else." She sighed.

"But don't you worry about me! I've never been one to be lonely, if you know what I mean." She winked. Soon Vontrice was telling her about her many men and the two laughed together over their conquests.

"Looks like we have more in common that art! We both know how to get our way with men." Vontrice told her when she found the ad in the newspaper. She was hoping that *Art Works* was owned by a man as she would have a better chance for the positon. When she saw the beautiful owner, she didn't think she would be hired.

As the evening wore on, Rebecca told Vontrice about Glen Booth. They were still meeting each other on the sly and both of them enjoyed the relationship. Rebecca did not want another husband and didn't want him to divorce Norma. But the more she saw Glen the more possessive and jealous he became. He wanted her all to himself and she wondered how long it would be before she would have to end it. He was getting far too serious, and although it was a boost to her ego to have his full attention, she was growing tired of him.

"Seeing a married man is dangerous business." Vontrice warned.

"I'm not worried about his wife. She's a little mouse of a thing. I don't know what ever attracted Glen to the woman in the first place."

"She doesn't have to be big to carry a gun!" said Vontrice. Rebecca laughed uncomfortably. It was difficult to imagine Norma wielding a gun.

"They have a teenage son. He's probably more of a threat. If he found out he might come gunning for me." She smiled.

"More likely, he'll shoot his father for breaking his mother's heart." Anthony would be broken hearted if he caught his father stepping out on his mother, but both were willing to take a chance… for now.

Vontrice shook her head. She had no idea how to begin a spiritual conversation with her boss. Would she be fired? Would Rebecca no longer want her around? And if she was to begin a conversation... what would she say? She knew little about the Bible and would not be able to answer any of her questions if she happened to show an interest.

She decided to ask John how to proceed when they met next week. It was obvious he wanted to begin a new relationship with her and she couldn't be happier. He was the man of her dreams and she knew in her heart he loved her. She thanked the Lord he had not found another woman and that his patience paid off. She laughed to herself when she thought of the date he planned. He was bringing over several small books that would help her in her daily walk and also a reference Bible to help her in her daily reading.

As she drew near her place of employment, Rebecca motioned for her to hurry. It appeared she was receiving a large delivery and it always rattled her a bit. She was always fearful that one of her art pieces would get broken by the bumbling hands of the delivery men. Everything was insured, but some things were priceless and irreplaceable.

"I'm so glad you're early, Vontrice. These fools are plopping things down as if they are sacks of potatoes!" she complained. Vontrice hurried into the shop and immediately began helping.

"Please set things down on the carpet over there and we will open the boxes." Vontrice immediately took charge and Rebecca was relieved. She should have thought of that herself as the delivery men set boxes on the coffee tables and desks. At least the soft carpeting would help cushion the pieces should they fall over.

"What is all this?" Vontrice was usually in the know when Rebecca bought new art pieces.

"Can you believe that the *Artful Connection* went out of business?" Rebecca announced happily. Vontrice had visited the establishment a few times and felt sorry for the owner. Mr. Gorsuch was getting older and no one seemed to know much about the man. The store was starting to look pretty run down and was not in the best part of town.

"I practically stole the merchandise from him!" she giggled.

"I paid pennies on the dollar, especially after I heard he was in financial difficulty with doctor bills stacking up." There was a time Vontrice would have celebrated with her, but today she felt sorry for the poor man trying to make a living. She made a mental note to pay him a visit. Maybe John could go with her. That would be best.

"Aren't you proud of me?" Rebecca couldn't figure out what was going on with Vontrice. She thought she would be clapping with excitement! Maybe she was having men problems. That could take the smile off any woman's face! It reminded her she was going to have to end it with Glen. Enough was enough! He was taking more and more chances to see her and as far as she was concerned, the affair had run its course. It had lost most of its excitement and was no longer fun, besides Rebecca had far too many offers to settle down with Glen Booth.

"You are quite the business woman, for sure! No one holds a candle to you!" Vontrice's voice broke her reverie and Rebecca smiled at the remark.

"We are going to be rich one day, Vontrice! You and I make quite a team. Just look at this place." She swept her arm across the room as she spoke.

"Between my purchases and your displays... there is no stopping us!"

"Yes, we are good together." Again there was no real enthusiasm in her voice and it troubled Rebecca. They had become good friends over the past few months and they had learned to depend and trust each other.

"Okay, spill it... what's going on? Are you having boyfriend troubles?" Rebecca asked.

"No, nothing like that."

"Well, something isn't right. You know you can tell me, Vontrice." She took her hand and led her to the small sofa nestled between two antique floor lamps.

"Are you sick?" she tried.

"No, I'm fine, really!

"You've been acting strangely for the few several weeks and I thought by now you might share whatever it is, but you haven't. You know I don't like to pry, but we're friends, Vontrice." She sounded a bit hurt and Vontrice had no idea what to say.

"Rebecca, I'm so thankful to be working here with you. You know a lot about antiques and have taught me so much! I just hope someday I will be able to return the favor!" Rebecca gave her a hug for her kind words.

"Vontrice, you have become invaluable to me. You don't owe me anything!" Satisfied that she had discovered the reason for her friend's mood, she quickly jumped off the couch to get them a drink.

"Let's toast to our continued success." Before she could run to the kitchenette and return with champagne, Vontrice called after her.

"Nothing for me, please!"

"Nonsense, you know I don't like to drink alone." Rebecca returned quickly with two champagne glasses and set them on the table before them. Vontrice prayed silently that she would know how to handle the situation, but she was uncertain. She didn't want to offend Rebecca but she didn't feel comfortable drinking alcohol with her boss.

"This is a lovely piece." Vontrice reached into one of the boxes and lifted out a beautiful crystal vase.

"Yes, it's worth a fortune! Even old Mr. Gorsuch had no idea what a treasure he had!" she laughed. Vontrice stood with the vase in her hand and began walking around the store. She wanted to distance herself from the champagne glass and also from Rebecca for fear she could see her displeasure.

"I think we should display it in the front window. It will attract attention and people will know we truly have the finest pieces money can buy."

"Excellent idea! I think there are a few other pieces in one of the boxes that will compliment it nicely." Rebecca added.

Soon they were both busy opening the delicate boxes and searching for the right location to exhibit them. Vontrice had mixed emotions each time she unwrapped an item. She was excited for Rebecca and knew the store would benefit from these remarkable pieces, but her heart was heavy for Mr. Gorsuch. He was a nice man who also had an eye for antiques.

Soon the store was bustling with people and Vontrice used the opportunity to take her untouched champagne glass to the kitchen and dump the contents. She knew it was a deceiving act, but it was the best she could figure out for the moment.

She hurried back quickly and began speaking to a potential buyer. No longer did she use her female persuasion to push the middle aged man into a sale, though she was certain it would take very little manipulation.

"I have to run an errand, Vontrice. Lock up if you have to leave the store." Rebecca called after her. Generally, they took turns leaving the store. Sometimes they would order lunch or one of them picked up lunch for both. On other occasions, if either had a lunch date, the other would stay behind. Rebecca appeared a bit flushed but left in such a hurry, there could be no prior discussion.

When the store was quiet, Vontrice took the small Bible John had given her and began thumbing through the pages. She had no idea where to start. He had mentioned starting with the gospels, but she felt like she was starting a novel in the middle and wasn't sure if that was the best place to begin. Eventually, she began in Genesis and shook her head as she read the account of Adam and Eve.

"I always thought it was a fairy tale!" she smiled to herself. In just a few short chapters she had plenty of questions. Why did the devil appear to Eve and not to Adam? Hmmm, maybe it took the devil to deceive a woman and only a woman to deceive a man! That seemed accurate.

She glanced at her watch and wondered what was keeping Rebecca. It wasn't like her to be gone for any length of time on such short notice. She didn't have children and her husband was deceased. She never spoke of siblings or parents so it didn't seem likely a family member called her unexpectedly. Her cell phone broke her reverie.

"Hi Vontrice, sorry to rush out like that." said Rebecca.

"Is everything okay?"

"It will be soon. I didn't have time to tell you, but Glen called and wanted to meet. He said it was important so I thought I better meet him before he did anything foolish."

"I can't believe I've been sitting here for over an hour and he hasn't showed up!"

"He hasn't called the shop, has he?" It wasn't likely, but anything was possible. She no longer trusted his judgment as he had broken many of the established rules over the last few months.

"Oh, he just pulled in. I'll call you later." Vontrice held the dead phone to her ear and shook her head. She worried about Rebecca's relationship with Glen. She knew it was a dangerous one.

"Glen Booth! I have been waiting for you for nearly an hour! What on earth has gotten into you?!" He jumped out of the car and in quick strides was standing before her with an angry face. He grabbed her roughly which was completely out of character for him.

"Nobody makes a fool out of Glen Booth!" he snapped as he pulled her within inches of his foul breath.

"Are you out of your mind? What's gotten into you?" Rebecca did her best to control the fear that was gripping her heart. It was obvious, he had been drinking and his slurred speech and blurry eyes only increased her anxiety.

"You really had me fooled, I'll give ya that!" he scoffed.

"I have no idea what you're talking about, but I am ending this conversation…and the relationship as well! I have no intention of seeing a drunk. It's over Glen." She began heading back to her car but he grabbed her from behind.

"It's over when I say it's over! I decide!" he slapped her hard and she realized she needed to change tactics before he became more brutal. She had never seen this side of him.

"I saw you with that good looking young man a couple of days ago."

"What are you talking about? She didn't have a clue.

"Don't deny it, Rebecca. I saw you give him a big hug and he drove away in a Mercedes! You were right on main street!" he growled.

"Glen, that was my accountant! He figured a way to save me some fees in my antique purchases and I gave him a friendly hug."

"You've read too much into it. He's been my accountant for several years and we are just friends!" She didn't dare tell him she had seen him for a few months before he got married. She considered it a harmless affair and they both were agreeable to end it.

To her surprise, he kissed her hand and closed his eyes, pressing her hand firmly on his cheek.

"I'm sorry! I want things to be good between us, Rebecca. The way they were when we first met. I want to be the *only* man in your life. I can't bear to think of you with other men." He whimpered.

"But I allow you to be with another woman, Glen. I never have given you a problem about your wife. I know we share you... and it's okay!" she said gently.

"I'll divorce her if you will marry me." He pleaded.

"Now, Glen, we've been over this before. I haven't been a widow for very long and I certainly am not looking for another husband." Glen glared at her and once again his entire demeanor changed.

"What exactly *are* you looking for?" he growled.

"I am looking for someone I enjoy and who I can care about."

"But not enough to marry them!" he scoffed.

"I was unhappily married... you are unhappily married. Why would either of us want to do that again? Isn't it better this way?" she tried.

"Better for you! I sneak around and lie to my wife while you can just come and go as you please. We wouldn't have to get married right away. If I were free, we could spend more time together. Maybe we could travel..."

"You have a teenaged son, Glen. You don't want to upset his life." She pulled out all the stops. She did not want him to leave his family.

"Between alimony and child support, you wouldn't have money to travel to the next town! Be reasonable. This way, you have the best of both worlds."

"You know what I think? I think you wouldn't want me around that much. I think you like the freedom of seeing me and anyone else you choose." It was far too dangerous to agree. She knew she needed to calm him down.

"I'll tell you what. Let's get together this weekend at my place and we'll go somewhere special for the weekend. How does that sound?"

"Really, Rebecca?" he sounded like a pitiful school boy and it was terribly annoying to her.

"Of course! I'll find a special getaway and we'll talk everything through and see what makes sense." She patted his cheek like a little boy.

"I hope we can do more than talk!" he said coyly.

"We always do!" she smiled through gritted teeth. She couldn't wait to dump him.

"Now, I need to get back to work. Call me on Friday and I'll have all the details worked out by then." She was already planning her excuse and would use Vontrice if she needed someone to verify her story. He pulled her into his arms and gave her a passionate kiss. She did her best to reciprocate.

"Just one more thing." he said.

"Whether you marry me or not, *we* are a couple. I will not tolerate you seeing anyone else."

"Now Glen, we've been all over this and..." to her surprise, he pulled a hunting knife out of his pocket.

"You are MY woman! I will not tolerate cheating!" She stood as still as a statue as the point of his knife touched her chin.

"MY woman... or no one's! I assure you, you don't ever want to forget that!" He threw the knife into the backseat of his car and patted her on the backside with a broad smile.

"See you this weekend." He drove away and she stood watching him for several minutes. She didn't trust her legs as she trembled with fear. She gingerly touched her chin and found blood on the tip of her finger. There was no doubt he meant business. She drug her wobbly body to her vehicle and fought back tears as she slid behind the wheel.

Slowly she pulled into the highway and began driving back to the shop. She shuddered as she recalled the look in his eyes. She beat her fist against the steering wheel.

"What a fool I am!" she chided herself. She should have known better. Glen had shared with her that though he had never actually hit his wife, he pushed her around from time to time. She was too stupid to understand he was giving her a warning.

She decided to stop off for a drink before she returned to work and one of her favorite places was along the way. The *Quick Stop* was well known for those who needed a quick drink on the way home from work. The customers were mostly regulars and rarely made the stop a 'quick' one.

The bartender was young and quite the ladies' man. He did his homework on all the regulars and when he realized Rebecca owned an antique shop he treated her royalty. He plied her with liquor, often at no charge. She was completely oblivious to his advances and believed he was genuinely interested in her.

"Ah, my favorite guest!" he cooed as she entered the dark establishment. Quickly he poured her favorite drink and slid it into her waiting hand.

"Thank you, Rigo." She smiled. Rodrigo was a handsome Latino with an eye for the ladies.

"What a pleasure to have you here so early in the day."

"I can't stay long but I sure needed a little pick me up before I return to work." Rigo frowned playfully.

"I was hoping you came because you couldn't stand to be away from me for another moment." He took her hand in his and she made no effort to remove it.

"I think you are in need of more than a drink. Perhaps Rigo can make those frown lines disappear." He offered. She giggled like a school girl and he continued his flirtation.

"Why don't you come back when I get off work? I know a cozy place where we can relax and... uh... unwind." She laughed at his attempt to seduce her. She remembered well the last time they spent time together. It was shortly after she began seeing Rigo that she decided to end things with Glen.

"Maybe it is exactly what I need." She said thoughtfully. Rigo glanced at his watch and hoped she would leave soon. He couldn't take a chance the females in his life would discover each other. He was meeting another middle aged woman who was quite wealthy and didn't mind throwing some of the wealth his way. He was able to buy himself a sail boat and in another few months would quit working in the bar altogether. But first he would see how much Rebecca was willing to spend on him.

He smiled to himself and applauded his manhood. How many men could keep this many woman happy?

"Why don't you get back to your business so you can finish early and we can meet later?" he tried. The last thing he needed was for Loretta to catch him holding hands with Rebecca.

"When do you get off work?" asked Rebecca in a sultry voice.

"I'll be done by 4:00 and we'll have the rest of the night. How does that sound?"

"Sounds perfect! I think it's exactly what I need." She smacked her empty glass on the bar and he leaned forward and gave her a quick kiss.

"Later lovely lady!" he whispered in her ear. Rebecca walked out of the bar feeling more like her old self. She held the door for a well-dressed middle aged woman who swaggered in like she owned the place. Rigo held his breath as the women crossed paths, and gave a sigh of relief once Rebecca was out of the parking lot.

Rebecca glanced at herself in the mirror. There was no mark on her cheek from Glen's hateful slap though the spot under her chin was still tender where the point of the knife penetrated her skin. No doubt she needed to get of this man. She was not quite sure how but she was definitely going to do so.

Rigo was in his late twenties to early thirties and was an expert with women. He took time to tell her repeatedly how beautiful she was and how privileged he was to be with her. He never told her he loved her nor did he tell her he was involved with anyone else, though it never crossed her mind that he could be. After all, he seemed completely taken with her and told her she was all he could think about.

Perhaps she could tell him of her dilemma with Glen. He might be able to help her, but she hated to let him know that she was seeing anyone else. She would never want to hurt him and was sure he would be devastated to know she was not seeing him exclusively.

By the time she returned to the shop, she was feeling like her old self again. She was pleased that Vontrice had been busy unwrapping and displaying the new merchandise. She should be able to leave work at a decent time and run into Rigo's waiting arms.

"Is everything okay?" Vontrice was concerned as she looked intently at her boss.

"Nothing I can't handle." When Vontrice continued to stare she rolled her eyes.

"Really, Vontrice! I am perfectly capable of taking care of myself." She sounded miffed. She nodded quickly and got back to work.

"I'm sorry... I met Glen and it didn't go well. End of story." She hated being so evasive, but she didn't intend to tell anyone what had just taken place... not even Vontrice.

"Maybe it's time to stop seeing him."

"You're absolutely right about that! I don't intend to ever see him again!" The words sounded good as soon as they left her mouth and she decided right then to never meet with him again.

"Good for you!" said Vontrice sincerely. It would be one less obstacle to cross once she began to speak to her about the Lord.

They worked in comfortable silence each knowing their part and were like a well- oiled machine. When the clock chimed four, Rebecca ran to the mirror and applied fresh make up.

"See you tomorrow. Have a good evening!" she sang as she patted her hair and smoothed her skirt. Vontrice stood motionless watching her and knew in her heart she was meeting a man. Obviously, she was not meeting Glen, but she knew somewhere out there a man was waiting for her.

Rebecca wasted no time calling Rigo the moment she was in the parking lot. It was time to find out how important their relationship was to him. Would he be upset to learn she had been seeing another man? Would he be willing to help her get rid of him?

She felt like a mobster as she thought of it. She didn't actually intend to harm him. She only wanted him out of her life.

Rigo gave her an address in an affluent area and she raced to get there. She had never been in this particular neighborhood and as she pulled into the driveway, she wondered if this was his home. He was waiting with a drink in his hand and a towel around his waist.

"There is a hot tub on the porch. I brought a towel for you as well." He kissed her neck and she was excited that he wasted no time.

"Sounds heavenly!" she sighed.

"First the hot tub, then I plan a massage that will relax every muscle." He smiled.

"You are the best, Rigo! The very best!"

"We haven't even discussed the 'best' yet. That is after the massage!" He teased. By the time she reached the hot tub, her clothing was strewn everywhere. Oddly, Rigo picked up each piece and put it on a chair with her shoes tucked underneath.

They stayed in the hot tub until their skin began to prune and then he whisked her out and onto a massage table. His gentle, firm hands smoothed across her neck and back and worked their way down her arms and legs. She was like putty and enjoyed every minute. Soon he carried her to the large bedroom a few feet from the massage table.

She wanted to tell him she loved him, but the words never came from either of them. She had rarely said the words to anyone, though her husband expected to hear them and after Glen stated his love for her, he expected to hear her say them back.

As she lay in Rigo's arms, she began to think of her dilemma with Glen. She was never going to see him again, though she was fearful and hesitant to end the relationship. Would he come to her place of business and get violent? Would he be watching for her as she left work and threaten her life? She shuddered at the thought of his sharp hunting knife piercing her chin.

"What is wrong, Rebecca? Have I done something to make you uncomfortable?"

"Of course not. You are just about perfect!" she kissed him passionately.

"You know you can confide in me." He hoped she was not

Karen Fertig

experiencing financial problems as he had already invested a great deal into this woman hoping for a return!

"Promise you won't be upset with me?" She held his hand tightly as she spoke. He held his breath. There were only two concerns. Either she had no money, or she was sick. As long as she was not contagiously sick, he was fine.

"Before I began seeing you, I was seeing another man." He fought to keep from laughing. Did she actually think he would care? He must be a better actor than he gave himself credit for.

"I see" he feigned hurt.

"He means nothing to me." Rigo frowned as an idea popped into his head.

"Perhaps I mean nothing as well." He said slowly with false emotion.

"That's not true! I care deeply about you, Rigo. I look forward to every rendezvous."

"I am but a poor man working at a bar. I offer you nothing but my heart." He knew it was an award winning performance and hoped it would pay off.

"I brought you to this house so you would not see my humble abode." She would have a coronary if she knew it was Loretta's home. She had to fly to Arizona on business and gave him a key to take care of her cat. He made sure she arrived at her destination before contacting Rebecca.

"You should have a home like this!" Rebecca kissed his cheek and hugged him to herself.

"You do not live in a home like this with bartenders' wages." Rebecca was also formulating a plan.

"Perhaps we can help each other." Rigo couldn't believe his luck. She seemed to be taking the bait wholeheartedly.

"We both seem to have a problem. You are obviously living well below your means. You are a smart young man with a bright future. You just need a nudge here and there." He nodded in approval and wondered what her money was about to do for him.

"As I said, I also have a problem. I want *you* to make it go

292

away." He was puzzled. He was a bartender and a ladies man… not a hit man!

"What are you asking me to do?" She saw the concern on his face and realized how her statement must sound.

"Don't look so worried! I am not asking you to kill anyone!" she laughed.

"No, what I am asking is that you pay Glen Booth a visit and tell him he needs to stop pestering me." He didn't like it. The last thing he wanted was an altercation with another man over a woman he cared nothing for.

"It will be fine, Rigo. He is an ant and you are a giant! He will not fight you. I assure you he is a coward."

"He does not have to be a big man if he carries a weapon." Rebecca hid her concern as she didn't want to scare Rigo. She hoped he was strong enough to fight Glen even if he was still brandishing a knife. He tried a new tactic

"You know, I could get myself killed, Rebecca. Any man who is involved with you will not give up easily. He may prefer to die rather than to give you up."

"That's not going to happen! Tell you what. You do this for me and I will set you up in a house that is every bit as beautiful as this one." Rebecca had quite a large savings and knew her recent antique purchases would bring three or four times the money she paid for them. She enjoyed living in the suite over her place of business. It met all her needs and she would rather travel than care for a house. After Chuck died, she did some renovations to make the suite more to her liking. She got rid of anything that reminded her of her late husband. In her opinion, he had the taste of a billy goat and despised his plywood rifle cabinet and shelves with endless ball caps he had collected over the years. She was not dumb enough to put the house in Rigo's name, but she would allow him to live there rent free. That should be enough… for now.

"Where would I find this Glen Booth?" Perhaps he could lie to her and never actually meet this man.

"He would like to meet me this weekend, but I will have *you* meet him instead. Just tell him that you are a private investigator that his wife hired and if he continues to see me, she will sue the pants off him." She laughed.

"Where are you to meet him?"

"I haven't told him a place yet."

"Why don't you tell him to meet you at the bar? I am not working this weekend and will meet him outside in the parking lot." Rebecca agreed and gave him a full description of Glen and his vehicle.

"What if he confronts his wife?"

"She will deny any knowledge of course." For an instant, Rebecca nearly called the whole thing off. What if he became violent with her? Could she live with herself knowing he had harmed her?

"Make sure you let him know that if his wife has so much as a bruise, he will go to jail!" Rigo nodded but was becoming more uneasy all the time. So, Rebecca knew the man he was to meet was a man of violence and was sending him to see him anyway. What else was she keeping from him?

Plans were tentatively made for Rigo to wait for Glen in the parking lot around 1:00 on Saturday. He was to carry a briefcase and download a restraining order document or reasonable facsimile as he needed to appear genuine!

"Tell him if he tries to contact me, he will get another visit from you and he will freeze like a deer in the headlights." She laughed. Rigo frowned. He didn't like it but if she kept her end of the bargain, he was willing to speak to Glen and hopefully, frighten him away.

Chapter 20 *View Two*

Bombastic hid behind two gigantic cinder blocks hoping he could escape Portentous' wrath. Word had spread that there were too many in his charge, who had been given sanctions but did not produce as they had promised. Portentous had been flogged repeatedly for his lack of productivity. Once again he had elevated the wrong one. Bombastic was full of unfulfilled promises and he would now face the same fate as Ominous. Most entering the abyss were immediately in torments awaiting their final sentence and destination. Not that anyone would ever be coming out of this horrific place. That had already been determined when they closed their eyes in death. There were no escape routes, no reconsideration, and there would be no pleading. Anyone who did not belong to their Enemy in life would not find Him in death. The rejected payment for their sinful soul could not be bartered or renegotiated.

On earth, Portentous had been one of the "Watchers" and was given special consideration for a short time. He trained and was given charge of many minions... for the moment. Somewhere deep inside he knew he had made the wrong decision, but there was no turning back now. He wanted to doom as many as possible but if the truth were known, he feared that if too many came at once, the Enemy would decide to return for His own and set things in motion that would lead to his final destruction. In time, he knew the Enemy would call out those who were His blood bought Bride. He would reign for a thousand years... but then... after the reign came to an end... Portentous would stand before the Almighty and his fate would be final and sealed for all eternity! He quaked in fear and immediately dismissed the thought. He never allowed his mind to rest there, and he did all that was in his power to make sure every person on earth never thought about such things.

Now he was on a rampage. His hate increased as he thought of the Enemy. He must doom as many as possible and bellowed for those in his charge to assemble themselves! Today, he would throw more into the deep abyss and let the rest watch in fear and trepidation! Those who hadn't produced would find themselves sizzling in torments and the rest would step things up!

Bombastic wanted desperately to bring Kate McDaniel and her family to Portentous. Though the Parker family as well as Glen Booth and Rebecca Benson were his assignments, the McDaniel family would be the bigger victory. Their doom would be applauded and every minion would want to be there to 'welcome' them. He salivated as he thought of the monstrous things each demon would do to them before sending them to the abyss. Mortals were not capable of administrating the indescribable torment that came with complete evil! Neither Hitler nor Nero could contrive such torture and they were masters on an earthly scale!

He shook with fear wondering if Portentous knew about Vontrice. It was easy to lose interest with those that loved their sinful lifestyle. She loved John Dunbar, yet she loved her sin more. She was of no real interest to him in that condition. She had no effect on those around her and he witnessed the argument that left John heartbroken as he discovered she had no interest in coming to the Enemy.

Portentous had warned them of becoming complacent. He was right! He didn't notice her quiet entrance that fateful Sunday morning when she listened to John's preaching and came forward. He was far too busy running through the auditorium causing distraction everywhere. He whispered thoughts into the minds of those he thought might be listening. He created doubt after each point of John's sermon. When Kate set fire to the downstairs classroom, he thought the people would begin pouring out of the church in fear. As usual, he underestimated that Blasted Book and the Power of the Enemy. He would pay dearly for it!

He could bring Colten and young Mac to the abyss. He would only need to nudge the Watcher to make it happen, but he knew it wouldn't be enough. He had nothing to report that would change his fate. There was only one thing left to do. LIE! Hmmm... he would tell Portentous that Lisa was pregnant! Perhaps he would expand the lie by telling them she did not know the father. Yes, he liked that! Was it Mac or Anthony? He laughed in spite of himself. Perhaps he could add a feather to his cap if he could cause the meeting between Rigo and Glen to go awry. If he could get Rebecca to attend the meeting, he might persuade Glen to kill them both! Ah yes... things could take a favorable turn!

Chapter 21 View One

Vontrice met John for dinner and he was amazed as she fired Biblical questions between each mouthful. He fought back joyful tears, as he listened to her enthusiasm. She had no embarrassment perching her Bible between them and pointing out verses that troubled her.

"I promise to answer your questions to the best of my ability, but you need to slow down! Your firing them at me too fast, girl!" he said lightheartedly.

"There was a time I thought they were fairy tales. I see things so different now." She said earnestly.

"That's because God gave you the light you were asking for to see the truth. He will give anyone the same light that wants it. Trouble is… most people don't want it. They want to be their own beginning and end and do what they please. They would like to think there will be no consequences to their choices. Sounds good on *this* side… unfortunately, it won't work out for them when they get to the other side."

"That's exactly how I feel! Like someone pulled open the shade and I can see clearly!" said Vontrice.

"I can't thank God enough." He said with a smile.

Along with her Bible questions, they talked about their day and their work. Both loved what they were doing. Vontrice told him how she wanted to witness to Rebecca but was not sure that was a good idea. She also told him about the champagne and how she had poured it down the sink.

"Eventually, she's going to catch on, Vontrice. Be ready with a compassionate answer. She may not be interested, but you can catch her attention and let her watch your changed life. Believe me, that speaks volumes to people."

"On one hand I feel like a different person, but I sure don't feel better than anyone else. I want to make a difference in lives... like you do!" John's lip trembled as she spoke. He loved her so much and was amazed at her transformation.

"You just be you... that will be enough. Pray before you open your mouth and make sure it is the Lord who is leading you. Don't try to get ahead of him in your zeal. He will tell you if you are the right person for the right time! I've seen it happen over and over. People mean well, but sometimes their zeal gets ahead of them. They want to see people come to know the Lord so bad, they push! But you don't push people into heaven and you don't badger them in. On the other hand, you can't get complacent and think things will just happen either." John smiled as he remembered his early days as a Christian. He wanted to win the world to Christ and though he didn't want to lose his zeal, he came to grips with the fact that things didn't work on his timetable.

He had such fear for his family that he began speaking and often preached to them every time they met. He gave them tracts, underlined Scripture he thought would help them to see their need and often became so distraught that they weren't listening that he pushed harder and harder. His heart was broken for them and his intentions were purely motivated. To his dismay, they became more resistant and no longer wanted to be alone with him. After shedding many tears and begging God to show him what to do, things began to change. He listened more and became more empathetic towards them. When they had problems, he told them he was praying for them and their needs and their hearts began to soften. No longer was he avoided but instead searched for especially in times of distress.

The day his youngest brother was killed in a fiery car crash, his entire family came to him for solace. John was very close to his brother and was crushed to learn the horrific details of his untimely death.

But John had shown his brother, Lloyd, how to become a Christian. It was John's first funeral and he was nervous and brokenhearted.

"I weep with you friends and family, but I do not weep without hope! You may think this funeral service is all about Lloyd. But it's really all about you! We no longer have a need to pray for Lloyd. Some of you may be angry with God for taking away our young brother. Oh family... if you could see him now! God has not been cruel to take my brother... God took him on ahead to his Saviour... to his reward! So you see, this is no longer about Lloyd. It is all about you! Perhaps Lloyd did not have the opportunity to share with each of you his wonderful salvation. But there is hope today! Today, those of you who have not come to the Saviour will have that opportunity.

You think Lloyd's life is over, but it is just beginning. My brother wants each of you to spend your eternity with him. You think there is nothing else you can do for Lloyd. Do you know there is? If you will come to the Saviour today, you will not only be reunited with my brother, and one day see him and the Lord who rescued you. But, your salvation will be added to my brother's reward! Can you imagine that? After you are gone out of this world you can still be racking up blessings and rewards? Think of those blessed preachers who have been gone for years. Each time someone reads or hears their sermons and comes to a saving knowledge of our Lord... they are racking up rewards! Now there's something to shout about!

There were several eulogies given and many pictures shared. John's missionary brother, Lincoln also spoke with grave concern for friends and family who might never see Lloyd again. It was their choice. It always comes down to choice!

John and Linc had earnestly prayed together for all those who would be attending Lloyd's funeral. Before an invitation was given, a beautiful young lady began walking up to the microphone. She had not asked to speak at the funeral, but all had been given the opportunity to pay tribute if they desired to do so. Linc handed her the mic.

"Some of you may not know me, but I am Gail Spicer. Lloyd and I dated all through college and planned to marry one day. I had many things in common with Lloyd. We both loved learning and had high aspirations of running our own company one day. I have a marketing degree and Lloyd has a degree in finance. We were a great match. I excelled in words, he in numbers. It was perfect!" she took a moment to wipe her eyes with a dainty handkerchief.

"You can imagine my surprise when we met at our favorite restaurant and he began… uh… preaching to me! I thought he was kidding. He was not. I thought it would pass. It didn't. I told him I was acquainted with many people who had gone through some kind of 'religious experience' and it always seemed to be temporary. In time, I found these same people back in the bar and living much as they did previously. Lloyd was not one of those people. Instead, his love for the Lord seemed to grow more with each passing day. He wanted me to know the Lord as he did. He wanted me to love the Lord as he did. I only wanted him to love me! I told him we were far too young to think about such things. There was too much life I wanted to experience. I didn't want anything to hold us back from anything we wanted to do. I argued with him and told him he was going to miss out on so many things if he continued on the path he had taken. He told me his biggest fear was what *I* was going to miss out on when my life ended! I thought he was making huge concessions. I thought he would be miserable as I thought of the things he chose to 'give up' but he wasn't. He told me he didn't give up anything. That was the difference. The more he drew near to the Lord, the less desire he had for the things that would not please Him." She began to weep and John put a comforting arm around her. John understood his brother's heartache as both of them let go of the women they loved.

"Today, I understand how fragile life is. I understand that death comes to all ages. My eyes have been lifted to a new plane and I want what my beloved Lloyd had in his life." With that, she handed Linc her microphone and knelt at the altar. John grabbed his Bible and ushered her into a quiet room where he could show her the Bible verses that led to new life in Christ.

"When so many of my family and friends came to know the Lord at Lloyd's funeral, I praised God how he used that tragedy to bring people to Himself! Oh, I still hurt when I think of Lloyd. He was a good brother and friend. He had a great sense of humor and was a bit of a practical joker too!" John laughed.

"What I'm trying to say is for you to keep learning and growing. Keep close the Word of God. Remember you are only a vessel to be used by the Master. Pray constantly for opportunities to speak to others about the Lord. Then don't let the opportunity slip away because you weren't tuned in!" he smiled.

"Never lose your zeal, Vontrice! Don't let this life take your eyes from the life to come."

"I used to get so irritated with you for constantly bringing up the Lord, but I have to admit, I always admired you. I just didn't think it was the life for me and to be honest, I didn't think I could do it. I had no idea that the Lord would make changes in my heart. I thought it would just be drudgery and a life without fun!" she admitted.

Tomorrow would be a very different day. John planned to meet Martin at the hospital to check in on Kate McDaniel. He prayed silently that she would be receptive to their visit.

It was disheartening to see her in such a state. Martin had tried in vain to contact Kate's husband. He had young Mac seemed to have vanished from the earth. John knew she would be devastated to find herself alone and could not believe her family could be so heartless.

Martin and Christine prayed fervently for the poor woman. The doctor believed with cosmetic surgery, he could repair her facial burns, but there wasn't enough undamaged skin left to replace burned areas on her arms and legs.

Martin confided his concern for her mental health. She was an extremely vain woman and was sure to believe her husband could not deal with her imperfections and left her. He also told John of her incessant babbling. It was if there was someone in the room speaking to her and the conversation was tortuous. At one point, she sat up in bed and tried to pull of IV's and bandages as she spoke of coming for her reward. Little did they know it was Bombastic appealing to her to end her life and come to him. He told her she would be given her 'just reward' for all she had accomplished.

The doctor said he would allow John and Martin to visit with her and promised she would be less sedated and able to talk with them. No one knew what to expect from her and it was quite worrisome.

Rebecca wished she could confide in Vontrice all that was to take place before the day came to an end. She felt nervous and jittery and needed a stiff drink, but she hated drinking alone and she was not about to offer Vontrice her fine champagne to see it poured down the drain! What had gotten into that girl… you would think she had some sort of religious experience! She laughed to herself, though she was not laughing the day she watched her friend pour an entire glass of her finest champagne into the sink. She was too shocked to speak.

She continued to check her watch, though only a few minutes had gone by since her last glance. She tapped it gently hoping somehow to speed up time! Rigo was to call the moment he finished speaking to Glen. What was taking so long?

Things were getting more and more out of her control and she didn't like it. Her phone rang incessantly and she decided not to answer. But that didn't seem like a good idea. She wanted him to be on schedule for their planned weekend together. She decided it would be better to answer the next call and spoke as if she was out of breath.

"Glen, are you there?" she asked.

"Yah, I'm here! Where you been?" he snarled.

"I'm so sorry! My phone is cutting out on me. I dropped it and it is giving me fits!" she laughed nervously. He wasn't buying it.

"Sure, and I suppose the phone in your store doesn't work either!"

"Now, you know I can't talk in front of customers, and we've been really busy…"

"Cut the bull, Rebecca! You're avoiding me!"

"Glen, you're jumping to conclusions…" he continued to cut her off as she spoke.

"I suppose you're too busy with all your customers to meet me this weekend, right?" He exploded.

"No, we are still on for the weekend. And I promise, I'll make it up to you." She said brightly.

"Really? We're still getting together?" He felt much better as the knot in his stomach began to release.

"Yes, yes, I have no intention of working this weekend. Tell you what. Why don't we meet for a drink at the *Quick Stop* say 1:00?"

"How about I bring whatever you want to drink to your place and we skip the bar and the outside company?" he laughed.

"We will have all weekend to be together!" she hadn't expected any resistance. She had to think fast.

"I told my friend, Vontrice, I would meet her there at 1:00 on Saturday so she could introduce me to her new beau! Now you can spare an hour or two can't you? I wanted Vontrice to meet my beau too!" she giggled knowing he would be happy to hear those words.

"All right! We can stop by for a quick drink. If you hens want to compare your guys, I understand!" Rebecca rolled her eyes. She couldn't wait for this to be over.

"Wait 'till I get my hands on you!" He sang merrily forgetting his former distress. Maybe she really had been too busy to pick up his call. She seemed anxious to meet him and that was all that mattered to him.

He decided to get a haircut and buy himself a stylish shirt or perhaps a jacket. He wanted Rebecca to stand with the better man leaving her friend embarrassed by the competition.

He was in a particularly chipper mood as he brushed his shoes and checked himself in the mirror. He was careful to leave early enough to miss breakfast with Norma. He packed a few things into a small valise and crept out of the bedroom unnoticed.

Norma had been told a small business trip would possibly detain him overnight. He thought they could work the details through earlier than expected and he would call her if things had not gone according to plan. Of course, he had no intention of getting home before Sunday evening.

In the meantime, Rigo was working on lies of his own. He was very competent with high computer skills and excellent software programs. He knew how to investigate his targets on line and spent an enormous amount of time gathering information. After he had been duped by a beautiful woman who appeared to be wealthy and affluent, but was actually playing the same game, he did his homework first.

He tapped his lip with his pencil as he read all he could find about Norma Booth. She certainly was not wealthy, skilled, or even remotely pretty. Her parents were not people of means... none were highly educated with the exception of a cousin. Hmmm, he lived in a nearby state, and was an attorney.

Rigo laughed when he discovered this cousin was a well-established divorce attorney. He not only won nearly all his cases, but his defendants received tremendous compensation. He was pleasantly surprised to see a picture of the elegantly dressed man with a wide smile. Apparently, Norma's brother had married a beautiful Cuban and her cousin, Calvin Jr. could pass as his own brother. Most people didn't know the difference between a Mexican, Cuban or Latino.

Rigo slicked his hair back with gel and selected the expensive suit Loretta had purchased for him when she wanted him to accompany her on a business trip. He told her he would be ashamed to be seen with the smartly dressed woman unless he was also attired in the same fashion. He thought she was a dope and hated to be seen with her.

Though he accompanied her during the business trip, he found time to 'play' while she attending required board meetings. He had the time of his life! There were many beautiful women who enjoyed his company and it took little to satisfy Loretta's requests. She was content to be seen with him and was often exhausted by the time evening came. He plied her with liquor and after she was snoring deeply, he snuck out for another evening of fun. He was smart enough to pretend disappointment that they couldn't enjoy the time together during the day, and she ate up every word. She gave him her credit card and enough cash to keep him occupied while she attended her meetings and he thanked her for her kindness!

This was going to be a piece of cake. He downloaded official looking documents for his beautifully engraved, genuine leather brief case. He specifically had the initials C.J.C. Calvin James Currothers emblazed boldly on the front. He smiled at his reflection. This could be fun! He would enjoy the masquerade.

On Saturday afternoon, he arrived early and watched for Glen to drive into the parking lot. Glen was obviously anxious as he was getting out of his car and heading to the door. He was almost twenty minutes early! Good thing Rigo arrived early as well.

"Excuse me, are you Glen Booth?" he asked with authority as he dashed to meet him and stood between him and the tavern door.

"I'm Glen Booth. Who are you?" Glen did not want to be detained, but it was obvious he was speaking to a sharp businessman and he needed to be cautious.

"My name is not important. I am here to tell you to stay away from Rebecca Benson. This is your only warning."

"Who are you and what is this all about?" Glen was angry, confused and more than a little scared.

"Perhaps you do not recognize me. I do not believe we have actually ever met. I am your wife's cousin and I assure you if you continue seeing Rebecca Benson, you will not have a family or a job! Look up my stats. You will be amazed at the settlements I have procured for my clients."

"Your clients?"

"I do not charge family. As a matter of fact, my cousin knows nothing about this. But word has come to me about your... your... sordid affair and I will not tolerate it!" He feigned disdain.

"This is none of your business, especially if my wife has not retained you." He tried.

"But you see, I have made it my business! I will not have my cousin humiliated while you cheat on her! I have also paid Ms. Benson a visit and she agreed to stop seeing you as she did not want to lose her antique business."

"Now wait just a minute! Are you threatening me? Are you threatening her?" He couldn't believe this was happening.

"If I want to see Rebecca, I will just have to divorce your cousin!" his mind was racing and he had no idea what to say.

"That would be a stupid idea. I assure you the results will be the same. If you choose to do such a thing, you will not be able to afford a one room apartment on a vacant lot. I know where you work and could cause enough difficulty there to have you fired. Perhaps you didn't know that the owner of your company is a model family man and I could paint such a picture…he would fire you on the spot! And last but not least, Ms. Benson is also used to living in a certain style and has no intention of losing everything to continue seeing you." The men stood glaring at each other for a few moments. Rigo had to suppress his laughter as he watched Glen's face contort. Rebecca was correct in her assumption. Glen was the Ant and he was the Giant!

"I suggest you get back in your car and go home to my cousin. Ms. Benson has already gone home."

"This is not over!" Glen sputtered, though he had no idea what to do next. He was already packed for his feigned trip.

"It is *all* over, my friend! You see, though cousin Norma is a sweet lady, I am not so sweet. I have learned to be tough as I fight with garbage like you. I work hard for my clients, but I will work twice as hard for family. I will chew you up and spit you into the sewer where you belong! And by the way, I will be checking on my cousin in the next few days. Should I see a mark on her or any indication of violent behavior on your part, I will lay aside my legal obligation for a time and you will find another kind of adversary. I can be a harsh enemy as I have helped many shall we say 'unsavory' people who owe me favors. Do we have an understanding?" Glen could only nod his shaking head as he slumped back to his vehicle and sped out of the parking lot.

Rigo got back into his vehicle and lay his head on the steering wheel as he laughed hysterically. Maybe he missed his calling. Perhaps he should go to Hollywood and stand toe to toe with the big boys!

The suit made him feel powerful and successful. He decided to take a little trip to reward himself for such showmanship.

Glen had no idea what to do. He didn't want to go home and was in no mood to see his family. He had never felt so defeated. His mind raced back to his confrontation with Rebecca's husband. The man could have killed him and no doubt wanted to!

After Chuck was killed in the accident, Glen saw Rebecca

frequently. In the beginning, she seemed as anxious to meet as he was, but he was no fool. The relationship had lost something. Rebecca was often aloof and unresponsive and he feared she was no longer interested. He realized how ridiculous his threats had been. He couldn't keep the relationship going through fear! Either she wanted to be with him or she didn't and forcing her by knife point underlined his desperation. Was he going through some kind of midlife crisis?

He pulled absentmindedly into the large parking lot of the local hospital and sat quietly behind the wheel for a few minutes, hoping to come up with a plan. It was too early to go home even if he wanted to and he didn't; he didn't want to go anywhere. He didn't even care that he wasn't going to see Rebecca. He closed his eyes and felt the hot tears trying to escape. His life was a mess.

"Glen, are you okay?" the voice of his pastor startled him back into the present.

"Oh… hello Preacher!" Glen gasped. How was he going to explain his presence?

"Are you going in or coming out?" Martin asked.

"I… uh… haven't decided." He laughed nervously.

"Why don't we have a cup of coffee together as you decide?" Martin laughed. He didn't want him to know about his conversation with Norma. She had been so excited to see the changes in her husband after the camping trip, but unfortunately, it was short lived.

"Oh, I don't want to trouble you, Pastor. I'm sure you've got lots of people to see in there."

"I'm meeting John Dunbar but I'm a little early. I've got time, Glen." There wasn't much he could do but follow Martin to the cafeteria. There seemed to be no logical explanation as to his appearance in the parking lot of the hospital. He knew no one that had been recently admitted. What could he possibly give as an explanation?

"I certainly hope Kate McDaniel is doing better than the last time I saw her." Glen nodded his feigned concern. He was so absorbed in his own problems that he had forgotten about Kate and the fire.

"What a terrible thing to happen to a beautiful woman like that."

said Glen. Martin sighed. The woman could have lost her life. Clearly, Glen's concern was a shallow one.

"It could have been much worse." Martin replied.

"Oh yes! I'm sure that's true." Glen barely realized how he must sound to the pastor. Martin paid for their coffee and they sat across from each other at a table by the window.

"How are things with you, Glen?" he began.

"Can't complain. I'm not in the hospital so I guess that's already a plus, huh?" he laughed.

"I haven't seen you much since our camping trip. We'll have to do that again sometime." He was careful not to sound 'scolding' as his only intent was to let him know he was missed. Glen had spent many weekends away 'on business' and Norma began questioning his frequent trips. Finally, in desperation, she called his boss and asked some questions. It was apparent, Glen had been telling lies. She worded her questions carefully as she did not want Glen's boss to think she was checking up on him. She told him she was concerned that Glen wasn't sleeping well and that perhaps he was sick. Had he taken on additional work that was too much for him? To her dismay, his boss let he know that Glen seemed distracted these days and though he had thought of giving him additional assignments, he decided against it.

When he told her that a couple of the guys were traveling but he decided to keep Glen at home, she nearly gasped. It was one thing to know the truth in your heart and quite another for someone to confirm it. She called Martin and told him her assumption. She wanted to find Rebecca and have it out with her, but she decided to counsel with her pastor before doing anything rash.

"Yes, I've been traveling more lately. I've missed being in church. I know Norma and Anthony love being there." He added.

"I hope you can be there Sunday. Norma and Anthony are singing a special and I know you will be blessed. I've heard them practicing."

"It just so happens I *will* be there. They really have a good blend when they sing together don't you think?" he added.

"Yes, they certainly do." Martin had been praying for the right words, but they just didn't seem to be forthcoming.

"There you are, Preacher. Am I late?" John hustled to the table to join the two men.

"Nope, I'm just a bit early." Martin said. Glen saw his opportunity to get away.

"Well, I'll let you two get on with your visits. It was nice seeing you Pastor, thanks for the coffee." Before he could make a move, John was at his side.

"I don't know if you remember me. I'm John Dunbar." The men shook hands as he spoke.

"I've heard good things about you. My wife and son were there the day you preached and they still talk about it." he smiled.

"We were just going to make a visit on Kate McDaniel. Please join us."

"Oh, no, I couldn't do that. You two go on ahead. You don't need me barging in." Martin was surprised that John seemed adamant to have Glen join them.

"We could really use another man of prayer." Glen smiled at the compliment. No one had ever referred to him that way and it made him feel important.

"Well, if you really think you want me along." Again, Martin remained silent as he listened to John's engaging conversation. He tagged along with them to the elevator and Martin was puzzled. Did John think Glen would be a spiritual presence? He seemed more of a hindrance.

By the time they reached Kate's room, Glen was having a change of heart. He didn't like hospitals or sick people and the last thing he wanted to see was a burn victim. Maybe she would be grotesque! How would he handle that?

Kate was asleep as they entered the room. She had been moved from ICU and though she was continuously monitored, she was doing well.

"Will she be okay?" asked Glen nervously.

"I think her burns are healing. There is no way of knowing

the extent of the damage to her arm. We are praying for complete mobility."

"What about her face?" asked Glen. John and Martin exchanged knowing glances. Of course, Glen would be concerned about her appearance.

"The doctor believes with skin grafts, she should have minimal scarring."

"I am more concerned about her mental scars." Glen noticed her agitation. She appeared to be speaking to someone in a dream.

"I've always followed orders. Done exactly as you requested." She whimpered.

"I should be rewarded, not condemned!' she cried.

"Kate, can you hear me?" John asked tapping her hand gently.

"Who in the world is she talking to? Is she dreaming?" Glen asked curiously.

"I only wish she were." Glen could feel the hairs stand up on his neck and arms. He wanted desperately to bolt, but was standing between John and Martin and was not certain his feet would take him anywhere.

"Kate, you're safe! No one can harm you! You are in the hospital and they are taking good care of you." For a few seconds she seemed lucid.

"Preacher? I'm sorry about the fire!"

"It doesn't matter, Kate. You're all that matters. Nothing else." Martin assured her. Kate nodded and then seemed to revert back to the trance like state, but John wouldn't allow it.

"No, you don't, Kate. You listen to *my* voice! You are safe! No one can harm you!" he spoke close to her ear and she twisted her head to look into his eyes.

"I don't know what to do! I have given my full allegiance and it was all for nothing! I am NOT SAFE!" she cried hysterically.

"You don't know what to do, but I do! Listen to me Kate. Jesus loves you..." immediately her bandaged hand went over her ear.

"NO! NO! NO!" she cried.

"He is your only chance, Kate! Without Him you are not safe!

Without Him you have no hope… you will be harmed!" Martin spoke gently but firmly and kept her hand away from her ears.

"It is too late! I can't!" she sobbed. John and Glen listened as Martin spoke Bible verses into Kate's unwilling heart. There were times she softened, and eagerly listened and then she became tense and terrified. Glen had never witnessed such an event in his entire life and was glued to the floor as he watched.

John began singing softly and Kate seemed to respond to his voice. Both men were kind and compassionate and it was obvious Kate was beginning to respond.

In the end, Kate bowed her head and prayed with Martin and John. She asked for forgiveness. She asked for mercy and she asked for redemption. Martin and John adjusted her bed and straightened her bedding from all the thrashing that had taken place. Kate fell asleep but there was a difference. She was at peace.

"I've never seen anything like that in my entire life! I'm not sure what I just witnessed!" Glen's head was reeling. He felt like he had been cast into a horror movie and though he had no lines, he felt the terror around him.

"It's not something people see every day. That's for sure. But just as heaven is real and our Lord Jesus is real… there is another dark reality. Most people live there life barely aware that they are following the instructions of one side or the other." Glen looked baffled.

"I know there are people out there that think evil lurks in every wind and are preoccupied with the devil and his minions. But at least they are aware! Every day we make choices that please one side or the other.

"But God is forgiving. Don't you always say that, Preacher?" Glen asked nervously.

"Yes, but maybe what I don't say enough is that there are consequences for every choice." Glen's throat tightened at the words. He didn't like to think about that part.

"Well she must be some evil kind of woman to be talking to demons of some kind. Are you telling me that Kate is possessed by some kind of … demon?"

"You don't have to be evil... just willing!" John interjected. Glen thought his hair would walk right off his scalp and his throat felt restricted.

"I can only tell you that Kate was definitely in a tortured state!"

"That seems like quite a leap! I mean maybe it's the medication that made her talk crazy!" he didn't want to accept the explanation. That was too far fetched in his mind.

"Unfortunately, I've seen this before. It is not from medication."

"What about the rest of her family? Do you think they are like Kate?" Glen dared to ask.

"Yes I do. I wish I could help them, but they are nowhere to be found."

"She seems to have quieted down. Maybe she'll be okay now." Glen didn't realize what he had witnessed and neither Glen nor Martin felt the need to continue the explanation.

"Only the Lord can give peace. Thank you for praying with us Glen." Said John knowing he had stood frozen during the entire thing.

"Glad to have helped." He lied.

"I guess I should get on home now." Glen shook their hands and began walking toward the elevator. Martin quickly caught up with him.

"Glen, I hope you won't discuss this with anyone else. It is a difficult thing to witness and sharing it is equally challenging. Glen nodded in agreement.

Glen returned to his car feeling weak and queasy. He had read many verses about heaven and enjoyed the picture of streets of gold and pearly gates, but he never envisioned the other side, at least not until today. It made perfect sense. Pastor had once taught a lesson about 'opposites' and he vaguely remembered the concept of equal and opposite. Big is the opposite of small. Wet... dry, tall...short, hot... cold but when he said... good, he did not want to say evil. He liked the idea of heaven but he didn't want to think of an opposite! Today, that opposite side had shown its ugly head and it gave him the creeps!

He drove home thinking about his life. He claimed to be a follower of Christ, he knew certain Bible verses, but he also knew in the depths of his heart... he was wicked. He was a cheater... he was a proud and arrogant man... he didn't deserve his family.

He pulled his car into the driveway and turned off the motor. He hadn't expected to feel such emotion as he watched Norma through the kitchen window. She and Anthony were making dinner together and it was obvious they were enjoying each other's company. He felt like such a fool! Chasing the wind! Slowly, he slipped into the house and entered the kitchen unnoticed.

"What's for dinner?" he asked quietly.

"Hey Dad, you're just in time! Mom and I made this new dish together. You're going to like it! Mom thinks it's a little too hot, but I know *you* won't think so. We've got a salad to go with it." To their surprise, Glen reached into the fridge and pulled out the iced tea. He had never helped with anything in the kitchen before and Norma and her son exchanged inquisitive glances.

When everyone was seated, Glen asked Anthony to say the blessing on the food. This was also completely out of character for the proud man. Generally, he could spit nasty comments and ridicule his wife and have no problem bowing his head for a pious prayer.

Glen ate quietly as he listened to his son and wife converse. Anthony spoke about his finals and also the baseball team. Norma told them about the missionary meeting she had attended. Glen smiled and nodded from time to time but made no comments.

"Are you okay, Glen?" Norma asked.

"You haven't said anything about your meetings. I'm so glad you didn't have to be away for the weekend." Glen bit his lip to keep from crying. He had no idea how much he should say.

"It's good to be home. There isn't any place else I would rather be." He said through trembling lips.

Anthony finished eating and decided to leave his parents alone to talk. Something was definitely wrong with his father and he sensed their need to talk without his presence.

"I've got homework to finish. I'll be in my room if you need me."

He said more for his mother's benefit. His father didn't seem angry, but there was something definitely on his mind. Was he leaving them? Anthony shook his head. No, he didn't believe that.

Somewhere in the back of his mind he knew his father wasn't faithful to his mother. He almost followed him at one point, but he had been praying about the situation and never felt compelled to trail behind him. What would he do with the information if he learned something? He would never be the one to break his mother's heart. So instead, he asked his mother if they could spend time praying for him. At first, she began to argue as she didn't want to put Glen in an unsavory light before his son. But her son's appeal for prayer was put in his heart from the Lord.

They began praying on a daily basis. Neither of them spoke ill of Glen. Their prayer was for a softening of his heart. They prayed he would be the man God created him to be. It gave both of them courage and hope to face Glen's moods and his constant weekend disappearance.

When Anthony left the room, Glen buried his face in his hands and wept. Deep sobs escaping as Norma rubbed his back and waited for him to compose himself. Her mind raced for conclusions. Was he ill? Dying? Perhaps he had been fired.

"I have been such a fool!" He sobbed. He pulled her into his lap and held her tight. She prayed she would have the right words to say to her broken hearted husband.

"Whatever it is, we'll face it together Glen." She assured him.

"I don't know if I can bring myself to telling you what an awful husband I've been. I don't deserve such a loving woman. I have seen myself as the wicked man I am and I wonder how you've been able to put up with it all these years." He cried.

"I love you, Glen. I have always loved you." She whispered softly.

"There is nothing good in me to love! He took a deep breath and closed his eyes. He barely knew where to begin to ask forgiveness. Should he tell her about his clandestine meetings with Rebecca?

"Glen, I know you've done things and I don't want to know the details. I thought I did. I thought I would want to hear every single offence… but in my heart I know you are done with that life. I don't want to live with the details or torture myself with the memories.

"Can you ever forgive me?" he held her narrow face between his hands and looked into her eyes. She was the most beautiful woman on earth.

"Yes, Glen. I forgive you." They held each other for a few minutes and both felt a release of emotion replaced with a great calm.

"I saw something today, Norma. I saw a person who was living a horrible, tortured life and though I felt sorry, I realized I am not living far from that myself." Norma looked puzzled but he could not explain.

"I think I've wasted enough of my life just fooling myself into believing I'm a Christian. Today I saw myself the way God sees me." She continued to stare at her humbled husband as he spoke softly about his genuine conversion. He knew many of the verses that tell a person their lost state and how they can know for sure they are accepted through the Saviour. They had been meaningless words for the most part. But today, he meant each word with his whole heart.

"Glen?" her heart leaped within her.

"I promise you, Norma, I will be a new husband! I will be a new father! I can't give you back the years I've wasted, but I will do my best to crdeate great memories with you… if you'll still have me!" She kissed him passionately in response.

That evening Glen, Norma and Anthony spent time around the Word of God and Norma knew her prayers had been answered.

"Mac! I can hardly believe my eyes!" Martin and John ran to his side.

"Yah, I would have been here sooner, but me and Dad have been real sick." He lied.

"Your mother was just praying that you would be here today." John announced with tears in his eyes.

"My mother was praying?" he asked in disbelief.

"Your mother has a lot to tell you, Mac." Martin prepared to leave them alone to talk privately.

"Please stay! I think you will be able to help me speak to my son." Kate cried.

"Mother, I'm so sorry I haven't been up to see you." Mac's voice cracked as he tried in vain to keep the tears from falling. It was strange to see his mother so vulnerable. She was still heavily bandaged, and reached out to him with her good arm. She had never shown such warmth to him, which only made the tears that much more difficult to suppress.

"I wasn't up to company anyway. I'm so glad you are here now. I can't tell you how happy I am to see you." Her voice was soft, filled with tenderness and nothing at all like the Kate McDaniel he had known all his life.

"But I'm better now than I have ever been in my life!" she added. Mac nodded absently wondering if the change in his mother was due to strong medication.

"That's wonderful, Mother. Maybe you will get to come home soon." As soon as the words escaped from his lips, he realized they no longer had a home. He had no idea where he would take her or how he would explain.

"Have they talked about releasing you?" Martin could see the alarm in his face and remembered the deserted house.

"No, they won't be releasing her until they are sure she is stable and there are no infections." Martin reported calming Mac's fears.

"Are you in pain, Mom?" She smiled at him and shook her head.

"Maybe a little, but I'm doing well. I have so much to share with you, Mac. I hardly know where to begin." She grinned.

"I'm afraid it's going to have to wait. It's time to change your dressing and your also due for more meds." The nurse interrupted.

"Preacher, John, could you both speak to my son for me. I will fill in the details when we can talk later." She blew her bewildered son a kiss as he trailed behind John to the nearest waiting room.

Surely this was some kind of performance his mother was giving. If it was... she should receive an award! He shook his head and noticed his thoughts were clear though sketchy in places.

"Is my mother going to be okay?" asked Mac.

"I think she is on the road to recovery, but she is going to have some tough days ahead." Martin replied.

"How bad are her burns? Will she be scarred?" John gritted his teeth. Why were people so obsessed with the outward appearance?

"She may not have much use of her right hand. Time will tell." Mac sucked in a deep breath. There was so much bandaging around her face, neck and arms, that he couldn't be sure of the extent of her injuries.

"Does she know?" He knew she would be devastated.

"Yes, she knows." John said flatly.

"You're sure she understands what has happened to her?" he tried again. She should have flipped out with the knowledge.

"She understands that she may have to do everything with one hand. She knows that though they will do their best with skin grafts, she may have scarring on her face, neck and legs. I hope you will be supportive and helpful as she recovers." Mac could only stare dumbfounded at the news.

"You asked if she understands what has happened to her. I think we need to explain exactly *what* has happened to her." John smiled and slowly, they filled in the details of his mother's conversion.

Mac appeared horrified as they slowly filled in each detail, and then seemed to dismiss the entire depiction. His mother was either on heavy meds, didn't understand what had happened to her or was trying to fool the preacher so the church wouldn't press charges. That was the only thing that made any sense!

"Now, my question to you, Mac. Where is your father?"

"Like I said, he's sick at home." Mac couldn't make eye contact as he lied to them once again.

"I've been to your home." Martin pressed.

"He's too sick to answer the door."

"You need to come clean with us, Mac. Not only have we been to your house, but you and your father picked it clean before you left." John interjected. Mac hung his head.

"We were going to come back for her." He wished that were true.

"Did you come back without your father?" Martin asked.

"Yes. I don't think he's coming back." Mac began to weep uncontrollably and John and Martin waited for him to regain his composure.

"The truth is I don't know what happened to my father. I can't remember. Not only can I not remember... I'm afraid to remember...I won't let myself remember!" Martin could see the fear in his eyes and wondered what had happened that was too frightening to remember.

"We need to figure out what to do when your mother is released. Why don't you tell us what you remember?" Mac told them how he and his father had practically ransacked the house taking anything of value and then headed to Massachusetts. He didn't tell them about the 'Watcher' as he didn't think they would understand.

"Is your father still there?" Mac couldn't be sure.

"That was where I left him." He replied.

"He didn't want to come back?" John asked. Mac shrugged.

"Does he know you came back?" John tried. Another shrug.

"This is where the memory falls apart." Mac tapped his temple lightly with his finger.

"What am I going to tell my mother?" he said through fresh tears.

"Don't tell her anything yet. We don't have enough answers and she's already been through quite a lot."

"Why don't you come home with me and have dinner. We'll sort things out together." Martin said.

"I appreciate the offer, but I don't want to see anyone right now."

"You only have to see my wife. The kids are gone this week. They went to teen camp." Mac recalled the announcement when he attended church and decided to take him up on his offer.

"I am planning to come back to the hospital tonight so we can check in on your mother together." Mac nodded. He needed to talk to her alone to get the *true* story. John and Martin parted company and committed the situation to prayer. They had become like brothers. As Mac and Martin traveled the short distance to the Parker home, Martin noticed Mac was increasingly withdrawn.

"Can I answer any questions you might have about your mother coming to the Lord?" Mac shook his head. He only trusted his mother's words.

"Mac, I want you to know I understand more than you might think. Your mother was sincere and I believe she genuinely wanted to … um… change sides." Mac stiffened. He wasn't sure how to respond.

"There was quite a battle going on within her mind and heart. I know that for certain. It appeared she was speaking directly to someone in the room that we could not see." Martin glanced at Mac's white face and knew he understood the meaning behind the words.

"Maybe it was just the medication."

"I'm not sure what you've been through, Mac, but I can assure you, your family has been on the wrong side. Your mother came to that conclusion." Mac nodded dully without comprehension.

"Think about it. Your mother has always done her best to hide the truth from us. She prided herself on fooling everyone. I know what she was involved in. Do you think for a minute she would confess those things and forsake them?"

"You don't know my mother…" Mac began.

"No, it is *you* that doesn't know your mother. She is not the same person. That is what the Lord does in a life." Mac stared out the window. He did not want to continue this topic. Perhaps it was a bad idea to go home with the preacher, but where else did he have to go? Fresh tears streaked down his face as he thought of his situation.

His mother would know what to do. She always did. She was the decision maker for the family and he and his father always went along with her. She was seldom wrong.

Christine added another setting to her table and prayed for direction. The situation was more than she could understand. How could Kate's family abandon her? Martin assured her there was more to the story and he would fill her in later.

Mac greeted her as if meeting her for the first time. He was silent and withdrawn and definitely not at all like the Mac they were acquainted with. Christine did her best to steer conversation away from the situation, but everyone knew there was the proverbial "elephant-in-the-room."

No one ate much, though Christine prepared a sumptuous dinner. Mac toyed with his food and stared at his plate as Christine talked about church camp and Martin spoke about events on the church calendar. The time passed slowly.

"I would like to get back to the hospital and see my mother." Mac announced.

"It's a little early for visiting time, but we can get an early start if you like." Mac thanked Christine for dinner and headed back to the garage without waiting for Martin.

The silent ride back to the hospital made both of them uncomfortable, but neither could think of anything to say. The few blocks seemed miles away and Martin was happy to pull his car into the familiar parking slot designated for clergy.

"I don't mean to be rude, but I would like to speak to my mother alone." Mac said sullenly.

"Of course, I think you *need* some time alone." Martin smiled. He would love to stay and listen in case Kate needed him to explain, but he didn't want Mac to think he put words in his mother's mouth.

By the time they reached Kate's room, she was sitting up in bed fumbling with her dinner. Her arm was wrapped tightly and she did her best to eat with the opposite hand. She had always been a very polished woman with grace and charm and this 'new' clumsy Kate was difficult to get used to.

"Hi Mom" Mac swallowed the lump in his throat as he watched his mother. It was depressing to see her. Part of her face was bandaged and though he wanted to ask... he truly didn't want to know the extent of her injuries.

"Oh, I'm so glad you're back! I'm getting my appetite back, but by the time I try to cut my food and get it into my mouth, it's cold! You know how I like my food piping hot!" she laughed. Mac remained grim and could only stare in disbelief.

"Could you be a dear and cut this up for me?" She let the knife and fork drop back into her plate and Mac had little choice but to cut things into bite size pieces.

"I'm feeling a little bit better every day and I think I should be out of here in no time!" she added pleasantly. Mac nodded without knowing what to say. Where were they going to go when she was released?

"I'm glad you're getting better, Mom." She stopped chewing and cocked her head to one side as she stared at her troubled son.

"Don't look so upset, Mac. I knew when you came back to see me... alone... that your father did not come back." Mac's eyes were wide with fear. He had no idea how to respond.

"Please tell me he didn't take you to Massachusetts!" Mac nodded; his mouth ajar in disbelief. How could she possibly know?

"You're lucky to have escaped with your life! He should have been smarter than that! The 'Watcher' in Massachusetts is the final stage of the journey! Thank God I got out!" she cried. For the first time, Mac realized it wasn't a hoax. His mother had actually done as the preacher said.

"I don't know what to say! I was hoping when Dad made it back…"

"Your father is dead, Mac." Kate said firmly showing no emotion.

"You don't know that. Dad might have gotten away, after all, I did."

"You don't know how fortunate you were to get away! That rarely happens. You know your father let me make most of the decisions. I would *never* have made that one." She hoped she was right, but wondered if she would have followed the same course.

"I hated to leave him behind, but I was a mess myself. I felt like I was in a fog and could barely concentrate long enough to get bus fare back home.

"My poor son!" Kate's tears were rare and Mac had no idea how to respond to this new woman.

"If it hadn't been for that preacher in the church where I was hiding, I don't think I would have made it back safely." To his amazement, his mother burst into a new flurry tears. She reached out to him with her good arm and pressed her bandaged face against his.

"Oh Mac! God answered my prayers! There was nothing I could do for you so I began praying for protection and that someone would come to your rescue!" He stood wide eyed as she continued.

"Don't you see, Mac? God allowed that preacher to find you. You said you were *hiding* in the church. I believe you were directed there as a result of my prayers for you."

"I would like to talk to your doctor, Mom." As if reading his mind, she answered his unasked question.

"I can assure you, this is not medication talking. I am clear headed and at this point, I am also clear hearted!"

"Maybe I'm the one who is still in a fog. For all I know, I might still be in Massachusetts." He said in a frightened voice.

"Mac look at me! You are here beside my hospital bed as a result of prayer. I broke the chains that I didn't even know were around me. I saw the other side, Mac. It broke me! Oh yes, our lives had many thrilling, exhilarating moments for sure, but Mac, at the end…" her lip quivered and she forced herself to continue.

"Think of what you saw in Massachusetts. Think of the 'Watcher' and your father." She could tell it was too painful and terrifying for her son to consider.

"Mac listen to me! You must do as I have done."

"After all you've taught me? Now you are doing a complete reversal?"

"After what you witnessed in Massachusetts, I would think it would take little convincing." He couldn't disagree with her.

"I taught you the only life I have ever known. My mother came from a similar background. We called ourselves a family, but Mac, I don't know if my mother even loved me. We lived the same life as you and your father. But when my mother died, it was a horrible event to witness."

"You've never spoken about your parents. I don't think I ever met them." Mac interjected.

"You were still a baby when they died. I should have known then that there were conditions for the lifestyle we chose. I tried to convince myself that we were smarter, wiser and I would never allow myself to think of anything else. There were those 'what if' moments, but I was enjoying life too much to think about it." she cried.

"We have a great life, Mother! The best! Now you want to trade it in?" he asked astonished.

"Yes! I was only living for the moment, but this life is brief! Fleeting! It's like a blip on a computer screen. So fast and then gone and barely remembered! I tried to convince myself that in the end we would also be victorious, but I know that's not true. I didn't want to believe it. I wanted to think that we could have the best on both sides. What a fool! What a ridiculous fool!" she sighed.

"I don't know what to say! It's hard to believe you're serious!" He threw his hands in the air and shook his head.

"I know how difficult this must be for you to understand."

"Try impossible!!"

"Mac, if you don't listen, you will end up just like your father. I wish I could have rescued him, but it's too late. His destination is final. I don't want that to happen to you." She pleaded.

"I can't just turn my back on everything I have ever known just because you ended up in the hospital. I think these preachers have talked you into this. Sure, that makes sense! They knew how vulnerable you would be! But wait until you get out of here, Mom. We can travel together as we've always done. I'll help you recover, I promise, and I'm so sorry I bailed on you!" Kate reached for her bedazzled son but he pulled away from her.

"I'll be back to see you soon, Mother. I promise" He ran from the room not knowing what to do next. He had no place to go and he had no intention of going back to the preacher's house. He would rather sit on the curb for the night. He headed for the elevator, but in his hurry, collided with John Dunbar who was stepping out of the elevator at the same moment.

"Slow down, son!" John laughed.

"Sorry, man, I didn't see you!" It was obvious, Mac was nervous and scared. If John didn't know better, he would think the boy was being chased.

"Can I give you a lift somewhere?" John asked keeping in step with Mac who seemed to have forgotten the elevator entirely.

"Ah, no, that's okay. I'll walk."

"Walk where?"

"I just need some air."

"It's raining."

"I won't melt."

"We need to talk." John took Mac gently by the arm and steered him into the cafeteria. Mac had only played with the food on his plate at the preacher's house, and couldn't remember the last time he had eaten.

"Look, I know you mean well, but I think I need to be alone. I got a lot to figure out."

"Yes, you most certainly do." John agreed. He bought a couple of hamburgers and added a large portion of fries with two soft drinks. He figured all teenagers were on the same diet.

"When do you think my mother might get out of here?" he ventured to ask. He thought it best for him to pick out the topic.

"I really don't know for sure. She's healing nicely though, so hopefully it will be soon. What are your plans when she gets out?"

"I think I'll take her someplace warm where she can relax and heal." He wanted to add... and come to her senses, but he knew better.

"That sounds nice. Do you have a car?"

"I'll get one."

"What about money?"

"You sure ask a lot of questions! I don't mean to be disrespectful, but I'll take care of my mother, okay? We'll figure it out together." John nodded casually and continued to pray. He knew anything he said would fall on deaf ears, so he held his peace for the time.

"I know you'll take care of her, Mac. She's your mother, after all." He smiled.

Mac wolfed down the burgers and tried to formulate a plan for the night. He had no place to go and refused to ask for assistance.

"Why don't you stay with me tonight?" John offered, as if reading his mind. Immediately, Mac's hand went up in protest.

"Thanks, but no thanks. I'll manage." He said a bit curtly.

"Tell you what. I promise if you stay at my house, we won't talk about anything. You can stay in my spare bedroom and watch television if it eases your mind." Mac let out a long breath of air and contemplated the offer. Where else did he have to go?

"If you're sure there will be no discussion about my parents, my plans or any of this new stuff my mother is yacking about." He said gruffly.

"I promise. I just want to lend you a hand, that's all. No discussions, no pressure, no expectations." Mac nodded in relief. He promised himself that if John didn't keep his word he would leave immediately. He nodded silently and finished devouring his food.

After they were finished eating, Mac reluctantly followed John to his car as they drove the short distance to his humble home. John was hoping to visit Kate before Mac crashed into him outside the elevator doors. He would call Martin later to let him know why he was detained; knowing Martin would make the visit on his own.

"There are fresh towels in the bathroom if you want to take a shower." John called to him as he rushed into the bedroom pointed out to him.

"Thanks, that sounds good." Mac closed his eyes and tried to remember the last time he took a shower, or changed his clothes. He had no idea. Maybe a shower would help to clear his head.

After peeling off his clothing, he adjusted the shower and allowed the spray to pound his aching body. To his surprise, his skin seemed to sting in multiple areas. He turned his arm over and saw scrapes in several places. His legs also had unidentified lacerations. Thankfully, there were no deep gashes. The cuts were just deep enough to sting like a swarm of bees.

Again his thoughts raced back to his father. No, no, no! He would not allow himself to go there. His mother said his father was dead. How could she know that? But his mother *always* knew! If she said he was dead... he was dead. Oddly there was little emotion connected to his father. Most of his interactions were with his mother. He knew about his father's affairs and unscrupulous business dealings, but he spent little time with him and as his mother had no problems with his infidelity, neither did he. His mother had been more influential, and though he never admitted it to anyone, he always wished she had shown him more love. He admired her and hoped to become more like her, but his whole life had turned upside down since the fire. His father was dead and his mother was a stranger to him. He gingerly toweled off and wrapped the towel around his waist. He hated to put on the same clothes, but he had no choice.

"Here are some sweats you can sleep in." John didn't wait for an answer, but tossed them on the bed.

"Thank you." Mac said softly. He liked this kind hearted black man and wanted to talk to him, but he was afraid he would push him for details he either didn't know or didn't want to know.

"You get yourself a good night sleep and I'll make you one of my special breakfasts in the morning." John shuffled off to his room and began to pray again for this young man. He truly wanted to rely on the Lord to tell him whether he should speak or remain quiet until

Karen Fertig

Mac opened his ears to him. He called Martin to keep him in the loop and both men prayed earnestly for Mac before they ended their conversation.

Mac slept well for the first time in days. He woke clear headed and alert, though it took a few minutes to remember where he was. He could smell bacon cooking and his mouth began to water. Slowly he slipped out of bed and found his way to the kitchen.

"Morning, Mac!" John said cheerily.

"What time is it?"

"Morning!"

"I don't think the sun is up yet!" said Mac staring out the window into the darkness.

"Hope you're hungry!" Mac sat down with a thump and began to dive into pancakes, sausages, bacon and scrambled eggs. He noticed John's bowed head and set his fork down. He didn't want to be rude to his host, though he had no intention of thanking anyone but John for his breakfast. John prayed a brief but heartfelt prayer and both men dug into their food.

"You are welcome to stay here until your mother is released from the hospital. You can come and go as you please. I just ask that you lock up before you leave. It will give you time to either look for a place for you and your mom and you'll be close to the hospital." There didn't seem to be a hidden agenda, and Mac knew it was the best solution for the moment. He needed to discuss future plans with his mother, but he didn't really want to talk to her in her present condition.

"I'm planning to visit her myself sometime today, would you like to go with me?" John asked.

"Um, maybe later. We have a lot to catch up on and I'll wait until everyone has made their visits." John understood the meaning but didn't push.

"I would like to talk to her doctors." He added.

"Of course, you need to be brought up to date with her condition and the expectations once she's released." Mac nodded and helped himself to another huge helping of food. John watched the ungrateful

328

young man scarf down food without asking if John would like more. He finished off the pancakes and picked off the rest of the bacon that was on the same plate with the sausage. Once he finished, he pushed his chair away from the table and left his dirty plate for John to take to the sink.

Mac walked out the front door without so much as a good bye or thank you and headed for the hospital. He didn't mind the walk and decided to talk to his mother's doctors rather than visit with her. Maybe he could figure out what had gotten into her. Perhaps he could convince her that she was under the influence of drugs and not having a 'religious experience' of some kind. The thought made him feel better. He was prepared to tell her that the doctor had given her a drug for pain that he was certain caused hallucinations. He needed to mix just enough truth with his lies that she would believe him. The concept made him laugh for it was exactly what his mother had taught him.

To kill time, he decided to walk by the ATM machine and withdraw some money. He had no intention of spending any more time with John than need be and would stop later to get some fast food. To his surprise, the machine did not grant his request, instead he received a paper stating there were insufficient funds for the transaction. Mac kicked the machine and tried again. He received the same explanation and no money!

Mac walked angrily into the hospital and demanded to see Kate McDaniel's doctors. The girl at the information desk could hardly believe this hostile young man was the same dazed and confused person she had recently directed.

Her doctors were anxious to meet with him and a bit angry as they recalled having no one to sign off on her surgery, though they realized he was her son not her husband. The doctors reviewed her chart with Mac and let him know that if she continued to improve, she would be released by the end of the week.

"Do you know what insurance your parents use?" asked the doctor.

"Sorry, I don't know anything about insurance. I'm sure she has the best though. My father will have no trouble making sure you and the hospital are paid for taking such good care of her." Mac figured they would leave the area and no one would see a dime.

"How heavily medicated is she? She seems to be talking out of her head." Mac snarled.

"At this point, she is only getting over the counter medication."

"Could there be a lingering affect from the meds from surgery?"

"There could be some residual effect, but I assure you it would be very minimal." That was not at all what Mac wanted to hear.

Both doctors flipped through charts to outline Kate's injuries, surgery and what was needed for a full recovery. Mac nodded sullenly.

"If you have any other questions, please feel free to give my office a call." He handed Mac a card and shook hands with the young man before finishing his rounds.

Mac entered his mother's room to find her sitting up in bed looking rested and alert.

"How are you feeling today, Mother?" he asked.

"I feel good enough to make plans to get out of here." She said cheerily.

"Great! Can you travel?" He couldn't wait to start a new life away from there.

"We aren't going to be able to go anywhere for a while, Mac."

"We can go slow, Mom, but I want to get out of here. Maybe we could go someplace warm. That would be nice for both of us." He smiled at the thought.

"That takes money." She studied him knowing he was holding something back.

"When was the last time you used your credit card?" she tried.

"I used it to buy a bus ticket from Massachusetts." Kate frowned.

"I tried to use it today, but I got this." He handed her the printout from the ATM.

"It seems we've been cut off." She frowned.

"Cut off? What does that mean?"

"It means, we don't have any more money."

"Maybe your card still works." He said hopefully.

"It doesn't work that way." She assured him.

"What are we going to do?" He had never known a time when they didn't have money.

"I always wondered if there would be a day when this would happen. I have some money stashed away. We'll be okay for a while." He nodded absently considering the implications.

"First things first! I need to get out of here." He had no idea where he would take her and couldn't bring himself to give her more bad news.

"I don't think your doctors are ready to release you yet." He said.

"Nonsense, I've already spoken to them and..." she searched Mac's face and knew there was more trouble brewing.

"Okay, spill it!" He shrugged in response.

"I can't fix it if I don't know about it, Mac!" she said pointedly.

"It's about the house... that is... we uh..." she held up her hand to quiet him.

"Do you still have your key?"

"Yah, I think so."

"Then you go back there right now and go to my bedroom. There are several shoe boxes in the closet with shoes in them. Pull the shoes out and lift the cardboard. There is money in each of them." Mac felt instant relief. Once again, his mother came to the rescue.

"I'll have to get someone to drive me."

"I'll ask John or the pastor to help you." Mac grimaced. He didn't want to spend time with either of them.

"You have a better idea?" he shook his head. He had few options.

"Get over there as soon as possible. I don't want anyone throwing things away or giving them to charity." She warned.

"I'll ask John to drive me tomorrow."

"No, you'll ask him today!" she said emphatically.

"Do you really think one day will make that much difference?" He hoped to come up with a different plan.

"Yes! We need to get everything of value out of that house today!" Mac nodded reluctantly.

"I think Dad took anything of value out of the house when we left for Massachusetts."

"And I'm sure your father took everything he could think of that was worth *anything*, but he would never think to look at my things. I never told him I kept money, and travelers' checks in shoe boxes. He would have flipped! But I knew the value of disbursement. You know the old saying 'never put all your eggs in the same basket'.

"Okay Mom. I'll get over there today. Then what are we going to do?"

"Let's take one step at a time. First we need to know how much money we have and then we'll be able to make some decisions."

"I think we need a fresh start! We will both think more clearly when we get out of this place." He smiled at the thought.

The inference was implied and Kate did not miss it. John warned her to go slowly with Mac. He was young and up until this point, he had only known one kind of life with one kind of parenting. The life she now embraced was foreign and undesirable to young Mac. She decided to hold her tongue and continue praying.

She noticed he never looked at her bandages and seemed repulsed by her injuries. She couldn't blame him. She had taught him to be self-centered and arrogant. Until a few days ago, she was self-absorbed as well. In her heart, she knew she would have made the same mistakes as Colten. She would have run out on him and gone to Massachusetts just as he had done. She knew his fate. She shuddered as she thought of the eternity that he had *just* begun. She thanked the Lord over and over that he not only opened her eyes to the truth, but had given her forgiveness! Somehow, she must find a way to make her son understand!

Chapter 22 *View Two*

Bombastic watched through the portal as Portentous taught his newest recruits. It was difficult to keep order as each one vied for position. Only their fear of Portentous kept them in check. The room was filled with hate that left a thick, putrid haze around them. It was too much evil to contain! Foolishly, each one boasted how he would defeat the Enemy Christ. Bombastic had made such claims, but somewhere in the depths of his being, he knew better. Experience taught him the limitations of his kind. Yet, he continued to spout the same lies for it was part of his very core.

"Who is moving up the ranks today?" Portentous asked. Several hands went up and Bombastic would have laughed aloud, but needed to protect his secrecy.

"Tell me why you should be elevated!?" He asked a fearsome, rheumy eyed minion.

"I have doomed all I was given!" he boasted.

"That's nothing... I not only doomed all I was given, I also tortured as many as possible before their final breath!" bragged yet another one.

"Very good! I hope the rest of you are listening!" Portentous said proudly.

"Perhaps he was not given as many souls to doom!" shouted a quiet voice. Apparently, this came from one who was not as successful.

"Are you calling me a liar!?"

"Yes! You are a LIAR!"

"ENOUGH!!!! We are all liars!" Portentous snarled, ending the debate.

"Tell us how you tortured your victims." Portentous salivated. The minion cleared his throat and stepped forward, enjoying the limited limelight.

"Let me tell you about Nancy. Ah, it is a wonderful story of defeat! For you see, Nancy was one of those grubby church bus kids that was pretty unlovable to begin with. She had an uncle who enjoyed watching Nancy develop into a budding young lady. I knew it would take just a little nudge to get him motivated to abuse her. He was troubled the first time he touched her inappropriately, but I helped him dismiss such thoughts. I told him he was a red-blooded young man who was merely teaching her what she should expect from mankind." He paused to laugh along with the dark crowd assembled before him.

"Of course, once the uncle tasted the forbidden fruit, he was hooked. It took more and more to gratify his lust and soon he was marked as a Pedophile. With all the modern technology, he was also marked as a predator and lost his job, his family and the last of his self-respect. I capitalized on his self-abhorrence and confusion." He remarked.

"Is that when you had him kill himself and come to us?" asked an excited voice.

"Naw, I wasn't done with him. That is what a novice would have done. I on the other hand, used this to my advantage! I screamed into his mind that it was all Nancy's fault. She had tried to seduce him! Of course, my lies were readily received, for mankind would rather blame *anyone* but themselves!" Again, laughter filled the air.

"I told him to find Nancy and kill her. If he would end her life... he could start fresh! He had no choice but to listen to my convincing voice. He listened easily to me, as I am a familiar voice and one he is used to obeying. He began a search for the girl who had ruined his life. By now Nancy was in her early twenties and was so demoralized by her uncle's behavior that she was putty in any man's hands. She found that none of the men in her life loved her and when she became pregnant, turned to abortion as the only option. Of course, this only added to her self-hatred." Portentous took note to move this one up the ranks.

"Nancy's uncle found her unconscious in an alley. Before he choked the life out of her, he slapped her awake to make sure she knew why he was ending her life. It was a fatal mistake. 'You ruined my life' he screamed as his angry hands gripped around her throat. Ah, but Nancy had been on her own for some time and found the world a cruel place. She kept a knife in her purse, for protection. She pulled out the knife and shoved it deeply into his chest. It was GREAT! I got a twofer" he giggled.

Bombastic snarled at the praise. He hated the story because it was not his own! He hated himself as he knew he should be telling such tales for the envy of all those listening! He roared loudly as the hate overwhelmed him and quickly ran for cover before he was discovered!

His only hope was to destroy Martin Parker, his family and his church! Filled with burning hate, he returned to earth with a plan of vengeance!

Chapter 23

"Did I ever tell you that you don't think clearly when you're sick?" Christine said as she bit her lip holding back an angry retort. Martin was a wonderful husband and father most of the time, but when he was sick, thought he was getting sick, or worried that something was wrong with his health... he was not easy to deal with. She would much rather deal with her children!

She did not come from a pampering background, and unless she could prove to her parents that she was ill, she went to school, finished her chores and did her homework. Of course, if she was actually sick, she was not allowed to go anywhere! As an adult, her family quickly learned, if Christine said she didn't feel well... take notice... she was known as a silent sufferer and for her to speak out meant she probably had waited too long to let anyone know how sick she was!

"Why don't we talk about this when you're not running a fever?" she smiled and rubbed his back.

"I am actually thinking very clearly! I think it might be time to get out of the ministry." He sighed.

"I thought it was a calling? Has God changed His mind?" she asked.

"Well, maybe it is time for a change. I've been at this church a long time Christine and to tell you the truth, they are wearing me out!" His voice was terse and unhappy.

In some ways, she was in total agreement. The battle could certainly wear you out! She wondered if Martin was harboring more bad news! It seemed to cast a shadow on anything good that was happening in their church. Ever since Kate McDaniel was released from the hospital and decided to once again attend their church, tongues began to wag! They thought people had forgiven Kate for setting the fire to the church, especially in view of all she suffered. Curiously, they found people were willing to pray for her when she was admitted to the hospital with 2nd and 3rd degree burns, but they did not want her to attend their beloved church she had tried to destroy!

When Kate came to church with her son, whispers could be heard in every pew. Many did not hold back their contempt, but narrowed their eyes in disdain. Kate held her head high as she knew she had been forgiven, but Mac was mortified! He had never experienced humility from either of his parents and hated every minute.

Martin could barely concentrate on his message and was horrified and more than a little irritated at the congregation. These were the people he relied on to pray! Yet, they were like Pharisees with their tongues wagging.

When he had had enough, he addressed it and it did not go well. There were many in the church that caused division. It seemed there was going to be a 'showdown' and it made Martin sick! They had never experienced a church split, but it certainly appeared that it was going to happen.

To his delight, Glen Booth was doing his best to speak to all that would listen. He used his own testimony as a tool and though it was painful, he felt the need to share his journey of faith. He prayed it would not hurt Norma to hear him speak so candidly of his despicable deeds, but she held his hand and smiled at the transformation.

"Martin, people are coming to know the Lord and we are a growing church. That says effective ministry to me!" The scowl on his face spoke volumes to her heart. She learned long ago that though you may have the right message, it may not be the right time to speak.

"Why don't you rest for a while and I'll bring you something to drink." She offered.

"Yah, sure." He murmured. She pulled a light cover over his shoulders and he turned to face the wall. Conversation was over.

"How's Dad feeling?" Chad asked as his mother shut the bedroom door softly.

"I think he just needs to rest for a while." Chad got the message. Leave him alone!

"Don't worry, I'm not going in there." He pointed to the bedroom.

"He about took my head off the last time I poked it in there." Chad retorted.

Christine wanted to defend her husband but couldn't think of a proper response, as she knew Martin could be testy when he didn't feel well.

"Is there something I can help you with?" she asked.

"Thanks, Mom, but I'll wait until Dad feels better. I don't think you can help me change the spark plugs in my car." They both laughed and it lightened the mood.

"Maybe you should check in on Lisa. I think she's getting what Dad has" said Chad.

"Really? She seemed fine this morning." She didn't think Martin was contagious.

"Let's just say she's got a lot of the same symptoms."

"Fever and aching joints?"

"I was thinking more of the nasty disposition, and general crabbiness!" he smiled. Christine shook her head and smiled at her son. They were as much alike as Martin and Lisa. Lisa was known to hide in her room without speaking to anyone if she had a bad hair day! Chad rarely complained. Christine learned the hard way to check on him after a rough game on the field. He had limped around with a broken ankle for nearly a week before she insisted on an x-ray. Another time he carelessly bandaged a bleeding knee that needed stitches. He had not cleaned the wound appropriately and in days the infected area caused him to be feverish.

"Maybe I should send Lisa in to see Dad. They can complain together." Christine almost giggled, but knew she needed to end this conversation. She never allowed her children to speak unkindly of each other and especially of their father.

"Your father will be fine in a day or two. I think we can forgive him if he is not in the best of moods! He certainly has a forgiving heart when it comes to the rest of us." Chad nodded in agreement. He admired his father is so many ways and never wanted to disappoint him, which made his present situation difficult to explain.

Sadly, Martin's illness was the consequence of a guilty conscience. Long sleepless nights along with overworked days and fast snacks left his body fatigued and ready for illness to make itself at home. He was in a place he vowed would NEVER happen, therefore, he could not forgive himself for he knew better and had counseled countless men for the very act! It all began so innocently... as most things do.

Martin had always been extremely careful when counseling women. He had seen far too many men in the ministry lose their families as well as their pulpits because they did not protect themselves. What he did not sufficiently protect himself from was the internet!

He certainly was no expert when it came to the web, and he had no idea how to prevent the countless 'pop-up' screens that appeared out of nowhere unannounced and uninvited. Normally, he deleted any of the undesirables as soon as they appeared, but for some reason, he found himself staring at the partially clad woman who seemed to be beckoning him. She looked vaguely familiar and he studied her for a few more seconds before realizing he was not really that interested in her familiar *face*. Instead of hitting the delete button, he moved her to his favorites! Eventually, he found himself looking forward to his private viewing, and it was taking longer to take his eyes from the screen. Like most pop-ups from the internet, there are a series of other websites attached, each a little more provocative than the first to tantalize men.

What had once been a harmless pop-up for which he had no control, became a source of shame as he realized how his mind drifted to the woman in his 'favorites' who he had visited on a daily basis. Several times he made attempts to delete her, but each time he looked at the sensual woman, he changed his mind. Over and over he told himself he was not harming anyone! He was definitely NOT cheating on his beloved wife as it was all imaginary. He would never meet this person even he knew her name and address. He just enjoyed looking at her. Maybe it improved his romantic time with his wife... who knew!! He certainly was making more advances toward Christine at the end of the day.

He knew his meeting last week with Glen Booth came directly from the heart of God. Since Glen's conversion, a 'new' man evolved. He became sensitive to the Lord's leading and even his family barely recognized the new Glen. He desperately wanted to please the Lord in all things and therefore set up sessions with Martin to help him move forward in his Christian life.

Martin could barely speak when Glen confessed to him how the internet had permeated his mind and how victory over sensual things seemed to elude him. Glen read Martin's series on pornography and as he spoke, the words were like sharp knives cutting his heart. When Glen read a portion of the chapter that dealt with the imprint pornography makes on a man's mind, Martin nearly broke into tears!

After Glen left his office, he immediately went to his computer with every intention of deleting the image that so often plagued his mind. Oddly, when he clicked on the woman, instead of repulsion, he gazed with admiration at the face and body of his unknown friend. Again, old impulses passed through his heart. He wasn't hurting anyone! Oddly, he refrained from removing her from his favorites. And in the passing days, he grew more sick of heart... and body and spirit. What in the world was happening to him??? Unfortunately, what was 'happening to him' was not of *this* world!

In the meantime, Bombastic tasted victory! He had done his best to create problems in each of their lives, with the exception of Christine. As an added bonus, instead of feeling drained from screaming into their minds, he found it made him much stronger! He had learned a great secret. *Prayerlessness not only brings defeat to the Christian, but it always brings victory to the dark side!* Bombastic was sure he had the Parkers right where he wanted them. If he could break Martin the rest would fall like a house of cards. He couldn't wait to boast of his evil deeds to Portentous and the other minions. He rehearsed his victories with the added mix of lies.

"Chad has been expelled from school for cheating! It has devastated the church youth group and completely humiliated his parents. Once he has been thrown out of the house, I will pursue him until I convince him to end his life." Bombastic laughed evily at his partial truth mixed with horrific lies. He was getting good at this!

"Lisa has become an addict swallowing large amounts of diet pills. She is just one step away from getting on the hard stuff and then her addiction will follow the same destructive course it has for all humanity. Once she is in desperate need of her drugs, she will be easily persuaded to pursue any method to satisfy her habit. Again the church and her parents will be devastated and humiliated." He beat his chest in triumph.

"I have saved the best for last." He howled

"The preacher has succumbed to pornography and is visiting all the websites to meet both men and women who have the same sensual appetite. There are several websites such as "Sex on the Side" and "Married but Lonely" and at the right time, I will expose him to the entire congregation." There was little truth in any of his words, but it only takes a grain of truth mixed with a pound of lies to get the job done! He salivated at the taste of success for he had forgotten Agnes and other prayer warriors who were begging God for victory!

Victory came to Martin in an unusual way. As he lay in bed sipping soup anguished in soul and spirit, he received a phone call from a dear friend and pastor who he and Christine had spent a great deal of time with over the years. Christine knew Martin would want to take his call no matter how he was feeling. Reluctantly, Martin took the phone and the terrible story unfolded.

"Martin my friend, I didn't want you to hear this from anyone but me." Carl's voice was thick with emotion and Martin was sure someone had died.

"I have resigned my pulpit Sunday and Martha and I are moving to Michigan where we will live with our daughter until I know what to do."

"Carl, what happened? Were you called to another area to serve?" he asked.

"How I wish that were the case. No, I have been relieved of my pastoral duties and rightly so." Martin sucked in a gulp of air and waited for his friend to continue.

"I have played the fool, Martin. Went in knowing full well it was wrong, but it didn't stop me." Again Martin waited for him to continue.

"Things start innocently, and I can always discern another man's situation, but when it came to my own... I was a total idiot!" He cried.

"Thank the Lord I have a good wife that is willing to continue with me. I know she is heartbroken and I pray she can forgive me." Martin wanted to console him, but his mouth was dry as newspaper and he could not seem to formulate a helpful sentence.

"Sin is so deceitful, Martin. Do you know that I thought the Lord understood my situation? Isn't that ridiculous? After all, I told myself... there were people coming to know the Lord on Sundays and I was still able to council others and minister to the hurting. What a joke!! The Lord used His word out of the mouth of a jackass just like he did in the Bible! He wasn't blessing my ministry... He was adding to His kingdom as His Word was spoken." Martin understood clearly what Carl was telling him. Too clearly! When he didn't answer, Carl assumed he was too emotional to speak.

"Guard yourself, Martin! Don't ever forget you have feet of clay!" Martin could feel the tears course down his cheeks. Yes, he was well aware.

"Is there anything I can do?" Martin stammered unsure how he could be of help.

"Yes, pray, pray and the pray some more! Not just for me and my family, but especially for those who proclaim God's Word."

"If there is anything you or Martha need, you know I am only a phone call away."

"Thank you for your friendship and your concern, Martin. Please forgive me for failing you."

"There is no need to ask *my* forgiveness, Carl…"

"I must ask for forgiveness for all those I have failed. Do you have any idea how horrible it was to stand in my pulpit for the last time and say good-bye? I looked at the faces before me and saw grief, fear, disbelief, and some well-deserved anger. I have hurt so many lives, Martin. Some are strong enough in the faith that they will weather this storm, but I fear some will fall by the wayside. I heard a member of my church say 'if the preacher can't live what he's preached all these years, what chance do I have?' Fortunately, I have many good, solid men that will handle things until they choose a new man." Martin's head was reeling. He envisioned himself standing before his own congregation.

"My pain was well deserved, but my poor wife! Oh, Martin, my poor wife!" he broke into sobs and Martin continued to wipe his own eyes, feeling his friends agony.

"Those were her closest friends! I humiliated my beloved, Martha. She walked out the church doors with me knowing it would be the last time she would ever see many of these dear people. I took all those years away from her and she didn't deserve any of it!" Martin's heart broke for his friend and by the time he hung up the phone, he understood that God was giving him a chance to make things right. It was quite a wakeup call!

Chapter 24

In the days that followed, there was a thorough 'house cleaning' among the Parker family. Martin pulled himself out of bed and after spending hours on his knees, knew he had once again received a clean slate from his Heavenly Father. He had no idea how he was going to speak to his family, but he had always been one to shoot from the hip without making excuses, and this time would be no different.

Before he met with Christine, he ran to his computer and without looking at the screen, pulled up his 'favorites' and hit the delete button. It made him feel *clean* again! He couldn't wait to delete the picture that wandered unannounced into his thoughts. There was not a single ounce of regret for discarding her. As a matter of fact, the very thought of looking at the familiar woman was loathsome.

Christine entered the bedroom while her husband was on his knees and quietly closed the door. Lunch could wait. She came back later and gently pushed open the door. Nothing had changed. Martin was still on his knees and she began to worry. Maybe he was *really* sick and had not shared it with her. She smiled at the notion, for her husband would tell her if he had a splinter in his finger and she was aware of any ache or pain he experienced on any given day.

"What's wrong, Martin?" Christine's compassionate gaze only increased his guilt.

He had no idea how to begin and once he closed the bedroom door he held her hand and looked into her eyes. How could he bring pain to this woman who he loved with his whole heart?

"I have something I need to tell you and it is not going to be easy for me to say or for you to hear." He began.

"For the last several weeks, I have had something on my computer that should never have been there. I of all people know how sinful …" he could barely continue as he thought of the hurt this announcement would bring.

"If you are talking about the woman in your 'favorites' I already know." Martin gasped! It never occurred to him that she might have come across his secret. As he thought about his actions, he shook his head. Christine had all the passwords and could view anything available. She was not on the computer very much and would have no reason to check his favorites or history.

"Why didn't you say anything?"

"I thought it might be Chad's 'favorite' and I didn't want to bother you with it until I was sure. Then we would talk to him together." She was too blindsided to continue. It never crossed her mind the 'favorite' could be her husbands.

"I'm so sorry, Christine. I don't know how it happened." He cried.

"I think you somehow forgot you are also a man who must guard himself." She hugged him to assure him that they would get passed this moment.

"Martin, I remember a day not long ago that you had met with a man who was battling with …um… moral issues. And you said 'I don't know how he could do that? Not at this point in his Christian life. He should be more grown in the Lord than that.' And I held my breath thinking that we are all one decision away from making hurtful, harmful and even despicable mistakes." Martin nodded slowly. Had he really thought he was beyond such things?

"I also remember you saying that though the Enemy can't read our minds, he laughs when we make ridiculous proclamations publicly and can't wait to show us how weak we are when he rubs our nose in our sinful choices."

"Yes, I remember saying that. Sometimes you think your words are for others and exclude yourself." He felt nauseated.

"Can you ever forgive me?"

"Yes, I forgive you" was her immediate response. Martin could hear the *hurt* in her voice and pulled her close.

Anthony stopped over to see Lisa and brought her homework. Chad filled him in and he was actually relieved. He had no idea what had happened to the sweet girl he loved to the unpredictable young woman that was kind one minute and yelling and screaming the next. He could finally make sense out of her mood swings.

Christine was happy for the company. Anthony had a great sense of humor and quick wit. He was always a pleasure to be around and the entire family welcomed his presence. He often came around dinner time and was always a welcomed addition. They loved to see how he was growing in his relationship with the Lord and his father played a huge part.

"Can you believe my parents are taking a cooking class together? And they love it. My mother's cooking has improved drastically, but it really doesn't matter anymore. My dad compliments my mother on... everything... her cooking, her hair, even her driving!" he laughed.

"I don't get compliments on my driving!" Christine nudged Martin.

"You haven't damaged the car... or the passengers... so I compliment your driving ability." Laughed Martin.

"I never thought I would see the day when my parents seemed happy. I mean my father is so loving toward my mom and I've heard her thanking the Lord so many times when she doesn't know I'm close by. It's wonderful!" all nodded in agreement.

"That's how I want it to be when I marry. I want my wife to know she is the best thing that ever happened to me and I want her to be happy she married me." Lisa and Anthony smiled at each other as he talked and both Christine and Martin knew they were smitten. Of course, they were still in school with college ahead of them, but they seemed more committed to each other as the days passed.

Glen was a true depiction of a changed heart. His infidelity haunted him at times, but Norma would not let him dwell there. She told him they should call the 'old' Glen by a different name not to be confused with the wonderful husband she was now married to. Martin had allowed him to give his testimony to men who were struggling and the Lord used him to bring many to a clear understanding of their salvation. Some had lost their way while others realized they were only playing a spiritual game. God blessed him for his penitent heart by giving him a new love for his plain little wife, Norma. He gladly burned the painting Rebecca had given him and found she no longer evaded his thoughts. He prayed someone would reach out to her with the love of Christ as he understood how desperate they were both chasing an illusion of love that would only be found in God.

Chapter 25

It seemed God *was* answering Glen's prayer concerning Rebecca. Little did he know that he was actually joining the prayers of John Dunbar and Vontrice. Rebecca truly loved Vontrice and knew she would be lost without her help, though they seemed to have less in common these days. Rebecca blamed John for the changes she saw in Vontrice and hoped it was just a phase she was going through. In the beginning, she spoke unkindly about John.

"Vontrice, I think you are beautiful and obviously attract all kinds of men. Why would you spend so much time on this 'religious' one?" she spat.

"You're right! I've attracted all kinds of men. Most of them hurt me and all of them used me!" she retorted.

"Okay, so learn from your mistakes and move forward. But come on, girl! At least pick one you can have fun with!" she nudged.

"John and I have a lot of fun together. We both love the outdoors and music…"

"What about having a stiff drink? I'll bet he absolutely forbids it!" Rebecca snorted.

"He doesn't forbid me anything!"

"Not yet, but rest assured if you keep spending time with him, he'll have to make you one of his little converts and then the fun will be all over!"

"John is not interested in making anyone 'his' convert, but he *is* interested in making converts for Christ." Rebecca put up her hand as if she were about to be assaulted.

"Not interested! You can hold the rest of the spiel for someone who wants to hear it!" Vontrice sighed as Rebecca marched out of the room angrily. There was nothing she could do but go back to work and pray for her misguided friend.

In the weeks to follow, Vontrice noticed there was a difference in their relationship. There was no more comradery between them, and Rebecca spoke to her more as a boss than a friend.

One night after dinner, John and Vontrice took a walk in the cool of the evening. With no destination in mind they walked aimlessly along happy to be in each other's company. The Lord had evidently directed their steps as they found themselves directly in front of *Art Works* and could see Rebecca through the window. She looked upset.

"Something is definitely wrong! Should we go in and talk to her?" asked John

"I don't know, John. Rebecca is not as open with me as she once was. I'm not sure she would like the intrusion." She worried that Rebecca would be angry and mean spirited with John for the interference.

"Maybe she needs a friend right now." Vontrice was reluctant, but John had already walked through the door leaving her to trail behind him. As they approached Rebecca, it was evident from her red rimmed eyes, she had been crying.

"Pardon the intrusion, Ms. Rebecca." John began.

"Oh, I didn't hear you come in. Did you forget something?" She asked Vontrice. It was her day off and rarely did she stop by when she was not working, especially now that she spent so much of her time with John. Vontrice was not sure how to approach her friend or how to begin a conversation.

"We were just taking a walk after dinner, not sure how we ended up here." She said sheepishly.

"I'm sorry. I'm not really up to company right now." Her eyes once again filled with tears and Vontrice impulsively reached for her and threw her arms around her.

"You're hurt! I'm so sorry!"

"It's nothing! I'll be fine!" Rebecca said flatly. John noticed she did not push Vontrice away, which was a good sign.

"I'll get over it. It's no big deal...really." Vontrice knew it had to do with a man. It always did! John prayed quietly for the right words and the right time to say them as he headed for the kitchenette to get Rebecca some water.

"Do you want to talk about it?" Vontrice asked gently.

"Nothing really to talk about. Apparently, I've once again made a fool out of myself." She talked softly and watched the kitchen. She didn't want John Dunbar to get wind of her conversation.

"I can be so stupid sometimes, Vontrice! You were right when you said you attract all kinds of men and most of them just use you!" she wiped her eyes again and shook her head in confusion. She thought she was smarter.

"Did you know I was going to set *this* one up in a nice house? Ooooh, that Rigo! He is a good actor, I'll give him that! I should have known that he was seeing every rich old woman that would pamper him!" She quickly told her about her clandestine meetings with the handsome bartender. He flattered her and she gave him expensive gifts for his feigned adulation. In her misguided enthusiasm she decided to surprise him with an unexpected visit. Her mistake was to show up at the same time as one of his other trysts. He did his best to keep the two women apart, but Rebecca was no push over. She knew the moment their eyes met her unexpected arrival did not bring him pleasure.

"Would you like to introduce me to your...friend?" Rebecca said hatefully.

"Oh, yes, of course, where are my manners." He smiled, but his crimson face betrayed him.

"Rebecca, this is my friend, Loretta." Loretta narrowed her eyes and looked Rebecca over as if she was a piece of rotten food that needed thrown into the garbage. The women put two and two together immediately and knew neither meant anything to Rigo.

"Sorry for the interruption. I can see I've caught you at a bad time. Rest assured it will *never* happen again!" Rebecca snapped as she clutched her purse and turned on her heel. She knew she needed to leave quickly, as she would rather die than let either of them see tears in her eyes.

"Rebecca wait!" Rigo shouted after her adding to Loretta's fury. By the time Rebecca crossed the parking lot and unlocked her car, she heard Loretta's Mercedes screech out of the parking lot. It made her smile through her tears, as she knew Rigo would have to find himself a couple more dimwitted women to take their place. The jig was definitely up!

Rebecca thumped the palm of her hand against her forehead. She was obviously losing her touch. She hated to think of how much she was going to miss Rigo. He certainly knew how to handle a woman. Too bad it was all a charade.

John took his time coming back into the room to give them privacy. He didn't want to embarrass Rebecca and continued to pray for the right words.

"I found some juice in your fridge. I thought it might refresh you." John said sincerely. She took it from his hand and stared into his compassionate eyes. No matter what she told herself or Vontrice, she knew she could not categorize him the same as the men she knew.

"Thank you." She said simply and drank deeply from the glass.

"It seems you have found yourself a good one, Vontrice. Good for you." She set the glass down and took a deep breath.

"There is nothing good about me, Ma'am. I'm just as despicable as any other man you ever met." Rebecca looked at him quizzically. Was he joking? Trying to evoke a response from her?

"I doubt that's true. You don't know some of the men I've known. Why they would think you walk on water!" she smiled.

"So, what's your secret, John Dunbar? Religion? Is that what it takes?"

"No, religion hasn't done much for anyone."

"What??? I thought you were all about religion!"

"Nope! You got it all wrong."

"So, you're not going to tell me that I need to go to church, stay away from bars, men, entertainment, music that doesn't have a religious theme blah, blah, blah!"

"Right now, I don't see that as your biggest need." She stared in silence wondering if she should end the conversation before he started preaching to her, yet there was something about this man that intrigued her. She knew in her heart he was sincere and that alone was different from any man she knew.

"Okay, I'll give it a shot. What is my biggest need?" Vontrice was shocked that Rebecca would ask such a question. She prayed as John sat quietly for a moment and knew he was praying for guidance before he spoke.

"Your biggest need is for love and forgiveness." Vontrice cringed as she waited for Rebecca to erupt. To everyone's surprise, including Rebecca's, she began to sob uncontrollably. In desperation she willed herself to stop, but her body would not cooperate. Great convulsive sobs continued to wrack her body.

"Love? Forgiveness? I doubt I know the meaning." She cried.

"I sense you've been deeply hurt, Ms. Rebecca. It goes back as far as you can remember and it has not allowed you to forgive." There was no condemnation in his voice and his tone was like a warm sunbeam on a frigid day.

"I don't want to talk about it." She stood up fully intending to walk out of the room. John held his arms out to her and for no understandable reason, Rebecca fell into them and laid her head on his shoulder and cried as she had not cried since she was a child.

"Shh now, you just take your time. This has been inside you for a long time and you need to let it out."

"I feel ridiculous!" she sniffed but Vontrice noticed she didn't push him away.

"It's probably the best thing you've done in years." He patted her back and she continued to cry softly into his shoulder with eyes closed tightly.

Images of a sweet Daddy with warm hugs emerged in her memory and she concentrated on each detail. She resembled her father who also had red hair and large green eyes and tons of freckles. She once teased him that if she could join all his freckles together, he would have the perfect tan!

The tall, redheaded man everyone called "Red" loved farming and Rebecca had faint images of riding on her Daddy's tractor as he cultivated fields or walking with milk pails to the barn as he teased "Bossy" to give her best and finest milk for his family. Most of the memories were like fuzzy snapshots.

There was no one in the world like her father and when he divorced her mother, she felt like she got divorced too. Her mother was not a 'maternal' sort and would rather spend her time with adults then with her children. Rebecca's brother reported their neglectful mother and before long, the authorities had placed her and her brother in separate foster homes.

Rebecca lived with her ailing Aunt who took her in to clean and cook. Aunt Melissa had asthma and was often in bed puffing on her inhaler. Rebecca thought she was an Indian who was smoking a piece pipe. Aunt Melissa had no children of her own and it was best. It didn't take Rebecca long to discover that Aunt Melissa might spend the week in bed, but when Saturday night came… she was out of the dance floor!

Rebecca's father tried to win custody, but the court always ruled in favor of her aunt as they felt she needed a woman to teach her and not her farmer father! She never knew what happened to her mother. There were conflicting stories. Some said she moved out of state and others said she left the country. Wherever she was, she seemed to have written off her children as none of them ever heard from her.

By the time Rebecca was thirteen she was dating and ran away with her first boyfriend at fifteen. From that time on, there was a series of boyfriends that came and went. She tried to find her father who would remain the love of her life, but her aunt told her he had died in a farm accident. She had no idea the whereabouts of her brother or whether he was looking for her.

Rebecca met her husband Chuck at an art gallery. She found him rather boring while he was totally mesmerized with her. After a few drinks, he became a little more tolerable and they spent the rest of the evening together. He didn't want to lose this beautiful woman, so told her immediately he would like to set her up with her own art gallery. Of course, she thought he was joking, until he flashed a large wad of cash her way. She had no idea that the money was not his. He had just cashed a payroll check for his father, but before bringing it home, he decided to flash some money around the important people at the gallery. It made him feel rich and important. No one needed to know he was his father's errand boy who lived on a meager salary. The large wad of cash he was flashing was his father's paycheck.

Chuck also lied about his inheritance. He didn't tell Rebecca his father was leaving him little of his wealth. His older brother, Simon was his father's protégé and would receive the lion's share of his father's estate. Chuck had always been a hot head with more brawn then brain and had his father not given him an insignificant position in his company; he would no doubt be on the welfare role.

Soon after they married, Rebecca discovered the ruse and her bitterness erupted like a volcano. There was nothing Chuck could do to repair the damage. Chuck's father agreed to buy an art gallery for her with the stipulation she had to stay married to his worthless son and that she allow Chuck to work in the gallery with her. He could at least put his minimal accounting skills to work. Rebecca agreed believing when the old man died, she would end the marriage.

When her father in law died, she found he was a brilliant man who took no chances. His attorneys had an iron clad will stating that Rebecca's art gallery would remain under her control as long as she was married to Chuck and that he worked there as well. There was money allocated to pay the mortgage on the gallery with an additional allowance to buy art for the gallery. There was no way she could possibly keep the gallery without Chuck's father's money. Again, she was stuck!

Her only happiness came from the gallery. She truly loved art and in time the artists knew her by name. Some had inspired her to try her hand with paint and water colors. She wasn't sure if she had real talent, or if her teachers saw it as an opportunity to show their work in her gallery. She began dating some of the artists and though

Chuck was pretty sure she was cheating on him, there was too much at stake to demand a divorce.

"I don't know why I am blubbering like an idiot!" Rebecca sniffled.

"You've had a lot of losses" said Vontrice remembering some of her childhood stories. She told her things so matter of fact that it never occurred to her anyone ever meant anything to her.

"I hardly remember most of the people in my life. My mother may know what became of my brother. The only person I would truly like to contact is my father, but I have no idea where he is either."

"Maybe I can help." Offered John.

"I doubt it! I tried years ago to hunt him down but it's always a dead end. I guess when you have such a common name it's too difficult." She sighed.

"Try looking for George Miller! You might as well look for John Doe!"

"There are many ways to search for people these days. Let me take a crack at it." said John. He had developed exceptional computer skills and it was time to put them to the test.

"Why would you want to help me?" she looked at the floor remembering all the cruel comments she had made to her friend.

"Hurting people are my specialty." John smiled.

"Too much hurt out there and too few willing to do something about it! I can't promise I'll find him, but I can promise I'll make a good effort!" She smiled at him and it was as if they had just met.

"My father was such a special man. My heart was broken when my parents divorced. My Aunt complained that he was taking her to court to get custody of me and I was on cloud nine! Even if the court wouldn't allow it… and they didn't … I knew he love me and wanted me!" fresh tears streaked her face but this time she didn't brush them away.

Vontrice kept waiting for John to share the gospel with Rebecca, but he seemed ready to leave without another word. She gave him a puzzled look as she stood beside him preparing to leave.

"Before I go, I would like you to read something for me." Rebecca froze in her steps.

"You're a smart woman, Ms. Rebecca. The word on this paper are pretty simple, but they are straightforward and to the point." She pushed his hand away.

"I told you I wasn't a religious person." She stated emphatically.

"And I told you religion never helped nobody! But the words on this paper are from God's Word and that's why it's important you read it." She took it from his hand and tossed it carelessly on the coffee table.

"If there is anything you don't understand my phone number is on the back. Call me anytime." He smiled as he headed for the door.

"See you in the morning." Vontrice said quietly. To her surprise, Rebecca reached out to her and gave her a bear hug.

"Thank you for being a friend!" Rebecca whispered through quivering lips.

"Good night, John Dunbar." She shook his hand formally and turned on her heel to go. She was exhausted and confused. She looked forward to thinking things through on her own.

As soon as they walked outside, Vontrice searched John's face for answers.

"She was listening, John! She was actually listening to you. Why didn't you present the gospel to her? There couldn't be a better time!" she said in frustration.

"I understand how you feel, but it wasn't the right time."

"How can you say that? You had her attention! She was listening to you!" she berated.

"Yes, and I was also listening! I was praying and listening to the Lord. It was not the right time." He said softly, understanding her desperation.

"What if she dies tonight? You should have told her, John!" she snapped.

"Do you trust me, Vontrice?" she sighed and slipped her arm through his. She trusted no one like she trusted John.

"Most people never take the time to pray earnestly for God's leading. Some have learned the life changing Scripture and can't wait to share it. That's wonderful, but truthfully, that is not the entire answer. There have been times I rushed ahead of God and pushed my way through the Bible hoping to lead someone to the Saviour. I was often frustrated when someone would allow me to show them the Word, but stopped me from continuing. Worse yet, I had some bow their heads and recite a prayer and I knew in my heart they just wanted me out of their hair. My heart was in the right place. There was nothing I wanted more than to see them come to know the Lord as Saviour."

"There is nothing like it, that's for sure." Vontrice chimed in.

"But I have also watched people under conviction. Not all of them weep, though there are other signs. I have looked into the eyes of those who knew they were guilty before a Holy God and believe me it is far different from those checking their watch or glancing at their cell phones."

"Aren't we supposed to warn them anyway?"

"Yes! I always leave the Gospel in written form for them and always include my phone number to answer any questions they might have."

"Do people call you?" Vontrice asked in astonishment.

"Yes, some do. I try to follow up on those who don't." He didn't want to discourage Vontrice in any way from speaking to others.

"I am excited for your zeal, Vontrice. Truly I am! Don't ever lose that or become complacent. You are to speak to as many as you can and are instructed to do so from the Scriptures. I am only suggesting that you earnestly pray before, and during your communication. I am as anxious as you are to see people come to Jesus, but you can't force it. There is just as much harm done when people have a false sense of security because they remember a time they 'prayed a prayer' and barely remember anything about that time. No conviction... no desire to live for the Lord..."

"Not everyone changes." Said Vontrice.

"This is true, though they should. Whether they change or not, the *desire* should have been there. That's what regeneration will do for a person. They may fail miserably, but the initial desire... the intent of the heart... was to make that life change."

"I understand what you're saying, I'm not sure I entirely agree."

"That's fine, Vontrice. You certainly don't have to agree. Just keep your heart tender so you hear the Lord's leading. That's all I am saying."

Vontrice had a restless night's sleep. She wanted to call Rebecca and ask her if she read the tract John left for her. She wanted to show her step by step how she could know for certain heaven was her home. Yet, she watched John as he spoke to Rebecca and as she carefully went over each piece of conversation in her mind, she was reminded that she too was praying fervently as John spoke to her friend. If John said it was the wrong time... she trusted him. She also realized she knew few people like John who had that kind of prayer life. She certainly didn't.

True to his word, John began searching for Rebecca's father. He decided to use the "Ancestry" app he was familiar with, and found several George Millers. It took several calls and mountains of dead ends, but eventually, he found a few possibilities. Two of them had daughters named Rebecca. One hung up on him before he could tell him the reason for his call. The other one began to cry and told him that his daughter had died long ago.

John persevered as was his nature. None of the leads seemed to be working out. Finally, he knelt beside his bedside and took it to the Lord, chastising himself for not asking sooner! As he finished praying, he looked closely at the scattered papers on his desk. Hmmm, the one that seemed to stay on his mind was from a discarded lead.

"Now, Lord, I know it aint this man. I have already called him and he told me that his daughter died long ago." Still, his eyes stayed focused on the paper with George Miller, daughter Rebecca, son Timothy. Immediately, he was on the phone, but not with George Miller.

"Ms. Rebecca can you tell me the names of your brothers and sisters?" he asked without telling her who was calling.

"This is John Dunbar, Ms. Rebecca." He said in a rush.

"I should have asked more questions before I started my search. That was stupid on my part. But I do have some leads and I want to follow up." He said quickly.

"I'm with a client, Mr. Dunbar." She said rather stiffly though she felt excited about the possibility of finding her father.

"Just name your siblings for me and I'll let you get back to your customer." He said hopefully.

"I had a brother named TJ, no sisters."

"Okay, thank you, ma'am. I'll get back to you." He shook his head as he stared at the information before him. This couldn't possibly be the right George Miller. She didn't have a sister and this wasn't the right brother. He shook his head baffled. Again he prayed earnestly for an answer and once again his eyes were drawn to the same paper.

"What am I missing?" he said aloud. He scrutinized each piece of information and made a discovery. He slapped his forehead as he realized the brother, she called TJ was probably Timothy James or Timothy Joseph. This could be the man he was looking for.

Though he wasn't exactly local, he lived about two hours away as close as he could calculate. He had never heard of the little town and was astonished to find it within driving distance.

Should he call first? What if the man didn't want to see him? What if he was the *wrong* man and he was wasting his time? Should he go alone or bring Vontrice with him for support? Again, John began to pray for direction. In his heart he was certain this man was Rebecca's father.

After lengthy research, he found the last known address for George Miller but could not find a phone number. Perhaps it was God's way of telling him to meet in person. Fortunately, Vontrice was available to travel with him. She could barely contain her delight.

"Do you think you have found her father?" she asked excitedly.

"Yes I do." He said firmly hoping she would not ask too many questions as he had few answers.

"Can I tell Rebecca?" she asked.

"I would prefer that you don't say anything yet. I have no idea what this man will be like or whether he will be agreeable to meet with me. What if he doesn't want to see Rebecca? No, I don't want to take the chance." Vontrice readily agreed.

"Okay, I won't tell her. You know she has been acting differently ever since your conversation with her the other night."

"Different... how?"

"I can't really put my finger on it exactly. She's ...um... *softer.*" It sounded strange but it seemed the right definition.

"Rebecca has always been, you know, kind of 'coarse.' And she prides herself on it! I remember how she practically did cartwheels when she bought Mr. Gorsuch's art at a cheap price. She would never pay what something is worth and loves the fact most people don't know she's almost stealing from them. She's always been ruthless and cutthroat! But the last few days, she has been, I don't know, kind and thoughtful!?"

"I think the Lord is working in her heart, Vontrice."

"I do too. I have to tell you it's not easy to work with her and not sit her down with my Bible. I keep thinking about what you said, but John, I also wonder if I should talk to her while she is in this state of mind!"

"If you believe the Lord has given you the opportunity, then I understand." He certainly didn't want to get in the way. He had never shared his heart before when it came to witnessing, as he feared he would not be understood. Worse, he was afraid people would use it as an excuse to keep their mouth shut instead of presenting the Gospel.

After her conversation with John, she went back to work and continued to watch her boss carefully. Yes, she was definitely different. She noticed when a little boy picked up an expensive art piece and his mother did not appear to have the means to pay for it, she carefully took the object from the boy and put it back in its place with no mention of 'you break it... you bought it.'

Vontrice smiled at Rebecca who brought the boy into the picture gallery and showed him some of the ones he would be most interested in. There was an artist who painted beautiful wild life; some so amazing they seemed to leap from the canvas. Vontrice could never remember a time her boss showed such kindness to a child.

When they finally had a break, Rebecca ordered lunch and closed the doors for a short time. The Deli could have made the lunches in advance as they ordered the same things day after day. It was all delicious and eaten quickly with snippets of conversation between mouthfuls.

"You were so kind to that little boy, Rebecca. I think you would have made a good Mom." Vontrice smiled.

"Me with kids?? Don't be ridiculous. I just didn't want him to break anything." She said icily. Vontrice was taken aback from her demeanor.

"I was hoping they would get out of the store before he touched anything else. I doubt his mother would have been able to buy an ashtray." She laughed, sounding like the old Rebecca she knew so well.

"Actually, she bought a very expensive painting."

"I hope you didn't take a check from her! It will no doubt bounce!"

"She paid in cash." Rebecca's mouth dropped open. She had no idea the woman had a nickel on her.

"People aren't always as they appear." Vontrice smiled.

"Jesus looked like a poor carpenter's son, but he was much more than that. He was the Son of God. He came to take away the sins of the world." She began.

"I think it's time to get back to work." The smile was gone from Rebecca's face as she hurriedly slipped back into her shoes and unlocked the front door. Vontrice noticed a pointed difference in her the rest of the afternoon.

Vontrice was excited to make the trip with John to find George Miller. She had a GPS in her phone, but John liked maps. They brought a few snacks for the trip and plenty of water. Neither John nor Vontrice drank soda, as John had convinced her of the importance of water.

They traveled in silence for a few miles before Vontrice spoke.

"I think you were right about Rebecca."

"Right about what?" she told him the entire story and sad ending. Rebecca did not want to appear vulnerable and when

Vontrice mentioned her interaction with the little boy in the store, she immediately changed course.

"I wouldn't worry about it Vontrice. Maybe she's sensitive about motherhood being she never had children or an example of a mother."

"That's probably true, but I went further by speaking to her about Jesus." She thought John would be upset with her, but that wasn't John's way.

"I wouldn't worry about that either. Now, if you started following her around the shop quoting the Bible to her, than we might have a problem."

"No, I didn't go that far!" she giggled. He could always take the sting out of things.

"Vontrice, God knows your heart. Don't fret about it. We will just stay on course and see if we can't find her Daddy." He smiled.

The next couple of hours were spent talking about all the Lord was doing in both of their lives. Vontrice was trying to memorize portions of Scripture that she found both soothing and challenging. She thought John was the smartest man she ever met and hoped he would ask her to marry him one day.

After several wrong turns, they eventually found the correct address. The road turned dusty and Vontrice covered her face with a scarf. She could already taste the grit between her teeth.

"Let's park here and walk up the drive. It doesn't look like there is much traffic coming in and out and I don't want to spook him." John said.

Vontrice was glad she wore her flats and walked gingerly across the stones as they headed to the house ahead. The house seemed to perch on top of a mountain and they leaned forward with every step as they made their ascent.

"Do you see what I see?" John asked. Vontrice shielded her eyes from the sun and squinted. She could see a man standing before a canvass painting. As they approached, they noticed the freckled arms of the painter, and though the hair was mostly white, there were signs it had once been red.

"Hello, we are looking for George Miller. Are you "Red?" asked John pleasantly.

"Who wants to know?" He continued to paint without giving them so much as a glance.

"There is another artist looking for you."

"That so... well I don't know any artist that would be looking for me." John took a few more steps to get a look at the picture and was quite taken aback. The colors were vibrant and the perfect strokes of his brush made the scene come alive.

"That is beautiful! Absolutely beautiful!" Vontrice said as she joined John for a look.

"Ya think so? Hmmm, maybe it's better than I thought." He smiled for the first time and seemed to relax a bit. He laid his palette on a stump in front of him and turned to view his guests for the first time.

"I don't get much company out this way. Who did you say is looking for me?" Vontrice turned to John. She held her breath afraid of his reaction.

"Is there a place we can talk?" asked John.

"I got nothing to hide. But I could use a drink. I suppose you could too." He added. Though he didn't exactly invite them, they trailed behind him to a modest house a few feet behind him. When he walked through the door, John noticed he left it open and they took the opportunity to get out of the sun.

"I got nothing fancy for you, but my artesian well produces some of the best tasting water around." He ushered them into the living room and they sat down on the sofa before them.

The house was well taken care of and though the furniture was older and a bit outdated, it was in good shape and the house was immaculate.

"John, look at the paintings on the wall!" John saw a young blonde girl with her arms wrapped around a beautiful Irish Setter.

"Did you paint these?" John asked as he took the glass from his host's hand.

"Yep, I painted everything you see. Some of the sculptures are mine too." He pointed to a lovely hand painted statue. John held the solid piece of wood in his hand and was amazed at the intricate detail of the carving as well as the complex colors.

"You carved it as well?" John asked.

"Of course."

"You have a lot of talent Mr....uh...what did you say your name was?" The men stood toe to toe for a few seconds observing one another.

"Are you George Miller also known as 'Red'?" asked John.

"I am." John gripped his hand and shook it as if he had found his long lost friend.

"Who is looking for me? I don't know any artists." Just then Vontrice gasped. All eyes turned her way as she stood before a picture on the wall.

"This little girl... can you tell me who she is?" John quickly joined her and both knew they had made an important discovery. Mr. Miller's reaction confirmed it.

"That was my baby girl, Rebecca. I haven't seen her in so many years and I painted that picture as one of the last remembrances I have of her." His voice shook a bit as the emotion gripped him once more. Sometimes he would stand before that picture drinking his coffee and praying once again that she was well.

"Mr. Miller, we know this little girl, though she is all grown up now."

"What are you saying? How can you be sure? Her mother told me she died in a plane crash years ago, but I could never trust anything the woman told me. I felt sure in my heart my little girl was still alive, but I thought it was just wishful thinking."

"I work for your daughter, Rebecca. She is a wonderful artist and owns her own gallery. She gave up ever believing she would see you again. I can't tell you how happy she is going to be to find you again!" Vontrice hugged him feeling as though she had found her own father!

"Wait until she sees you and finds out she gets her artistic ability from you!" said Vontrice in tears.

"Now hold on just a minute. She thinks I walked out on her and maybe I did. Lord knows I tried to find her, but that miserable aunt of hers wouldn't give me a lick of information and tried to lie along with her sister. Trouble is they never got their story straight. Her aunt said she died coming home from Europe when she was on spring break in school, but her mother said she died when she was a little girl. I tried to press her but she wouldn't budge."

"Rebecca knew you loved her and wanted to get her away from her aunt. She has wonderful childhood memories of the farm." Red bit his lip to keep back the tears. He couldn't believe she was alive and wanted to see him.

"We are about a two hour drive from here. Is it possible for you to leave for a few days?" asked John.

"Now hold on there. I don't know either one of you and as far as I know you could be scamming me." He didn't believe that was true, but on the other hand, he knew it was a crazy world and many were taken in by crooks and … worse!

John couldn't believe in his excitement to find the man, he would have to convince him he was acting on his daughter's behalf. Vontrice saved the day.

"Let's sit down and talk." Said Vontrice gently. She told him every scrap of information she had ever been told and produced a picture of the gallery and Rebecca standing beside her at an art festival. But the clincher was the stories. John told the story of the little girl walking to the barn with her Daddy to see old "Bossy" He also remembered her Aunt Melissa had asthma and Vontrice remembered Rebecca's story of joining his freckles together to make the perfect tan. George was convinced!

"Her brother lives in Ireland. He wanted to meet my relatives and once he saw the beautiful country, he never came back to the States. I hear from him around the holidays but not much else.

"If I'm going to make a trip, I need to make a couple of phone calls." As soon as he left the room Vontrice clapped her hands excitedly.

"What about you, John? Are you going to call Rebecca?"

"I'll call her when we get close." He knew she would have

difficulty working with the anticipation of seeing her father again, and he thought it best to wait.

They decided to ride together and by the time they reached their destination felt like close friends!

Chapter 25 *View Two*

"We are superior to these weak mortals." Portentous bellowed.

"How then is it possible for any of them to win?" asked a timid voice in the darkness.

"If any of them are winning, then someone is not paying attention! Someone hasn't done their homework!"

"And let me assure you, if any of your assignments are winning... you will be cast into the abyss immediately! I am through teaching and training those who are not heeding my words!"

"No one should be slipping through your mangy fingers! DO YOU UNDERSTAND?" he bellowed.

"How many times can I tell you to capitalize on their weaknesses? But always remember... it starts in the mind! It is a domino effect. The heart controls the mind and the mind controls the actions!"

"Today, we have several minions on trial. They have been warned and they have continually failed." His voice shook the air and those closest trembled in fear as the lineup began. It was truly a mock trial used only as a fear tactic.

"What do you have to say for yourself?" Portentous bellowed to the first in line.

"I have done my best! I just need more time!" cried the offender.

"You are out of time!" Portentous screamed over the thunderous clapping.

"Wait! Wait! Let me explain!" He whimpered.

"I was given church members! It is not fair when so many have been given atheists!"

"As I recall, you begged to show your prowess! If the truth be known, you had a desire to alieve me of my position! But you gave a pitiful performance!

"You did not capitalize on their frailty!"

"But...but... no one can stand against them when they pray!" he scoffed.

"Do you not understand there is no power in their hunched over demeanor? No power in their rigid-rehearsed-many-worded-so-called-prayer? You must stay while they bring out prayer beads or even that Blasted Book and watch and listen!" he screeched!

"I don't understand! When they are praying, we have no authority, no voice, no control!"

"That is only if they are *truly* in prayer!"

"How do we know the difference? We can't actually read minds!" he pouted.

"You don't know the difference? You really don't know the difference? No wonder you are on trial!"

"Tell us how to know the difference!" several voices inquired at once.

"YOU CAN TELL THE DIFFERENCE WHEN THE ENEMY SHOWS UP~!" Boos and hisses were heard throughout as Portentous continued.

"The Enemy *always* comes when His people humble themselves before Him!"

"So, don't be frightened away just because you think these frail people are actually praying much less trusting... hit them hard when they are merely on the outskirts of prayer. Tell them it does no good. They are not worthy of answered prayer! Their Master doesn't care anyway! Flood their minds with their to-do lists! Remind them constantly of all they have to accomplish in a day. Most of them never ask the Enemy for help in their day to day anyway! They are prideful people who take credit for all the Enemy has given them and then cry for more benefits! Never satisfied!! Use it!!"

"Send me back! I will do better this time. I understand now!" pleaded the minion.

"Too Late! Too Late! Take him away!" the cheers were deafening as one by one those who failed were thrown into the darkness.

"Who is next?" Portentous loved watching them squirm and all enjoyed the torment.

"Please let me explain before you make your final judgment!" Portentous puffed out his chest as the minion bowed before him.

"I am on the verge of taking down a very well-known enemy! It may look like I have failed, but this is not true!"

"Continue... but this better be good!" snapped Portentous.

"I was given a large church congregation as I have already climbed the ladder from apprentice." The look on Portentous face made him shudder. It was not wise to sound more promising than your adversary and Portentous was a well-established adversary.

"Of course, I could never ascertain the level of power and understanding such as yourself! Why you are a legend!" Portentous took the bait and allowed him to continue.

"The church seemed to be growing until the preacher became ill and allowed his nephew to become the pastor. Unlike his Uncle, the nephew only had the appearance of a follower. I watched him as you have directed, and you're wise council paid off. The nephew began to make demands of the people to benefit himself and many of the congregants were in desperate need of food and shelter for their family. No one dared speak against the new preacher and he and his deacons used scare tactics to keep these people in check. Why one of the women was actually molested by this so called preacher while her husband worked two jobs to put food on his table. When the woman told her husband, he said that the preacher was always right and never to be questioned!" He had to wait until the howls dissipated before finishing his tale.

"The woman was angry with her husband and it escalated into a huge fight. I was worn out speaking to both of them as quickly as possible. I told the woman her husband could not possibly love her and allow this to happen. I told the man the woman was violating her rights as a wife and member of the church. They were easy targets. She was too emotional to pray and he was too frightened of the church deacons to stand up for her."

"Finally, to shut her up, he hit her with a mallet and killed her!" He howled!

"Then why are you on trial?"

"I was supposed to bring the preacher here. That was my assignment. But truly, I feel I can continue to help him wreck more homes. Why should he be brought here so soon? He will have eternity to suffer!" Portentous looked over the accusations that brought on the trial. He discovered the answer.

"You were to bring the uncle down. He was influencing these people at one time. But I can see he is of little value at this time. The nephew has completely taken over and the uncle is too weak to be of much influence. I am going to allow you to continue!" Portentous swaggered importantly.

However, this was a mistake. They would later learn of the error when the uncle, though bedridden, called a number of members along with the police, and had his nephew arrested. After fervent prayer, many found their way back to the Lord Christ and began to make a difference in their community.

Portentous shuffled through more violations before coming across Bombastic's defeats. It angered him that he had not been able to find him. He seemed to be one step ahead of him each time he would have brought him to trial. In desperation, he decided to use the violations as a teaching tool for the others.

"The violations I am about to read to you tell a story that will not be tolerated! Many of you are familiar with Bombastic and his claim to be superior to you. I assure you...he is not! He has been given far too many chances and failed each time!" He strutted about as the story began to unfold.

"You must be very watchful when it comes to those who have given their allegiance to the Enemy! They have a way of leading others away from us! This will not be tolerated!" He bellowed.

"Bombastic has allowed Kate McDaniel to slip away from us. She was once one of our very own! A pity really! She was beautiful, sensual, and persuasive! A combination for success. But Bombastic thought she was unreachable. Be that a lesson to you!!!! No one is unreachable until they have made their way to us!" he snapped.

"We still have a chance with young Mac, but it will slip through our fingers if someone, other than the incompetent Bombastic, doesn't do something soon! We have already lost Vontrice! This cannot be tolerated! Learn from this mistake! Vontrice should have been killed by one of her vicious lovers, but as I recall, someone thought it was better to keep her alive so she could bring John Dunbar down! Miscalculations! Costly Miscalculations!! Costly, Intolerable, Miscalculations!!" Portentous was livid at the thought.

"Now Vontrice and John Dunbar have teamed up to win Rebecca to the Enemy! I do not want this to happen! Surely one of you numbskull's can prevent this from happening!" Several began to spout off what they would do if given the chance. He surveyed the area and found no one he deemed promising. Must he do everything himself? Perhaps it would teach them a lesson and give him a bit more affluence.

"I will handle this myself and give a full report. Make no mistake! I will bring my spoil with me when I return!" Immediately, there was thunderous applause for his eloquent speech. But would he be able to deliver? They were no match for him... but he was no match for the Enemy. He must be careful. If he was wise enough to tread slowly, they would depend on themselves and never see danger ahead! Portentous threw back his head and laughed heartily. He could taste their defeat!

Chapter 26 *View One*

John felt anxious the moment they piled into his car. He had the sensation of walking through a thick web and his movements were as if he was walking waist deep through water.

"Would you mind if I rode shotgun?" asked George as he neared the vehicle.

"I guess in the excitement, I am feeling a bit queasy." He slipped in the front seat without waiting for an answer leaving Vontrice no choice but to ride in the backseat.

"I need to make a phone call before we leave. I won't be long." George and Vontrice were sure he was calling Rebecca, but it was his brother, Linc, he needed.

"John, do you know what time it is?" Lincoln sounded a bit miffed until John relayed the information.

"Get Vontrice and that George fella if he can pray. We need to bring this before the feet of the Lord" ordered Linc. John knew he made the right call. Though he felt there was some kind of warfare going on, he wasn't sure without talking to Linc first.

Soon Vontrice, George and John were huddled around John's phone listening to Lincoln's prayer on their behalf. John noticed the shock on George's face as he stood with his hands folded under his chest. John and Vontrice held hands as Lincoln's voice permeated the air in prayer. John prayed as well and Vontrice smiled and said 'Amen' when they were done.

"We are only going a couple hours' trip. You think that was necessary?" asked George.

"Yes! I know it was." John smiled at his skepticism. It didn't bother him and he noticed immediately the difference in his movements. No longer did he feel weighed down, and though George was silent, he also noticed there was no hint of nausea as they traveled.

John asked several questions about farm living, art, and sculpting. George relaxed more as they sped down the highway and soon filled them in with several animated details from his earlier days to the present.

"You've had quite a life, George" said John.

"I suppose I have." He said reflectively.

"Call me Red, all my friends do." Vontrice smiled at the comment. She prayed they would all become friends and more.

"What about you, are you two married?" John grinned from ear to ear as Vontrice giggled.

"Not yet, but it is definitely in our future."

"What ya waiting for? You aren't getting any younger and if you aren't careful, this pretty girl is going to have other suitors." He warned.

"So, you don't think anyone would be after me... just the girl!" John teased.

"Seriously? You better grab her quick!" they all laughed as if they were close friends jabbing in fun.

"I assure you, I am quite serious about making her my bride." Though Vontrice knew he felt that way... it was reassuring to hear him say it.

"Well, I have to warn you. I knew a fella that dated a girl for years and always talked about making her his wife, but as the years went by, she began to doubt it would ever happen. Another man began to date her and the next thing we knew, she got married to him. As you can imagine, her previous beau was quite upset about it."

"When he demanded an answer from her, she said 'if you wanted it, you should have put a ring on it." Red laughed.

"If you would have told me yesterday that I would be hopping in a car with a couple strangers and going for a trip to see my supposedly dead daughter, why I would have laughed you right off my front porch!"

"I'm not usually a very trusting sort. I have never done anything like this before."

"So, why did you decide to come with us?" Red was quiet for a while as he tried to think of a good answer.

"I can't really tell you I have a good explanation. I mean you two don't look like ax murderers, but these days that doesn't mean anything."

"Can I tell you why I think you decided to travel with us?" asked John.

"Vontrice and I prayed that we would find you and that you would also believe our strange story. Believe me, you weren't easy to find, and until we actually met you, we weren't sure if you were the right George Miller.

"You a preacher?"

"No, I'm not a preacher. I am a Christian cleverly disguised as a Paramedic" Vontrice laughed at Red's astonished face. He had never met anyone so outspoken about their faith.

"I never met anyone like you, John. I wish I had faith to believe something I can't see. This world has given me a pretty cold shoulder. I guess it tainted me." He said thoughtfully.

"Can't argue that this world can be difficult with lots we can't understand, that's why it's so important to know what lies ahead, once we leave this world."

"I don't think anyone can know until they get there" said Red.

"You can't wait that long or it will be too late." Vontrice interjected.

"Don't misunderstand. I think there is a God of some kind. Don't know if it matters which one we call Deity. I mean we are the ones that put a name to it. God may not refer to himself as God. He may have a name we can't even pronounce. God is an easy name. Any man can say a word with three letters." John could tell Red had given this some thought.

"And Jesus? How does He fit into your thinking?" asked John.

"I've done a little research. He was definitely here on earth at one time. There is a historical record."

"Not sure I believe all his claims. No doubt he was a great man, philosopher, and teacher. But that doesn't make him God."

"Then he was a crazy man. Is that your opinion?"

"No, I never said he was crazy!" said Red appalled he would think such a thing.

"Wouldn't he have to be one of the craziest men on earth to claim to be God in the flesh?" Red didn't like this line of reasoning, though he could not dispute it.

"I never thought about it that way. It doesn't fit, does it?!"

"There is only one reason Jesus came to earth. Would you like to hear?"

"It's a long drive, got nothing else going on... I'm listening." Red slouched back in his seat with arms folded across his chest as if he was about to take a snooze. But it didn't deter John. He began speaking about his beloved Saviour, and before long, John was wide eyed and totally interested in every word. John spoke with reverence, gratitude and love for his Saviour and he was totally in awe of his words.

"That's a lot to chew on." Red leaned back in his seat and Vontrice was disappointed that the conversation seemed to be over. John glanced in the rearview mirror and mouthed 'it's okay.' If he needed time to 'chew' he would wait and pray. There were many more miles to travel and he felt certain the conversation was far from over.

Vontrice gazed out her window and silently prayed for both Red and Rebecca. If only John could make them both understand their need, but she knew only God could change their hearts, and they would need to be willing.

When John pulled the car into a gas station, he decided it was time to call Rebecca. Red was asleep with his head resting against the window so the timing seemed perfect. If Rebecca didn't respond favorably, he certainly didn't want Red to hear it.

Vontrice stood beside John as he pumped gas, and he gave her his best smile. There were times he had to focus his mind away from his beautiful girlfriend, or he would not be strong enough to wait until they were married to keep themselves pure.

"Rebecca, can you talk?" John asked as soon as she answered the phone.

"I can talk for a few minutes. Though if my assistant were here, I would have more time!" she laughed easily and John thanked God for the change in her.

"I'm bringing her back to you, Rebecca. Just as fast as my car will get to you, and she is not the only one I'm bringing... I found him, Rebecca and I'm bringing him with me." He ran so quickly over the words, she wasn't sure if she heard him correctly.

"Slow down, John! Who are you bringing with you?" she could feel her heart pounding in her chest.

"I found George Miller, better known as Red." He laughed.

"How can you be sure?" It seemed like the impossible dream and she didn't want to get her hopes up.

"Rebecca, he is an artist too! I've seen his painting and sculptures. He painted a picture of you that we decided to bring along." It sounded too good to be true and she just couldn't get her head wrapped around the idea.

"John, an artist's picture of a young girl is not proof!"

"The picture is of a pretty little red-haired girl named Rebecca. He painted it after your mother and your aunt tried to convince him that *you* had died." He heard her gasp and realized he was giving her too much information over the phone.

"Listen, we'll be there in another half hour or so. I'll let your Daddy speak for himself. But I can promise you, he was as skeptical as you are."

"I'm going to have to close early!" she laughed and felt lighter hearted than she had since she was a little girl. Could they have truly found her father?

Red opened his eyes as they neared their destination. They were all a little nervous as they pulled up to *Art Works*. He glanced at John wondering if he had made a mistake. He didn't want to get his hopes up yet his throat was tight and heart pounding.

"Let's get this over with. If this is my Rebecca, I need to know." He said matter of fact disguising his emotion the best he could.

Before he reached the door, it burst open and there stood Rebecca with searching eyes scrutinizing every inch of the man before her.

"Rebecca? Can it really be you?" As soon as she heard his voice she leapt into his arms nearly knocking them both to the ground.

"Daddy! Oh Daddy! I thought I would never see you again!" she cried as he smoothed her hair and held her close.

"I would know you anywhere!" they said simultaneously.

"Please come in and see my gallery." She hooked her arm through his and led him inside.

"Looks like we've been left in the dust!" laughed John as Vontrice hooked her arm through his to join them.

Vontrice had already made the decision to take care of the gallery without Rebecca's help to give her all the time she needed to visit with her father. Unfortunately, it was a very busy day and people were milling around every inch of the store. John did his best to help, but knew little about art and its worth. The best he could do was keep customers occupied until Vontrice could get to them. Fortunately, he knew how to run a cash register and was comfortable behind the counter wrapping art pieces and making change.

When the store emptied, they took a much needed break and joined Rebecca and her father. They were talking and laughing as if they had only been apart for a short time and were catching up.

"I don't know how you did it, John Dunbar, but I will be eternally grateful!" she said through her tears of joy, as she gave him an uncharacteristic hug.

"He tells me he did it by praying." Red announced as he watched his daughter's face. Was she praying too? Was he the only one who questioned God?"

"Yes, that sounds like John." Rebecca commented.

"Were you praying with him?" he ventured to ask.

"I suppose I have in some ways. I prayed he would find you, and I must tell you it was a little strange for me to do so. I am not a church going person and lightning would probably strike if I made an appearance." She laughed nervously.

"I must tell you that I promised if John were able to find you... because of his prayer... then I would listen to what he had to say about God." Vontrice could barely contain her enthusiasm.

"Now that's funny, because I told God I would think about the things John told me on our travel here if at the end of this journey I was to find my daughter!" he covered his eyes to hide his tears and John knew there was more he hadn't shared.

"Truth is, my second wife was a lot like you John. She was a bit on the 'preachy' side, and went to the little country church not too far from my home. She wanted me to go with her but I was stone cold about it. Do you know what I used as my excuse? I told God that if I found my little girl, I would come to church and be like Martha. Over the years I just got colder."

"I think it's time I opened my Bible and we looked at the Word together." With that, John sat between them and showed them passage after passage. They both had questions and John did his best not only to give them answers, but show them where the answers were to be found.

"I don't believe in a literal hell!" Rebecca announced without much conviction.

"What happens to those who will not accept the Lord's payment for their sin? You do believe in sin!?"

"Of course I believe in sin... I'm practically the poster child!"

"You didn't answer my question."

"I think they go back to dust and ashes and never get to experience heaven."

"You believe in heaven but not hell?"

"Yes. I think a good God doesn't send people to some horrible place."

"He is a good God. That is why Jesus paid the penalty for sin. He took your place and mine." She looked unconvinced.

"Let's try something. I will say some words and you give me the opposite."

"Up" said John

"Down" said Rebecca

"Square"

"Round"

"Short"

"Tall"

"Hot"

"Cold"

"Pretty"

"Ugly"

"Fat"

"Skinny" They were on a roll as John threw in the last one.

"Heaven" There was a few seconds of silence and then...

"Hell" she said quietly. Everything had an opposite.

"If you think about it Rebecca, dying and going back to dust and ashes is not that bad! And if that's all that happens then why not get all you can get in this life? If you only have one chance to get it all before you're in the ground ... live it up!!"

As Vontrice prayed silently for both of them, she knew there was understanding, acceptance and desire to become a child of God. It took her breath away!

Both Red and Rebecca gave their heart to the Saviour and Vontrice cried for joy as she hugged them both. At last her boss understood the changes she saw in her life.

Red stayed for a few days and Rebecca showed him every nook and cranny of her art gallery. He burst with pride at her accomplishments and she felt like a little girl again getting her daddy's approval.

Red knew enough about the art world to be very helpful. He could spot an antique from a replica and knew how to price merchandise. They made a wonderful team.

"Daddy, you must bring your artwork to my gallery. I want to display it!" Rebecca announced with pride.

"Don't know if it's worth anything. I am just a local artist... nothing fancy. And there are pieces I don't want to part with." He was thinking of the picture he had painted of her that hung on his living room wall.

"If you don't want to sell some of them, then I want you to replicate them so I have them in my gallery. Some of them will remain on my walls and we'll sell other pieces."

"I can't wait for you to see the picture he painted of you, Rebecca. It is fabulous!" Vontrice remarked as she described the painting in detail.

"Don't get excited, it's really not that good. Maybe you will let me paint a new one of you. I tried to envision what you might look like as an adult, but you are more beautiful than even imagined you would be!"

"Thank you, Daddy!" she said with a rare blush.

"You look a lot like your mother, Rebecca. At least you got all her pretty parts." He laughed.

"Hope you didn't inherit her ability to lie and deceive." The room fell silent as each one knew of distinct times she was guilty of both. Red knew somehow he had hit a nerve.

"It's all in the past anyway! I don't need an account and I'm not giving you one." He smiled.

"I wonder if you'll make the trip back with me, Rebecca. I really need to get back home. I've got a neighbor feeding my dog and I don't want him to feel taken advantage on! I would like you to see my home and there are a few people I would like you to meet." Immediately, her eyebrows raised he gently touched her hand as he spoke.

"We can talk as we drive and I'll answer any questions you might have. I would also like to call your brother once we get home and have a conversation with him. Hope he's sitting down!" he laughed.

"I would be happy to travel with you. Vontrice can handle everything until I get back."

"Is everything okay, John? I know you drove me here, but I thought it would be nice if Rebecca drove me back home" said Red. John seemed distant and his solemn expression made him feel uncertain. He was anxious for his daughters to meet. Was he wrong? Was this not the right time?

"Truthfully, I am feeling anxious about your return trip."

"Don't worry, I'm good at directions. I know I snoozed on you but believe me I can find my way back home" said Red.

"Do you remember that before we took our trip, I called my brother, Lincoln?"

"Yes, I remember how weird I thought that was at the time."

"I know this is a lot to take in… but…not everyone is happy that you decided to trust the Saviour." Vontrice could feel her skin prickle with each word and wondered how John could explain himself to such new believers.

"The Bible says that even the angels rejoice when someone trusts the Lord and gives his heart to Him, but just as there is good, there is evil." He watched John and Rebecca as he carefully selected each word.

"Do you think we're in danger traveling back to my home?" asked Red bewildered. John wasn't sure how to answer. Were they in danger? Once again he felt the sinister pressure of a world he could not see.

"When do you plan on leaving?" asked John.

"Was thinking tomorrow would be good. You know I just stashed a few clothes in a travel bag as I didn't think I would be staying long. At this point, I need to wash the clothes I'm wearing or buy new ones." He laughed easily among family and friends.

"I would like to see you off if that's okay" said John.

"We would like that, wouldn't we, Rebecca."

"Yes, of course!" Vontrice gave John a quizzical look. She knew him too well, and his stilted conversation with Red and Rebecca was a bit unsettling.

John and Vontrice left father and daughter to continue their conversations alone. Vontrice and John said their goodbyes as they closed shop for the day. She was extremely tired but ecstatically happy too. It would be nice to slip into a hot bath and relax for a while.

"Something's troubling you, John. What's wrong?" she asked as soon as they were alone.

"I can't really explain it… but I am feeling the same as I did when I called Lincoln."

"Do you think they are in danger?"

"Not sure. I just know I want to be there in the morning before they leave on their road trip."

"I thought at first it was just me! I began getting a headache and then nausea. I wasn't sure if I would be sick in the backseat, but George already slipped into the front so I had little choice."

"Everything changed after the phone call with Lincoln. He always seems to change the atmosphere." She laughed.

"I hope you will get to meet him one day. He is an amazing man."

"You're pretty amazing yourself, Mr. Dunbar!" she kidded.

"You know I have given a lot of thought to my brother's prayers. I mean, I pray all the time, but when Linc prays it just seems like heaven comes down to meet him." He sighed with admiration.

"I'm always second guessing situations, but Linc just seems to know! And when *he* is praying… darkness just has to leave! It can't reside in his presence or his words because he is speaking to the Lord, and it just feels like the Lord comes to meet him half way!"

"You are more like your brother than you think. When you pray, I settle down inside. There is a calmness in your words because you trust the Lord and have close fellowship with Him. I love it!" said Vontrice sincerely.

"And I love you… in case you don't know." She smiled.

"I never grow tired of hearing it. I guess that's the way it is with the Lord. He never tires of hearing our sincere prayers and our heartfelt love for Him."

Early the next morning, John and Vontrice were back at *Art Works* as Rebecca scurried around trying to pack a suitcase.

"Slow down, girl! You aint moving in with me, we're just going for a short trip." Red laughed. Rebecca's suitcase was crammed full of clothes, shoes, and jewelry.

"Oh, Daddy, you know so little about me!" she giggled.

"I always pack more than I need. I change my mind a lot and you never know if the weather will be agreeable. I would rather have too much than not enough."

"You got enough stuff for two women. My place is not fancy and there are no highfalutin restaurants around either."

"Daddy, this is how I always dress. It may not seem like casual attire to you, but it is it me."

"Casual attire is coveralls and boots" he laughed at her turned up nose.

"Okay, you two. Let me put your suitcase in the car" said John.

"If you can lift it!" laughed Red.

Chapter 27

John called Martin on his way to work and filled him in on all that had happened since they last saw each other. Martin smiled with delight as the stories unfolded. It never grew stale or unimpressive. Each soul was worth so much! He delighted in each detail.

"I've been rambling on for quite a spell here. Why don't you tell me what's going on at your end." John laughed as he glanced at his watch.

"Nothing that rivals your stories, that's for sure! You've had quite an adventure!

"Anything new with Kate and young Mac?" John asked tentatively.

"Yes, Kate is out of the hospital and she came to church with Mac, though he didn't look too pleased to be there. People were hovering around Kate. Some were happy to see her and were genuinely pleased that she was recovering from her wounds. But, you know, there are others that were not so happy to see her. Christine had a talk with the ladies and asked them to be kind and gentle with Kate. Norma Booth has been very gracious and has helped me talk with some of the ladies that are having a difficult time dealing with all that has happened. It's not every day that someone starts a fire in your church."

"She almost paid with her life! Hopefully, that will build some compassion." Martin agreed, though that didn't always happen.

"Mac is supposed to come over tonight and spend some time with Lisa and Chad. They are both praying for him. At this point, he is so confused."

"How is Kate doing?"

"Physically, she is healing nicely. I know it's been hard on her to face the church and she asked for a time to speak openly about her experience, but I asked her to wait. I don't think it's the right timing."

"Hmmm, I wonder." John's mind was racing. Perhaps it was the best timing!

"You disagree?"

"Perhaps after Mac has spent time with you and your family, it might prepare him for his mother's testimony. Perhaps his heart will be more open."

"That is my prayer. I told her I would give her an answer in the next couple of days."

"I will also be in prayer!" John smiled as he knew he could be on his knees 24/7 and still never run out of prayer requests, as well as prayers of gratitude.

"I have another matter to discuss with you." John cleared his throat before he blurted out…

"I want to get married."

"Yes, I am aware of that." Martin laughed.

"I mean I want to get married right away." For a moment, Martin wondered if something had happened between John and Vontrice that pushed the marriage forward.

"I don't want to spend another day or night away from the woman I love. I hate saying good bye in the evening and returning home to my empty home and to be honest with you, it is getting more difficult to keep my mind right." Martin smiled as he listened to John struggle to find the right words to express himself.

"When would you like to get married? I am not sure when the church is available."

"We just need to get the license and have you perform the ceremony. I will make sure my mother attends and will call Linc so he can listen. I don't know if Vontrice has anyone that needs to be there."

"Okay, that will make things simple and easy. You tell me when you have the license and I will make sure to perform the ceremony."

John hoped Vontrice was serious about tying the knot quickly as he wanted to do it today!

John knew he was looking at a twelve hour shift to thank those that covered for him in his absence. Sometimes he wished he had become a missionary like Linc, so he could devote all of his time to those he wanted to minister to. But the job was rewarding and the Lord used him constantly.

Martin had a full schedule as well but deliberately crossed off the end of his schedule to be home tonight. He was sure his wife and children would need all the reinforcements possible when dealing with Mac.

As usual, Christine prepared a wonderful dinner for them and though Mac entered the house a little sullen, his mood seemed to change as Lisa and Chad began joking and catching each other up on the day.

"How is your Mom doing?" Chad asked. Immediately the smile was removed from Mac's face. Chad realized his mistake. He didn't want to ruin the mood.

"I'm glad she's out of the hospital." He said quickly.

"Yah, she seems to be on the mend." Mac said softly.

"So, are you ready for the big history test? I can barely keep today's date in my mind, let alone remember what happened a hundred years ago!" Lisa chimed.

"History is important none the less." Martin said.

"You don't want to repeat mistakes they made in history and if you don't remember what happened, you will!" Christine added.

"I don't mind remembering what happened, but why do we have to know the exact date? Who cares if it was December 1, or December 31! As long as you know what happened and how it affected everyone, I don't know why we have to know those details." Lisa argued.

"I think you're just lazy!" laughed Chad.

"I remember the important dates, like your birthday!" she laughed.

"Now that was an important day!" Chad teased. Soon Mac was chiming in with his own jibes and the mood was playful once again.

"I'm glad you came over tonight, Mac. Your teasing is a lot more fun than hearing my children fuss at one another." Christine kidded.

"Thanks for inviting me. I have enjoyed myself." He said sounding a bit surprised.

"Why don't we make plans to go to the baseball game next month? I could get tickets and we could make a day of it. It's a Saturday game and it's about sold out."

"Sounds good, but I'm not sure if I will be around in another month. My mom and I haven't decided what we're going to do once she's done with all her doctor appointments." Lisa and Chad exchanged nervous glances. They didn't want him to leave the area without the opportunity to talk to him about the Lord. Chad glanced at his father for direction.

"There is still time, Chad. Why don't you get the tickets anyway? If Mac can't make it, I'm sure you won't have any trouble finding someone else to go with.

"I hate to think of you moving away, Mac. Hopefully, that won't happen anytime soon." Martin added.

"We never stay too long in one place. Maybe my family just gets restless." He smiled. Nothing had been mentioned about his father and he dreaded anyone asking about him. He told people that his father was looking into a job in another state and pumped it up big. Supposedly, a major company wanted his father to run the corporation and become their next CEO.

"If my father gets this new position, we'll be moving soon." he added. Speaking of his father made him sad and angry and brought terrible memories to the forefront that he tried his best to repress.

"I should be going. I am not ready for the history test and I best get studying those annoying dates." He smiled at Lisa and she remembered how much she enjoyed the attention of this handsome young man. But that was over. So much had happened since he tried to date her. She was crazy about Anthony and no one else could turn her head.

"Why don't you study with me and Lisa? We can take turns finding out how much we don't know!" he laughed.

He stayed much later than anticipated and enjoyed himself far more than he ever thought possible. Lisa and Chad treated him like a close friend and expected nothing in return. He winced a little when Chad jokingly told his sister that he remembered some of the history dates because he *prayed* they would stay in his head. He tried to convince himself that there was no value to praying, but he couldn't quite shake it off.

Lisa noticed he had lost most of his self-confidence. He didn't strut around like the proud peacock they were familiar with. His joking did not have the usual double meaning or cutting edge.

After they said good night to Mac the two looked for their parents. They wanted to share great news, but neither of them approached Mac about his need of Christ. To their amazement, Martin smiled as if the night had concluded with a great spiritual feat.

"Mac is changing, that is obvious." Martin said.

"I really looked for an opening to talk about his mother, but I just couldn't find one. I don't think he wants to talk about his mother anyway. It seems to make him uncomfortable." Chad said.

"I think the night went just the way it was intended. You see, Mac needs friends like you. He needs to see that we are not playing some kind of church game. He needs to see *real* Christians living *real* lives for a *real* Savior."

After hearing what had taken place between the teens, Martin called Kate and asked her to prepare her testimony for Sunday. He let her know that they would be in prayer. It was decided to keep the information from Mac for fear he would find an excuse to stay home.

Kate worked for hours on her testimony, praying constantly for the Lord to use it to bring Mac to Himself. She didn't care if the church ever forgave her misconduct. She felt deserving of any biting words or unforgiving spirit; though it was difficult to attend in the very sanctuary she almost burned down.

Sunday morning came quickly and Kate nervously hid her testimony in her Bible. Mac did his best to remain distracted as Martin preached. He painted such a dramatic picture of Christ as the Savior and Mac held tight to the pew in front of him during the invitation. He couldn't wait to bolt! To his surprise after everyone was seated, Martin asked his mother to come forward. Mac's heart was thumping in his chest. He glared at her as she walked forward to the platform and stood behind the pulpit. Was she going to embarrass them more by speaking to these people? Yes she was!

He narrowed his eyes and hoped she could see the disdain he felt as she began smoothing out the papers of her testimony. Kate had always taken the lead and was *always* in control...but not today.

Her words took his breath away. He wanted to hate this soft, compassionate woman, but instead he found something coming alive within his heart. She spoke as effectively as she ever did! Strong, powerful words that gripped her audience...but this time her words were not an attempt to persuade the hearer to join forces with her. Her words were about Jesus, the loving Savior she had come to trust and turn her life completely over to his control.

Unless you walked in her shoes on the dark side, you could never know what she experienced. It was like being in the darkest dungeon without a glimmer of light. Never seeing anything without a dark shroud encapsulating everything; and coming into the light a step at a time. She felt like a blind man who had his eyes healed and could see color and shapes for the first time. It was truly miraculous.

Mac's heart melted. He had never really had a mother. Kate and Colten were called mother and father, and taught him to be self reliant and egotistical. There was never warmth or affection between any of them. Brad gripped Mac's arm and asked him if he would like to know the Saviour as his Mother did. Without a word, Mac followed Brad into a small room in the back of the church and after pouring over several Scriptures; Mac too bowed his head and bent his will and his way to a loving Savior.

For Mac it was a slow, painful act. His body seemed to quake at the thought of turning his life over to the Lord. He had never known such fear and believed he would die if he dared to do such a thing. If it had not been for his mother's testimony, and knowing in his heart that this was a completely different woman... he could never have taken the necessary steps. On one hand, he could feel himself tremble with fear as he thought of leaving the only life he had ever known. He felt pulled and prodded to remain in the life he had chosen so many years ago as he followed his parents' leading.

Colten was dead! He was certain of that. Though he would not allow his mind to drift back to those horrific unreal memories, he knew in his heart he never wanted to remember! He shook his head several times as he felt the strong urge to run! Over in over he could hear 'Don't do it! Don't do it! Don't do it!!!! As Portentous screamed and pulled at his heart.

The entire church seemed to celebrate and Kate and Mac were welcomed with open arms. Mac was elated! Kate cried softly as she watched her son welcome the King of Kings into his life. Mac, on the other hand bawled like a baby. He couldn't remember the last time he shed a tear. Perhaps when he was a small child and hurt himself, but this was completely out of character. The tears seemed to come from somewhere deep in his soul. Huge sobs that wracked his body seemed to release something in the depths of his being. He felt free! Absolutely free... for the first time in his entire life!

While the congregation continued to celebrate, John ran into the parking lot to call Linc. It was always his first thought. It rarely occurred to him that he was half way across the world and probably sleeping. Besides, Linc would want to know! He dialed quickly and was surprised to hear a sleepy voice on the line.

Chapter 27 View Two

Portentous could not believe how many things went awry! "They should all be DEAD!" he screamed into the air. He was not a novice; he was at a much higher level and considered a teacher to those deemed worthy of consideration. These were the ones that had their fate on hold for a time. No one in their army wanted to investigate the final chapters of the Enemy's Words. It was not that they had not heard them, but they vowed not to believe them. Of course, this made no sense when they knew the Enemy was incapable of lies and their great leader was incapable of truth.

Perhaps in the final analysis, "pride" was the answer. When a man is full of pride, he believes things about himself that are total lies. Mankind was not capable of the full embodiment of pride. His kind was. Therefore, in *total* pride, they could believe that the Enemy would be defeated and they would be victorious, for PRIDE believes such lies.

Portentous stepped forward to rehearse what he believed the number One lie...

"As we gather together, we must continue to doom mankind! Study your assignments! They sleep...you do not! Watch their expressions, their body language, the slight smirk as they listen; the haughty voice! Do not miss anything that can be useful!

"We have done a marvelous job telling them over and over there is NO GOD! Many have bought in to such nonsense as it pleases them to think they are not accountable to anyone! But alas, there have been many renown scientist who pursued truth. It was quite exciting in the beginning as we were sure they would publish journals to disprove the existence of God. Unfortunately, in their quest for the truth... they came to KNOW the truth!! Now they are publishing for the Enemy and how they KNOW He exists!"

"Why don't we just burn that blasted Book so no one can read the Enemy's Words?" someone asked.

"We have done that through the centuries. We have had bonfires with the Enemy's Word, but we have never been able to get rid of it!" Portentous screamed in anguish as he remembered the many defeats.

"What if we torture and imprison all that will speak on the Enemy's behalf!"

"That too has been done since the first believer was found. But alas... adversity only makes them stronger. In fact, they have found the Enemy's presence in ways they never experienced during the good times. No, that is not the answer!"

"You are smiling, Portentous, does this mean you know the answer?" He nodded his shaggy head and puffed his chest before making his final point.

"Listen, and listen well!" He bellowed forcefully.

"We will allow them the Blasted Book, and we will even let them toy with the question of the Enemy's existence!" He grinned evilly.

"BUT... WE WILL TELL THEM THE LIE OF ALL LIES....

YOU HAVE PLENTY OF TIME!!!!!!!!!!!!!!!!!!!!!!!!!!!" BWAHAHAHH!

Is that the lie you have fallen for????????

Printed in the United States
By Bookmasters